The Missing Merchantman

by

Harry Collingwood

The Missing Merchantman
by Harry Collingwood

Copyright © 2024

All Rights reserved.

No part of this publication may be reproduced, stored in a retrieval system, or transmitted in any form or by any means, electronic, mechanical, photocopying or Otherwise, without the written permission of the publisher.
The author/editor asserts the moral right to be identified as the author/editor of this work.

ISBN: 978-93-68095-34-7

Published by

DOUBLE 9 BOOKS

2/13-B, Ansari Road
Daryaganj, New Delhi – 110002
info@double9books.com
www.double9books.com
Tel. 011-40042856

This book is under public domain

ABOUT THE AUTHOR

Harry Collingwood was an English author best known for his adventure novels, particularly those with maritime themes. He was a prolific writer, producing a wide range of novels, short stories, and travel writings. Many of his works reflect his fascination with the sea and the lives of sailors, often emphasizing bravery, adventure, and moral integrity in the face of danger. Collingwood's works were quite popular during his lifetime, and he became known for his detailed depictions of naval life and shipwrecks, as well as for his well-developed characters who often found themselves in life-or-death situations. His writing style is often direct and focused on action, making his novels appealing to readers who enjoyed adventure stories with strong plots and vivid settings. One of Collingwood's most famous works is Dick Leslie's Luck: A Story of Shipwreck and Adventure, which showcases many of the themes that ran through his writing—survival, resilience, and human endurance. His other notable works include The Pirate Island and The Log of the "Flying Fish", which also explore nautical adventures, often with an emphasis on exciting exploits at sea.

CONTENTS

Chapter One
Introductory 7

Chapter Two
On board the "Flying Cloud" 17

Chapter Three
The plotter at his work... 28

Chapter Four
A meeting in mid-ocean 38

Chapter Five
The derelict barque... 48

Chapter Six
The springing of the Mink.. 60

Chapter Seven
Anxious days... 70

Chapter Eight
Sibylla the hostage.. 85

Chapter Nine
The Captain's denunciation 96

Chapter Ten
Refuge Harbour 109

Chapter Eleven
An important discovery... 121

Chapter Twelve
Mr Gaunt goes on an exploring expedition 133

Chapter Thirteen
A visit to the wreck 142

Chapter Fourteen
    Gaunt's pontoon raft 152

Chapter Fifteen
    Captain Blyth and young Manners reappear 161

Chapter Sixteen
    The skipper goes in chase of a strange sail 172

Chapter Seventeen
    The Malays! 185

Chapter Eighteen
    An anxious night at the fort 196

Chapter Nineteen
    Doomed to die 208

Chapter Twenty
    A daring plan successfully executed 221

Chapter Twenty One
    The arrival home of the "Flying Cloud" 231

Chapter One
Introductory

This story opens on a glorious day about the middle of July; and Weymouth, with its charming bay, was looking its very best. A gentle southerly breeze was blowing; the air was clear—just warm enough to render a dip in the sea the quintessence of luxury—and so laden with ozone and the wholesome scent of the sea that to breathe it was like imbibing a draught of *elixir vitae*. The east land was in itself a picture as it stretched across the horizon in front of the town, its lofty chalk-cliffs and swelling downs, the latter dotted here and there with a solitary farm-house or a clump of trees, gleaming softly through the clear transparent atmosphere in a thousand varied hues of green, and creamy white, and ruddy neutral, which gradually merged into a series of delicate pearly-greys as the eye followed the bold outline to where Saint Alban's Head sloped down into the azure sea. The noble bay, gently ruffled by the morning breeze, shimmered and sparkled brilliantly in the strong unclouded sunlight, its rippling wavelets chasing each other shoreward in long lines until they plashed with a soothing murmur into mimic breakers upon the broad, smooth, firm expanse of sand, whereon happy children were disporting themselves, barefooted, with boat, and spade, and bucket, to their innocent hearts' content.

The proprietors of the bathing-vans were doing an excellent business, their lumbering vehicles jolting noisily down into the water with scarcely a moment's intermission. The band, drawn up in front of the hideous statue to George the Fourth, which so greatly disfigures the town, was discoursing, fairly well, a selection of good music; a long line of chairs on the sands was fully occupied by loungers, mostly ladies, reading, or amusing themselves by watching the antics of the thronging children; the broad promenade was crowded with people on pleasure bent. Light skiffs and neat well-appointed sailing boats were darting hither and thither along the surface of the glancing waters; and farther out, at a distance of about a mile from the shore, some half-a-dozen or more yachts of various rigs and tonnage were lying at anchor, with their club burgees gaily fluttering in the breeze, and most of them with mainsail hoisted, or with other preparations actively going forward toward getting under weigh for a day's cruise.

The delightful little watering-place, it has been said, was looking its best; or at least this was the opinion expressed by a young man who, accompanied by his father and sister, walked up the esplanade on that particular morning, on his way to the railway-station *en route* for London by the ten o'clock South-Western express—his luggage having preceded him on a hand-truck.

As the young man happens to be the hero of the present story, it may not be amiss to describe him somewhat particularly.

Edward Damerell, then—for that was his name—was, at the date of our introduction to him, within a month of reaching his nineteenth year; and he had hoped to spend his birthday at home with his father and sister, the only relatives he possessed on earth, but circumstances had ordered it otherwise. He stood just five feet seven inches in his stockings; was as stout-built and shapely a youth as one need wish to see, though it was evident that he had not yet attained his full growth; his frank, handsome, albeit sunburnt face was lighted up by a pair of keen, honest grey eyes and crowned by a close-cut crop of crisp, curly, flaxen hair—a good-tempered, pleasant-looking fellow enough, true as steel, brave as true, and, having been already three years at sea, as smart a seaman as ever trod a plank.

His father was his exact counterpart, with the comparatively trifling difference that he was not quite so tall as Ned; was broader in the beam, and, as of course might be expected, much older-looking, though the appearance of age was due principally to the grey with which his hair and bushy whiskers (which latter appendages, by the by, Ned was still without) was thickly dashed; the old gentleman's eye being as keen and bright as his son's, and his step almost as springy.

Edward Damerell, senior, it may be as well to mention, was a naval lieutenant, retired upon half-pay. He had seen a great deal of service in his youth, principally on the West Coast of Africa and in the China seas, and had been fairly fortunate in the matter of acquiring prize-money—to which circumstance he was indebted for the exceedingly comfortable little cottage on the hill overlooking Newton's Cove, which he had inhabited for some twenty-five years, having purchased and settled down in it upon his marriage and retirement from the service.

His daughter Eva was a beautiful girl, as good as she was beautiful, and the very apple of her father's eye—which is all that need be said of her, as she plays no part in the events which it is the purpose of this narrative to chronicle.

Young Edward Damerell, born and brought up within sight and sound of the sea, early manifested a natural desire to tread in his father's footsteps by following the same profession. To this the old gentleman made no very serious objection, but he would not hear of his son entering the navy. The service, he insisted, had been ruined by the introduction of steam and armour-plates. Moreover, he had discovered, to his cost, that without money and influence, and plenty of both, a man stood but little chance, in these piping times of peace, of making any great amount of headway up the ratlins of promotion. "So," said he, "if Ned chooses to go to sea, he will have to enter the merchant service, where good seamen are still, and always will be, required."

And this Ned did under the most advantageous circumstances, as "midshipman-apprentice" on board an Australian clipper belonging to the "Bruce" line, in which employ he was duly serving his time—very creditably, indeed, to himself and to the officers who had the training of him, if the report of the skipper, Captain Blyth, was to be believed. And he was now, on this particular morning, leaving home once more, after a month's leave, to join a brand-new steel-built clipper called the *Flying Cloud*, the latest addition to the "Bruce" fleet, of which ship Captain Blyth had been given the command.

As the lad arrived opposite King Street, the point where he would have to turn off and leave the esplanade and the "front," as the inhabitants term it, he paused a moment, looked longingly to right and left of him at the long terraces of neat houses facing the sea, at the "Nothe" on the opposite side of the harbour, at the sands, the bay, and the long stretch of bold coast to the northward and eastward, and sighed regretfully at the thought that he was about to leave the place once more for so long a time. He was enthusiastically attached to his profession—as every lad must be if he would make his way in the world—but he was also attached to the place of his birth, and infinitely more was he attached to his father and sister; and though he was too manly to express sorrow at his departure, the feeling was there and would not be altogether ignored. It was, therefore, with but an indifferently successful assumption of cheerfulness that he exclaimed:

"Well, good-bye, old town! Who knows how many weary leagues I shall have to travel, and through what hardships and perils I may have to pass, before I tread your streets again!"

And, linking his arms in those of his father and sister, he crossed the road and passed down the street to the railway-station.

Poor Ned! when he spoke so lightly he little knew that the words had so prophetic a meaning.

In due course he arrived in London, and, chartering a cab, made the best of his way to his new ship, which was taking in cargo in the London

Docks. On arriving alongside his first act was naturally to give a scrutinising look at the craft and to mentally compare her with the *Bride of Abydos*, his former ship; and much as he thought of the latter, he was almost reluctantly compelled to admit that the *Flying Cloud* greatly excelled her in every point most highly prized by a seaman. She was the very latest exponent of the shipbuilder's art, and of the success which has attended the efforts of the naval architect to combine, in the highest degree, a large carrying capacity with perfect sea-going powers and super-excellence in point of speed. She was just a nice, comfortable, handy size—twelve hundred tons register—steel-built, and of exceptional strength, classed 100 A1 at Lloyd's; a beamy rather than a deep vessel, with very fine ends. And an innovation had been introduced in her construction in the shape of a pair of deep bilge-keels, which her designer asserted would not only very greatly modify her rolling, but would also cause her to hang to windward like a yacht. She was an exceptionally pretty model, with a full poop, and was full-rigged, her stability being most satisfactorily demonstrated by the fact that her skysail-yards were aloft and crossed notwithstanding the circumstance that she had only just begun to receive her cargo. She was painted grey, with a broad white riband and painted ports, her top-sides being black. She carried a very handsome, well-executed carving of a woman, with long, streaming hair and fluttering drapery, under her bowsprit, by way of figurehead; and Ned noted with deep satisfaction, that instead of the double topsail-yards now so common in large ships, she was fitted with single revolving yards for patent reefing topsails.

He was interrupted in the midst of his admiring scrutiny by a hail from Mr Bryce, the chief-mate, who, after a somewhat off-hand welcome, informed him that he was wanted to assist in receiving and taking account of the cargo, which was coming down too rapidly to be dealt with by one man. Stowing away his "dunnage," therefore, in the after deck-house, and flinging his bedding into the berth which he selected for his own occupation, he quickly rejoined the mate, who furnished him with book and pencil, and stationed him at the after hatchway to take account of everything which passed down that receptacle.

As soon as the work of the day was over and the hatches had been put on and secured, Ned made his way to Captain Blyth's lodgings, and reported himself as having returned to duty.

He had observed, with some surprise, that the stevedores had left a large vacant space in the centre of the main hatchway, and at the very bottom of the ship; and he had once or twice wondered, during the course of the afternoon, what could be the nature of the cargo for which this space was being reserved. That it must be something heavy he knew, from the fact that the bottom of the hold had been selected for its stowage. The secret, however (if secret there was), came out next morning, when several very heavy cases of peculiar shape were brought alongside; which cases turned out to contain twelve steel 14-pounder breech-loading rifled field-pieces, with mountings, etcetera, complete, and several hundred rifles, sword-bayonets, etcetera, for the use of the colonial volunteers. The nature and destination of the contents were legibly enough set forth in stencilled lettering on the outside of the cases, and they very naturally attracted a considerable amount of curiosity as they were carefully hoisted out of the trucks and lowered into the ship's hold. Among the onlookers Ned soon noticed a swarthy-complexioned man, who wore gold rings in his ears, and was dressed in a very natty suit of dark blue cloth—evidently a seaman in shore-going togs—who manifested quite an unusual amount of interest in the cases and their handling, and who finally climbed into the trucks and lent a hand in the slinging of them, exhibiting in the performance of his self-imposed task a very considerable amount of smartness and seamanlike dexterity. And when the cases were all at length safely deposited in their destined place on the dunnage in the bottom of the hold, the man was observed narrowly scrutinising the ship herself—hull, spars, and rigging—with just that appearance of intelligent and appreciative interest which a smart seaman would be likely to bestow upon so handsome and well-appointed a craft as was the *Flying Cloud*.

The cargo came alongside with very satisfactory rapidity, and on the morning of the eighth day from that on which Ned joined, hopes were entertained that the evening would see the loading of the ship completed and the hatches put on for good and all. The swarthy-complexioned man had been seen on the quay alongside two or three times since the loading of the guns. He had evidently taken a fancy to the ship; and Ned was therefore by no means surprised when, on the morning in question, he again appeared, and, seeing Captain Blyth on the poop, stepped on board, and approaching the skipper asked if the crew had all been shipped. They had not, as it happened; so, after a short conversation, which seemed to give complete satisfaction to both parties concerned, the man was instructed to present himself at noon that day at the shipping office to sign articles.

"Rather a smart fellow, that," observed the skipper to the chief-mate, as the man swung himself lightly on to the rail and stepped thence ashore. "I'm very glad to have fallen in with him; he is an A.B., and has been twice round the Horn, so he ought to know his business. And he tells me that there are five other men, former shipmates of his, and good, smart, active, willing men, staying at the same boarding-house with himself, who, he believes, will be willing to ship with us for the voyage; so I hope we shall have a good crew."

Mr Bryce assented, and dutifully echoed the skipper's wish; but it was with a tone and manner which seemed to indicate that he did not feel very greatly interested in the matter; and Captain Blyth, when he went ashore shortly afterwards, felt more than ever sorry that his former mates were not to be with him on the forthcoming voyage. For, it must be explained, the late chief-mate of the *Bride of Abydos* had been promoted to the post of master of that ship—or *captain*, as the masters of merchant ships like to be called—and the second-mate had met with an accident, and was lying disabled in an hospital. However, it could not be helped, and Captain Blyth was obliged to content himself with the hope that Mr Bryce—who had come to him with a very good recommendation—would turn out to be a better chief-mate than, at the moment, seemed likely.

The *Flying Cloud's* crew were shipped that day, and they comprised a second-mate, a steward, a cook, a carpenter, a sailmaker, a boatswain and boatswain's-mate, eight A.B.'s (or able seamen), including the swarthy man—whose name, by the way, was entered upon the articles as Joshua Williams—and his five shipmates, and ten ordinary seamen. These, with the captain, chief-mate, and four midshipmen-apprentices, made up a crew of thirty-one, all told; which, exclusive of the captain, cook, steward, carpenter, and sailmaker, neither of whom kept watch, made up a crew of thirteen hands in a watch, none too many for a full-rigged ship of the size of the *Flying Cloud*, with such a spread of canvas as she could show to the breeze.

During the afternoon Ned made a little journey up into the Minories, to the studio of a clever marine artist to whom he had given a commission to paint the portrait of the ship; and when he reached the place he was much gratified to find that not only was the picture finished, but also that it was a capital representation of the *Flying Cloud* as she would appear at sea under all plain sail upon a taut bowline. Her ensign was shown flying from the peak; the house-flag—a large square white flag, with blue border, blue Saint Andrew's cross, and a large letter B in red in the centre—floated from the main-skysail-mast-head, and her number from the mizen, in response to a signal from another ship seen in the distance. It was a very spirited picture, and as Ned paid down its price, and gave instructions for its immediate despatch to his father's address, he felt that the money had been well laid out.

The hatches were put on, and, with the exception of the after-hatch, battened down that evening; and, whilst this was being done, Captain Blyth made his appearance on board, accompanied by a friend, a certain Captain

Spence, who had been invited to take a farewell glass of wine in the *Flying Cloud's* saloon. Captain Spence was in command of a very fine ship, named the *Southern Cross*, some two hundred tons larger than the *Flying Cloud*. She also was in the Australian trade; and though the two ships belonged to rival lines, and there was intense emulation between the skippers of the "Bruce" and the "Constellation" clippers, Captains Blyth and Spence were old and sincere friends, and the rivalry between them was all in good part. They had long been secretly anxious to have a fair race together; but hitherto circumstances had been against them. Now, however, their opportunity had come, for the *Southern Cross* had also been loading in the London docks for Melbourne, the port to which the *Flying Cloud* was bound, and, like the latter, was to haul out of dock with the morrow's tide; and the two skippers had each made a bet of a new hat that his own ship would make the passage from Gravesend to Port Phillip Heads in a less number of hours than the other, which bet was now to be ratified over their parting glass of wine. The *Southern Cross*, however, would get the start by about one day, as the *Flying Cloud* was to call at Tilbury Fort to take on board a quantity of ammunition for the guns and rifles which she was carrying out, and Captain Spence was cherishing an inward hope that a fine easterly breeze which had been blowing for some days would carry him well down channel and then chop round from the southward in good time to baffle his old friend during the passage of the *Flying Cloud* through the Downs. A somewhat curious and amusing characteristic of the friendly rivalry between the skippers was that, whilst each implicitly believed in his own ship, he affected a faith in the superior qualities of the other, and framed his remarks accordingly. So when the little farewell chat and the parting bottle of wine had come to an end, and Captain Spence rose to go, he held out his hand with:

"Well, good-bye, Blyth, and a pleasant passage to you. You will catch us somewhere in the neighbourhood of the Line, I expect, if not before; and, should the weather be fine, I hope you will come on board and dine with me, and make the acquaintance of my passengers, who, I assure you, seem to be very capital people."

"Thank you very much," was the response; "but you know very well that this poor little ship has no chance whatever with such a spanking craft as the *Southern Cross*. Look how deep we are in the water; and we don't even know our proper trim. Then, too, the glass seems inclined to drop a little, which probably means that the wind is going to haul round from the southward, which, with the twenty-four hours' start you will have, will carry you down channel nicely enough, whilst we shall be hung up in the Downs. So that, altogether, I consider you ought to reach Melbourne about eight days, at least, ahead of us, which will give you ample time to tell them that we are coming."

And so, with mutual protestations of disbelief in each other's prognostications, the rival skippers laughingly shook hands and parted.

On the following morning the two ships hauled out of dock, the *Southern Cross* leading, and proceeded down the river in tow, the one anchoring off Gravesend to take her passengers on board, whilst the other went alongside the wharf at Tilbury Fort. The ammunition was all ready for shipment, as it happened; and, securely packed in copper-lined cases, was that same afternoon carefully stowed on top of all in the after hatchway, whence, if necessary, it could be easily and quickly removed and launched overboard in case of an outbreak of fire. The *Southern Cross*, meanwhile, with her tug hanging on to her, had only paused long enough to allow of her captain going on shore and fetching off her passengers, when she had proceeded. The *Flying Cloud*, on the other hand, having now completed her cargo, and battened down everything, shifted her berth and anchored off Gravesend pier; but, as it had not been expected that she would receive quite such quick despatch at Tilbury, the passengers would not be on board until the following morning, so there was no alternative but to wait for them. In the meantime there was plenty for the crew to do in getting the decks cleaned up and everything made ship-shape; and this task was so satisfactorily performed, under the supervision of the mates, that Captain Blyth's spirits rose, and he began to hope that he had secured not only a good crew, but good officers as well. He was also particularly pleased to notice that the steerage passengers—twelve in number, all men, who had joined the ship in the docks on the preceding evening—though a rough-looking lot, were scarcely as bad as they looked, evincing a distinct inclination to make themselves useful and to assist the crew as much as possible.

On the following morning, directly after breakfast, Captain Blyth proceeded on shore in his gig to look up his passengers; and about ten o'clock they were seen approaching the ship, a shore-boat being in attendance with the trunks, portmanteaux, etcetera, which contained their immediate necessaries (the bulk of their luggage having been sent on board whilst the ship was in dock). Upon this, the windlass was at once manned, the cable hove short, and the tug signalled to come alongside and take the tow-rope. These preparations were still actively in progress when the two boats pulled alongside the ship; and by the time that the passengers had reached the decks and their luggage had been passed up, the tug had received the tow-rope and had passed ahead, and the anchor was reported ready for tripping. The shore-boat was then discharged, the gig hoisted up, the windlass was again manned, the paddles of the tug began to revolve, the anchor was broken out of the ground, and the long voyage had at length actually commenced.

The saloon passengers were seven in number (quite a pleasant little family party, Captain Blyth averred), and they consisted of a Doctor and Mrs Henderson, with their daughter, Lucille, aged six; Miss Sibylla Stanhope, Mrs Henderson's sister; Mr and Mrs Gaunt, and their son, Percy, aged seven.

Dr Henderson was a medical man who, notwithstanding his undoubted ability, had found it difficult to establish a satisfactory practice in England, and was therefore going to try his fortune in the southern hemisphere, taking his family and his wife's orphan sister with him; and Mr Gaunt was a civil engineer on his way to the colony to take up a lucrative professional appointment. They were both clever, quiet, unassuming men, very gentlemanly in manner, but with nothing particularly striking in their appearance; the kind of men, in fact, of whom it is impossible to predict whether they will, in case of emergency, turn out to be heroes or mere useless incumbrances.

The ladies were very much more interesting. Mrs Henderson was a very handsome, dark-eyed young matron of medium height, and a temper as perfect as her form; in short, a very charming person altogether. Miss Stanhope bore a very marked resemblance to her sister, except that she was much younger, being barely eighteen years of age; but there were not wanting indications that her charms would one day even surpass those of the lovely Mrs Henderson Mrs Gaunt was a *petite* blonde, very pretty and engaging, and an excellent foil to Mrs Henderson, the two ladies being of exactly opposite types of beauty. Of the children no more need be said than that they were light-hearted, joyous, and just well-behaved enough to show that their parents did not intend to spoil them if it could possibly be helped.

The first act of the saloon passengers, on reaching the deck, was to inquire for their respective cabins, of which they at once took possession, and forthwith set about arranging in such manner as they judged would prove most convenient during the long journey they had before them. The trunks uncorded, and the heavier work done, the gentlemen had it gently insinuated to them by their fair partners that they were rather in the way than otherwise; and they accordingly adjourned to the poop with the youngsters, where, over a cigar, they soon made acquaintance with each other and with the ship's officers. By luncheon-time they had mutually arrived at the conclusion that they were likely to get on exceedingly well together, that the captain was a capital fellow, the mates but so-so, the midshipmen very gentlemanly lads, and the ship everything that could be wished; and that, on the whole, they were justified in expecting the passage to be as pleasant as it was likely to prove long. The ladies, meanwhile, had been busy below, and had found time not only to convert their somewhat cramped quarters into perfect bowers of comfort and convenience, but also to follow the gentlemen's example, by cultivating mutually friendly relations; so that when the little party sat down to luncheon they felt almost as much at home with each other as though they had been acquainted for the best part of their lives, instead of for a few hours only.

Chapter Two
On board the "Flying Cloud"

The weather was gloriously fine; much too fine, indeed, to suit Captain Blyth, for, as he and his friend Captain Spence had foreseen, the easterly breeze which had prevailed for so long had at length died completely away, leaving the surface of the river as smooth as a sheet of polished silver. The air had grown much warmer, a sure precursor of a southerly wind; and the ladies had, in consequence, changed their dresses immediately after luncheon, discarding the woollen fabrics in which they had embarked and substituting for them dainty costumes of cool, light, flimsy material, arrayed in which they established themselves for the afternoon on the poop.

It was somewhat late that night when the *Flying Cloud* rounded the North Foreland; and, as Captain Blyth had feared, the little breeze which had sprung up with the setting of the sun was all out from the southward. There was, however, a capital moon, almost full; the tide, too, was in their favour. So, instead of anchoring in the Downs until next day, as had been his first intention, he determined to keep on; and all sail was accordingly made upon the ship as soon as the tug had cast off the tow-rope. A stretch was made across the channel towards the French coast, in the direction of Gravelines; and great was the satisfaction of all hands when they found that the ship, on a taut bowline, and with only wind enough to heel her some six inches under every stitch of plain sail they could set upon her, was slipping along through the water at the rate of fully five knots, and that, too, so cleanly that the ripple under the bows was inaudible to the men on the forecastle unless they put their heads over the side and listened for it, whilst scarcely a whirl or a bubble was to be seen in the long smooth wake which she left behind her.

The breeze continued scant all night, notwithstanding which the *Flying Cloud* was, at eight o'clock next morning, as close to the French coast as Captain Blyth cared to take her, and she was accordingly hove about, the wind so far favouring her that it was confidently hoped she would weather Beachy Head and so pass out clear of everything. With the rising of the sun the wind gave promise of freshening, which promise was so far fulfilled that by noon the ship was skimming along at a pace of over nine knots an hour, she being at the time just abreast of Calais. The breeze still increasing, and the tide being again in their favour, Cape Grisnez was passed little more than an hour later; and then, running out from under the lee of the land, the swell of the channel almost immediately began to make itself felt. The full strength of the wind at the same time also became apparent, and the ship, now heeling over sufficiently to send the water spouting up through the scupper-holes with every lee-roll, increased her pace to a fair, honest ten knots, steering "full and by." Captain Blyth was simply enchanted with the performance of his new command, feeling fully convinced (though he did not yet venture to give utterance to his conviction) that in her, that hitherto invincible clipper, the *Southern Cross*, would at length assuredly find she had met her match. By three o'clock Dungeness was broad on the lee-bow; by four o'clock it was fairly abaft the beam; and when the passengers went on deck after dinner they found the ship in the act of weathering Beachy, though without very much room to spare, the wind evincing an inclination to veer round from the westward. At eight o'clock next morning, when Ned came on deck to keep the forenoon watch, he saw that he was on familiar ground, the ship being about midway between Saint Catherine's Point and Saint Alban's Head, the high land at the east end of the Isle of Wight looming like a white cloud on the horizon astern, or rather on the starboard quarter, whilst Saint Alban's gleamed brilliantly in the bright sunlight on the starboard bow. The ship was still close-hauled on the larboard tack and going about six knots, the wind having headed her somewhat during the night and fallen lighter. The weather was magnificent, and everybody was in capital spirits. Captain Blyth was pleased because, though the ship was not just then travelling at any great speed, he had at all events got half-way down the channel; the passengers were pleased because they were having such a splendid view of the coast—with the prospect of getting a still better view later on in the day, as Ned informed them—and most pleased of all was Ned himself, because he not only looked forward to getting one more glimpse of dear old Weymouth itself, but also hoped to be able to make his near vicinity known to his father.

Noon found the *Flying Cloud* abreast of Saint Alban's Head and within half a mile of the shore; and, this bold promontory once rounded, all hands found themselves face to face with that magnificent panorama of rolling downs, smiling valleys, tiny strips of snow-white beach, and lofty precipitous chalk-cliffs, which help to make the scenery of Weymouth Bay one of the fairest prospects within the boundaries of the British island.

The ship was reaching right down along the coast at a distance of little more than two miles from the shore, and though it was now his watch below, Ned undertook to point out the various objects of interest as they crept into view, such as Warbarrow Bay, with Lulworth Castle nestling among its surrounding trees; Lulworth Cove, with its bold, rocky entrance; the noble natural archway of Durdle Door; the curious Burning Cliff, and so on; and when they were off the latter he made bold to ask Captain Blyth's permission to hoist the ship's colours, explaining that he would like his father to see the vessel and to know that he was so near at hand. Ned was a very great favourite with the skipper; moreover, the latter and Ned's father were old friends. The cheery answer given to this request, therefore, was:

"Yes, certainly, my lad; show our bunting by all means. We shall then be reported as having passed, and the owners will be glad to learn that we have crept so far on our way."

Armed with this permission Ned lost no time in getting out the flags and hoisting them exactly as they were represented in the picture he had sent to his father, and which he knew must be in the old gentleman's possession by this time.

That afternoon old Mr Damerell and his daughter were, according to their usual custom, on the Nothe, Eva with a piece of dainty embroidery work wherewith to amuse herself, and her father with his somewhat ancient but trusty telescope, without which, indeed, he was scarcely ever seen out of doors. They had hardly reached the old gentleman's favourite point of look-out when his quick eye detected the ship reaching down along the east land, and even before he had adjusted the telescope he had a presentiment that she might be the *Flying Cloud*. He had received a hastily-scribbled line or two from Ned—forwarded by means of the shore-boat, which had taken off the passengers' luggage at Gravesend—which had made him acquainted with the day and hour of the ship's sailing; and his long experience and intimate acquaintance with the navigation of the Channel, aided by his habitual observation of the weather, enabled him to follow the subsequent movements of the *Flying Cloud* almost as unerringly as though his eye had been on her the whole time. In one particular only had his calculations been inaccurate, and that was in the *speed* of the ship; he had not reckoned on her being either so fast or so weatherly as she had proved to be, and his reckoning located her as being at that moment within sight of but to the eastward of the Wight. When, however, he saw a large ship, loaded, and evidently by the course she was steering, bound out of the channel, and when he further noted the clean, white, new appearance of the stranger's canvas, the peculiar painting of her hull, and the very marked similarity of appearance which she bore to the picture at that moment hanging in the place of honour on the walls of his snug little parlour, he was quite prepared to admit a possible error in his calculations sufficient to account for the appearance of the ship where she actually was; and when he saw the colours hoisted, he had, of course, no further doubt upon the matter. The ship, it is true, was heading so obliquely towards him that he could only see the house-flag at her main-skysail-mast-head; but that was quite sufficient. The broad snow-white field, the blue border and cross, and the large red B in the centre, were plainly distinguishable through his telescope; and turning to his daughter he said, with just a faint tremor of excitement in his voice:

"Eva, do you see that ship reaching down under the east land, yonder?"

"The one you have been watching so intently, father? Yes, I see her," was the reply. "What a noble object she looks, with her white canvas gleaming in the sun! It is not often that we see such large ships as that so close in with the land, is it? I wonder where she is going!"

"She is bound to Melbourne. She is called the *Flying Cloud*, and she has a young gentleman named Edward Damerell on board her, who, I'll be bound, is at this moment intently looking in this direction," answered the old gentleman decisively.

"Oh, father, you can't mean it!" exclaimed the young lady impetuously, though she knew very well that her father *did* mean it. "Pray let us make haste down to the boat and go out to meet him."

Her father looked irresolute, took another glance at the ship, then shook his head sorrowfully.

"It would be of no use, my dear," he said. "Before we could reach the boat and get her under weigh yonder ship will have tacked, and fast as the *Eva* is she would never catch her in this light breeze. No; we must be satisfied to remain here and see as much of the *Flying Cloud* as we can. Perhaps when the ship goes about we may even succeed in catching a glimpse of dear Ned himself through the glass."

At this moment the loud clanging of a bell, which was being rung somewhere down in the harbour, smote noisily upon their ears.

"The very thing!" exclaimed Eva, starting eagerly to her feet. "Come, father, we have not a moment to lose! That is the first bell. The *Victoria* is to make an excursion to the Bill this afternoon, and if we go on the trip we shall surely pass not very far from Ned's ship."

"Capital!" exclaimed the old man cheerily. "Come along, my girl; we are neither of us rigged exactly in a style suited to our mingling with swells; but never mind, we shall both pass muster, I dare say, and, whether or no, we have no time to shift our canvas."

And away went the pair, without more ado, making the best of their way toward the steps which lead down the side of the hill to the quay, whence they took a boat across the harbour, the second bell from the steamer admonishing them that they had no time to spare. They reached the pay-gate in good time, however, took their tickets, and ascended to the hurricane-deck just as the captain of the boat climbed to his own private bridge. The last bell rang, a few belated excursionists came rushing breathlessly down, and whilst they were scrambling for their tickets the *Flying Cloud*, now within two miles of the town, was seen to tack. The laggards hurried on board, the gang-plank was drawn ashore, the ropes were cast off, the engines made a revolution or two astern to cant the steamer's head toward the centre of the harbour, and then away the excursion party went, the band on board at the same moment striking up a lively tune.

By the time that the *Victoria* had reached the harbour's mouth Mr Damerell was able to see that they had started at exactly the right time. The *Flying Cloud*—a beautiful sight, as she now appeared broadside-on to them, reaching across the bay, with the afternoon sun gleaming brilliantly upon her immense spread of canvas—was slipping along through the water at a speed of about six knots, and it was apparent she would pass the breakwater-end at about the same moment as the *Victoria*. But the excursion steamer's usual course was through the opening in the breakwater, and not out round its end; and if she now took that direction the trip would be spoiled, so far, at least, as Mr Damerell and his daughter were concerned. The old gentleman looked round, and saw that Captain Cosens, the veteran commodore of the little pleasure fleet, was in command, and to him he determined to make his wishes known. The captain was talking to some of his lady passengers when Mr Damerell approached him, but looked up at once and spoke on recognising an old friend.

"Good-morning, Mr Damerell," said he. "What fair wind blows you on board the *Victoria*? It is not often that you favour us with your company. A noble vessel that, isn't she?" indicating the *Flying Cloud*. "I take it she is an Australian liner."

"Yes," said Mr Damerell, "that is the *Flying Cloud*, my son's ship, you know, Captain—"

"What! your son aboard?" interrupted the commodore. "Starboard, Tom, starboard a bit, boy! and pass as close to leeward of that ship as you safely can. It's not often we have the opportunity to treat our passengers to a sight of a clipper under all plain sail, so, as the water is smooth, and we can do so with safety, we will do it to-day; it will be something of a novelty for them. And perhaps," he added, his kindly grey eyes beaming sympathetically, "you may be able to get another glimpse of Ned as we pass. Come upon my bridge, Mr Damerell, you will see better, and he will see you all the quicker too."

The ship and the steamer now rapidly approached each other; and soon after passing the breakwater-end, the latter shot across the stern of the former and ranged up on her lee quarter. The word to "ease her" was passed below into the *Victoria's* engine-room; and Mr Damerell and Eva had the opportunity of not only seeing, but also of exchanging a few words with Ned, who had soon espied them on the steamer's bridge, and had placed himself in the mizen-rigging for the purpose. The pleasure party on board the steamer were meanwhile thoroughly enjoying the unwonted sight which the *Flying Cloud* presented, with her ponderous but shapely hull, lavishly adorned with gilding at the bow and stern; her clean, well-ordered decks resplendent with glittering brass-work, and polished teak and mahogany fittings; her handsome boats, fresh painted, with the house-flag emblazoned on their bows, and canvas covers neatly lashed over them from gunwale to gunwale; the lofty masts, the orderly but intricate maze of standing and running-rigging; and the towering spread of canvas which seemed to reach almost to the clouds. Many of them had never in their lives before seen a ship of any size under her canvas and fairly at sea; and now they were brought into close proximity with one which was not only "a clipper," but, as the affable captain of the steamer explained to his numerous questioners, one of the finest, if not the largest, of that class of vessels afloat. The little group of passengers on the poop, seemingly so thoroughly comfortable and so completely at home, naturally attracted a considerable amount of attention, the children especially; and one enthusiastic lady on board the steamer was so completely carried away by the influences of the moment, that she tossed to little Percy Gaunt a basket of freshly-gathered flowers which she happened to have with her, which the little fellow deftly caught, and with a laughing "Thank you very much!" at once handed to his mother. Then, the brief conversation between father and son being brought to an end, the signal for "full speed" was given, and the steamer drew ahead, the band on board playing "A life on the ocean wave," and the vessels separated with much waving of hats and handkerchiefs on both sides. The steamer was of course the first to reach the Bill, the *Flying Cloud* being partially becalmed under the high land of Portland; and when the pleasure party again passed her, it was at a distance of about a mile, the ship steering a course which would take her well clear of the Shambles shoal.

"Bill," said Captain Cosens, when the two vessels were again abreast, "jump aft, my lad, and dip the ensign!"

The ensign was dipped three times, the salutation being promptly responded to by the clipper; and then her colours were hauled down as, catching a freshening breeze, she gracefully inclined to it, and swept grandly out to seaward.

Such was Mr Damerell's last farewell to his son, on this eventful occasion at least. Poor old gentleman! well was it for him that he so little dreamed of what that son was destined to pass through before they two again should meet! Little, as they lost sight of her, did the light-hearted throng on board the *Victoria* guess at the horrors of which that noble ship was to be the theatre.

On clearing the Bill of Portland, and once more getting the true breeze, it was found by those on board the *Flying Cloud* that the wind had veered some points further to the westward, and was now almost dead in the teeth of their course down channel. There was a red-hot ebb tide running, however, which was so much in their favour, and Captain Blyth held on upon the same tack, pushing out toward mid-channel so as to get the full benefit of it. The ship was heading well up to windward of the Channel Islands, so that she was not doing at all badly; and the wind having veered so far, the skipper was in hopes it would veer still further, and so give him a favourable slant down channel after his next reach in for the land. Nor was he disappointed; for tacking at six o'clock to avoid the flood, which he knew would soon be making, he found himself, at ten o'clock that night, some four miles to the westward of Beer Head, the wind heading him more and more as he drew in with the land. On again tacking, it was found that the ship was heading well up for the Start, which was passed about four bells in the morning watch; when, feeling themselves at length safe for a fair run out of the channel, the ship's departure was taken, together with a small pull upon the weather braces. A course was given the helmsman which would carry the ship well clear of Cape Finisterre, and away went the *Flying Cloud* to the southward and westward, reeling eleven knots off the log with all three skysails set. By three o'clock in the afternoon, Captain Blyth's reckoning placed the ship off Ushant. They now began to feel the regular Atlantic roll, and shortly afterwards the wind, continuing to veer, worked round so far to the northward of west, that they were not only enabled to get another good pull upon the weather braces, but also to set studding-sails on the starboard side, when away went the ship plunging and rolling across the Bay of Biscay at a pace which amply justified her name, and sent all hands into ecstasies of delight. And the climax of their happiness was reached when, just about sunset, a large steamer, which had been in sight ahead since noon, was triumphantly overhauled and passed, though she, like themselves, was under all the canvas she could show. Captain Blyth was simply in a beatitude of bliss; he walked the poop to and fro, rubbing his hands gleefully, chuckling, and audibly murmuring little congratulatory ejaculations to himself, fragments of which—such as—"new hat—astonish that fellow Spence above a trifle, I flatter myself—reach the Heads a clear week before him," etcetera etcetera—Ned Damerell caught from time to time as the skipper trotted past him.

In the forecastle, too, there was great jubilation that evening. Jack dearly loves a speedy ship; and now that they had had an exemplification of what the *Flying Cloud* really *could* do when she had a fair chance, all hands were fully agreed that she was by far the fastest ship they had ever sailed in.

Williams, the man who had assisted at the loading of the guns on board, was especially enthusiastic upon the subject.

"My eyes! mates, what a pirate-ship this craft would make!" he ejaculated when at length all hands' catalogue of praises seemed to be about exhausted. "Why, if she was mine I'd make my fortune—ay, and that of all hands belonging to her in less than six months!"

This remark produced a general laugh. "Why, Josh, bo! you don't mean to say as how you'd go piratin' if so be as this here pretty little ship was yourn, do you?" asked Tim Parsons, a great burly, bushy-whiskered seaman, who was seated on a sea-chest on the opposite side of the forecastle.

"Why—no, I don't perhaps exactly mean *that*," was the reply. "And yet—I don't know—why shouldn't I? There's worse trades than pirating, let me tell you, boys?"

"Ay, ay? Is there? I should like to hear you name a few of 'em," objected Parsons.

"Well, then," said Williams, warming to the subject, "to go no further than this identical fo'c's'le where we're now sitting, I mean to say that the trade of sailor-men like ourselves is a precious sight worse. We're hard worked, badly fed, badly paid—not, mind you, that I'm finding fault with the treatment we're getting aboard here—far from it—the grub's good enough for anybody; and, as to work—well, we haven't seen much of that yet. But this I *will* say, I don't like the looks of either of the mates, and as for the skipper, why, he's a good enough man, but this ship is going to spoil him. Now you mark my words if she don't—he's just finding out that he's got a flyer under him, and what will be the consequence? Why, he'll be everlastingly carrying on, driving the ship all she'll bear, carrying on to the very last minute, and then it'll be 'all hands shorten sail' to save the spars, instead of handing his canvas in good time, by which means the watch could do all the work. Now, you wait a bit, mates, and you'll see I'm right."

There were several melancholy shakes of the head at this, indicative of a belief on the part of the shakers that these prognostications would prove only too true.

"But what's all this got to do with piratin'?" persisted Parsons.

"Oh—well—why, everything," returned Williams. "Here we are, as I was saying, hard worked, badly fed, and badly paid; whilst if we was the crew of a pirate clipper we should have nothing to do but trim sails, we should live upon the fat of the land, and in six months, if our cruise was a lucky one, we could chuck up the sea and live like princes ashore for the rest of our days."

Parsons burst into a hearty laugh.

"Why, Williams," he said, "I wouldn't ha' believed you was such a greenhorn. You can't *mean* what you're sayin', shipmate. I don't suppose you've ever been a pirate, and I'm precious certain I never have—or I don't believe we should either of us be sittin' in this here snug fo'c's'le to-night—so I reckon neither of us knows very much about the business. But anybody, not a born fool, must understand without much tellin' that a pirate's life wouldn't be worth havin'. As to work, he'd have to work just as hard as any of us, with the chance of bein' shot at a minute's notice by the skipper or either of the mates, if he didn't happen to do his work just exactly to their likin'. Then he'd be in constant dread of bein' overhauled by a man-o'-war, and mayhap strung up to the yard-arm; he daresn't venture into a civilised port, to save his life. And then, what about the murders he has to commit? Faugh! no piratin' for me, thank 'ee."

"Nobody's wanting you, Tim Parsons, or anybody else, to go pirating" was the rejoinder. "I was only talking about the thing in a general sort of a way. But, though, as you say, I never was a pirate myself, I happen to know that the trade ain't quite such a bad one as you'd make out after all. First and foremost, there's no occasion for murdering at all. 'Dead men tell no tales,' we know; but there's ways of stopping the telling of tales without cutting men's throats. There's islands enough scattered about here and there quite out of the regular tracks of ships, the natives of which don't see the colour of canvas once in a lifetime; what's to prevent a pirate-ship landing her prisoners there? They'd have a jolly enough life of it in such a place, and be out of harm's way. Then, as to work, I should keep just enough prisoners aboard to do all the rough, dirty work, and let my regular crew have easy times of it. And with such a ship as this, for instance, what need to be afraid of a man-o'-war, even if there weren't a dozen ways of bamboozling the 'gold-buttons,' which there are. Then, as to going into port—that's easy enough managed by a man with a good head-piece on his shoulders; and, as I was saying, a lucky six months' cruise, and your fortune's made. Then, what do you do? Why, you watches your chance, scuttles your ship some fine night when the weather's favourable, and goes ashore with your swag, as a castaway seaman whose ship has sprung a leak and foundered. Pooh! don't tell me. The thing could be easy enough done."

"Then, I s'pose you're one o' those chaps who wouldn't mind layin' hands on other people's goods?" quietly inquired Parsons.

"Ah! I see you've misunderstood me altogether, or you wouldn't ask such a question as that, shipmate," replied Williams. "No—if you mean by 'laying my hands on other people's goods,' would I go to any of your chests and help myself—I would not. I'm not a thief; I'm as honest as ever a man here. You've got nothing in any of your chests, I reckon, but what I call *necessaries*—things a man needs and has a right to have. But—it may seem a strange thing to say, mates, yet it's what I think—no man has a right to more than he needs of anything whilst other people have to go short. Why, for example, should some people have more cash than they know how to spend—and that, too, without working for it—whilst we poor sailor-men have to strive night and day, in fair weather and foul, just to keep soul and body from parting company? I say it ain't fair; things ain't evenly divided, as they should be. We've just as much right to ride about in a carriage as any of them swells ashore—we're just as good men as they are—and if I had the chance I'd think I was doing no wrong to help myself to a little of their spare cash to make myself comfortable with. That's what *I* think about it."

"Ay, ay," muttered one or two, "that sounds fair enough when you come to overhaul the thing in all its bearings."

Others maintained silence; they instinctively recognised the falsity of Williams' logic though their intellects were not acute enough to enable them to put their fingers on the weak spot. Others, again, shook their heads dissentingly. But Parsons, the irrepressible, after looking at Williams in blank surprise for a moment or two, broke out in a tone of mingled contempt and raillery:

"There, there, you've said enough, man; and now you'd better clap a stopper over all. You're an uncommon smart man, Williams,—I won't deny it—almost *too* smart, it seems to me,—and you've just been talking like this to give us an idee, as it were, of your smartness. You argufy like a lawyer, shipmate, there's no mistake about that; but you can't persuade me that you believe a single word of what you've been sayin'. Why, man, if you hadn't already proved yourself to be the primest seaman and the most willing hand aboard this here dandy little hooker I'm blest if I shouldn't almost be inclined to believe you was a Socialist. Pah!" and he spat contemptuously on the floor of the forecastle.

"There goes eight bells," he continued, "and on deck we goes, the starboard watch. Whose wheel is it?"

Chapter Three
The plotter at his work

The little forecastle conclave made their way out on deck without waiting for the formality of a call; and, there happening to be no sail-trimming to attend to, and every prospect of a fine night, they made themselves as comfortable as circumstances would permit under the shelter of the bulwarks and elsewhere, excepting, of course, the man whose trick at the wheel it was and the look-out, the latter of whom stationed himself on the topgallant-forecastle, to windward, whilst the former went aft. The men broke up into little knots, some to smoke, some to chat, and some to snatch a cat-nap—if they could elude the vigilance of the second-mate, which they had already discovered was no very difficult achievement. The two apprentices in the watch were keeping a look-out in the waist, the one to windward and the other to leeward.

Williams and another man, named Rogers, lighted their pipes and settled themselves on the lee side of the deck, just forward of the fore-rigging, where they maintained a sort of perfunctory look-out on the lee-bow whilst smoking and chatting.

"I say, Josh," began Rogers, in a low tone of voice, "don't you think you pitched matters just a trifle too strong in the fo'c's'le just now? Seems to me, mate, that you spoke out plainer than was altogether wise by way of a starter. If 't had been me, now, I should ha' felt my way a bit; talked more in a general sort of a way, you know. I tell you it fairly took my breath away to hear you rap out about piratin' right off the reel. I'm afraid that chap Parsons 'll get suspicious next time any thing's said."

"Yes," Williams admitted, "I did overrun my ground-tackle a trifle; no mistake about that. Parsons sort of provoked me into it. But don't you trouble; it'll give the thing a start, and set the hands talking together; and as for Parsons, you'll see I'll put everything right next time we have a yarn together. He called me 'smart,' and he's right; I'm a precious sight smarter than he gives me credit for being, 'cute as he is. And there's no harm done; I could see that I've given some of 'em a new idea or two to overhaul and think about. I think that, even now, I could name three or four in our watch who'll prove all right when the time comes."

There was a great deal more said in the same strain which need not be repeated; the pith of the conversation has been given, and will suffice to suggest to the intelligent reader the idea that, even thus early in her first voyage, there was something radically wrong on board the *Flying Cloud*.

To the superficial eye, however, everything seemed to point to a prosperous voyage. The wind continued slowly but steadily to haul round from the northward, and by nine o'clock in the evening of the fifth day out the good ship, with a breeze at about due north and fresh enough to necessitate the stowing of all three skysails, was off Cape Finisterre and bowling along upon her course with studding, sails, from the royals down, set to windward, and reeling off her knots in a manner which caused the mates to stare incredulously at the line every time they hove the log.

As for the little party of passengers in the saloon, they were delighted—charmed with each other, with the captain, with the midshipmen, with the crew—who seemed to them an exceptionally smart and steady set of men—with the ship, and with the weather; with everything and every body, in fact, but the two mates, who both proved to be very disagreeable men. There had not been a single symptom of *mal de mer* among them, though the motion had been pretty lively during the passage across the Bay of Biscay; and by this time they had thoroughly settled down and become almost as perfectly at home in the ship as though they had been born on salt water. The gentlemen chatted, smoked, walked the poop, and played chess together, romped with the children, or read aloud to the ladies whilst they reclined in their deck-chairs and pretended to work, and otherwise made themselves generally useful. This was the usual disposition of their day from about nine a.m. to about eight o'clock p.m., the married ladies very frequently joining in their husbands' post-prandial promenade on the poop until the latter hour, when, the air getting cool, the whole party would adjourn to the saloon, and, Dr and Mrs Henderson producing their violins and Mr Gaunt his flute, Mrs Gaunt or Miss Stanhope would open the piano which formed part of the saloon furniture, and the sounds of a very capital chamber concert would float out upon the evening air, to the great delectation of Captain Blyth, the officer of the watch, the helmsman, and—in a lesser degree, because less perfectly heard by them—the watch clustered forward on the forecastle-head.

In this quiet, methodical way life went on with the occupants of the saloon for some time; but at length ambition entered into and seized upon the imagination of Miss Stanhope, and she determined to learn to steer.

Hour after hour had she watched the helmsmen standing in more or less graceful attitudes at the wheel, with their sinewy hands upon the spokes, now drawing them gently toward them a few inches only to push them as far away again a minute or two later. It looked ridiculously easy; yet there was grandeur in the thought that, by these simple, effortless movements, the destiny of the ship and all within her was to a large extent controlled. There was something almost sublime, to her imagination, in the ability to "guide the furrowing keel on its way along the trackless deep," as she expressed it to herself; and she determined she would learn how to do it.

At length, making her way up on the poop one glorious evening after dinner—the ship being at the time about in the latitude of Madeira, and close-hauled on the starboard tack, with a nice little eight-knot breeze blowing, and everything set that would draw, from the skysail down, and with the water as smooth as it ever is under such circumstances—she descried Ned standing aft at the wheel, with his left arm resting on its rim, his right hand lightly grasping a spoke at arm's-length, and his eye on the weather leach of the main-skysail, as he softly hummed to himself the air of a song she had sung a night or two before; and the young lady at once arrived at the conclusion that this afforded an excellent opportunity for her to take her first lesson. So she walked aft, and opened the negotiations by saying:

"Good evening, Ned." (Everybody on board, fore and aft, called the lad Ned; so she naturally did the same.)

"Good evening, Miss Stanhope," replied Ned, straightening himself up and doffing his cap with a sweep which would not have disgraced a—a—well, let us say, a Frenchman; "what splendid weather we are having! Here is another glorious evening, with every prospect of the breeze lasting, and perhaps freshening a bit when the sun goes down. If it only holds for forty-eight hours longer I hope it will run us fairly into the trades."

"I hope it will, I am sure," said Miss Stanhope, "if 'running fairly into the trades' is going to do us any good. I presume you are referring to the trade *winds*, about which Captain Blyth has been talking during dinner."

"Precisely," acknowledged Ned.

"Could you not *tie* that wheel, and sit down comfortably, instead of standing there holding it as you are doing?" inquired Sibylla, by way of leading up gradually to the proposal she intended to make.

Ned laughed. "It *looks* as though one might as well do so," he said. "But you've no idea how capricious a ship is. I've not moved the wheel for the last ten minutes, and look how straight our wake is. Yet, if I were to lash this wheel exactly as it is now, it would not be half a minute before the ship would be shooting up into the wind."

"How very curious!" remarked Sibylla. "And yet, so long as you hold the wheel the ship goes perfectly straight. How do you account for that?"

"I watch her," answered Ned, "and the moment I detect a disposition to deviate from the right course I check her with a movement of the wheel. The slightest touch is sufficient in such fine weather as we are having at present."

"I see," remarked the young lady. "The ship is as obedient to her guide as a well-trained child. And it seems easy enough to guide her. I believe I could do it myself."

"Certainly you could. Would you like to try?" said Ned, who at length fancied he could see the drift of his fair interlocutor's remarks.

"I should very much," answered Miss Stanhope. "But I did not like to ask, fearing that such a request would be a transgression against nautical etiquette."

"By no means," said Ned. "Captain Blyth is one of the most gallant of men; he would never dream of opposing so very reasonable a desire on the part of a lady—at least, not *now*, when no possible harm can come of it. If you will take my place on this raised grating, I shall be delighted to initiate you into the art. *This* side, please—the helmsman always stands on the weather side. That is right. Now grasp this spoke with your left hand, and this with your right, so—that is precisely the right attitude. Now, you feel a slight tremor in the wheel, do you not? That indicates that the water is pressing gently against the rudder—the ship carries a small weather-helm, as a well-modelled and properly rigged ship should—and if you were to release the wheel it would move a spoke or two to the right, and the ship would run up into the wind. Now, at present we are steering 'full and by,' which means that we are to steer as near the wind as possible, and at the same time to keep all the sails full. You see that small sail right at the top of all on the mainmast? That is the main-skysail. It is braced a shade less fore and aft than the other sails; so if you keep it full you will be certain to also have all the rest of the canvas full. Now you will observe an occasional gentle flapping movement of the weather leach of that sail—the *edge* of it, I mean. That indicates that the sail is just full and no more; and you must keep your eye on that weather leach and maintain just precisely that gentle flapping movement. If it ceases, the sail is unnecessarily full, and you are not keeping a good 'luff,' and you must turn the wheel a shade to the right; if it increases, you are sailing rather too near the wind, and must press the wheel a trifle to the left. Do you understand me?"

"I think so," answered Sibylla, compressing her lips, grasping the spokes tightly, and concentrating her whole attention upon the weather leach of the skysail.

She proved an apt pupil; and though for the first ten minutes or so the course of the ship was a trifle erratic, and steering in a straight line proved to be not quite so simple and easy a matter as she had deemed it, Miss Sibylla soon caught the knack, and at the end of half an hour the *Flying Cloud* was making as straight a wake again as though the best helmsman in the ship had her in hand.

"Why, this is *splendid!*" exclaimed Ned. "You are evidently a born helmsman—or *helmswoman*, rather—Miss Stanhope. Permit me to congratulate you on your success. Not a man in the ship could do better than you are now doing. I foresee that, before long, whenever any extra fine steering has to be done, we shall have to request you to take the wheel."

"Thank you; that is a very neatly turned compliment," remarked Sibylla. "But I am afraid I do not wholly deserve it. For the last five minutes I have been steering, not by the little sail up there, as you told me, but by that small dark object right ahead. It is so much easier—"

"Small dark object! where away?" interrupted Ned. "Ah! I see it. Sail ho! right ahead Mr Bryce," he reported to the chief-mate.

The mate, who was sitting smoking on a hen-coop, to leeward, close to the break of the poop, rose slowly to his feet, walked to the weather side of the deck, and, shading his eyes with his hand, looked ahead, but was apparently unable to see anything.

"There she is, just over the weather cat-head!" exclaimed Ned, as he placed himself in line with the mate.

"All right! I see her," responded the mate, as he at length caught sight of the small purple-grey spot on the south-western horizon, and he sauntered back to his seat.

At this moment Captain Blyth made his appearance on the poop. "Did I hear a sail reported ahead, Mr Bryce?" he asked, as he reached the poop.

"Very likely. There *is* one," answered the mate, without offering to point her out.

Captain Blyth looked annoyed at this boorishness of speech and conduct, but it was habitual with the mate—he apparently knew no better—the skipper was becoming accustomed to it by this time, and, without noticing it, he walked aft and said:

"Where is she, Ned?"

Ned pointed her out.

"Ah, yes," said the skipper. "Is she coming this way, think you?"

"I should fancy not, sir," answered Ned. "It was Miss Stanhope who first sighted her; she has been steering by her for fully five minutes; and had yonder ship been coming this way I think we should see her more distinctly by this time than we do."

"I'll bet any money that it's the *Southern Cross*!" exclaimed the skipper with animation. "Get your glass, Ned, my boy, and slip up as far as the fore royal-yard, and see what you can make of her. I'll stay here, meanwhile, and see that Miss Stanhope doesn't run away with the ship."

And as Ned hurried away to execute his errand, Captain Blyth turned to Sibylla and laughingly began to banter her upon her new accomplishment.

Active as a cat, Ned soon reached the royal-yard, upon which he composedly seated himself, preparatory to bringing his telescope to bear upon the stranger. A little manoeuvring sufficed him to find her; but she was so far away—quite fifteen miles—that he could make out nothing beyond the fact that she was apparently a ship of about the same size as the *Flying Cloud*. He remained on his elevated perch watching her for fully a quarter of an hour, a period long enough to satisfy him that both ships were standing in the same direction, and then he descended.

"Well; what do you make of her?" demanded the skipper, as the lad joined him on the poop.

Ned stated fully all that he had seen and all that he surmised—for a sailor is often able to shrewdly guess at a great deal when he sees but little; and when he had replied to the somewhat severe cross-examination to which he was subjected, Captain Blyth reiterated his former opinion:

"It is the *Southern Cross*, for a cool hundred! Mr Bryce"—to the mate—"be good enough to muster the watch, sir, and see if you cannot get those sails to set something less like so many bags than they are at present."

There had been a pretty heavy shower earlier on in the evening, which had sensibly stretched the new canvas, and now that it was again dry it hung from the spars and stays, as the skipper had said, "like so many bags"—a terrible eye-sore to a smart seaman—yet the mate had apparently not noticed it; or, at all events, had made no attempt to have the matter rectified.

Mr Bryce made no reply; but, rising nonchalantly from his seat, he went slowly down the poop ladder and sauntered into the waist, where he came to a halt, and shouted:

"For'ard, there! lay aft here, all hands, and take a pull upon these sheets and halliards, will ye!"

"Confound the fellow!" muttered Captain Blyth. "I told him to muster *the watch*; and he must needs set all hands to work."

The men moved aft, very deliberately, clearly in no amiable mood at being given such a job in the second dog-watch, and began upon the main tack and sheet, gradually working their way upward, and from thence forward.

"What did I say, mates?" commented Williams, as they slowly brought the canvas into better trim. "This is the 'old man's' work—this swigging away upon sheets and halliards just upon night-fall; and there he is upon the poop looking as black as thunder, because, I suppose, we're not more lively over the job. And what's it all for? Why, simply because that young sprig, Ned, happens to sight a sail ahead of us; and because we happen to be a smart ship the skipper won't be satisfied until we've overhauled her. This is just the beginning of it; it'll be like this every time we happen to see anything ahead; you mark my words."

"D'ye twig the new helmsman?" laughed another, jerking his head aft to direct attention to Sibylla, who still held the wheel.

"Ay, ay, mate; we see her," answered Williams, who seemed to think himself called upon to play the part of spokesman. "We see her; and a pretty creature she is. But do you think, mates, she'll ever give any of *us* a spell when it's our trick? Not she! It's all very well when it's a smart young sprig of an apprentice—or midshipman, as they call themselves—that she can laugh and talk with; but it's a different matter with us poor shell-backs. The swells won't have anything to say to *its*."

"Now, you're wrong there, Josh, old shipmate, as I can testify," spoke up Jack Simpson, a smart young A.B. "Mrs Henderson and Mrs Gaunt has both spoke to me; and it was only a night or two ago that, when it was my wheel, Mr Gaunt gave me a cigar; and a precious good one it was too, I can tell ye."

"Ay; and I suppose when he handed it to you he made you feel as if you was a dog that he was giving a bone to; didn't he?" said Williams.

"No, he didn't; not by a long ways," answered Jack. "He looked and spoke like a thorough-bred gentleman; but he was as perlite and civil as ever a man could be."

"Civil!" grunted Rogers. "Well, I don't make no account of that; it's his business to be civil. He's what they calls a civil engineer; though hang me if I know what an engineer wants aboard of a sailing ship."

"How come *you* to know he's a civil engineer?" demanded another man.

"Because, d'ye see, mate," replied Rogers, "I was one of the hands as was told off to pass the dunnage up when the passengers came alongside; and I read on one of the boxes 'Mr William Gaunt, C.E.' The mate saw it, too; and he says to the skipper, as was standin' close alongside of him, says he:—

"'Mr William Gaunt, C.E.'—what does C.E. stand for? And the skipper, he says: 'What, don't you know? Why, C.E. stands for Civil Engineer, which is the gentleman's purfession,' says he. And that's how I come to know it, matey."

"Well, civil or not civil, I maintain he ain't a bit better than any of us," insisted Williams; "and I want to know by what right he or anybody else is to be allowed to give themselves airs over the likes of us. Can he do anything that any of us can't do? Answer me that if you can," he demanded defiantly.

"Ay, that can he, my lad," spoke up Parsons, promptly. "Why, he's one of them people that builds railroads and bridges and harbours, and the likes of that. Civil engineers is among a sailor's best friends, shipmates. Look at the scores of snug harbours they've built where there was nothing but open roadsteads before. There's Colombo, for instance. Look what a snug spot they've made of that. Why, mates, I was lying at Colombo once before that harbour was built, and we had to keep watch and watch all the time we was there, just the same as if we was at sea, just to take care that the ship didn't strike adrift and go ashore. And now, look at the place! Why, you're moored head and starn; and some ships don't keep even so much as an anchor watch all the time they're there. Don't tell me! A civil engineer's a man of eddication, boys; and that's where he goes to wind'ard of chaps like us. Look at the skipper, again. Any one of us could take him up and toss him over the rail, so far as hard work's concerned. But you give him his charts, and chronometers, and sextants, and things; put him aboard of a ship, and tell him to take her clear round the world and bring her back again to the same place, *and he can do it*. Why? Eddication again. It's *eddication*, mates, that makes swells of men, that enables 'em to earn big pay, and makes 'em of consequence in the world. There'll be no such thing as equality in this world, Josh, as long as one man lets another get ahead of him in the matter of eddication. Them's my sentiments."

And Parsons was right, lads. Simple, homely, and unpolished as was his language, he had succeeded in giving utterance to a grand truth; one which all boys will do well to lay to heart and profit by to the utmost extent of their opportunities.

It occupied the men fully until eight bells to get the canvas trimmed to Captain Blyth's satisfaction; after which the watch below retired to the forecastle and to their hammocks.

During the night the wind freshened somewhat, hauled a trifle, and came a point or two free, in consequence of which, when the passengers made their appearance on deck next morning to get a breath or two of the fresh sea air before breakfast, they found the ship bowling along at a regular racing pace, with weather braces checked, sheets eased off, and every possible studding-sail set on the weather side. The strange sail was in sight, and still ahead—a shade on the *Flying Cloud's* lee-bow, if anything—but the distance between the two ships had been reduced to something like nine miles. Like the *Flying Cloud*, the stranger was covered with canvas from her trucks down; and it was evident, from the circumstance of her still being ahead, that she was a remarkably fast vessel. Captain Blyth had been on deck from shortly after sunrise, and, notwithstanding a somewhat windy look in the sky, had himself ordered the setting of much of the additional canvas which his ship now carried. After getting matters in this direction to his mind, he had gone up into the fore-top with his telescope and spent fully half an hour there inspecting the stranger; and when he descended and met his passengers on the poop, he announced that though still too far distant to permit of actual identification, he was convinced that his first supposition was correct, and that the stranger ahead was none other than the *Southern Cross*.

"And he knows us, too," he added with a chuckle; "recognised us at daybreak, and at once turned-to and set his stunsails. But let him, ladies and gentlemen; we have the heels of him in this weather, and we'll be abreast of him in time to exchange numbers before sunset to-night."

In this assertion, however, Captain Blyth proved to be reckoning without his host; for as the morning wore on the breeze freshened considerably, obliging him to clew up and furl his skysails one after the other, and then his royals, which seemed to give the leading ship an advantage. For, whilst by noon the distance between the two vessels had been reduced to about seven miles, after that hour the stranger was, by the aid of Captain Blyth's sextant, conclusively proved to be holding her own. It was an exciting occasion for all hands; the passengers entering fully into the spirit of the time and exciting Captain Blyth's warmest admiration by the sympathetic interest with which they listened over and over again to his story of the long-standing rivalry existing between himself and the skipper of the *Southern

Cross, with its culmination in the bet of a new hat upon the result of the passage then in progress. Mr Gaunt even went so far as to unpack his own sextant—an exceptionally fine instrument—and to spend most of the time between luncheon and dinner on the topgallant forecastle, in company with the skipper, measuring the angle between the stranger's mast-heads and the horizon. Sometimes this angle grew a few seconds wider, showing the *Flying Cloud* to be gaining a trifle, then it lessened again; but when dinner was announced the two enthusiasts were reluctantly compelled to admit that, if gain there was on their side, it did not amount to more than a quarter of a mile.

Captain Blyth, however, though somewhat crestfallen at the non-fulfilment of his boast, was still confident in the powers of the ship; but the weather, he explained, had been rather against them that day, the wind had been just a trifle too strong for the *Cloud* to put out her best paces, whilst it had been all in favour of the other and more powerful ship. But the wind had continued to haul during the day, working more round upon the weather quarter with every hour that passed, and he was of opinion that they had caught the trades; the sky looked like a "trades'" sky, and, if his opinion proved correct, he anticipated that as the wind hauled further aft, so would the *Flying Cloud* decrease the distance between herself and her antagonist.

Chapter Four
A meeting in mid-ocean

Mr Bryce, the chief-mate of the *Flying Cloud*, was one of those unfortunate men who are always more or less in an ill humour. He was, like poor Mrs Gummidge, "contrairy," and so disputatious that it was almost impossible for anyone to make a statement that he would not either deny outright or strive to prove fallacious. He had a permanent quarrel with Fate, which he considered had not treated him in accordance with his high deserts; but as Fate was rather too intangible for him to satisfactorily vent his spleen upon it, he made his fellow creatures Fate's substitute, and never missed an opportunity to vent his spleen upon them instead. And, as he was a vulgar, surly, ill-bred fellow, he was able to make himself excessively disagreeable when he seriously set about the attempt, as he did when he discovered Captain Blyth's anxiety to overhaul the ship ahead. He did not—he *dared* not—set himself in opposition to the skipper, because that would have made matters unpleasant for himself; but he promptly saw that, by affecting to share the captain's anxiety, he could at one and the same time inflict great annoyance upon him and a large amount of unnecessary labour upon the crew, or at least upon that portion of it which constituted the larboard watch. Luckily for this watch it happened that they had to do deck duty only from midnight until four o'clock a.m. on this particular night, so Mr Bryce had only four hours in which to worry them. But during that four hours he did it most thoroughly. His first act on taking charge of the deck at midnight was to glance aloft, then he looked into the binnacle, after which he walked forward and had a look for the *Southern Cross*. That ship, or at least the ship which Captain Blyth averred to be the *Southern Cross*, was just discernible, a faint dark blot upon the star-lit sky; but in that imperfect light it was quite impossible to say whether she was gaining or being gained upon. The chief-mate, however, affected to believe the former, and exclaiming, loud enough for the men to hear him:

"Tut, tut, this will never do! the stranger is walking away from us, and the skipper will make a pretty fuss in the morning," he there and then began forward with the flying-jib, and made the watch sweat up every halliard throughout the ship, and the same with the sheets of the square canvas.

Then, the wind having hauled still further aft, a pull was taken upon all the weather braces; the jib, staysail, and trysail sheets were next eased up a trifle; and, finally, all three skysails were set, only to be clewed up and furled again just before the expiration of the watch. This kept the men pretty busy for the greater part of their four hours on deck, highly exasperating them—which was what the mate intended to do—and producing a general fit of grumbling among them, for which he cared not one iota.

Whether Mr Bryce's excessive zeal was productive of good results or not it is scarcely possible to say—the alterations he effected in the set of the canvas were so trifling that, with the ship running off the wind, it is probable they were not—but, be this as it may, the fact remains that at daylight next morning the stranger, still ahead, had been neared to within about four miles.

Captain Blyth, as might be expected, was on deck early that morning—before, in fact, the watch had begun to wash down the decks—and, observing that the stranger was carrying skysails, he immediately ordered his own to be set, the sails, small as they were, being capable of doing good service now that the wind was so far aft. He was in the most amiable of humours; for not only was he getting a trifle the best in the race, but the look of the sky was such as to convince him that he had undoubtedly caught the north-east trades, and that he was therefore certain of a good run at least as far as the line. His enthusiasm at the breakfast-table became almost wearisome, though his passengers listened to him with the most indulgent good-nature; but it was a distinct relief to them when he rose from the table to superintend on deck the setting of the larboard studding-sails, which had now become possible through the wind drawing dead aft.

This change of wind was slightly disadvantageous to both ships, much of the fore-and-aft canvas becoming useless, whilst even the square canvas on the foremast was partially becalmed by that on the main; but it soon became evident that, relatively, the *Flying Cloud* was a gainer by it, the distance between the two ships now lessening perceptibly. By noon they were separated by a space of barely half a mile, by which time the identity of the stranger had been established beyond all doubt. Captain Blyth hastened, therefore, to get and work up his meridian altitude, hoisted his ensign at the peak, and, as both ships appeared to be steering admirably, proceeded to edge down within hailing distance of the *Southern Cross*.

By half an hour after noon the two ships were abreast of each other, and divided by a space of little more than a hundred feet of water. The passengers—of whom the *Southern Cross* carried twenty in her saloon—were mustered, in their fine-weather toggery, on the poops of the two ships, eyeing each other curiously at intervals, but chiefly intent upon the impending ceremony of "speaking," the two captains having established themselves in their respective mizen-rigging. At length, when the two craft were as close to each other as it was prudent to take them, Captain Blyth took off his cap, bowed, and said:

"Good-morning, Captain Spence! This is a pleasant surprise for us; we scarcely hoped to see you before reaching Melbourne. What has happened to detain you on the way?"

"Good-morning, Captain Blyth! I am very glad we have fallen in with each other so early in the voyage," answered Captain Spence. "I have been looking out for you during the last three or four days, for, with such very fine weather as we have had lately, I expected you would completely outsail us. How has the wind been with you? We have had it light and shy, so far, during the entire voyage, except for the little slant we got down channel on our first day out."

"Ah, yes!" remarked Captain Blyth; "you had the advantage of us there. We had to beat the whole way from the Foreland to the Start."

"An advantage which is more than counterbalanced by your beautiful model and your brand-new canvas," observed Spence. "Our sails are so worn and thin that we can almost see through them; the wind goes through them like water through a sieve. But I am just about to shift them for a new suit, when I hope we shall be able to keep company with you at least as far as the line, where, if, as is most probable, we fall in with calms, I hope you and your passengers will do me the favour to come on board and dine with us."

"That we will, with the greatest pleasure; and you and your passengers will, I hope, favour us with a return visit—*if, when you have bent your new canvas, you do not run away from us altogether*," retorted Blyth. "Meanwhile," he continued, raising his voice as the *Flying Cloud* drew gradually ahead of the *Southern Cross*, "I am afraid we must say good-bye for the present, as we seem to be slipping past you."

With this parting shot Captain Blyth again raised his cap politely, and stepped down out of the rigging on to a hen-coop, and from thence to the poop; and so the little verbal sparring match between the rival skippers ended, each flattering himself that he had had the best of it, and that he had come out well in the eyes of the little audience before which he had been performing.

One thing, however, was certain, the *Southern Cross* had sailed twenty-four hours before her rival, and had by that rival been overtaken and passed—fairly outsailed; and whether Captain Spence's somewhat laboured explanation of this circumstance satisfied his passengers or not, it assuredly did not satisfy himself. He was fain to confess—to himself—that the hitherto invincible *Southern Cross* had at length been subjected to the ignominy of defeat. The thought was unendurable; there could be no more happiness for him until the stain had been wiped from his tarnished laurels. And to do this with the least possible loss of time he at once went about the task of shifting his canvas, for which, as the ship was now running dead before the wind, he could not have a better opportunity. It was a heavy task, and all hands were set to work upon it, the steerage passengers—ay, and some of the gentlemen in the saloon also—so far identifying their own interests with that of the ship as to volunteer their services in the pulling and hauling part of the work, which enabled the skipper to send two strong gangs aloft. But it was all of no use—just then, at least. The fact was that the older suit of canvas was not nearly so unserviceable as Captain Spence chose to consider it, and the substitution of the new suit was therefore without appreciable effect—the result being that when night closed down upon the little comedy the people on board the *Southern Cross* had the mortification of seeing the rival ship hovering on the very verge of the horizon ahead of them.

On board the *Flying Cloud*, on the other hand, apart from her commander there was no very great amount of enthusiasm. The passengers were merely placidly satisfied at having outsailed a notoriously fast vessel; whilst the mates and crew were, or affected to be, supremely indifferent to the circumstance. Captain Blyth, however, made ample amends in his own person for the indifference of everybody else. He was simply exultant. Whatever might happen in the future, nothing could rob him of the right to boast that he had beaten the *Southern Cross* in a fair trial of sailing, with the two ships side by side. And with regard to the future, also, he was tolerably sanguine. It had been conclusively demonstrated that the *Flying Cloud* was the faster ship of the two before the wind and in ordinary trades weather, which weather he could now depend upon until he reached the region of the calms about the line; and it was also possible that, walking away from the *Southern Cross* at his present rate, he might get a slant across the calm belt which the other ship would miss, and a consequent start from thence into the south-east trades of nobody could say how many days. And if the worst came to the worst and he were overtaken in the calm belt, the two ships would at least make a fair start of it again from the line, when he was not without hopes that the extraordinary weatherliness of his own ship would enable him to keep the advantage already won. So that, looking at the matter in all its bearings, he was not only fully satisfied with the past and present, but hopeful for the future. At the same time, knowing by his recent experience how hard a ship to beat was the *Southern Cross*, he fully realised that he must neglect no means within his power to secure to himself the victory. Nor did he. Had his life and fortune both been staked on the result of the race, he could scarcely have manifested more eagerness. Indeed, he rather overdid it, imperilling his spars by carrying a heavy press of canvas up to the last moment possible; which, as the north-east trades happened to be blowing rather fresh, involved a great deal of clewing up, hauling down, furling, and subsequently re-setting of his lighter sails, and a consequent amount of extra work for the crew which was anything but to their taste.

A week passed thus; but on the seventh day following that on which the *Southern Cross* had been spoken, and within an hour or two of the time when the skipper, having worked up his meridian altitude of the sun, had expressed to his passengers a confident hope that they would have crossed the line by the time that they retired that night, the wind began to fail them, and by eight bells in the afternoon watch the ship was lying motionless on a sea the surface of which was smooth as polished glass, save for the undulations of the ground-swell which came creeping up to them from the northward and eastward. The sky was hazy but without a cloud, and the temperature of the motionless atmosphere was almost unbearably oppressive, the pitch melting out of the deck-seams and adhering to the shoe-soles even beneath the shelter of the awning which was spread over the poop.

"Well, ladies and gentlemen," said Captain Blyth as he joined his passengers at the dinner-table that evening, "here we are in the Doldrums, fast enough, and no mistake. The nor'-east trades brought us so close up to the line that I was in hopes they'd be accommodating enough to carry us over it. However, we mustn't grumble. We're within sixty miles of the Equator, whilst on my last outward voyage I was left becalmed close upon two hundred miles to the nor'ard of it. And we're not alone in our misery; I counted no less than fifteen sail in sight from the deck just before dark, but I couldn't make out the *Cross* among 'em. I am in hopes of getting a start across and into the south-easters before she comes up."

"How far astern do you think she is just now, captain?" asked Mrs Henderson.

"Not an inch less than one hundred and fifty miles, ma'am," answered the skipper. "And if she brings the trades as far down with her as we've done—which is doubtful—she can't reach the spot sooner than nine o'clock to-morrow evening. So we've twenty-six hours the start of her now, and I'm going to do my best to keep it."

The saloon was far too hot for the passengers to hold their usual concert there that evening; they therefore adjourned to the deck, and lounged there to the latest possible moment. It was a glorious night—brilliant star-light with a young moon—the combined light enabling them to just dimly make out here and there the hull and sails of one or another of their companions in misfortune, the side-lights, green or red according to the position of the vessel, gleaming brightly and throwing long, wavering, tremulous lines of colour along the polished surface of the water. On board one of these vessels, about a mile distant, someone was playing a concertina—very creditably, too—and singing a favourite forecastle ditty to its accompaniment; and it was surprising how softly yet clearly the sounds were conveyed across the intervening space of water. Singing and playing was also going on among the more distant ships; but the sounds were too far removed to create the discord which would have resulted had they been near enough to mingle.

On board the *Flying Cloud* all was silent save for the persistent "whistling for a breeze" in which Captain Blyth indulged, mingled with the rustle and flap of the canvas overhead, and the patter of the reef-points occasioned by the pendulum-like roll of the ship. The water was highly phosphorescent; and the two children, carefully looked after by Mr Gaunt, were delightedly watching from the taffrail the streams of brilliant stars and haloes produced by the gentle swaying movement of the ship's stern-post and rudder, when far down in the liquid crystal a dim moon-like radiance was seen, which increased in intensity and gradually took form as it rose upwards until it floated just beneath the surface, its nature fully confessed by the luminosity which enveloped it from snout to tail—an enormous shark! It remained under the ship's counter, lazily swimming to and fro athwart the ship's stern, just long enough to allow the rest of the passengers to get a good sight of it, when it suddenly whisked round and darted off at a tremendous pace toward one of the other ships, leaving a long trailing wake of silver light behind it. A moment later, the sound of a heavy splash at some distance was heard; and whilst the little group of horrified spectators on board the *Flying Cloud* were still speaking of the terrible aspect presented by the monster a shout and a shrill piercing scream came floating across the water, followed by more shouting and sounds as of the hasty lowering of a boat.

"Hark! What can that mean?" ejaculated Mrs Gaunt.

"Sounds as though there was something wrong aboard the barque yonder, sir," reported one of the men to the chief-mate. (Captain Blyth happened to be below at the moment.)

"Well, it's no business of ours if there is," answered Mr Bryce, not attempting to move from his seat.

"Did you ever know such a brute as that man is?" whispered Mrs Gaunt to Miss Stanhope.

"Never," was the reply. "That I am free from any further association with him will be my most pleasant reflection when I leave the ship."

The flash of oars in the phosphorescent water showed that a boat had been lowered from the barque, and she could be faintly seen pulling about for some time afterwards; but at length she returned to the ship. The cheep of the tackle-blocks could be heard as she was hoisted up, and that ended the incident for the night.

On running into the calm the *Flying Cloud* had, of course, been stripped of her studding-sails in order that she might be ready to meet the light variable airs which were all she would have to depend upon to help her across the calm belt; and about nine o'clock that evening one of these little puffs, accompanied by a smart shower of rain, came out from the westward, lasting nearly an hour, and enabling the little fleet to make some four miles of progress on their several ways, some of the vessels being bound north, whilst the others were making their way in the opposite direction.

The following morning dawned with another flat calm; but that the crews of the several ships had not been idle during the night was shown by the scattered appearance of the fleet. Six of the fifteen sail counted by Captain Blyth on the previous evening were hull-down to the northward, in which direction three more vessels had put in an appearance during the hours of darkness; but these three were all in a bunch and about twelve miles to the northward and westward of the *Flying Cloud*. A solitary sail had also hove up above the southern horizon during the same period, and the remaining nine were scattered over an area of about seven miles; the barque before referred to being nearest the *Flying Cloud*, but a shade to the southward of her, showing how partial had been the light airs encountered during the night.

About four bells in the forenoon watch, that day, a few light cats'-paws were seen stealing over the surface of the water from the southward, and the sails of the several vessels were properly trimmed to meet them. The *Flying Cloud* happened to be heading to the westward, whilst the barque was heading east when the little breeze reached them, in consequence of which the two vessels began to approach each other on opposite tacks as soon as their canvas filled. Captain Blyth had been informed of the mysterious incident of the previous night on board the barque, and he now announced his intention of speaking her if the breeze lasted long enough to bring the two vessels within speaking distance. It was at first doubtful if this would be the case, but when the two vessels were within about a cable's-length of each other a somewhat stronger puff came up, dying away again just as the *Flying Cloud* was slowly passing under the barque's stern.

The usual hails were exchanged, by means of which each captain was made acquainted with the name, destination, port sailed from, number of days out, and so on, of the other vessel (the barque turning out to be the *Ceres*, of Liverpool, bound from that port to Capetown); and then Captain Blyth continued:

"Was anything wrong on board you last night? Some of my people thought they heard some sort of a commotion in your direction."

"Yes," answered the skipper from the barque. "I am grieved to say that we lost one of our best men. The poor, foolish fellow—unknown to me, of course—took the notion into his head to jump overboard, with the idea of swimming round the ship. He jumped from the starboard cat-head, and had very nearly completed his journey when he was seized by a shark and carried off from under our very eyes, as it might be. We lowered the gig and gave chase, but the boat could not get near him, and at last the fish dived, taking the man down with him, and we never saw any more of either. Good-bye! if we don't meet again I'll be sure to report you when we get in!"

The vessels gradually drifted apart, and the short colloquy was brought to a close.

"Good heavens, how horrible!" ejaculated Gaunt, turning to his fellow-passengers, who, with himself, had heard the short history of the tragedy. "That must, undoubtedly, have been the identical shark we saw. Being in the water he, of course, heard the plunge of the unfortunate man before the sound reached our ears, and at once made off, as we saw, in that direction. How little we dreamed of the fatal errand on which he was bound as we watched him disappear! Truly, 'in the midst of life we are in death.'"

Shortly before noon a black, heavy, thunderous-looking cloud worked up from the southward, and, when immediately over the ship, burst with a tremendous downpour of rain, but with no wind. Seeing that the fall was likely to be heavy, Captain Blyth ordered a couple of studding-sails to be opened out and spread to catch the water as it fell, and so copious was the shower that not only did they succeed in completely refilling all the tanks, but, by plugging up the scupper-holes the men were actually enabled to enjoy the unwonted luxury of a thorough personal cleansing in the warm soft water, and also to wash a change of clothing. The ladies and children, had, of course, been driven below by the heavy downpour; but they were not forgotten, Messrs Henderson and Gaunt taking care to promptly secure a sufficiency of water to afford each of them the treat of a copious fresh-water bath.

Between sunrise and sunset that day, the *Flying Cloud* contrived to make nearly eight miles of southing, and a small slant of wind during the night enabled her to make about fourteen more. When morning dawned they were again becalmed; but the sky was overcast, and it was evident that a heavy thunder-squall was working up from the eastward, and Captain Blyth was in hopes that when it came it would do them good service. He was on deck at daylight, eager to see if he could discover any traces of the *Southern Cross*; and great was his jubilation when, after a most careful scanning of the horizon from the main-topgallant-yard, he failed to detect anything at all like her in sight.

By breakfast-time the aspect of the sky was so threatening that Captain Blyth gave instructions to have all the lighter canvas taken in, leaving the ship under topsails, courses, fore-topmast staysail, jib, and mizen. It was well that he took this precaution, for just as they sat down to breakfast it began to thunder and lighten heavily, and about ten minutes later, a terrific downpour of rain followed. The rain suddenly ceased, and the murky darkness of the atmosphere as suddenly gave place to a vivid yellow light, a change which caused the skipper to spring to his feet and rush out on deck without even the pretence of an apology to his passengers for so abrupt a movement. On reaching the deck his first glance was to the eastward, the direction from which the light emanated, and he then saw that the heavy veil of black cloud—which now completely overspread the heavens—was in that quarter rent asunder, leaving a great gap through which was revealed a momentarily increasing patch of pale straw-coloured sky. The water was every where black as ink save beneath this livid streak, but there it presented the appearance of a long line of snow-white foam advancing toward the ship with terrific rapidity.

The second-mate, who was in charge of the deck, was standing on the poop regarding this phenomenon with a doubtful expression of visage, which gave place to one of unmistakable relief when he saw the skipper on deck.

"That looks like a squall coming down, sir"—he began. But Captain Blyth had no time to attend to him just then; he saw that there was not a moment to be lost, and turning his back unceremoniously upon Mr Willoughby he shouted:

"Stand by your topsail-halliards here, the watch! Hurry up, my lads, or we shall lose the sticks! Let run, fore and aft!"

The men, who saw what was coming, and had been expecting the call, sprang at once to their stations, let go the halliards, and then helped the revolving yards down by manning the topsail-clewlines, by which means the three topsails were snugly close-reefed by the moment that the squall burst upon them. There was no time to do more or Captain Blyth would have taken the courses off the ship. As it was she had to bear them; and so heavy was the squall that during its height the vessel was compelled to run dead before it. Her head was, however, brought to the southward the moment that it was safe to do so, and away she went like a frightened thing, tearing through the surges with her lee gunwale under. The first fury of the squall was spent in about a quarter of an hour, but it continued to blow with great violence until noon, when the gale broke and the crew were able to take a pull of a few feet upon the topsail-halliards. By eight bells in the afternoon watch the ship was under whole topsails once more, with a clear sea all round her and a rapidly clearing sky; and at ten o'clock that same evening, when Captain Blyth entered the saloon, after personally superintending the setting of the topgallant-sails, he announced not only that there was every prospect of a fine night and a steady breeze, but also that he believed they had caught the south-east trades.

Chapter Five
The derelict barque

The next morning demonstrated the correctness of Captain Blyth's surmise; for daylight found them with the breeze still steady at about east by south, and so fresh that they were compelled to keep all their skysails and the mizen-royal stowed. Needless to say, everybody was delighted at having slipped through the Doldrums so easily; even the chief-mate almost allowed himself now and then to be betrayed into an expression of dawning amiability; and, as for Captain Blyth, his exuberance of spirits threatened at times to pass all bounds. He believed it quite impossible that the *Southern Cross* could now cross the line in less than three days, at least, after himself; and the way in which the *Flying Cloud*, against a fair amount of head sea and on a taut bowline, was steadily reeling off her eight, nine, and sometime even ten knots per hour, with her really extraordinary weatherliness, quite convinced him that he could beat his antagonist in any weather which would permit him to show his topgallant-sails to it.

This state of general satisfaction and good humour was at its height, when about ten o'clock on that same morning, a man who was at work on the weather fore-topsail-yard-arm hailed the deck with:

"On deck, there! There is a wreck, or something like it, broad on our weather-beam, and about nine mile off."

Captain Blyth was on deck, and so was Ned; and the skipper immediately ordered that young gentleman to go aloft with his glass to see if he could make out the object.

Ned was soon in the main-topmast cross-trees, from which elevated stand-point he was at once enabled to make out the whereabouts of the supposed wreck with the naked eye, and he was not long in bringing his glass to bear upon it.

"Well, Ned, my hearty," hailed the skipper, when the lad had been working away in a puzzled manner with his telescope, "that you see something is perfectly evident. What d'ye make her out to be?"

"It is not very easy to say, sir," replied Ned. "The light is so dazzling in that quarter that I can see nothing but a dark patch; but it looks more like a vessel on her beam-ends than anything else. But, if it is so, she is lying over so much that her sails are in the water."

"Phew!" whistled the skipper. "We must have a look at her; it will never do to leave a ship in such a fix as that. Can you see any people on board her, Ned?"

"No, sir," was the answer. "But if there *are* people on board it would be impossible to make them out from our present position."

"No, no," muttered the skipper, "I don't suppose it would; of course not. Hark ye, Ned; just stay where you are, my lad, and let me know when we have brought the wreck a good couple of points abaft our beam, and in the meantime take a look round with your glass and see if you can make out anything like a boat anywhere."

"Ay, ay, sir," replied Ned, settling himself into a comfortable, easy position in the cross-trees, somewhat to the secret trepidation of Miss Stanhope, who was watching his movements with a great deal of undemonstrative interest, and who every moment dreaded that the young man's careless attitude, coupled with the pitching of the ship, would result in a fall. Nothing of the kind, however, happened; and in due time Ned hailed:

"I think we can fetch her now, sir. I can make her out much better than I could a quarter of an hour ago; and I believe she *is* a ship on her beam-ends. I can see nothing of boats in any direction, sir."

"Very well," replied Captain Blyth. "Stay where you are, nevertheless, and continue to keep a bright look-out. We will tack the ship, if you please, Mr Bryce."

"Ay, ay, sir. Hands 'bout ship!" responded the chief-mate; and in a minute or two the men were at their stations.

"All ready, sir!" reported Mr Bryce Captain Blyth walked aft to the mizen-rigging, signed to the helmsman, and gave the word:

"Helm's a-lee!"

"Helm's a-lee," responded the men, lifting the coiled-up braces and so on from the pins and throwing them down on the deck all ready for running.

The ship shot handsomely up into the wind; and the word was given to "raise tacks and sheets," quickly followed by the other commands; and in a couple of minutes the *Flying Cloud* was round and heading well up for the wreck, whilst the crew bowsed down the fore and main tacks simultaneously with the aid of a couple of watch tackles.

To the honour of Captain Blyth be it said that, though his interest in the race between his own ship and the *Southern Cross* was as ardent as though his very life depended upon its result, not one single murmur escaped him on account of this delay; for delay it certainly was. No; apart, perhaps, from the passengers, he of all on board betrayed the most anxiety respecting the crew of the distressed vessel.

In an hour the *Flying Cloud* was hove-to abreast and close to leeward of the wreck, which proved to be a fine wooden barque, copper-bottomed, on her beam-ends, as Ned had reported, with her masts lying prone in the water. There was no sign of any one on board her; nevertheless Captain Blyth ordered one of the gigs to be lowered, and instructed Mr Bryce to proceed to the wreck and give her a careful overhaul. At Mr Gaunt's own request that gentleman accompanied the mate.

A VISIT TO THE DERELICT BARQUE

The little party had some difficulty in boarding the derelict, for she was lying broadside-on to the wind, with her masts pointing to windward; and though there was no very great amount of sea running, there was still sufficient to make boarding from to windward an awkward if not an absolutely dangerous matter, in consequence of the raffle of spars and cordage in the water. But they succeeded at last; Mr Gaunt and the mate contriving to gain a footing in the main-rigging, whilst the boat with her crew backed off again out of harm's way. The task of examining the vessel, now that they were actually on board her, was even more difficult and dangerous than that of boarding, the ship lying so far over that her deck was perpendicular. By getting out on her weather side, however, and by means of ropes'-ends, they eventually succeeded in penetrating first to the cabin, and then to the forecastle (both of which were on deck); but in neither was there any one to be found. There were, however, in the cabin, signs—such as open and partially empty boxes and trunks, with articles of wearing apparel scattered about—which seemed to indicate that the vessel had been very hurriedly abandoned; and the state of these articles was such as to lead Mr Gaunt to the conclusion that the abandonment had taken place within the previous twenty-four hours.

Having so far completed their examination, the boat was signalled to again approach, and a few minutes later the party found themselves once more on the deck of the *Flying Cloud*, the chief-mate briefly reporting that the barque was undoubtedly abandoned.

"Then," said Captain Blyth, hesitatingly, "I suppose there is nothing more to be done but to hoist up the boat and fill away upon our course again?"

"No; I suppose not, sir," replied Bryce, in a tone of voice which very sufficiently indicated his supreme indifference.

"Very well," said the skipper, "man the—"

"Excuse me, Captain Blyth, but may I offer a suggestion?" interrupted Mr Gaunt.

"Assuredly, my dear sir," responded the skipper; "what suggestion would you offer?"

"Well," said Mr Gaunt, "if I may be permitted to say so, it seems a great pity to leave that fine ship there, to be possibly run into by and perhaps to occasion the loss of another ship; or, as an alternative, to eventually founder. So far as I could perceive, the hull is as sound and tight as ever it was, and, by the way she floats, I do not believe she has very much water in her; and with regard to her spars, her fore and main-topgallant masts are snapped off short by the caps, which appears to be about all the damage done in that direction. Now, why should you not right her, pump her out, man her, and send her into port? If her cargo is valuable, as is likely to be the case, it would put a handsome sum of salvage money into your pocket."

"So it would, sir," replied the skipper. "I was thinking of that just now, but couldn't exactly see how the thing is to be done; and as Mr Bryce seemed to have no idea of any such thing, why I concluded it must be impracticable."

"By no means, I should say," observed Mr Gaunt. "We engineers, you know, are constantly accomplishing things which other people would be disposed to pronounce impossible; and I confess I see no great difficulty in this case. I believe the barque is only held down in her present position by the weight of the water in her canvas."

Mr Gaunt then indicated to the skipper the means which he thought would be likely to prove successful; and Captain Blyth, though somewhat doubtful of the result, was sufficiently impressed to express his willingness to try the experiment, Mr Gaunt volunteering—to his wife's secret dismay—to assist by taking charge of a small working party on board the derelict.

To work all hands accordingly went. The gig once more shoved off for the barque, which was boarded by the energetic engineer and four men, who took with them a coil of light line, an axe, and, of course, their clasp knives. The little party got out on the weather side of the ship, in the main-chains, uncoiled their line, and were then all ready to commence operations. The gig, meanwhile, returned to the ship, and received on board a large but light new steel towing hawser, which was coiled down in long flakes fore and aft the boat, and with this she once more went alongside the barque, to leeward of her this time, however—that is to say, alongside the vessel's upturned bilge. A rope's-end was hove into her by the little working party in the main-chains, and by this means the end of the hawser was hauled on board, and, with some labour and difficulty, eventually made fast round the mainmast head, just above the truss of the main-yard. This done, a signal was made to the *Flying Cloud*, which had meanwhile drifted some distance away, and the ship thereupon filled her main-topsail and bore up, waring short round upon her heel. At the same time the crew hauled up the courses, clewed up royals and topgallant-sails, and, in short, reduced the canvas to the three topsails, jib, and spanker. She was now upon the larboard tack. Having stood on a sufficient distance, Captain Blyth went in stays, and the ship was again headed for the barque. Now came the only delicate part of the operation. But the skipper was an accomplished seaman, and he managed his part of the work to perfection, bringing the *Flying Cloud* up alongside the barque so close to leeward that there was only bare room for the boat between the two hulls; and at the proper moment the main-topsail was backed and the way of the ship stopped. A rope's-end, to which the other end of the hawser was attached, was then promptly hove from the boat alongside and smartly hauled inboard over the ship's bows, and several turns of the hawser were taken round the windlass-bitts. Then, by carefully manipulating the canvas, the *Flying Cloud* was brought head to wind, or with her bows towards the derelict, until, dropping to leeward all the time, the hawser was tautened out and a strain brought upon it. The topsails were then laid flat aback, and the result was awaited with some anxiety; the boat meanwhile remaining alongside the derelict to take off Mr Gaunt and his little party in the event of any accident happening. For a few minutes no visible result attended these manoeuvres; but at length a shout from Mr Gaunt of "Hurrah, there she rises! Be ready to let go the hawser on board there when I give the word" was followed by a barely perceptible indication that the vessel was righting. The movement increased; and then, still gradually, the masts rose out of the water until they were at an angle of about forty-five degrees with the horizon, when the vessel recovered herself so suddenly that the little party on board had to cling on for their lives or they would have been flung into the sea. A heavy roll or two followed, and the vessel then settled upon an even keel once more, with the water pouring in torrents out of the canvas down on to the deck, and wetting Mr Gaunt and his crew to the skin. Captain Blyth was personally superintending his share of the operations from the *Flying Cloud's* forecastle, and at the proper moment the end of the hawser was cast off and let fly overboard, to be recovered later on by the gig.

The first thing the engineer now did was to heave-to the barque as well as he could with his scanty crew; his next act was to sound the well, with the result that a depth of five feet of water was found in the hold. This, however, was not so formidable a matter as it at first sight appeared; for, the hold being tightly packed with cargo, the water could only get into the interstices, and a comparatively small quantity would consequently show a large rise in the pump-well.

A strong gang was now sent on board the barque, with the chief-mate in command; and the pumps were at once manned. A quarter of an hour's work at these sufficed to show that the vessel was making no water (that which was already in her having doubtless made its way in through the topsides and down the pump-well whilst the craft was on her beam-ends); the men therefore went to work with a will, and by eight bells in the afternoon watch it was reported that the ship was dry.

Mr Gaunt, meanwhile, made his way into the cabin as soon as the mate took charge, and proceeded to give the place a general overhaul, with the object of ascertaining who and what the vessel was. He succeeded in finding the log-book, log-slate, and the captain's desk, with all of which he proceeded on board the *Flying Cloud*. The articles were placed in the hands of Captain Blyth, who forthwith sat down to examine them, with the result that the barque was found to be the *Umhloti* of Aberdeen, her commander's name being Anderson. She was from Port Natal, bound to London, thirty-three days out when discovered; and her cargo consisted of hides, ivory, indigo, coffee, sugar, and wool. She was therefore a very valuable find, well worth the time and trouble they were devoting to her. The last entry on the log-slate had been made at eight o'clock on the previous morning; and the log-book had been written-up as far as noon on the day preceding that. Captain Blyth had therefore no difficulty in arriving at the conclusion that the vessel must have been capsized in a very similar squall to that which had struck the *Flying Cloud* on the previous day, and at about the same moment. This surmise was confirmed by the fact that when Mr Gaunt had entered the captain's state-room he had found the chronometers still going, though nearly run down. He had, of course, at once taken the precaution to wind them afresh.

Having brought the pumps to suck, the next task of the men on board the *Umhloti* was to clear away and send down on deck the wreck of the fore and main-topgallant masts, with all attached, a couple of hands being at the same time deputed to give the store-room an overhaul to ascertain whether the contents had been damaged or not by water. Everything was luckily found to be in perfect order there, the water not having risen high enough in the hull to reach the lazarette. This being found to be the case, nothing now remained but to man the vessel and dispatch her on her homeward way.

Captain Blyth had already thought out his plans in this direction. And when it was reported to him that the barque could part company at any moment he went forward, and, mustering the steerage passengers, told them he had not only observed their efforts to make themselves useful on board, but had also noticed that those efforts had been crowned with a very fair measure of success; he would now, therefore, ship the whole of them for the passage, if they chose, paying them ordinary seamen's wages from the commencement of the voyage. So good an offer was not to be lightly refused; and, after a few minutes' consultation together, the men unanimously declared their willingness to accept it. This made the rest of the business quite plain sailing for the skipper; and, closing with the *Umhloti*, he hailed Mr Bryce to say that he intended to send him home in charge, and that he was to ascertain how many of the men then with him would volunteer to return to England. A crew of fourteen hands, all told, was soon made up, Tim Parsons and two of the apprentices being of the number; and just as night was closing down the two vessels parted company, Captain Blyth, Ned, and the saloon passengers taking advantage of the opportunity to send home letters to their friends, the skipper taking the precaution to enclose them all in his dispatch to his owners, lest Mr Bryce, in his indifference, might neglect to post them. It may as well be mentioned here that the *Umhloti* arrived safely in England about a fortnight later than the passengers and crew who had abandoned her; and that the letters she carried duly reached their destination.

The changes rendered necessary by this drafting off of so large a proportion of her crew involved certain promotions on board the *Flying Cloud*, in which promotion Ned, to his intense gratification, was made a sharer, he being appointed acting second-mate *vice* Mr Willoughby, who was promoted to the post of chief, whilst Williams was made boatswain's-mate.

The ship being now once more close-hauled, with the south-east trade-wind blowing steadily, and only a very moderate amount of sea running, Miss Stanhope regarded the occasion as propitious for the perfecting of herself in the art of steering; and she accordingly practised with great assiduity. Ned, of course, by virtue of his promotion, was no longer required to take his trick at the wheel—he was now the officer in command of the starboard watch—but Sibylla did not allow that circumstance to interfere in the least with her plans; on the contrary, she rather made it subservient to them. For, whereas she had before been obliged to wait for her lesson until Ned's trick came round, she now simply watched her opportunity, and whenever she saw that the young man had nothing very particular to do, she would go up to him and say, "Mr Damerell, is it convenient for you to give me a steering-lesson?" Whereupon Ned would make a suitable response, and, accompanying the young lady aft, would say to the helmsman "Here, Dick, or Tom, or Harry", as the case might be, "go forward and do so and so; Miss Stanhope wishes to give you a spell. When she is tired I will let you know, and you can come aft again and relieve her." Upon which the seaman, with an inward chuckle and much carefully suppressed jocularity, would shamble away for'ard, fully convinced by past experience that he need think no more about the wheel until his trick should again come round. By the time that the ship had run through the south-east trades, Sibylla could steer her, when on a wind, as well as the best helmsman on board; and, proud of her skill, she then began to long for the opportunity to try her hand with the ship when going free. This opportunity came, of course, in due time;

and, though the fair helmswoman at first found the task far more difficult that she had ever imagined it could possibly be, she soon developed such extraordinary skill that Ned's prophecy at length became literally fulfilled, Captain Blyth gradually getting into the way of turning to Miss Stanhope when any exceptionally fine steering had to be done—as, for instance, when some contumacious craft ahead persistently refused to be overhauled—and saying, "I am afraid there is no resource but to invoke your aid, my dear young lady; we shall never overtake yon stranger unless you will oblige us with a few of your scientific touches of the wheel." Whereupon Sibylla, looking very much gratified, would make some laughing reply, and forthwith take the wheel, keeping the bows of the *Flying Cloud* pointing as steadily for the strange sail as though they had been nailed there, always with the most satisfactory result.

It was perhaps only a natural consequence of Ned's assiduous "coaching" of Miss Stanhope in the helmsman's art that the formal relations usually subsisting between passengers and officer should to a certain extent have given place to a kind of companionship, almost amounting to *camaraderie*, between these two young people. The seamen were almost, if not quite, as quick as their skipper in detecting what was going forward; and it is not very surprising that, with their love of romance, they should forthwith regard the handsome young mate and his pupil as the hero and heroine of an interesting little drama. This view of the affair afforded the men for'ard intense gratification. Ned was exceedingly popular with them; and the tars regarded the conquest with which they so promptly credited him almost as a compliment to themselves, and a triumph to which each might claim to have contributed, even though in ever so slight and indirect a way. It will be seen later on that this fancy on the part of the crew was the means of placing Sibylla in a most trying situation.

A few days later a sad fatality occurred. The ship was somewhat to the eastward of the Cape, going nine knots, with her topgallant-sails furled, the wind blowing very fresh from the northward, and a tremendously heavy swell running. Captain Blyth, the mate, and Ned were all on the poop, busy with their sextants, the hour being near noon, when, the ship giving a terrific lee-roll, Mr Willoughby lost his balance, and, gathering way, went with a run to leeward. Whether the accident was due to the poor man's anxiety to preserve his sextant from damage or not can never be known, but certain it is that, from some cause or other, he failed to bring up against the light iron protective railing which ran round the poop, overbalancing himself instead, and falling headlong into the water.

A shriek from the ladies, who witnessed the accident, and the shout of "Mate overboard!" from the helmsman caused the skipper and Ned to lay their instruments hurriedly down on deck and run aft to the lee quarter, where the first thing they saw was the unfortunate man's hat tossing on the crest of a sea about a dozen yards astern.

"He can't swim a stroke," exclaimed Ned to the skipper; and then, before the latter could stop him, the gallant fellow took a short run, and plunged headlong into the foaming wake of the ship.

"Down helm!" exclaimed the skipper to the man at the wheel, springing at the same time to the lee main-brace, which he let fly. The men forward, meanwhile, having heard the cry of "Mate overboard," rushed aft to the braces, and in another minute the ship was hove-to, with her mainsail in the brails.

This done, Williams, who was perhaps the keenest sighted man in the ship, sprang into the mizen-rigging, and, making his way with incredible rapidity into the top, stood looking in the direction where he expected to see the two men.

"D'ye see anything of them, Williams?" shouted the skipper.

"Yes, sir; I can see *one* of them," was the reply; "but which one it is I can't tell. It must be Ned though, I think, for he seems to be swimming round and round, as though looking for the mate."

"Keep your eye on him, my man; don't lose sight of him for a single instant!" shouted the captain. Then, turning to the men, who were clustered together on the poop, he exclaimed: "Now then, men, what are you thinking about! Out with the boat, my hearties; and be smart about it!"

The men moved to the tackles and threw the falls off the pins down on to the deck, talking eagerly together meanwhile; then one of them turned, and, stepping up to the skipper, said:

"Who is to go in the boat, sir? I must say I don't care about the job; and the others say the same. We don't believe we could get away from the ship's side in such a sea as this."

Captain Blyth stamped on the deck in his vexation and despair. It was only too true; the boat would to a certainty be stove and swamped if any such attempt were made; and that would mean the loss of more lives. What was to be done? Leave two men to perish he would not, if there was any possible means of saving them.

"Can you still see either of them, Williams?" hailed the captain.

"Yes, sir; I can still see the one I saw at first; but not the other," was the reply.

"We *must* pick him up, if possible," exclaimed the skipper. "Up helm, my man; hard up with it. Man the main-braces, and fill the topsail!"

At this juncture Sibylla, who had not heard the first part of the skipper's speech, stepped up to Captain Blyth, ashy pale, and gasped:

"What are you going to do, captain? Is it possible you are going to be inhuman enough to leave that poor fellow there *to die*?"

"No, my dear," was the answer. "I am going to save him, if it is in human power to do so. You go below, now, like a good girl, and persuade the others to go too; this is no sight for a woman to look upon."

But Sibylla could no more have gone below than she could have flown. She walked aft, and stood at the taffrail with tightly-clasped hands and starting eyes, looking eagerly astern, her whole body quivering with an agony of impatience at what seemed to her the tardy movements of the ship.

As a matter of fact, however, the *Flying Cloud* had never proved herself more handy, or been worked more smartly than on that precise occasion; had she been sentient she could scarcely have yielded to her commander's will more readily than she did. Keeping broad away until she had good way on her the skipper watched his opportunity, and, signing to the helmsman, the wheel was put over, and the ship flew up into the wind, tacking like a yacht, Williams at the same time making his way up on to the royal-yard, in order that the main-topsail might not interfere with his range of vision. In effecting this change of position, notwithstanding his utmost care, he contrived to lose sight of the diminutive speck on the surface of the water; and when Captain Blyth again hailed, asking him if he still saw it, he was compelled to answer "No." An anxious search of about a minute, however—a minute which seemed an age to Sibylla—enabled him to hit it off once more, and he joyously hailed the deck to say that the person—whoever it might be—was still afloat and broad on the lee-bow.

"Keep her away a couple of points," commanded Captain Blyth; "and pass the word for the boatswain to muster all the light heaving-line he can lay his hands upon. Range yourselves fore and aft along the lee bulwarks, my lads, and let each one stand by to heave a rope's-end with a standing bowline in it as soon as we get near enough. How does he bear now, Williams?"

"Straight ahead, sir. Luff, or you will be over him! It is Ned, sir."

"Luff!" said the skipper. "Man the main-braces, some of you, and stand by to heave the main-yard aback."

Captain Blyth then sprang upon a hen-coop, and peered eagerly out ahead.

"I see him!" he eagerly exclaimed at last. "Back your main-topsail. Luff, my lad; luff and shake her! So, well there with the main-braces, belay all; and stand by fore and aft with your ropes'-ends. Look out, for'ard there; now *heave*! Missed him, by all that's clumsy! Try you, the next man. Missed again; line not long enough. Steady, men, steady, or you'll lose him yet. Now, look out, Ned, my lad! Heave, boatswain, and let us see what you can do. *Well* hove! Pay out the line, pay out smartly—ha! lost it. Tut! tut! this will *never* do. Well done! he has it this time! Let him slip it over his shoulder; that's well. *Now* haul in—handsomely, my lads—and mind you don't lose him."

Half a minute more and poor Ned, gasping for breath, speechless, and too exhausted to stand upright, was dragged triumphantly up over the side and seated on the deck, where, of course, all hands instantly crowded around him. Doctor Henderson, however, promptly interfered, and, taking charge of the patient, was soon able to pronounce that, barring exhaustion, the poor fellow was all right; upon which the anxious little crowd dispersed, Sibylla retiring to her state-room, locking herself in, and gaining relief to her overwrought feelings by abandoning herself to a perfect tempest of hysterical tears.

Under the doctor's skilful treatment Ned was soon sufficiently restored to answer a few questions, when he stated that though he had remained continuously on the watch from the moment of his rising above the surface after his first plunge to almost the moment of his being picked up, he had never caught a single glimpse of the mate, and that it was his impression the unfortunate man must have been hurt in his fall, and that he had never risen above water again. Notwithstanding this statement the ship was kept hove-to for another half-hour, with a man on the look-out on each topgallant-yard; when, nothing having been seen of the missing man during that time, Captain Blyth reluctantly gave up the search, and, wearing round, the ship once more proceeded on her voyage.

Chapter Six
The springing of the Mink

The deplorable fatality mentioned in the last chapter necessitated a further rearrangement of the official duties on board the *Flying Cloud*; Ned being advanced still another step and made acting chief-mate, or "chief-officer" as it is the custom to dub this official in the merchant service, whilst another apprentice—a very quiet, steady young man named Robert Manners—was promoted to the post of second-mate thus rendered vacant. Although these two posts—the most important and responsible in the ship next to that of the master—were now filled by two young men whose united ages fell short of forty years, the arrangement appeared to work in the most thoroughly satisfactory manner. The lads performed their onerous duties efficiently; the crew were as orderly and obedient as heretofore, and not a single sinister omen or indication manifested itself to arouse anxiety in the mind of the skipper. To add to Captain Blyth's satisfaction, the island of New Amsterdam was sighted and passed on the morning of the tenth day succeeding the loss of the unfortunate Mr Willoughby, and that, too, in a direction and at an hour which precisely verified the prediction of the captain, who rather prided himself upon his skill and accuracy as a navigator.

For several nights previous to this occurrence the skipper had been losing a great deal of rest; he had been too anxious to sleep, knowing that during his absence from the deck the ship was in absolute charge of one or the other of two lads whom he remembered, as though it had been but yesterday, joining him without a particle of experience. But as day after day, and night after night passed, and he saw what excellent use those two lads had made of the training and instruction he had so conscientiously bestowed upon them, he had gradually grown less anxious. And now, with fine weather, a fair breeze, and New Amsterdam sighted and passed, the poor fagged skipper once more knew what it was to enjoy an easy mind; and as he bade Ned "good-night" on the poop, about five bells in the first watch, he announced, in tones loud enough to be distinctly heard by the man at the wheel, that he intended to treat himself to a whole night's sleep, and that he was not to be called or disturbed unless for something out of the common.

When, therefore, about three o'clock next morning, he was aroused from sleep by a gentle tap at the outer door of his state-room, Captain Blyth's first coherent thought was: "I wonder what is the matter now!" It was nothing to do with the weather—unless the sky had assumed a threatening aspect—for, by long force of habit, he had acquired the power of detecting, even during his soundest sleep, any such important change in the state of the elements as a material increase of wind or sea, and, though the sleep from which he had been aroused was as sound as it ever falls to the lot of a seaman to enjoy, he had been quite conscious all the time that neither the sough of the wind in the rigging nor the steady swinging motion of the ship had become intensified. It was, therefore, in a somewhat peevish tone that he inquired:

"Well, what is the news?"

"Will you please step for'ard, sir, and see what ails Bob—young Mr Manners, I mean, sir?" said a voice which the skipper recognised as belonging to one of the seamen. "He's on the fo'c's'le-head, a cussing and carrying on as if he was mad, sir; and two of the hands is holding him down so's he sha'n't fling hisself overboard."

"Whew!" whistled poor Captain Blyth in dismay. "All right, my man; I'll be out there in a brace of shakes! What can be the matter with the poor lad?" he soliloquised, as he hastily drew on his most necessary garments. "A fit, perhaps, brought on by over-anxiety. Well, I won't disturb anybody until I see what it is; then, if necessary, I must rouse out Dr Henderson."

And, as he came to this conclusion, the worthy man softly opened his state-room door and stepped out on deck.

The night was dark, there being no moon, whilst the star-lit sky was almost blotted out by the squadrons of fleecy cloud which swept with stately motion athwart it. Yet there was light enough to reveal to the skipper a dark blot on the forecastle, which he knew to be a cluster of men; and toward these he hurriedly made his way. Before he could reach them, however, two bare-footed men stepped softly out behind him from the galley; and whilst one seized and pinioned his arms behind him, the other flourished a large-headed, short-handled hammer over his head whilst he whispered fiercely in the ear of the paralysed skipper:

"Give but a single outcry, and I'll spatter your brains about the deck." Then he added, somewhat more gently: "No harm is intended you, Captain Blyth, but we mean to have the ship. We *will* have her; and were you to raise an alarm it would only cause bloodshed, which we are most anxious to avoid. Where's Nicholls? Here, Nicholls, this man is your prisoner; get the bilboes and clap them on him. And—mind—I shall hold you responsible for his safekeeping!"

"But—but—Williams," stammered poor Captain Blyth, who now identified the speaker, "what is the meaning of all this? I—I—don't understand it!"

"No time to explain now," was the answer. "Tell you all about it later on if you care to hear. Come, lads, away aft with us, and let us secure our other prisoner!"

In obedience to this command, the mob of mutineers who had clustered about the door of the forward deck-house—into which the unfortunate skipper had been thrust—melted away, and Captain Blyth found himself left alone with his jailer and young Manners, the latter being bound hand and foot, and lying gagged in one of the bunks which had been vacated when the steerage passengers were drafted into the forecastle.

In the midst of his bewilderment and dismay the skipper still retained enough presence of mind to note, by the light of the single lantern which illuminated the place, that his young subordinate was suffering severe discomfort from the presence of the gag—a large belaying-pin—in his mouth; and, turning to the man Nicholls, he pointed out that, unless the crew wished to add the crime of murder to that of mutiny, it would be advisable to remove the gag at once.

"Well, sir," said the man, civilly enough—he was one of the former steerage passengers—"I don't know what to do about that. I'd be willing enough to take the thing out of the young gentleman's mouth, but my orders are strict; and if anything was to happen through my meddling you may depend upon it I should be made to suffer for it."

"If that is what you are afraid of, my good fellow," said the skipper, "you may remove the gag at once. Nothing *shall* happen, I promise you. The crew have possession of the ship, safe enough; and, bound hand and foot as we two are, we can do nothing to recover her. So out with it at once, my man, unless you wish to see the poor lad suffocate before your eyes."

This was enough; the gag was at once removed, the skipper at the same time cautioning Manners against any ill-timed attempt to raise an alarm, and then Nicholls was questioned as to the reasons for the mutiny.

"Well, sir," was the reply, "I don't rightly understand the ins and outs of the thing, myself; but Williams has been talkin' to the men, and, accordin' to his showin', labourers and mechanics and sailors have been robbed and cheated out of their rights time out o' mind. So the long and the short of it is that we've all took a solemn oath to stand by one another in an attempt to get what rightfully belongs to us."

"What rightfully belongs to you?" exclaimed the skipper in bewilderment. "I don't understand you, my man. You surely do not pretend to say that *I* have defrauded you of anything to which you are entitled? A certain amount of wages is, of course, due to you in respect of work already performed; but it is the custom to pay seamen only when they arrive at the port of discharge—"

"Oh, yes, sir; we understands all that, of course," interrupted Nicholls. "It ain't that at all, sir; it's—"

Captain Blyth, however, was not destined to learn just then what "it" was, for at this point the conversation was broken in upon by the reappearance of a party of the mutineers, headed by Williams, and having poor Ned among them as a prisoner.

"There, Ned, there's the skipper. In you go, my lad, and stow yourself alongside of him; and that will complete the party," exclaimed Williams cheerfully, as he thrust the lad unceremoniously through the doorway of the deck-house. "Now take the gag out of his mouth," he commanded; "but I caution you," he continued sternly, addressing himself particularly to Ned, "that if either of you utter a single outcry I'll blow his brains out without hesitation." And as he spoke he drew from his pocket a revolver which he began deliberately to load.

"You are carrying things with a high hand, my fine fellow!" observed Captain Blyth fiercely; "but I warn you at once that you are only preparing a halter with which to hang yourself. The fact that something is wrong on board here will infallibly be discovered by the first man-of-war which falls in with us, and your punishment will speedily follow. Hear me, men," he continued, raising his voice and addressing the crew generally; "I don't in the least understand your motive for behaving in this extraordinary fashion; but cast me and my two mates adrift, and I promise you on my word of honour that I will listen patiently to whatever complaint you may have to make, and will redress any wrong which you can show has been done you."

"Spare your breath, skipper," answered Williams quietly. "We haven't done this thing in a hurry, and we're not to be talked out of it in a moment; and perhaps the sooner you understand that the better. No, sir; we've no fault to find with you or anybody else aboard here. The fault lies with them who've robbed, and cheated, and ground down the likes of us for centuries; and the time has now come when the few of us as belongs to this ship's fo'c's'le intend to help our selves to what we've as good a right as anybody to have. As to punishment, why, we've agreed to take our chances about that; and as to men-o'-war, how many have we fell in with, so far, this voyage? We'll take our chances about them too. Josh Williams may be no scholar, cap'n, but he knows a thing or two—he knows enough to be able to take care of his own neck, and of the necks of them that trust him too."

"My good fellow, you don't in the least know what you are talking about!" exclaimed Captain Blyth.

"Enough said, sir—enough!" interrupted Williams. "All the talking in the world won't undo what's done. We've put our heads into the noose, but we're not fools enough to sway away upon the yard-rope; so you may spare yourself the trouble of further talk, and us the trouble of listening to you. Now the present time is as good as any to tell you what our plans are so far as you are concerned; so please pay attention. We're all hands averse to bloodshed, and we intend to work our business without it, if possible—you understand, *if possible!*—so, instead of cutting your throats and heaving you overboard, we're going to land *you*, Captain Blyth, on some island or another where you'll be able to pick up a living, but from which you won't be likely to get away until long after we've done with the ship. Young Manners there we shall clap ashore on some other island four or five hundred miles away from you, skipper; and the passengers we shall put ashore somewhere else, where they'll not be likely to get us into trouble or to send trouble after us. As for Ned, here, we intend to keep him with us to navigate the ship."

"Do you?" ejaculated Ned. "Then understand at once and for all that I decline to remain with you. What! do you suppose I will mix myself up in any way or associate with a pack of rascally mutineers? I'll see you all hanged first!"

"Well crowed!" ejaculated Williams approvingly with a hearty laugh. "My eyes, lads, what a skipper he'd make for us if he could only be persuaded to join! But we won't ask you to do that, Ned," he continued in the same bantering tone. "You can follow your own inclinations in that matter—join us or not, just as you please; but remain with us and navigate us you *shall* and *will*, whether you like it or not."

"Never!" declared Ned resolutely. "You may pitch me overboard if you choose, but I will never do a single hand's turn to help you in any way."

Williams did not appear to be in the least disconcerted at this declaration; he simply sat down by Ned's side and whispered earnestly for some minutes in the lad's ear.

As the communication progressed poor Ned first flushed deeply, then grew as ashy pale as the sunburn on his cheeks would permit; his eyes dilated with horror, and when Williams had finished the lad struggled to his feet and gasped out:

"You villain! you infernal scoundrel! Cast off my lashings, and, lad as I am, I will thrash you before all hands for daring to make such an infamous proposal to me!"

For the first time that night Williams showed signs of anger, but, quickly checking himself, he said:

"Well, if that card won't take the trick, I have another that will!" And again he sat down and resumed his whispering.

It was evident by the expression of his countenance that this time Ned was not only horrified but also thoroughly frightened; and when Williams ceased the poor lad hung his head and murmured in a scarcely audible voice:

"Enough! you have conquered! though I can scarcely believe you *could* be so inhuman—to those poor children, too! But remember! if, after what you have promised, the slightest insult or injury is offered to any one of them, I'll—I'll—"

"There, that will do!" interrupted William. "I've pledged you my word, boy; and I hope to have you with us long enough to convince you that I *never* break it. But mind! I must have you faithfully do whatever you are told to do, in return. And now, as we thoroughly understand each other, you may go back to your berth and turn in until morning; and then I shall expect that when the passengers make their appearance you will tell them what has happened aboard here, and also mention our intentions about them. And be careful to make them clearly understand that, whilst we are all against bloodshed, the slightest suspicious action on their part will be looked upon as treachery, and treated as such. Cast our new sailing-master adrift there, some of you, and let him go back to his berth."

Williams' order was promptly obeyed; and Ned, half-dazed, rose to his feet, advanced to the door, and then stopped. "What about Captain Blyth and Mr Manners?" he asked. "What are you going to do with them?"

"They will have to put up with such accommodation as they can find here until we have an opportunity to land them," was the reply. "But make your mind easy on their account, Mr Damerell; their comfort will be properly looked after, and no harm will come to them *unless an attempt is made to retake the ship*. In such a case as that I won't answer for the consequences. The blame for whatever happens must fall upon the shoulders of them that bring it about."

Ned was obliged to be content with this; and with a heavy heart he turned and left the deck-house, not daring to look his commander in the face, and feeling as guilty in his new dignity as though he had voluntarily thrown in his lot with the mutineers, notwithstanding the fact that pressure had been brought to bear upon him which he was equally powerless to avoid or to resist.

Ned's first act, on returning aft, was to enter Captain Blyth's state-room, with the object of securing the keys of the arm-chests; but the mutineers seemed to have been beforehand with him, for the keys were gone. He next sought the lock-up tin box in which the ship's papers were kept; but here, too, the mutineers had been ahead of him, for the box, as also the captain's desk, was missing. Being thus foiled in the only matters which occurred to him at the moment, he left the state-room, closing the door after him as silently and reverently as if the captain's dead body had been lying there, and reluctantly returned to his own berth. Not to sleep, of course, that was utterly out of the question, the poor lad was so overwhelmed with consternation at the unexpected seizure of the ship, and with dismay at the way in which he had been compulsorily identified with the movement, that he just then felt as though he would never be able to sleep again. No; sleep and he were strangers, at least for the time being, so he flung himself down on the sofa-locker and tried to think. But for the first half-hour or so even the power of thought was denied him. The catastrophe had been so utterly unattended by any warning that it was like a levin stroke falling from a cloudless sky, and for the moment Ned found himself unable to recognise it as an actual fact. Over and over again he stood up and shook himself to ascertain whether or not he was really awake, or whether his disjointed cogitations and the cause of them were only parts of an ugly dream. At length, however, his mind grew clearer, the disastrous reality of the whole business finally asserted itself, and he then began to cast blindly about him for the means of rectification. But, alas, the longer he thought about it, the more hopeless did the situation appear. He began to see that Williams had only spoken the simple truth when he asserted that the mutiny was the result of long premeditation. They had laid their plans well, the scoundrels! and had carried them out with such consummate artifice and attention to detail, that as Ned turned over in his mind scheme after scheme for the recovery of the ship, it was only to realise that each had been anticipated and provided against. At length, baffled and in despair, he gave up, temporarily, all hope of effecting a recapture, and allowed his thoughts to turn in another direction. "What was to become of the passengers?" True, Williams had guaranteed for them perfect immunity from molestation, the price of this privilege being on Ned's part true and faithful service as navigator of the ship for the mutineers, but a time was to come when the passengers would be landed on some out-of-the-way spot, doubtless, and exposed to countless perils from hunger, thirst, exposure, and worse than all, perhaps the nameless horrors of a captivity among savages! And yet Ned felt that they would be in even greater peril so long as they remained on board the *Flying Cloud*. The mutineers seemed peaceably disposed for the moment certainly, but how long would that state of things continue after they had gained access to the liquor on board? Ned shuddered as his excited imagination pictured the scene of bloodshed which might be enacted within the next twenty-four hours, and he finally began to realise that even falling into the hands of a tribe of savages might not prove to be the very worst evil possible for those poor weak women and children. His next thought was that they must be got out of the ship with all possible expedition. Ha! but that involved the necessity for saying "good-bye"—for a parting! Well; what of that? He had said "good-bye" before now to plenty of pleasant people, both on the Melbourne quays, and on the dock walls at London. But, somehow, this time it seemed different; he did not know how it was, but these people seemed *more* than friends, the ladies especially; for them he felt that he entertained a regard as tender, almost—or quite—as that which he felt for Eva, and this now made the idea of parting so distasteful to him that, as his mind began to dwell upon it, the feeling amounted almost to agony. And this, too, quite apart from the sensation of indignant disgust with which he regarded Williams' unscrupulous resolution to involve him and his fortunes with the future career of the mutineers. But it should not be; he would outwit the rascals somehow, and join the little party of passengers when they were landed, even if he had to steal over the ship's side, drop overboard, and swim ashore as the vessel sailed away.

Whilst cogitating thus, the returning daylight surprised him; and shortly afterwards he heard a movement in the saloon which told him that the gentlemen were about to make their appearance on deck to indulge in the usual matutinal "tub."

He opened his state-room door and entered the saloon with a cheery "Good-morning, gentlemen!"

"Good-morning, Mr Damerell," was the equally cheery reply; and then Mr Gaunt, happening to notice the lad's worn and haggard appearance, exclaimed:

"Why, good heavens, Ned, what is the matter? Are you ill?"

"Hush!" said Ned. "No, I am not ill, Mr Gaunt, but I am in great trouble and perplexity. I have passed through a rather startling experience during the night; and"—in a low tone of voice, so that the ladies, if awake, might not hear him—"I have bad news to communicate. Will you kindly step into my cabin for a moment?"

The two gentlemen passed into the state-room and seated themselves on the sofa-locker, Ned following and closing the door after him.

"Now, Ned, what is it?" asked the engineer. "If I may judge from the expression of your countenance the matter is serious; and, if so, out with it at once. You need not be afraid of startling us, I fancy."

"You *will* be startled, nevertheless, I expect," was the reply. "The matter is simply this. The crew have seized the ship, and poor Captain Blyth and Mr Manners are at this moment close prisoners in the deck-house for'ard!"

The two gentlemen stared first at each other, and then at Ned, in the utmost perplexity. For a moment or two they were both so completely astounded that neither could find a word to say. At length, however, the engineer so far recovered his powers of speech as to ejaculate:

"But—but—good heavens! what will become of the women and children? And how is it, sir, that, if what you state be true, *you* are free—as you apparently are?"

"You are all perfectly safe—I hope and believe—at all events for the present. And the price of your safety is a promise on my part to faithfully navigate the ship to the best of my ability for the mutineers," answered Ned with quivering lips; and then suddenly and completely overcome by a sense of his desolate and desperate situation, the poor lad turned away, buried his face in his hands, and burst into tears.

Doctor Henderson appeared to be too thoroughly paralysed with surprise and consternation to say or do anything just then; but Mr Gaunt at once rose to his feet, and, laying his hand kindly on the young fellow's shoulder, said:

"There, don't give way, Ned, I ought not to have spoken so harshly, but I was rather 'taken aback' as you sailors say. Sit down, my lad, and tell us all about it, and then we must see if we cannot devise a means to recover possession of the ship, and restore their freedom to poor Captain Blyth and Mr Manners."

Quickly recovering his self-control, Ned seated himself on the edge of his bunk, and briefly related to his astonished listeners all that had occurred during the preceding night, winding up by saying:

"As to retaking the ship, I am afraid there is scarcely a chance of our succeeding in that, for the entire crew seem to have been completely won over by that fellow Williams, and to be thoroughly united in their determination to try their fortunes as pirates—for that, as I understand it, is what it all amounts to; so you see there are only our three selves against all hands for'ard—for they seem determined to keep poor Captain Blyth and Manners close prisoners until they can be landed somewhere—and what can we three do against so many? Moreover, I have been ordered to particularly impress upon you that, whilst the mutineers are at present extremely averse to bloodshed, anything like a suspicious action on your part will be looked upon as premeditated treachery, *and treated as such*. Those were Williams' very words. So, whilst I shall be only too glad to take my part in any feasible scheme which you may be able to devise, I feel it my duty to warn you that we must all act with the utmost circumspection."

This announcement made the gentlemen look rather blank again.

"Um!" at length said Mr Gaunt. "The further we advance with this business the more serious does its aspect become. I have no very great fancy just now for being landed anywhere but at Melbourne; nevertheless, as matters now are, I can easily conceive a state of things which would make us glad enough to be all safely quit of the ship, even if we had to leave her for a raft. We must be circumspect, as you say, Ned, ay, even to the extent of not being seen talking much together. But we will keep our thoughts busy, and if a scheme occurs to either of us that person must contrive an opportunity to communicate it as briefly as may be to the others. Meanwhile, you will be doing good service if you can manage to sound the better-disposed portion of the crew, with a view to ascertaining whether it would be possible to win them back to their allegiance. And now, Henderson, the best thing we can do, I think, will be to return to our respective cabins and break this news as gently as possible to our wives; they *must* know it—it would be quite impossible to long conceal the fact of the mutiny from them—and we are the most suitable bearers of the intelligence to them. Well, good-bye for the present, Ned, and do not forget that you may depend upon us at any hour of the day or night. Is not that so, Henderson?"

"Yes, certainly, of course," was the reply. "I am too much astonished to say much just now, but I shall not be found wanting when the time for action arrives. Good-bye, Ned!"

And with a cordial shake of Ned's hand, the two quiet, unpretending-looking men filed out and re-entered their respective cabins.

Chapter Seven
Anxious days

Upon learning the news of the mutiny the ladies were, as might be expected, overwhelmed with consternation and dismay, feelings which were intensified when it was further intimated to them, through Ned, that Williams intended henceforward to take up his abode in the cabin, and that he should expect all the passengers to favour him with their company at meals, and, in fact, whensoever he might choose to join them. So impertinent a message naturally excited at the outset a great deal of indignation; but Mr Gaunt—who seemed to rise to the occasion, and who, immediately upon the occurrence of the crisis, instinctively assumed the direction of affairs—soon brought the little party to reason when they assembled in the saloon for a hurried conference, by pointing out to them that, for the present, at least, they were quite helpless, and that, therefore, instead of struggling against what was unavoidable, their best plan would be to humour the whims of the mutineers, so long, of course, as they were not too outrageous, and to quietly bide their time in the hope that an opportunity might present itself for turning the tables upon the crew. And he emphasised his proposition by so many convincing arguments that, when breakfast was announced by the steward, the entire party presented themselves at table, the ladies making such a successful effort to conceal their perturbation as to thoroughly astonish Williams when that worthy made his appearance and established himself at the head of the table.

"Good-morning, ladies and gentlemen," said he, making a not ungraceful bow as he seated himself. "Hope you all slept well."

"Thank you," said Mr Gaunt; "yes, I believe we all enjoyed a fairly good night's rest; thanks to our ignorance of what was going forward."

"Ah, yes," answered Williams with a somewhat constrained laugh and an obviously embarrassed manner; "yes, we took the liberty of making a change or two for the better during the night."

"For the better?" repeated Gaunt. "Pray how can you demonstrate that the changes you have effected are for the better?"

"Well, I'll tell you," answered Williams. "I'm glad you've asked, as it gives me an opportunity to explain the why and the wherefore of our acts, and to show you that we are not, after all, quite such villains as I daresay you now think us. First and foremost," he continued, "I suppose I need not point out to gentlemen of your intelligence and experience that sailors—foremast men, that is to say—lead the hardest lives and are the worst paid for it of any set of men living?"

"Well," said Mr Gaunt, "without being prepared to go so far as that I am quite willing to admit that the life of a seaman is a hard one. But what has that to do with your mutiny? In the first place, I suppose you joined the ship voluntarily; and, in the next, it seems to me, from what I have seen, that you have been made as comfortable on board here as was possible under the circumstances. Your food has been good and sufficient, your quarters are dry, airy, and comfortable, and surely it would be difficult to find more considerate officers than Captain Blyth and his mates?"

"All very true, so far as it goes," answered Williams, "but would *you* like to be a seaman before the mast?"

"No," said Mr Gaunt, "I frankly admit I should not; otherwise, I suppose I should have been a seaman, and not a civil engineer. But the life was of your own choosing, I presume?"

"Yes, it was, and I don't complain of it," said Williams. "The thing I complain of is, that, seeing what a life of hardship and peril ours is, we do not get paid a half nor a quarter enough. What would be the use of ships without sailors to man them? We are just as necessary to a ship as her captain; yet look at the difference in his pay and ours! I say it is not fair; it is rank injustice; sailors have just been *robbed* all these years, and the long and the short of it is that the crew of this ship means to get back part of what has been stolen from them by the dishonesty of shipowners."

"But, my good fellow," exclaimed the engineer, "you are taking an altogether wrong view of the question. Admitting that you are as necessary to the ship as her captain, you entirely overlook the important fact that *one* captain is sufficient for a ship, no matter how large she may be, whilst *one* seaman alone is of very trifling value; hence the difference in the scale of pay."

It was clear enough from the expression of the mutineer's face that this view of the question had never before been presented to him; he was completely "taken aback," and for a minute or two could find absolutely nothing to say.

"Well!" he exclaimed at last, "it is clear enough that it is no use for an ignorant man like me to try to argue with an educated gentleman like you; you are bound to go to wind'ard of me the very first tack, and I was a fool for attempting it. But there are other matters which, in my opinion, fully justify the step we have taken."

"The fellow may *call* himself an ignorant man, but his language is that of a person who has enjoyed at least some of the benefits of education," thought Gaunt. But he merely said:

"Indeed! May I ask what they are?"

"Certainly. The question is just this. Why should I, and thousands like me, have to work and slave for a bare living, whilst there are others who never do a stroke of work in their whole lives and yet have houses, and land, and money, horses and carriages—in fact, all that heart can wish for? Is this fair, or right, or just?"

"Assuredly it is," was the reply, "and so, I think, you will admit, if you will give the matter a moment's consideration. It is not your fault or mine that you and I do not occupy the enviable position in life to which you have just referred; it is the fault, if fault there be, of our ancestors. They did not happen to be money-getters, and therefore, if we wish to enjoy the advantages attendant upon the possession of a fortune, large or small, we must get the fortune for ourselves. Just look at the question for a moment from the millionaire's point of view. If you happened to possess a fortune would you consider it fair or just that you should be called upon to divide it evenly with everybody worse off than yourself? For that, I fancy, is the idea you have in your mind."

This was another poser which Williams evidently found it wholly impossible to answer. He hung his head in deep and perplexed thought for some minutes, and at length said:

"It is quite impossible for me to argue with you, as I said before; but the long and the short of it is this, we have made our plans, and we intend to carry them out, right or wrong. But you need have no apprehension for yourselves. We have no intention to prey upon private individuals; and though we shall be obliged to land you on some spot from which it will be impossible for you to escape, we will deliver up to you the whole of your private property, and also furnish you with means to protect yourselves and to preserve your lives, so far as we have the power."

And without waiting to discuss the question further, the mutineer rose from the table and beat a somewhat precipitate retreat.

"Had you any hope of convincing the fellow?" asked the doctor, when the little party once more found themselves free to converse unreservedly.

"No, I cannot say I had," answered Gaunt; "but I thought I might so far shake his purpose as to make him hesitate about his future plans, and so give us a little more time in which to act. But it is evident enough that he has no wish to be convinced; if, therefore, we are to do anything we must make our arrangements speedily. Come on deck and have a smoke, old fellow."

The ladies had no fancy for being left alone just then; the entire party, therefore, children included, adjourned to the poop. Williams was then standing in the waist talking to the boatswain, to whom he appeared to be giving some instructions; but on observing the movements of the passengers he signed to Ned, who was standing near, to follow him, and hastily made his way into the saloon.

"Bring me the captain's charts," he said, as soon as Ned joined him. The charts were produced; and after carefully looking them over Williams selected a track-chart of the world, which he carefully spread out on the table.

"Now, show me whereabouts we are," he said.

Ned indicated the position of the ship by making a pencil dot on the paper, and a long period of anxious study on Williams' part followed.

"What is the course to the Straits of Sunda?" was the next question.

Ned told him; whereupon Williams left the saloon, and a moment later was heard altering the course of the ship in accordance with Ned's information. He then returned to the saloon, and unrolled a chart of the North Pacific, which he pored anxiously over for fully a quarter of an hour, finally huddling the charts all together in a heap, with the remark, "That will do for the present;" which Ned construed into a token of dismissal, and accordingly left the cabin.

Day followed day with little or no variety, the weather continuing fine all the time, and at length the *Flying Cloud* arrived within a few days' sail of the Straits of Sunda. Ned now spent on deck every moment he could possibly spare from sleep, as he was not without hopes that hereabout a man-of-war might be fallen in with; and he was resolved that, in such a case, it should go hard but he would make some effort to communicate to her the state of affairs on board.

And, as a matter of fact, they actually did sight a frigate on the day upon which they entered the straits. But Williams was not to be caught napping; he too had evidently contemplated some such possibility, and had taken such precautions as not only rendered it impossible for anyone to make a private signal, but had also arranged such answers to the signals usually made on such occasions that the frigate was completely hoodwinked, and passed on her way without attempting to send a boat alongside.

This was a terrible disappointment, not only to Ned but also to Gaunt and the doctor, each of them having confidently reckoned upon a certain deliverance in the event of a man-of-war being fallen in with.

They now recognised that in Williams, whether educated or not, they had a man of no ordinary acuteness to deal with; they realised that, though apparently free as air to act as they pleased, an unceasing watch was being kept upon them, and they felt that henceforth they must not place any dependence upon the hope of help from without. They all, therefore, individually and collectively too, so far as they had opportunity, began to plot and scheme; in the hope of being able to hit upon some plan which might enable them to recover possession of the ship, going even to the perilous length of sounding the least unpromising of the crew in the hope of finding at least a few of them open to either persuasion or bribery. But it was all of no avail. The men proved not only unresponsive but suspicious; and they were also wholly unsuccessful in their efforts to communicate with Captain Blyth, of whom they could not get so much as a sight, much less speech with him.

"It is of no use for us to try any further," at last said Gaunt, when talking matters over with the doctor. "We have tried our best, but Williams is too acute and too strong for us. I have noticed a certain something in his manner within the last day or two which tells me that we are standing on very perilous ground, and we must drop the whole affair before worse comes of it. We must not forget that the women and children have only us to look to for protection in this awful strait; it will never do for us to attempt anything which might result in their being left to the tender mercies of those ruffians forward. The only thing we can now hope for is a speedy and safe deliverance from their clutches by being landed somewhere; and we must pray that they will be induced to land us on some spot where we may not only be able to make ourselves safe, but also to secure the means of living."

Meanwhile the ship passed safely through the Straits of Sunda, along the south coast of Borneo, and so into the Java and Flores Seas; Williams maintaining a ceaseless and anxious watch upon Ned as the lad daily pricked off upon the chart the position of the ship, and frequently altering the course with the evident object of inspecting certain islands, probably to ascertain whether they were suitable for landing his unwelcome guests upon. Several islands were visited, but none of them proved satisfactory. Some were found to be inhabited by savages, whose demonstrations at sight of the ship were so unmistakably hostile that it would have been obviously only murder thinly disguised to have landed any white person there, whilst others seemed deficient in the means of sustaining life. Wandering thus about the ocean a fortnight passed away, and Williams began to grow impatient; so much so indeed that he at length proposed landing the passengers on the next land seen, let it be what it would. But to this the crew would not agree: they were as yet young in crime, and were determined that, since the passengers *must* be got rid of, they should at least be given a fair chance. A compromise was at length come to, by which it was agreed that the search should be continued for three days longer, after which the unlucky passengers were to be landed on the first land seen, there to take their chance. This matter was decided at a council composed of the entire crew, on the evening of a day whereon no less than three islands had been fruitlessly visited; and at the close of the discussion Ned was summoned and the chart consulted. At Williams' request the area already examined was pointed out, and then, after much discussion, a course of due east was decided upon, in order that a new tract of sea might be explored. On this course the chart showed a clear sea for something like three hundred miles ahead of them. Everybody was therefore much astonished when at daybreak next morning land was descried right ahead at a distance of only about ten miles.

The discovery was of course first reported to Williams, who seemed greatly disconcerted by it.

"Call Ned," said he.

Ned was duly summoned, and soon made his appearance on the topgallant-forecastle, upon which Williams had already established himself, and from which advantageous stand-point he was watching the approach of the ship to the land.

"What do you call that?" demanded Williams, pointing ahead, as soon as he became conscious of Ned's presence beside him.

"Land—unmistakably land!" exclaimed Ned, shading his eyes with his hand to get a clearer view.

"And do you know how far the ship has run during the night?" angrily demanded the mutineer.

"Not far, I should think; perhaps fifty or sixty miles," replied Ned, glancing aloft and away toward the horizon to note the appearance of sea and sky.

"And did you not tell me only last night that we had a clear sea to the eastward of us for something like three hundred miles? Yet there is the land; and if it had happened to blow fresh during the night we should perhaps have run upon it before making it out in the dark. How do you account for your being so strangely out of your reckoning?" sternly asked Williams.

"I am not out of my reckoning," hotly retorted Ned; "and I cannot account for the appearance of that island except upon the supposition that this particular portion of the ocean has never yet been thoroughly examined, and that therefore the island ahead has never been observed and set down on the chart. One thing at all events is certain, and that is that, as I said last night, the chart shows a clear sea a long way ahead of us."

"Bring the chart to me, and let me have another look at it," growled Williams.

Ned produced the chart and spread it out on the deck, when Williams kneeled down and examined it for some time with very evident suspicion, not scrupling at last to hint pretty plainly his impression that Ned had deliberately intended to cast away the ship. Of course Ned indignantly repudiated any such intention, and at length apparently succeeded in partially reassuring Williams, who finally grumbled out; "Well, if what you say be true, the only conclusion we can come to is that yonder island has never yet been visited by civilised beings; and if that is the case it is all the more suitable a spot on which to land some of our useless live lumber. So go aft and tell the passengers to pack up their traps at once, as I am about to put them ashore. And tell the boatswain to open the after-hatch and to purse these people's dunnage on deck all ready for sending ashore with them. I am quite tired of running about looking for a suitable spot for them, and will look no further. They will have to do the best they can yonder, savages or no savages."

Ned hurried aft to the poop, on which the little group of ladies and gentlemen was congregated, and delivered his message, adding:

"I am very glad—in some respects—that you are going, for I may now tell you that unconsciously you have been in some sort acting as hostages for my good behaviour, and I have been dreadfully afraid that some involuntary slip on my part might complicate matters for you. When once you are all safely out of the ship I shall feel more at liberty to take a few risks, if I can see that any good is likely to arise therefrom. I was at first in hopes that Captain Blyth and young Manners would have been put on shore with you, in which case I would have joined you, even if I had had to swim for it; but I am afraid Williams—the scoundrel—intends to land them elsewhere, in which case I am sure it is my duty to stick to the ship so long as they remain on board. But, at all events, I will try to give you the latitude and longitude of the island before you leave us, for, if I mistake not, you, Mr Gaunt, can navigate?"

"Yes," said Gaunt, "I am a fairly good navigator, and not a bad seaman, in an amateurish sort of way, you know. But do not trouble about the position of the island. I have here," producing his watch, "an excellent chronometer, showing Greenwich time, and books and instruments among my luggage which, with the aid of sun, moon, and stars, will enable me to obtain all the information I need. True, I have no charts; but I have a capital atlas, which will serve our turn, so far as finding our way from place to place is concerned. And now, Ned, whilst we have the opportunity, let me say that we all thoroughly understand the peculiar and difficult position in which you are placed on board here, and that we consider you have conducted yourself admirably and with remarkable discretion from the very commencement of this deplorable business of the mutiny. And if, as is by no means improbable, you should by and by find yourself involved by your involuntary association with these mutineers in a situation of difficulty or peril, we shall be most happy and willing to bear testimony to that effect, if we happen to be in a situation to do so. We shall of course endeavour to escape from our island prison; and should we succeed, our first act on reaching a civilised country will be to make to the authorities a full and detailed report of all the circumstances of the mutiny, so that a man-of-war may be sent out in quest of the ship. But I think it will be well for *you* to do the same, for your own sake. You can perhaps manage it by writing an account of the transaction, sealing it up in a bottle, and throwing the bottle overboard when you happen to be in some well-frequented ship track; not forgetting to state in your report the position of the island on which we are landed, as well as that of the spot on which poor Captain Blyth and young Manners may be put on shore. And now, as we may not have another opportunity to say it, good-bye, my dear lad, remain honest and true to your duty, as you have been hitherto, and leave all the rest to God, who will not allow you to suffer for the faults of others. Good-bye, Ned, and God bless and guide and deliver you from all evil. Amen."

Gaunt then shook Ned heartily by the hand, after which the others stepped forward one by one and did the same, each saying a hopeful word or two to cheer and encourage him under the pang of parting, which it was evident enough the poor lad felt keenly. Sibylla hung back until all the others, the poor children included, had spoken their farewell, and then she too advanced and held out her hand. She was very pale, and the small shapely trembling hand which Ned grasped in his was icy cold; but however keenly she may have felt the parting under such terrible circumstances she contrived to maintain at least a semblance of outward composure, though there was a tremor in her voice which she found it quite impossible to control. She murmured a few low half-inarticulate words of farewell, gave Ned's hand a slight involuntary pressure ere she released it, and then hastily retreated to her state-room.

As for poor Ned, on releasing Sibylla's hand he turned and staggered out of the cabin, looking like a man who had been suddenly struck a numbing blow, and feeling as he might have felt had the saloon been a felon's dock in which he had just received his death-sentence. This miserable parting, though he had been constantly expecting it any time within the previous fortnight, and though he honestly believed—as he had said—that he was glad of it, now seemed to have come upon him with startling suddenness, and it had called up with it an unexpected feeling of bitter anguish for which he was wholly unprepared, and for which he found it difficult to account. It was not, he thought, that he had conceived for these people an exceptionally warm friendship; he had made many friends during his sea-going career for whom he had felt quite as strong a regard, yet when the time for it came he had been able to say farewell with a cheery voice and a comparatively light heart. But now it seemed altogether a different matter; though the sun still shone brilliantly, as of old, and the warm soft wind still roughened the sapphire sea and caused it to laugh and sparkle as joyously as ever, the whole world looked dark, cheerless, and gloomy to him, and he felt as though he had suddenly become the victim of some terrible calamity. In the endeavour to get rid of the horrible feeling of depression which had thus unaccountably seized upon him, Ned went and hunted up the boatswain, and delivered Williams' order respecting the removal of the passengers' baggage from the hold; after which he mounted the poop, on which Williams had by this time stationed himself. But, actuated by the new and peculiar feeling which was just then so strongly asserting itself within his breast, the lad could think only of the mysterious island ahead, and of those who were so soon to be landed upon it; and his imagination, powerfully stimulated as it just then was, already pictured the little party abandoned there, and reduced to the most primitive state of self-dependence, given over to battle for their very existence as best they might: houseless, exposed to a thousand perils, and destitute of even the commonest necessaries of life until such could be provided by their own exertions. There was one—and only one—grain of comfort to brighten the gloomy prospect as it presented itself to Ned's mental vision, which was that Mr Gaunt seemed to be a man of infinite resource; one of those extremely rare individuals who can never be taken wholly by surprise, and who no sooner find themselves confronted by a difficulty than they are ready with a remedy for it. The doctor, too, though a singularly quiet and unassuming man, struck Ned as one who, his work once fairly cut out for him, would go manfully through with it. But what could two men, however resolute, do in the position they would soon occupy, unless well provided with arms, ammunition, and tools? And, determined to let slip no opportunity to help those in whom he was so strongly interested, the lad turned to Williams and said:

"As I suppose you do not intend to turn these people adrift without arms, or the tools with which to construct for themselves some sort of a shelter, would it not be well to look up a few things for them at once, so that the ship may not be detained in a position of danger when the landing takes place?"

"Arms! tools!" growled Williams. "Who spoke of supplying them with either?"

"Nobody," answered Ned; "but you cannot surely be thinking of putting them ashore without them?"

"Now, supposing that you had the management of this job," snarled Williams, "what would you give them?"

"Well," said Ned, "I should let them have one of those spare topsails out of the sail-room; a couple of rifles apiece, including the women, with plenty of ammunition, two or three axes, a hammer or two, and a few bags of nails."

"Oh! you would, eh?" sneered Williams. "And what use do you suppose all those things would be to them?"

"The sail," said Ned, "would serve them for a tent until they could build a house, the tools would enable them to build the house, and the arms would give them a chance to defend themselves if attacked, as well as to provide themselves with food."

"Well, yes, that's true," answered Williams, rather reluctantly. "Very well," he continued, "go and rout the things out; and let me see them when you have got them together."

Without waiting to give the fellow a chance to change his mind, Ned hurried off, and summoning the boatswain and his gang to his assistance, soon had the topsail on deck; after which he procured the keys of the arm-chest and selected not ten but a dozen rifles, fitted with bayonets, a goodly stock of ammunition, three new axes with helves complete, a couple of shovels, two hammers, half a dozen bags of nails, mostly large, a coil of inch rope, an adze, and a quantity of tinware—as less liable to breakage than crockery. And, as a suitable finish to the whole, he topped off with a case which he routed out from the lazarette, and which bore on its side the legend "assorted tinned meats."

Breakfast was by this time ready; and on its being announced, Williams ordered Ned to take charge of the deck, and, in the event of anything noteworthy occurring, to report to him at once. Ned was by no means sorry to be thus left to himself for a short time; but, fully alive to the exceptional nature of the responsibility laid upon him at that particular moment, deemed his proper position just then to be in the fore-top. And, first procuring his telescope, thither he quickly made his way.

The ship was by this time within about five miles of the land; and the first thing the lad noticed, on reaching his more elevated post, was that the sea was breaking heavily all along the shore. Hailing the boatswain, who was on deck, Ned instructed that functionary to report this circumstance to Williams, who, in consequence, soon made his appearance on deck again.

"Fore-top, there!" he hailed; "how far are the breakers off the shore?"

"About a mile, I should say," answered Ned.

"Do they look too heavy for a boat to go through them?" was the next inquiry.

"Yes," answered Ned; "there is nothing but white water all along this side of the island."

"Very well," said Williams, "stay where you are, and keep your eyes peeled; we must try the lee side of the island, that's all. Lay aft here, my lads, and man the lee braces. Down with your helm, there, you sir, and let her come by the wind. Brace sharp up, my bullies; we mustn't leave the hooker's bones on yon island if we can help it. Well, there! belay all! How is that, Ned; shall we weather the southernmost point, think ye?"

"Yes," answered Ned, "and plenty to spare, if there is no current to set us to leeward."

The island was now to leeward of the ship, stretching along the horizon on her larboard beam, the northern extremity being well on her quarter, whilst the southern end, with an outlying reef, lay about three points on her lee-bow. Anxious to see and learn as much as possible of the place which was to be the—possibly life-long—abode of those who had suddenly seemed so dear to him, Ned again had recourse to his telescope, with which he forthwith proceeded to carefully scan the island.

It measured, from north to south, about six miles, as nearly as the lad could estimate it; what its measurement might be in the other direction it was not then possible to say. The land was very high, especially toward the centre of the island; and one of the first things which attracted Ned's attention was a remarkable cliff, apparently quite perpendicular, which traversed the island from north to south, seemingly about four hundred feet high, and which sprang sheer out of the ridge of a lofty hill which appeared to form the back-bone, as it were, of the island. This cliff seemed to Ned to divide the island into two distinct parts; for it terminated, both to north and to south, in a terrific precipice falling sheer down to the sea, which foamed and chafed at its base. This gave the island a most peculiar appearance, suggesting the idea that at some distant period of the world's history a mighty convulsion had occurred, rending the rocks violently asunder and forcing a portion of them—namely, that which formed the land in sight—far above the level of the rest. To the eastward, or landward of the remarkable cliff already referred to, Ned could see the steep conical summit of a lofty mountain, apparently about four miles inland; but the cliff was too high to allow of his seeing any other portion of the island beyond it. The land was covered with wood from the base of the cliff clear down to the inner margin of the beach, and, with the aid of his glass, Ned could detect the feathery fronds of cocoanut and other palms, as well as the less lofty foliage of the useful banana. Meanwhile, the ship had by this time reached a point which enabled the lad to make out that the long line of breakers which had first attracted his attention inclosed a bay about a mile wide and nearly that depth, the water of which was quite smooth and unbroken inside the inner line of breakers. And whilst examining this bay, with the idea that a knowledge of it might be useful to his friends, Ned's eye was arrested by an object on the inner edge of the reef, and almost in smooth water, which a more careful inspection showed him to be a wreck. This discovery he determined not to report, but to communicate, if possible, to the little party before they were landed. And, to make more certain of being able to do so, he there and then tore a leaf out of his pocket-book and jotted down a few notes respecting his observations, which he thought they might be glad to have.

At length the ship handsomely weathered the most southerly extremity of the island, this proving to be a bold projection in a vertical cliff, the summit of which towered in some places to a height of nearly sixteen hundred feet above the sea. This cliff extended along the whole southern seaboard of the island, towering highest at the point where it met the curious transverse cliff before mentioned, and gradually becoming lower as it neared the eastern end of the island, which now showed itself to be about eleven miles in length from east to west. With the exception of the mountain, the conical top of which Ned had seen over the summit of the transverse cliff, that cliff seemed to be the highest part of the island; though the rest of it was also hilly, gradually sloping, however, to the eastward until it terminated in a beautiful white sandy beach, on which Ned soon saw that a landing might be effected without difficulty.

As soon as Ned had piloted the ship into a position where she might be hove-to with safety, Williams called him down on deck, on reaching which he was summoned aft.

"Now then!" exclaimed Williams, "let's give this cargo" - pointing to Ned's collection of miscellaneous articles for the passengers' benefit—"an overhaul. You seem quite determined that they shall not want for much, by the look of it."

"Of course not; why should they?" demanded Ned. "They are not going on shore to please themselves, but to please you; and it is only right that they should be supplied with everything necessary to make themselves thoroughly comfortable. They ought not to be allowed to want for *anything*."

Williams admitted that there was some truth in that argument; and, after inquiring what uses certain of the articles were expected to be put to, ordered the boat to be lowered and manned, and everything to be passed down into her. When this came to be done, however, there proved to be, with the luggage, too much for one boat; so, rather than incur the delay which would be entailed by the making of a second trip, Williams, with many expressions of dissatisfaction and impatience, ordered the second quarter-boat to be lowered.

At length everything was pronounced to be in the boats; and nothing remained but for the passengers themselves to pass down over the side. They had, previously to this, asked and been refused permission to say farewell to Captain Blyth, there was therefore nothing further to detain them, and Mr Gaunt now advanced to the gangway, where he paused for a moment in order to protest formally against being thus landed in a part of the world from which there seemed little or no hope of their being able to effect their escape. The protest was, of course, utterly ineffectual, as they quite expected it would be—indeed it was only made because they wished it to be clearly understood by all hands that they were not leaving the ship of their own free-will—and when the engineer had finished speaking, all that Williams said in reply was:

"That is all right. And now, as there is a fairish amount of swell running, I would recommend you two gentlemen to go down into the boat first, so as to help the ladies and children down, and to see that none of them fall overboard."

This was such sound advice that the engineer at once followed it, Ned at the same time pressing forward, and, under cover of a pretence of wishing to shake hands with him for the last time, slipped into his hand the pencil note he had prepared. The transfer was effected unobserved; and the doctor next stepping forward, soon found himself safely in the boat beside his friend. The children were next carefully handed down by Ned; after which, at a sign from Williams, first Mrs Gaunt and then Mrs Henderson followed. There now remained only Sibylla to complete the party; and she was in the act of advancing to the gangway, when—to the unspeakable dismay of those most concerned—Williams, who was standing on the rail, gave the order for both boats to shove off, at the same moment leaping down off the rail on deck. His extraordinary order must have been anticipated, so promptly was it obeyed; and before even Gaunt could recover from his momentary surprise, the boats were fifty yards away from the ship and heading for the shore, whilst the cries of the hapless deserted girl rang fearfully out over the water after them.

The feeling of dismay naturally excited in the breasts of the unfortunate passengers by this singular episode was of the briefest possible duration, and was immediately succeeded by one of vexed astonishment, that by what seemed like a cruel and inexcusably careless oversight, a sensitive girl should have been subjected to even the most temporary alarm; and whilst Mrs Henderson started to her feet with clasped hands and wide-open startled eyes, Gaunt laid his hand on the tiller, and jammed it hard over, as he exclaimed authoritatively:

"Back water, the starboard oars! pull, the port! round with her, men! You have left Miss Stanhope behind!"

The men, looking surprisedly at each other, proceeded to obey the order, upon which the new second-mate, who was in charge of the boat, started to his feet, and prefacing the inquiry with an oath, demanded:

"Now then, you sodgers, what are you about? Who commands this here boat? Give way, you swabs, and bend your backs to it, too, or there'll be trouble for some of you when you gets back to the ship. It's all right, sir," he continued, addressing Gaunt; "the young lady is to stay where she is.

It was all arranged by Williams and a few more of us about half an hour ago, whilst you was all busy packing up your traps in the cabin. The fact is like this here: None of us foremast hands understands anything about navigation, so we've been obliged to press young Ned into the sarvice; and we knows as how his heart ain't in the job, and Williams sort of suspects that he'd play us a scurvy trick if he dared. As long as you was with us he was all right, because, d'ye see, Williams told him that if he played us false you'd be made to suffer for it; but it suddenly struck him just now that when you was all put ashore where should we be? So he and two or three more of us had a palaver together, and the long and the short of it is that we decided to keep the young woman with us as a 'hostage,' Williams calls it, whereby we shall keep the whip hand of the lad, as you may say. So all her dunnage was passed down into the after-hold again on the quiet, and if there's anything of hers in either of the boats we've got to take it back aboard again. And Williams' very last orders was that I was to be sure to tell you that you wasn't to worry about the young lady, because we've all agreed that she shall be treated as a passenger with the greatest possible respect, and not be interfered with by anybody."

"Oh, my poor sister—my poor lost sister!" moaned Mrs Henderson, burying her face in her hands as she burst into a passion of hysterical tears; and whilst Mrs Gaunt did her best to soothe and comfort her unfortunate friend, Doctor Henderson and the engineer sought by every means in their power to induce the boat's crew to return to the ship and give them an opportunity to try their persuasive powers on Williams, with the object of obtaining Miss Stanhope's release. Their efforts proved utterly vain, the men positively refusing to go back; but hope was not entirely abandoned nor their efforts suspended until they had landed, and the boats were fairly out of ear-shot on their way back to the ship.

Chapter Eight
Sibylla the hostage

Sibylla no sooner heard Williams' order for the boats to shove off than she intuitively divined the horrible fate in store for her; and, resolved to effect her escape at any and every hazard, she darted toward the gangway, determined to fling herself into the sea rather than be left alone and unprotected in the midst of that gang of lawless men. But Williams was too quick for her; he saw her movement, anticipated her intention, and, leaping down off the rail, flung his arms around her, exclaiming:

"Avast there, my pretty one; you are to stay with us! Nay, it is no use to struggle; you will not be allowed to go, so you may as well submit quietly to your fate. Curse the girl—how she fights! Stand still, will you, and listen to me! The boats are already a hundred fathoms away from the ship; there are half a dozen sharks cruising round us—I saw them not five minutes ago; and if you were silly enough to jump overboard, as you seem inclined to do, you would be torn to pieces before we could even think about picking you up."

"Better that than to remain here at the mercy of such wretches as you!" gasped Sibylla, still struggling feebly, for her strength was almost exhausted.

"Well said, my beauty," laughed Williams; "you are a rare plucky one, and no mistake. I like to see—"

"Hands off, Williams!" exclaimed Ned, as he stepped coldly forward to the rescue. "What do you mean, sir, by such dastardly conduct? Do you call this keeping faith with me?"

"Yes, of course I do," exclaimed Williams. "I don't want to hurt her if she'll only keep quiet. Here, Ned, you take charge of her. She'll be quieter with you than with me, perhaps; and see if you can persuade her that she will be better off here than overboard among the sharks. As to keeping faith with you, my hearty, why, I've done the best I could. Those friends of yours, that you seem to have taken such a tremendous fancy to, have been treated just as well since we took the ship as they were before. We've lost nearly three weeks cruising about trying to find a good place on which to land them—and a perfect paradise of a spot we've found for them at last; nobody could wish for a better—and, now that they are turned adrift, I've landed them with an outfit complete enough for them to start a regular colony. What more would you have! Haven't I yet done enough to satisfy you?"

"No, certainly not," answered Ned, inwardly grieving now that he had not ventured to add to the scanty "outfit" several other articles which he had felt would have been of the utmost value to the marooned party, but which he had feared to include lest the whole should have been refused them. "No; this young lady was one of the party, and was included in my stipulations. Yet you have detained her on board here, a prisoner."

"Ah, well! the less said about that, perhaps, the better," remarked Williams. "I quite intended to have landed her with the rest of them; but that island looming up ahead this morning—when you told us only last night that we had a clear sea ahead of us—looked so queer that we held a consultation, and came to the conclusion that, for our own safety's sake, we ought to keep somebody aboard here to act as a sort of hostage to secure us against treachery on your part; and, as we didn't think it would be right to separate husband and wife, or parents and children, why, you see, there was only this young lady left for us. And, whilst we are talking upon this subject, shipmates," he continued, turning to the rest of the crew, whose curiosity had brought them about the little party, "let me say, here and now, that Bill Rogers, Bob Martin, and myself agreed this morning that she must be kept among us for the safety of the ship and all hands. You all know—for no secret has been made of it—that Ned, there, has been kept with us, not of his own free-will, but because we required somebody to navigate the ship for us. And you know, too, or I know, that the lad has just that amount of spirit in him that he wouldn't hesitate to cast away the ship and all hands—himself included—or to play us any other awkward trick if he saw a chance of spoiling our plans for the recovery of a few of the good things that we've been defrauded out of. Now, so long as this young girl is all safe and sound we have nothing to fear from his treachery, because, d'ye see, I'm going to tell him and her—as I do now—that any act, or even suspicion, of treachery on *his* part will be followed by the young woman being turned adrift by herself in the dinghy; and, rather than see her come to harm, he will be faithful to us, and carry out our orders to the best of his ability. But if evil comes to her we shall lose our hold upon him at once—I say all this before him because I've studied him and know him, and I want him to understand as much—and it has, therefore, been agreed that any man who interferes with the young lady will be shot at once and on the spot. So, now, mates, as you've had the whole affair explained to you, it is to be hoped you'll shape your behaviour accordingly."

"Stop a moment!" exclaimed Ned, as Williams waved his hand by way of dismissal to his little audience, "it seems, from what Williams has said, that Miss Stanhope has been detained a prisoner solely on my account. If that be really the case, I wish to say that, if you will release her and put her on shore with her friends on the island yonder, I swear to you that, though I will never take part in any piracies or other unlawful acts which you may commit, I will in every other respect be absolutely faithful to you, and will navigate the ship whithersoever you will, to the best of my ability. This is no light sacrifice for a young man in my position to make; yet I will make it cheerfully, and take any oath of fidelity you may choose to impose upon me."

"It is no use, Ned; we can't—we dare not do it," answered Williams. "You mean what you say—*now*—I don't doubt; but if you ever had a chance to betray us, as you may have, you wouldn't be able to resist the temptation. No; the matter has been fully talked over, and the young lady must stay."

Ned was about to make a further effort on Sibylla's behalf, but the girl herself stopped him.

"Humble yourself no more to these men!" she said; "it will be of no avail, I can clearly see. And trouble not yourself on my behalf. God is able to protect me even here; His will be done!"

She turned away, and Ned, offering his arm, half led, half supported Sibylla into the cabin; and, as he poured out and offered her a glass of wine from a decanter which stood in one of the swinging trays over the table, he exclaimed:

"Oh! Miss Stanhope, what can I say, or how express the sorrow and regret I feel at the knowledge that it is through me you are placed in this terrible position. Believe me—"

"Say no more, Mr Damerell, I entreat you," interrupted Sibylla. "I know that you have no cause for self-reproach; we are both equally unfortunate. For, if I am detained on board this ship a prisoner, so are you; your prospects in life are as completely blighted as mine. And I have at least the comfort of that man's assurance—in which I believe he was quite sincere—that I shall be treated with consideration and respect. Indeed, terrible as must be my position here, I am by no means sure that I am not safer where I am than is my poor sister on that lonely island. What may be her fate and that of those who are with her who can tell? to what dangers and privations will not they be exposed? It is terrible only to think of it. And now let me thank you for your noble and self-sacrificing efforts just now on my behalf. Come what will, I shall never forget them, nor shall I ever forget that you have proved yourself our true and staunch friend, forgetting yourself and all your own trouble and peril in your anxiety to help and befriend us. Tell me, do you think there is any possibility of our ever being able to make our escape from these dreadful people?"

"Well," said Ned, "I should not like to raise hopes which may never be fulfilled, but I think there *is* just a possibility of it. You must not build too much on what I say, because it would be idle to deny that our future is beset with difficulties and perils. The absence of your brother-in-law, the doctor, and Mr Gaunt is an irreparable loss to us, to say nothing of that of the captain and young Manners, both of whom will, I feel sure, be landed somewhere within the next few days. But do not despair; perhaps, when Williams has rid himself of them, his vigilance may relax. I should, under any circumstances, have tried to escape, and you may rest assured that, as your deliverance seems now to depend almost wholly upon me, my thoughts will more than ever be given to the project. What you have to do is to think as little as may be upon your present situation and to keep up your spirits. A chance *may* come to us at any moment—and I believe it *will* come, sooner or later. We must therefore be on the watch and hold ourselves ready to take advantage of it when it comes. The accidents—if I may call them so—of the sea are countless; we shall, by and by, be constantly hovering in the regular track of other ships, and that, in spite of all their vigilance, may afford us an opportunity to make our situation known. Or we may be captured; for, if the rascals carry out their present plans, it will not be long before we shall have all the men-of-war in these seas after us. Or we may, perhaps, be able to effect our escape in a boat. That gig of ours, in which our friends have been sent ashore is a splendid boat; and if we could get away in her whilst in some well-beaten ship track, with a good stock of provisions, we might well hope to be picked up in the course of a few days. That, however, I should only propose as a last resource. But the more I think of it the less hopeless do our prospects appear; so keep a good heart, Miss Stanhope, and hope for the best. By the by, do you know how to use a pistol?"

"Yes," said Sibylla, "I know how to use a revolver. Duncan has—or had—a pair; and when we were at home he taught Rose and me how to fire them, putting up a target in the garden for us to shoot at. Why do you ask?"

"Because—although I think there is not much ground for apprehension—it will do no harm if you have a weapon upon which you can lay your hand in case of need. I have a pair of small revolvers which, though they are not very formidable weapons for long-distance shooting, are tolerably effective at close quarters, say within thirty yards or so. I will give you them—they are in a case, with cartridges and so on all complete; and I should like you to keep them always loaded and handy. And now, if you feel sufficiently composed to be left alone, I think I will go out on deck again and see how matters are progressing there."

When Ned reached the poop, to which he naturally directed his steps, he found Williams there, fuming at the protracted absence of the boats, which could clearly be seen, with their noses hauled up on the sandy beach, and the two boat-keepers sitting in lazy attitudes on their gunwales, quietly smoking. That the remainder of the crews were not delayed by assisting the marooned passengers to "shake down" was evidenced by the fact that the latter could be seen grouped together on a little grassy knoll, the ladies and children seated upon boxes, whilst the two men were vigorously attacking with their axes a couple of young straight-stemmed palms at no great distance.

"What can the rascals be about?" growled Williams impatiently. "I'll bet anything they are off skylarking in the woods, instead of hurrying back to the ship, as they ought. For'ard, there! pass the word for the boatswain to clear away one of those signal-guns. We'll give them a shot by way of a reminder to quicken their motions."

The gun was cleared away, loaded, and fired—not once but nearly a dozen times before the laggards appeared. They were seen at last, however, hurrying down to the beach, in little straggling groups, one after the other, and finally the boats pushed off and headed for the ship.

A quarter of an hour later they were alongside; and in another moment the two men who had been sent away in charge stood on the quarter-deck, confronting their angry chief.

"Come, Rogers I come, Martin! what the mischief have you been about, keeping us dodging in the offing all this while?" demanded Williams fiercely. "Hook on the tackles, and let us be off," he continued.

"Wait a minute, cap'n," answered Rogers; "we've a bit of news for you that I expect you won't particularly relish. One of the men has cut and run; and it was hunting for him that kept us ashore so long."

"Who is if!" demanded Williams.

"Why, it's Tom Nicholls, one of the steerage passengers that Blyth shipped after we fell in with that barque on her beam-ends."

"So he has bolted, has he, the white-livered hound!" ejaculated Williams furiously. "Well, he shall not escape us. Take your boats' crews, both of you; give each man a rifle and half a dozen rounds of ball cartridge, and pull ashore again and hunt the cur until you find him, and bring him aboard here to me, dead or alive! I'll anchor the ship and wait for you, if it takes you a week to do the job."

"Ay, ay, we'll get him before the day is over, never fear!" exclaimed Rogers, apparently in high glee at receiving the brutal order. "Come along, mates, and get your rifles; it isn't every day that we get the chance of such a spree as a man-hunt!"

The boats' crews had, during this short colloquy, scrambled up the ship's side to the deck, and had gathered round the speakers, curious to see how Williams would receive the news of the loss; and it was to these that Rogers had addressed himself.

They did not, however, appear to by any means enter into the spirit of the thing, hanging back so coldly unresponsive to the mate's jovial invitation that the latter paused in blank astonishment.

"Why—why—what the—" began Rogers, when he was brusquely interrupted by one of the men, who stepped forward and said:

"Get somebody else to go in my place, matey. I don't understand man-huntin', as you calls it, and should only make a poor fist at it, I'm afraid."

"Same here," said another. "I never done anything of the sort yet, and don't know how to set about it."

The others were expressing themselves to the same effect, when Williams darted forward, and, seizing the first speaker roughly by the collar, savagely demanded:

"Look here, you scoundrel, do you mean to say that you *won't* go?"

"Ay, ay, shipmate, that's just exactly what I *do* mean," was the answer, given good-naturedly enough. "But take your hand off my collar," the man continued more sternly. "Two can play at that game, you know; and I doubt whether you are man enough to thrash me."

Williams, white as death with passion, prudently withdrew his hand from the man's collar, and stepped back a pace or two.

"What does this mean?" he demanded. "Are you going to mutiny, men, before our cruise has even commenced?"

An insolent laugh greeted this inquiry; and the man who had just spoken answered:

"Call it what you like, Cap'n Josh; mutiny is as good a name for it as any other, I reckon. And what I mean is, that I, for one, ain't goin' ashore on no man-huntin' expedition. There was nothing said about man-huntin' when the articles for this here cruise was drawed up; and what I say is, if Tom Nicholls wants to cut and run, let him do it."

"Ay, ay; so says I," added another of the men. "He never entered into the thing with no spirit, anyhow; and if he'd rather be ashore there than makin' his fortune aboard here with us, why, let him stay ashore, says I. 'No manhuntin'' is my sentiments."

Several of the other men now declared themselves to the same effect, whereupon Williams, finding himself in the minority, said, with as perfect an assumption of indifference as he could command at the moment:

"Very well, lads; just as you please. It was of you, not of myself, that I was thinking. The work will be so much the heavier for you if Nicholls is allowed to escape; but, if you do not mind it, I am sure I need not. If, as you say, the fool prefers slaving ashore there for a bare living to making his fortune with us afloat, let him go. Up with the boats, and be smart about it! Up with your helm, abaft there, and let her go off square before the wind! Square the main-yard; and away aloft there, some of you, and rig out the topmast and topgallant-studding-sail booms!"

These orders were rapidly obeyed. The ship squared away before a freshening breeze; and two hours later the island was left so far astern that a landsman might easily have mistaken it for a grey cloud on the edge of the horizon.

The ship was kept running to the eastward all that day under studding-sails, and by sunset had travelled a distance of nearly seventy miles. At that hour, however, Ned requested that sail might be shortened and the ship allowed to go along under easy canvas during the night, urging the experience of the morning as a reason for caution whilst navigating that comparatively unknown sea. Williams at once assented to the suggestion, remarking immediately afterwards to Rogers, with a self-satisfied chuckle:

"That was a rare good move of ours, Bill, to keep the young woman aboard. See how cautious Mr Ned has grown all of a sudden! You may take my word for it, there will be no more tumbling over islands so long as she remains aboard of us."

As it happened, it was just as well that the precaution was taken; for at midnight, just as the watch was being relieved, breakers were discovered ahead, and the ship was only brought to the wind just barely in time to avert a disaster. But even then the craft was by no means out of danger; for, when an attempt was made to claw off from the reefs to leeward, it was soon discovered that the vessel was embayed, other reefs being found to exist both to the northward and to the southward of her. For a few minutes something very like a panic took possession of the mutineers; but Williams proved himself equal to the occasion, stilling the tumult by a few brief authoritative words, and promptly ordering a man into the chains with the lead. Soundings were taken and a sandy bottom found, with just the right depth of water for anchoring. So the cable was roused on deck and bent on to the best bower, the ship making short reaches to the northward and southward meanwhile; and as soon as everything was ready a position was taken as nearly as possible midway between the reefs, and the anchor let go in twelve fathoms of water, with sixty fathoms of chain outside the hawse-pipe. The canvas was securely furled, the watch set, with one man told off to tend the lead-line which was dropped over the side to show whether the anchor held securely or not, and then nothing remained for them but to wait, with what patience they could muster, for daybreak.

This was a somewhat trying ordeal; for the night was pitch dark—the moon being new and not a star visible, the sky overcast, and the wind fresh and at times gusty. Moreover, they could form but a very vague idea of the dangers by which they were surrounded, the chart showing nothing but a clear sea; and, to further increase their anxiety, there was a heavy ground-swell rolling in from the westward, which caused the ship to bury herself to her hawse-pipes. Altogether, what with the uncertainty of their position, the inky darkness, and the ominous roar of the breakers all round them, it was a very anxious time for everybody on board the *Flying Cloud*.

At length, after what seemed an eternity of darkness, the harassed watchers caught the first faint signs of returning day. The forms of the clouds became dimly perceptible along the horizon to the eastward; then the cloud-bank itself broke up, revealing little patches here and there of soft violet-tinted sky, which rapidly paled, first to a pure and delicate ultramarine, and then to a soft primrose hue before the approaching dawn. The leaden-tinted clouds imperceptibly assumed a purple hue, then their lower edges became fringed with gold; and presently a long shaft of white light shot from the horizon half-way to the zenith, tinging the higher clouds—now broken up into a crowded archipelago of aerial islets—with flakes of "celestial rosy red," and in another moment the golden upper rim of the sun's disk flashed on the horizon, sending a long path of shimmering radiance across the bosom of the heaving, restless sea; and it was day.

The awkward character of the predicament in which the ship was involved now became sufficiently apparent. To the eastward and astern of her a small island, measuring about two miles from north to south, was seen. Its shores were indented and rocky, the surf beating upon them with great violence; and between it and the ship, at a distance nowhere greater than a mile, there lay an extensive crescent-shaped reef, almost completely encircling the unfortunate craft. The swell, rolling heavily in from the westward, hurled itself with appalling fury upon this reef, the far-reaching expanse of white water revealing distinctly the extremity of the peril through which the ship had passed during the previous night. Indeed, it was difficult to understand how she had escaped at all, for the opening between the two horns of the reef was so narrow that he would have been a bold navigator who would willingly have risked the passage, even in broad daylight.

Williams' first act was to summon Rogers and Martin, in whose company he paid a visit to the fore-topmast cross-trees, where the trio devoted a full half-hour to a careful and critical examination of the ship's position. Fortunately there was no occasion for haste, the anchor maintaining a firm grip of the ground, notwithstanding the occasional heavy plunges of the ship when some exceptionally big roller came sweeping in unbroken through the narrow channel in the reef. It was possible, therefore, for the mutineers to weigh well the advisability of the steps they contemplated, and to act with due caution. The cross-trees afforded a clear and thoroughly comprehensive view of the entire reef; and from this lofty stand-point the position of the ship was seen to be much less critical than it had appeared to be when viewed from the deck below. The *Flying Cloud* was, in fact, found to be lying in about the centre of a natural harbour. True, it was rather a wild berth for a ship, especially in the particular spot which she then occupied— this spot happening to be exactly opposite the opening in the reef and fully exposed to the unbroken run of the sea—but it was seen that by moving her half a cable's-length either to the north or south the craft would be sheltered by one of the arms of the reef, and, with a couple of anchors down, might hope to ride out a moderately heavy gale in safety.

This was all very well, and very satisfactory—so far as it went—for it relieved their minds of all anxiety respecting the immediate safety of the ship. But, safe as she might be for the moment, the spot was not one in which a prudent mariner would linger one unnecessary instant; and Williams' only anxiety just then was how to get out.

The channel into this natural harbour trended as nearly as possible due east and west; and, with the wind as it then stood, the ship, in order to get to sea, would have to make a series of short tacks to windward. But the opening was so narrow and tortuous that the little party in the cross-trees considered it exceedingly doubtful whether this would be possible with so lengthy a ship as the *Flying Cloud*; and, for the moment, it looked very much as though they would have to remain where they were until a change of wind should occur to release them.

At length, however, an expedition in the gig to the mouth of the channel was decided upon, and Ned—who had already distinguished himself by the exhibition of an altogether exceptional aptitude and dexterity in his handling of the ship—was instructed to join the party. The boat was soon lowered and manned, and, with Williams, Rogers, and Ned in the stern-sheets, pulled away towards the entrance. They had had the precaution to provide themselves with a hand-lead; and as soon as the channel was reached a very complete set of soundings, from end to end and over its entire width, was taken under Ned's supervision. The result was unexpectedly satisfactory, no detached rocks being found in the fairway, whilst a tolerably even depth of water, nowhere less than five fathoms, and extending right up alongside the edge of the reef, prevailed throughout the entire length of the channel.

The progress of this survey was watched with the utmost anxiety by Williams—who, indeed, actually took the soundings with his own hands; and upon its completion he was so intensely gratified at the way in which this important service had been executed that he actually went the length of stammering out a few half-intelligible words of thanks to Ned.

The only question now remaining for settlement was, whether it would be prudent to make the attempt to work the ship out to sea. All hands were most keenly anxious to get clear of the place, for, safe as the ship just then undoubtedly was, they knew that it might prove a death-trap to them if it came on to blow heavily from the westward; but they also had the sense to know that a single mistake or miscalculation on the part of the person working the ship would send her on to the reef, a hopeless wreck.

Rogers and the boat's crew were unanimously of opinion that the project was an impossibility; Williams expressed his belief that the thing *might* be done, but he at the same time frankly confessed that he had not faith enough in himself to undertake the responsibility. Ned prudently kept his opinion to himself until he was directly appealed to, when he modestly said that, with a smart hand at the wheel, a keen look-out aloft to warn him of the presence of any sunken rocks which might perchance have escaped their search, and a lively crew at the sheets and braces, he believed he would be able to work the ship into open water.

"Then," exclaimed Williams with an oath, "you shall try your hand at the job. But remember," he added, "if the ship touches anywhere, though it be only lightly enough to just graze the paint off her bottom, you may look out for squalls!"

"Now, look here, Williams," answered Ned hotly, "if you want me to do my best for you, you had better be somewhat more sparing with your threats; and unless you withdraw what you have just said I shall decline to have anything to do with this matter. The task you have asked me to undertake is a most difficult and delicate one. I am quite willing to do my best, if you see fit to intrust me with the care of the ship, but it is a case in which even so slight a matter as a temporary flaw in the wind may bring about a very serious accident. If, therefore, I am to make the attempt, it must be with the distinct understanding that I am not to be held responsible for anything which may happen."

"What d'ye think, mates? dare we trust him?" asked Williams, appealing to Rogers and the other men in the boat.

They said they thought that Ned's objection was quite fair and reasonable; and Rogers, unceremoniously changing places with Ned, whispered something in Williams' ear, whereupon the latter said:

"Very well. Will you swear, Ned, to honestly do your best to get the ship out of the fix she is now in, and to navigate her safely into open water?"

"Certainly I will, if you wish it," answered Ned, "but a little reflection would convince you, I think, that I must be as little anxious as any of you to be cast away in such an unpromising spot as this."

"All right, then," said Williams; "we'll chance it. Give way, men, for the ship."

A quarter of an hour later all hands were once more on board, the boat was hoisted up to the davits, and the word was passed to man the windlass and heave short.

Chapter Nine
The Captain's denunciation

"Now, Ned," said Williams as the windlass-pawls began to clank, "you are in charge of the ship, mind, until she is in the blue water once more; and all hands, myself included, are ready to obey your orders, whatever they may be. You want a smart hand at the wheel, you say, and another as a look-out aloft. I intend, therefore, to take the wheel myself; and Rogers, who has the quickest eye on board the ship, will station himself on the fore-topsail-yard to watch for the rocks you spoke about. The rest of the hands will be stationed at the sheets and braces, with orders to let go and haul the moment you give the word. So, with this arrangement, if anything goes wrong you will not be able to say that any of us were to blame."

"All right," cried Ned, "I am quite satisfied with the arrangement; and I will do my best, as I said, to take the ship safely through. As there is a good steady breeze blowing I shall work her under topsails, topgallant-sails, jibs, and spanker, with the courses in the brails ready for an emergency, but not set; as presently, when we get into the narrowest part of the passage, our boards will be so short that the men would not be able to get down the tacks and sheets before it will be time to heave in stays again. When the cable is shortened in to twenty-fathoms let the hands go aloft and loose the canvas."

"Right you are," said Williams, turning away and walking forward to superintend operations on the forecastle.

The men roused the cable in to the inspiring strains of a lively "shanty;" and before long Rogers' voice was heard announcing the news that the twenty-fathom shackle was inside the hawse-pipe.

"Away aloft and loose the canvas" was now the word, upon which the men deserted the windlass; and whilst some swarmed aloft to cast off the gaskets from the upper sails others laid out upon the jib-boom to loose the jibs, the residue scattering about the decks to attend to the calls of their shipmates aloft to "let go the main-topgallant-clewlines" and to perform other similar operations of an equally mysterious character—mysterious, at least, to Sibylla, who, at a hint from Ned, had ventured out on deck to look abroad upon the unwonted scene, and to watch the passage of the ship through the reef.

In thus summoning Sibylla from the seclusion of her own cabin Ned honestly believed that his only motive was to do the poor girl a service. He said to himself that she would be far better on deck, breathing the fresh air and stimulated by the healthy excitement of a little peril, than she would be if she remained below cooped up in a stuffy state-room, fretting her heart out over matters that neither she nor he could help. Moreover, he was anxious that she should become accustomed as quickly as possible to the novelty of being the only woman on board, and accustomed, too, to the idea of coming and going as freely about the decks as she had done before the mutiny. And if, in addition to these motives, there lurked another far down in the depths of Ned's heart, making him anxious that Sibylla should see for herself how valuable, and indeed indispensable, his services were to the mutineers, who shall blame him?

With the usual amount of bustle on board a merchantman the canvas was at length set, the yards braced in the manner necessary for casting the ship, and the men returned to the windlass—Williams walking aft and standing by the wheel, whilst Rogers and Martin remained on the forecastle to superintend the operation of getting the anchor. Williams was evidently very much pleased at the prospect of getting out to sea again, for as he passed Sibylla he raised his hat with more grace than could have been expected of him and wished her "good-morning!"—a salutation which the young lady silently acknowledged with one of her most stately bows.

Presently the cry came from Rogers:

"Anchor's aweigh, sir."

"Very well," said Ned; "rouse it up to the bows smartly, cat it, and then range along your cable all ready for letting go again if need be. Flatten in your larboard jib-sheets for'ard; man your larboard fore-braces and brace the headyards sharp up. Hard a-starboard with your helm, Williams—she has stern-way upon her. And you Rogers, away aloft and keep a sharp lookout for sunken rocks. Martin will see to the catting of the anchor."

Fully alive to the necessity for prompt obedience to the orders which had been given them, the crew sprang to their several stations and did their work with a smartness which would have been creditable even on board a man-of-war; and in another minute the ship had paid handsomely off on the larboard tack, with her after-canvas clean full.

"Let draw your jib-sheets," now shouted Ned; "let go your larboard and round-in upon your starboard fore-braces, and then lay aft here, two or three of you, and haul out the spanker. Steady the helm and meet her, Williams. Keep everything a-rap full and let her go through the water. What is the latest news from the anchor for'ard there?"

"The stock is just coming out of the water, sir," answered Martin.

"That is right; up with it as smartly as you can, lads," urged Ned. Then to Rogers:

"How are things looking from aloft, Rogers?"

"All right, sir—no rocks anywhere in the way as I can see, and deep water right up to the edge of the reef," came the answer.

"That is well," commented Ned, walking to the lee rail to note the speed of the ship through the water, and also to judge more accurately her distance from the swirling masses of white water which marked the position of the reef.

She was nearing the rocks fast and was already within a cable's-length of them; and the men forward were beginning to cast anxious glances aft, fearing that Ned was cutting his distance too fine.

But Ned knew perfectly well what he was about; with the utmost calmness he gave the word "Stations!" and then, as the men sprang to obey the order, he glanced aloft at the canvas. Williams was performing his share of the work with the skill of a most accomplished helmsman, and all the canvas was clean full.

Now came the ticklish part of the business. If Ned's judgment failed him here the ship was as good as lost. He took one more glance at the breakers and then gave the word:

"Ready about!" followed immediately by the customary "Helm is a-lee!" at the same moment signing to Williams to put the helm down.

The wheel, under the influence of a single vigorous impulse from Williams' sinewy arm, went whirling round until it was hard over, when he caught and grasped the spokes and held it there. The ship swept gracefully up into the wind with her white canvas fluttering so violently as to make the stout craft tremble to her keel; and, shaving the reef so closely that a vigorous jump would have launched a man from her rail into the breakers alongside, she forged ahead and finally paid off on the opposite tack.

So far, so good. The ship was, however, still in the comparatively spacious lagoon inside the reef. The crucial test of Ned's ability would come when she passed into the narrow tortuous channel leading through the reef to the open sea. But that one trial had sufficed to demonstrate to Ned that the ship, even under the comparatively small amount of canvas then set, was under perfect command; and he was, moreover, just at that moment in that peculiar state of exhilaration both of mind and body when no task seems impossible. It was not likely, therefore, that, with Sibylla's bright eyes regarding him with an eager curiosity—which to him seemed not wholly devoid of interest—he should shrink from any ordeal, however difficult.

But there was a peculiarly trying spot to be passed just at the inner extremity of the channel, and the ship would probably reach it on her next board. It behoved Ned, therefore, to dismiss from his mind all thoughts not strictly appertaining to the business in hand; and, like the sensible, practical fellow he was, he did so. Standing on a hen-coop, with one hand lightly grasping the mizen-topmast backstay, he sought and soon found the spot, which he carefully watched until he considered that the ship had run far enough to reach it on the next tack. He then gave the word "Ready about!" and immediately tacked the ship. The exceeding awkwardness of the passage consisted in the fact that, at the particular point referred to, the channel through the reef for a length of about sixteen hundred feet was only about three hundred feet wide, whilst its direction was dead in the wind's eye as it then blew. Hence it was quite impossible to work the ship through this narrow "gut" in the ordinary way. Two small coves of unbroken—and therefore deep—water had been discovered on the north side of this narrow passage during the preliminary exploration; but they trended in the wrong direction and were so very narrow that Williams, on seeing them, at once declared them useless for all practical purposes. Ned, however, thought differently, and it was indeed upon the existence of these two indentations that he based his hope of success in an effort that, under other circumstances, it would have been sheer madness to attempt.

The ship tacked with the same admirable precision as before, and on gathering way was found to be looking well up for the entrance to the narrow channel. The distance to be traversed was no great matter, and Ned consequently kept all hands at their stations; but the anxious looks which they cast, first at him and next at the formidable barrier of rocks to leeward, showed plainly enough how completely puzzled they were as to the manner in which Ned was to deal with the difficulty which faced him. In less than five minutes from the moment of tacking the ship reached the opening, and as she glided across the narrow channel Ned signed to Williams to put the helm gradually down. The result was that the ship shot easily up into the wind; and the moment that all her canvas was a-shiver Ned ordered the helm amidships. This manoeuvre caused the ship to shoot for a considerable distance along the channel right in the wind's eye; and before she entirely lost her way she had, as Ned had calculated she would, forged past the opening giving access to the first cove or indentation in the reef. The square canvas was now thrown flat aback and the ship soon gathered stern-way, when, by a judicious and skilful manipulation of the helm and braces, a stern-board was made and the vessel backed into the indentation and to its farthest extremity, a distance of about two cables'-lengths. The yards were then braced round and the canvas filled on the starboard tack, when, the ship gathering headway, she went booming down the indentation again and rushed once more into the narrow channel; when, having by this manoeuvre acquired sufficient "way" or momentum, the same tactics were a second time resorted to in order to get her past the second indentation, upon emerging from which she entered a wider reach of the channel where there was room to work her in the ordinary way. Thenceforward there was no further difficulty, except that in one rather awkward spot a sunken rock was encountered, which Ned, being duly apprised of its position by Rogers, avoided by the masterly execution of a half-board. A quarter of an hour later saw the *Flying Cloud* gliding out of the last reach of the channel to windward of everything, and five minutes afterwards Williams resigned the wheel to the man who had gone aft to relieve him, and resumed command of the ship; saying to Ned as he dismissed him:

"You have done exceedingly well, young gentleman; and I thank you not only for myself but also for all hands. It was, no doubt, your foresight and the caution you gave us last night that saved the ship from wreck on yonder reef; and you have this morning got us out of a difficulty which a slight increase of wind would have made a most serious one. We are very greatly indebted to you; and if ever you should require a favour at my hands remind me of this morning, and if it is possible to grant that favour with safety to ourselves it shall be granted. And now, tell me what you think of yon island as a dwelling-place for Captain Blyth?"

"I should think it would serve fairly well," said Ned, inwardly rejoicing at the prospect of the skipper being put on shore within such comparatively easy reach of the other party. "The island is large enough to support a hundred people, for that matter. It is as much out of the way as any other place we are likely to fall in with; and I have no doubt but that round on the lee side of it we shall meet with smooth water and a beach upon which to effect a landing."

"So I think," returned Williams. "At all events," he continued, "we will run round to leeward and have a look at the place. And in the meantime you may as well go and tell the skipper and young Manners to hold themselves in readiness to leave the ship—if the place looks promising I shall land them *both* here. And when you have spoken to them you may look out a few things—as well as all their own belongings—which will help to make them comfortable. We have no ill-feeling toward either of them, and it will be a satisfaction to remember that we left them with the means of taking care of themselves."

"All right," said Ned; "I will do so." And he hurried away upon his errand, which he was anxious to fully accomplish whilst Williams' extraordinary fit of good-nature still remained upon him.

Captain Blyth and young Manners were, it will be remembered, confined in the forward deck-house; and thither Ned at once made his way. The sliding-door was closed, and secured by a hasp and staple which had been put on since Ned had last visited the place. Withdrawing the pin and folding back the hasp, the lad slid the door open and entered—to start back horrified at the sight which met his gaze. The two prisoners were there, with their feet in irons, the skipper being seated on one side of the small table which occupied the centre of the berth, and Manners on the other side. It was not their condition, however, nor the fact that they were in irons, which startled Ned; they were clean and comfortable-looking enough, both in person and in dress, to show that they had been fairly well looked after; it was the dreadfully haggard and worn look of the skipper. The poor fellow looked twenty years older than when Ned had seen him last; he was wasted almost to the condition of a skeleton. The skin of his forehead and the outer corners of his eye-sockets was furrowed and wrinkled and crow's-footed like that of an old man of eighty; and his hair was thickly streaked with grey.

As Ned entered, both prisoners rose to their feet, and Captain Blyth, stretching out his hand in welcome, exclaimed with emotion:

"At last—at last! I *knew* you would be true to me, Ned, my dear lad—I said so, over and over again; did I not, Manners? And now you are come with good tidings; I can see it in your face. What is it boy! Out with it. I have been terribly shaken by this villainous mutiny, but my nerves are yet strong enough to bear the shock of good news, so out with it; do not keep us in suspense, dear lad."

It was pitiful to Ned to listen to the yearning tones of anxious entreaty in which the poor fellow uttered those last words, and to feel that he had not a single scrap of comfort to offer; but his task was before him. He had to execute it, and he determined to do it as gently as possible, and to put matters in the most hopeful light he could on the spur of the moment.

"Yes," began Ned, "I *have* come with what I hope will prove to be good tidings, though, perhaps, they may not strike you as such at the outset; and I deeply regret to say that they are certainly not such as you seem to have been looking for. The ship is still in the hands of the mutineers, notwithstanding all the plotting and scheming of Mr Gaunt, Doctor Henderson, and myself;

Williams and the rest of the people have been too watchful for us to take them by surprise, and we were not strong enough to attempt force with them. And now—the passengers, all but Miss Stanhope, being landed, as I suppose you know—I fear that the poor *Flying Cloud* will have to remain in the rascals' hands; at all events until we get into more frequented waters, when you may depend upon it I shall make desperate efforts, and leave no feasible plan untried to secure the capture of the ship. But, in the meantime, I have been instructed by Williams to inform you that you are to hold yourselves in readiness to be landed on the island yonder, which you may see through the starboard window. This, I hope, will be good news to you both, for you will at least be *free*—free not only from your present confinement, but also free to act; free to devise and to carry out means for your escape from the island, and your speedy restoration to civilisation. I am instructed to say that all your personal effects will be rendered up to you; and I have orders to get together a few things to make you comfortable. So now, if you will name what things you would most desire to have, I will jot down a list of them, and do all I possibly can to ensure your getting them."

"So—so; that is how the land lies, is it?" remarked the skipper thoughtfully, when Ned had brought his story to a close. "And, pray, what are they going to do with *you*, young gentleman, if I may presume to ask?"

"Don't speak like that, Captain Blyth, I beg," protested Ned, deeply hurt by the tone of suspicion in which the skipper's question had been put. "I am just as helpless as yourselves in this matter. They have determined to keep me on board to navigate the ship for them; and, with a malignant ingenuity which would never have occurred to anybody but Williams, they have also detained Miss Stanhope to act as hostage and security for my fidelity and good behaviour, informing me that anything like treachery, or even a mistake on my part, will be visited upon *her*."

"Poor girl! poor girl!—and poor lad, too, for that matter!" ejaculated the skipper. "Forgive me, Ned, if for a moment I fancied that you had been led astray by those scoundrels and tempted to cast in your lot with them. I might have known better; but this mutiny seems somehow to have strained my mental faculties until sometimes I almost think they are stranded and ready to carry away altogether. It is the first time that anything of the kind ever happened to me; the first time. Ah, well!—but I must not let these thoughts run away with me; our time together is short, and I have one or two questions to ask you. And, first of all, when and where did you land the passengers?"

"We landed them yesterday," answered Ned; "did you not know it? I thought it would be quite impossible to keep that fact from your knowledge."

"No, Ned, not quite impossible. I heard the boats lowered, and caught a few words here and there, which gave me an idea of what was happening; but we were shut up here with that surly fellow, Carrol, as guard over us, and he would neither tell us anything nor allow us to so much as glance out through the side-light to ascertain for ourselves what was going on. So you landed them yesterday, eh?"

"Yes," said Ned; "on an island exactly one hundred miles due west of us—"

"Stop a moment," interrupted the skipper; "let me make a mental note of that. 'One hundred miles due west of us;' that is to say, one hundred miles due west of the island where we are going to be landed. Is that it?"

Ned nodded.

"Very well," continued the skipper, "I shall remember that. Do you think you can bear that in mind, Mr Manners?"

"Certainly, sir," answered Manners. "That is an easy thing to remember."

"Very well," said his superior. "Now go on, Ned, and tell us what the island is like."

Ned gave as accurate a description as he could of the place, supplementing it with a careful pencil sketch from memory on a leaf torn from his pocket-book, showing the island as it would appear to a person approaching it from the eastward, and winding up with the statement that he believed it would be possible to distinguish the top of the mountain—the highest point of the island—from the spot where they were, on a clear day.

"Thank you, Ned; that is capital," said the skipper, with renewed animation, as the lad finished his statement and handed over the sketch. "Now," he continued, "do you know what I mean to do?"

"I fancy I can guess," answered Ned. "Unless I am mistaken, it is your intention to rejoin the passengers as soon as possible."

"Precisely," agreed the skipper. "You could not have hit it off more accurately if you had tried for an hour. Yes; these villains are going to put it most effectually out of my power to do my duty to my owners, but they shall not prevent me from doing my duty to my passengers. Manners and I will make our way to that island as soon as ever we can knock something together to carry us there. Poor souls! I hope they will manage to keep soul and body together until we can get to them. After that I flatter myself that matters will not go so very hard with them after all."

"Quite so, sir," said Ned. "From the moment that Williams announced his intention of putting you ashore here, the thought has been in my mind that it would be a good thing for all hands if you could manage to join Mr Gaunt and his party."

But whilst he said this, the lad could not help smiling at the unconscious egotism displayed by the skipper in his last remark; Ned's own private opinion being that, with a man of such inexhaustible resource as the engineer had proved himself to be, at the helm of affairs, the little party on the island were likely to get on almost as well without Captain Blyth as with him. He had, however, far too much respect for his commander to allow this idea to reveal itself either in his speech or his manner.

"Very well," said the skipper, in reply to Ned's last remark, "you now know our intentions, so I will trouble you, Ned—since I understand you to say that Williams has commissioned you to look out a few things for us—to look out as good a supply as you can of such things as will enable us to carry out our plans. We shall want first a small supply of provisions and water to carry us along until we can get into the way of foraging for ourselves. Next, we shall want arms and plenty of ammunition. And, after that, our wants, I think, will be confined to a few useful and handy tools, and as much rope and canvas, and as many nails as you can persuade them to spare us. If there is anything else you can think of which will be likely to be useful, just heave it into the boat with the rest of the things, will ye?"

"Ay, ay, sir, I will," answered Ned. "You may rely upon my doing the very best they will allow me to do for you. And now, sir, as time presses, and I may not have a better opportunity, let me say good-bye to you both. God bless you, Captain Blyth, and you, too, Manners, and may the day not be far distant when we shall all meet once more in peace and safety."

"Good-bye, Ned, dear boy," answered the skipper, with deep emotion; "good-bye, and God bless *you* and that poor dear girl who shares your cruel captivity. May He preserve you both, protect you from all evil, and, in His own good time, accord you a happy deliverance from the wretches who now hold you in bondage. We have had no time to talk about yourself and your own plans for the future; but I have no fear for you, boy. Yours is an old head though it is on young shoulders; and I firmly believe that by and by you will somehow manage to handsomely give the rascals the slip and carry off that poor girl with you. Good-bye, my lad, once more; good-bye and God bless you!"

Ned grasped the outstretched hands which were offered him and, too deeply moved for speech, wrung them silently, after which he beat a hasty retreat, and forthwith set himself about the task of providing as plentiful a supply as he dared of all those articles which the skipper had enumerated.

Ned had scarcely finished his task when the ship rounded-to under the lee of the island, which was now discovered to be a small affair of about three miles long by two miles wide, or thereabouts, its greatest elevation being perhaps two hundred and fifty feet above the sea-level. Like the island on which the passengers had been landed, its most rugged face seemed to be turned to the westward, the eastern side sloping gradually to the water's-edge, where it terminated in a smooth sandy beach, upon which a landing might be effected without difficulty. For a distance of about half a mile inland from the beach the ground was carpeted with a smooth velvety green-sward, the rest of the island appeared to be densely wooded.

"That will do!" exclaimed Williams, as he closed his telescope, after a long and searching examination of the place; "the spot is quite large enough to enable a couple of men to pick up a living upon it, and I see no sign of savages anywhere about. Lower away the quarter-boat and bundle those things down into her. Have you looked out all you think they will need, Ned?"

"Yes," said Ned, who was most anxious that his collection should not be subjected to too close a scrutiny—"yes, I think they may perhaps manage to rub along and make themselves fairly comfortable in time with what I have put out for them. And, if I may be allowed to offer a suggestion, I would advise that the landing should be effected as speedily as possible, for when I was in the saloon just now I noticed that the glass showed a slight tendency to fall, a warning which ought not to be neglected in these seas."

"Ay, ay, that's true enough!" ejaculated Williams, in some alarm. "Look alive with the boat, there, you, Martin tumble the things in, and let's get the job over as quick as possible."

"No, no," said Ned, "there is no need for *quite* so much hurry as all that, and I must beg that you will handle those cases carefully or their contents will be spoilt or wasted and two human lives placed in jeopardy, which *you*, Williams, I know, would be the last to wish. If you have no objection I will superintend the loading of the boat myself, and whilst that is going forward I hope you will allow Captain Blyth and Mr Manners to step into the saloon and say good-bye to Miss Stanhope. It can cause no possible harm, and I am sure the young lady would like it."

"Very well," said Williams, after a moment's consideration; "I have no objection. Rogers, let the prisoners' irons be knocked off, and then send them into the saloon until the boat is ready to take them ashore."

Sibylla was at that moment on the poop affecting to inspect the island through her own private binocular, but in reality—having overheard Williams' announcement of his intention to land the two officers there—

watching for an opportunity to say good-bye to the hapless men. Ned, whose intuition was peculiarly quick and sensitive where this young lady was concerned, had divined her wishes in an instant, hence the suggestion he had thrown out; and the moment Sibylla heard that her desire was to be granted she hastened down into the saloon to await with a beating heart and swimming eyes the arrival of her two friends.

In a few minutes Captain Blyth and Bob Manners entered the cabin, accompanied by and apparently in the custody of Rogers, who seemed undecided whether to go or stay during the progress of the interview.

Sibylla detected the fellow's state of indecision in a moment, and at once helped him to make up his mind.

"Thank you, Mr Rogers," said she, with one of her most radiant smiles. "Oblige me by placing chairs for the two gentlemen, if you please; and would you be so kind as to close the door as you pass out—so that we may not be interrupted, you know?"

"Yes, miss, cert'nly," stammered the bewildered Rogers, nastily fulfilling her bidding, and as hastily effecting his bungling retreat.

"Oh, Captain Blyth, I am so pleased to see you—and so sorry!" burst out Sibylla, as she clasped the skipper's hand and gazed tearfully into his care-worn face. "How you must have suffered all this cruel time, pent up there in that horrid, *horrid* place! Do you know, I have tried, oh, ever so many times, to get permission to go and sit with you and cheer you up a bit, but those dreadful wretches would not allow it; and at last Ned—that is—I mean—Mr Damerell said perhaps I had better not try any more, as my evident sympathy with you might only make them angry and result in your further ill-treatment. And now they are going to put you on shore on a wretched desert island—as they did with my poor sister and Lucille and—and the rest yesterday, and you are come to bid me good-bye."

"Yes, my dear, yes," said the skipper huskily, "that is just about the sum and substance of it. But don't you trouble about us, or about your sister and the rest of them either for that matter. We shall be all right, never fear. The island yonder, though it is but a small strip of a place, is not exactly a desert by what I could see of it as I came aft; there is grass and trees—and, no doubt, water—upon it; and where such things are to be found it ought to be no very hard matter for a couple of handy men like Manners here and myself to pick up a living for a month or two, which is as long as we intend to remain upon it. For, hark ye, my dear," continued the skipper, sinking his voice to a whisper of mystery, "the moment that this ship is fairly out of sight we are going to set to work upon a boat, and as soon as ever she is finished it is our intention to make sail for your sister's island. Ned has told me its whereabouts; and if they can only hold out until we reach them they will be all right afterwards. And, by this day twelvemonth, if all goes well, we will not only be, all hands of us, back among civilised people, but we will have half the men-of-war of the British navy scouring the seas in search of you. Do you think you can manage to hold out for so long, my dear?"

"I don't know," said Sibylla, somewhat ruefully, "a year is a long time, isn't it? However," she continued, rather more cheerfully, "I hope we may not have to wait so long as that; Mr Damerell is wonderfully clever—as well as brave and gentle—and I know he is always thinking of some plan of escape, and he speaks so cheerfully and hopefully that I cannot but believe he will succeed. And if he does not we are still not absolutely helpless. The mutineers are quite as much in Mr Damerell's power as we are in theirs, for he says that not one of them possesses the least knowledge of the science of navigation, and he therefore believes that, for their own sakes, they will be civil to us both."

"Well, you are a plucky girl to keep up your spirits so well, and no mistake!" ejaculated the skipper admiringly. "I am glad to see it, and shall now be able to say good-bye with an easier mind. Keep up your courage, my dear, and trust in God; He is as well able to take care of you here as anywhere else, and He will, too, I am convinced. And, after God, my dear girl, put your trust in Ned; he is a true gentleman and a brave, clever lad. He will outwit those rascals yet, you mark my word; and when he gives them the slip he is not the sort of lad to secure his own safety and run off, leaving you in the lurch, so—"

"Boat's all ready, and waiting, gents, so look alive, please," here interrupted Rogers, poking his head in at the cabin door, and as hastily withdrawing it again.

"Well, then, the time has come for us to say good-bye," resumed the skipper. "I have said pretty nearly all I wanted to say, and the rest is not of much consequence. I am glad I have had the opportunity for this little chat, and more glad than I can say to find you so brave and hopeful. Keep up your courage, my dear young lady; put your trust in God, and whatever Ted tells you to do, do it at once and without asking any questions, because whenever the moment for action comes, it will be suddenly, unexpectedly, and there will be no time to spare for explanations. And now, good-bye, my dear girl; good-bye, and God bless you."

In another moment the parting was over, and the two men stood at the gangway, beneath which the boat was lying loaded and manned, and only waiting for them to step into her before shoving off for the shore.

Young Manners at once went down the side and seated himself in the gig's stern-sheets, and Captain Blyth prepared to follow him. As he stood on the rail, however, he turned and faced the men, who had all gathered in the waist to witness his departure, and raised his hand for silence; a signal which was instantly obeyed.

"Just a word or two before we part for ever, men," he said. "You have a noble ship under your feet, and you are doubtless flattering yourselves that when you have once fairly rid yourselves of my presence, your troubles—whatever they may be—will all be at an end. You are mistaken, however. Until you and I are parted your crime is not irreparable; it is even now not too late for you to repent and make restitution, and so stave off the punishment which *must* follow the consummation of your wickedness. You have a noble ship under you feet, I say; and you probably think that in her you can defy the law, and laugh to scorn the idea of capture. But, men, whether you believe it or not, *there is a God* whose power is great enough to overturn your best planned schemes in a moment, and think not that He will allow your sin to go unpunished, or your plans for future crime to prosper. At the moment when you least expect it—when you are feeling most secure—His vengeance will fall upon you as a consuming fire. In His hands I leave you."

And turning his back upon the mutineers, Captain Blyth quietly descended the side-ladder, seated himself alongside Manners, and gave the order to shove oh.

Chapter Ten
Refuge Harbour

Captain Blyth's valedictory speech was not without its effect upon some at least of the mutineers, who regarded each other with startled eyes, which dumbly but plainly asked the question:

"Is what we are doing worth the risk?"

Williams—who, it need scarcely be said, was one of the hardened ones upon whom the skipper's words produced no impression—saw plainly what was passing in the minds of the others, and hastened to annul the effect produced.

"That was a very clever speech of the old man's—very clever," he remarked sardonically. "There was only one fault about it, and that was that he didn't speak the truth. He spoke of our seizure of the ship as a crime. Well, maybe it is, according to the law, but we all know by this time that the laws are made in favour of the rich and against the poor; and we know, too, that law is not justice. For my own part, when I perform an act of justice I don't feel very particular about whether what I am doing is legal or illegal, if it is *just* it is quite sufficient to satisfy my conscience. The law, shipmates, is nothing—is no safe guide for a man's conscience, for we know that many a wrong, cruel, and unjust act is still perfectly legal—more shame to those that have the making and the powers of the laws in their hands. If you and I had been dealt with *justly* instead of merely legally, the money that bought this ship and cargo would have gone into our pockets as wages for the toil and hardship, the suffering and danger that we have been daily exposed to, instead of going as profit into the pockets of the merchants. Therefore I maintain that in seizing this ship and her cargo we have acted with strict justice, inasmuch as that we have merely taken possession of what ought in justice to have been ours at the outset—we have repaid ourselves a portion of the wages that we have been defrauded of during the many years that we have followed the sea. Why, mates, is it fair, or reasonable, or just, to ask a man to risk his life every day, as we do, for *three pounds a month*? Why, if our wages were *three pounds a day* it would not be too much. Reckon that up, you Bill Rogers, for all the years you've been following the sea, and how much will it amount to? Why, a precious sight more than your share of this ship and her cargo. But, lads, we've agreed to have our dues, and we'll have them, too, every penny of them; and if our only way of getting them is by turning pirates, why let the blame rest with those who have driven us to it. Justice is our right, and we will have it, let who will suffer for it, and upon that point we are all agreed. Aren't we, shipmates?"

"Ay, ay, of course we are—certainly, give us justice—give us our just rights, we want no more," murmured the men in response to Williams' appeal.

"There is only one thing I should like to know," remarked one man timidly, "and that is, how we are going to manage without murder if we're going into the pirating business?"

"Ha! is that you, Tom?" remarked Williams satirically. "You are a cautious one, *you* are; don't want to run your neck into a noose, eh? Well, you are quite right, shipmate, quite right. But you need not trouble yourselves, any of you, there will be no murder. I have a plan whereby we can avoid all unpleasantness of that kind, and still make ourselves perfectly secure, and I will explain that plan to you in due time, but not now; there are more important matters claiming my attention at this moment. Where is Ned? Here, Ned, bring out the chart and spread it upon the capstan-head, and you, lads, go to your stations."

Upon which the men retired, their torpid consciences silenced, and themselves more than half convinced of the righteousness of their actions. As for Ned, he muttered to himself as he went off to get the chart:

"Clever fellow—very; a regular sea-lawyer! Wonder who he is, and what he was before he took to the sea? Shall have all my work cut out to get to windward of *him*."

Ned soon returned with the chart, which he spread open upon the capstan-head as desired, when Williams and Rogers approached and regarded the document with looks of the profoundest wisdom.

"A queer-looking spot, isn't it?" remarked Williams to his companion, indicating with a rapid motion of his finger the entire area of ocean lying between Celebes, New Guinea, and the northern coast of Australia.

"Very queer!" assented Rogers, with a solemnity in keeping with the subject.

Whereupon the pair once more inspected the chart for several minutes with the same look of preternatural wisdom as before, to Ned's intense but covert amusement.

"Very well," said Williams at length, as though he had finally settled some knotty point to his complete satisfaction. "Now then, Ned, where are we?"

Ned placed his finger on a blank part of the chart and answered, "Just there."

"Yes," agreed Rogers, profoundly, "that's the very identical spot."

Williams glanced at Rogers with a broad smile of amusement, fully aware that the latter understood a chart about as well as he understood Sanscrit, and then turned to Ned with the remark:

"Now the next place we want, Ned, is a good harbour where the ship can ride it out safely in all weathers, where we can heave her down, if need be, to clear the weeds and barnacles off her bottom, and where we can build stores and what not."

"Ah!" remarked Ned. "That is a place which has yet to be found."

"Yes, of course, we know that," assented Williams sharply. "The question is, where ought we to look for it? Of course you understand it must be a place quite out of the regular track of ships, and not likely to be visited."

"In that case," said Ned, "I know of no better place to search than our present neighbourhood. You see that the sea all round the spot where we now are is marked 'Unknown,' which means, of course, that very few ships navigate these waters, and I fancy that such can scarcely be said of many other parts of the ocean except such as lie pretty close to the North and South Poles."

"Very well," said Williams, "in this matter we must trust to you, and we will therefore search this 'unknown' part of the sea. You know best how it should be done, so give your orders, and I will see that they are carried out."

"In that case," said Ned, "my advice is this. The wind is still westerly, and a favourable opportunity is therefore afforded for the prosecution of our search to the eastward. Now, from our main-royal-yard a man can see very nearly twenty miles—far enough, at all events, to make out any land at that distance suitable for your purpose. I would propose, then, that we should work a traverse to the eastward, sailing, say, one hundred miles on north by east a half east course, and then wearing round and sailing two hundred miles on a south by east a half east course. This will enable us to examine a strip of sea two hundred miles wide, whilst our northerly and southerly tracks will never be so far apart but what we *must* sight any land which happens to lie within that two-hundred-mile-wide belt. I would continue the search for say two hundred or two hundred and fifty miles to the eastward; and then, if you fail to find what you want, we must return and begin a systematic search to the westward, unless indeed you feel inclined to take the risk of venturing into better known waters. At night I would heave the ship to, with her canvas so balanced that she will make no headway; and in this way, I think, we may manage to pretty thoroughly explore the proposed track."

"Yes," said Williams thoughtfully, "that seems a very good plan. What do *you* think of it, Rogers?"

"Capital!" observed Rogers approvingly; "couldn't be better. If there's any islands about we're bound to find 'em that way."

The man spoke in a tone of such thorough conviction that Williams turned and scrutinised his face, as though wondering whether, perchance, the fellow really happened to dimly understand the matter about which they were talking, but the stolid features revealed nothing; so turning away again with a quick smile, he said:

"Very well, Ned, we will try your plan and see what it leads to. Ah! here comes the boat; they are just shoving off from the beach. Lay aft here some of you; overhaul those davit-tackles, and then stand by to hoist up the gig."

A quarter of an hour later the boat arrived alongside; she was hoisted up, the main-yards were swung, and the ship glided away on a north by east a half east course.

By sunset the ship, with the wind on her quarter, had run a distance of about fifty miles, when she was brought to the wind and hove-to for the night. At daybreak next morning the quest was resumed; and at noon the ship wore, her appointed distance of one hundred miles being completed. This mode of procedure was persevered in until noon of the seventh day after that on which they had landed Captain Blyth and Bob Manners, during which interval several islands had been sighted and examined without result, when, at the time named, Ned discovered by observation that the ship was two hundred and five miles north-east by east of the island which was now the home of those unfortunates. He had just completed his observations and calculations when the look-out aloft reported land on the port bow.

Williams went aloft to take a look at the reported land for himself, and invited Ned to accompany him. The journey to the royal-yard was soon accomplished, and the land was seen. It lay on the horizon like a faint grey cloud; indeed so thin and misty-looking was its appearance that an untrained eye would assuredly have mistaken it for a bank of vapour; but its outlines were so sharply-defined, and its shape so unchanging, that the experienced eyes of the gazers recognised it at once for what it was—namely, good solid earth. It was a long distance off, however—fully forty miles away according to Ned's estimate—and from its spread along the horizon it seemed to be an island of considerable size. The ship was at once headed for it; but it was five bells in the afternoon watch before it became visible from the deck, and at sunset the ship was still six miles distant to the southward of it. By that time, however, it had become apparent that it was an island of some nine or ten miles in length, with a pretty regular height of about four hundred feet above the sea-level; and its appearance was so promising that it was resolved to heave-to the ship for the night and give the place a thorough examination on the following day. The vessel was accordingly hove about, with her head off the shore; sail was shortened to the three topsails, jib, and spanker, the main-yard was laid aback, and then all hands, except the officer of the watch and a couple of hands to look out, were allowed to go below for the night.

At daybreak on the following morning the *Flying Cloud* was once more hove about and headed for the land under the same canvas which she had carried during the night, one hand being sent into the main-chains with the sounding-lead. Soundings, in twenty-five fathoms, were struck at a distance of about eight miles from the island; and thenceforward the water shoaled pretty regularly up to a mile from the shore, at which point a depth of five fathoms was met with. This was on the south side of the island, about two miles from its westernmost extremity, and abreast of an inlet which had previously been discovered with the aid of the ship's telescope. The vessel was now again hove-to, and, a hasty breakfast having been despatched, the gig was lowered and manned; and Ned, accompanied by Rogers, and supplied with a sounding-line and compass, was despatched in her to make a thorough examination of the place.

The boat pulled in, and at length entered the inlet, passing abruptly from the open sea into the shelter afforded by a bold rocky headland about one hundred and fifty feet in height, round the base of which, and over a short projecting reef, the heavy ground-swell dashed and swirled and seethed in snow-white foam with a hoarse, thunderous, never-ceasing roar. This inlet extended in a north-west direction for a distance of a mile and a quarter, its width decreasing from half a mile at the entrance to rather over a quarter of a mile at its inner extremity, with a tolerably regular depth of five and a half fathoms, until within half a mile of its inner end, where the water shoaled to four and a quarter fathoms. The scenery was very striking and beautiful—a sheer precipitous cliff, varying from one hundred and fifty to three hundred feet in height, towering out of the clear translucent water on their larboard hand as they passed in, whilst on their starboard hand the ground sloped gently upward from the water's-edge for a distance of about a mile and a half inland, where it cut the sky-line as an undulating ridge some four hundred feet in height. The outer or seaward face of the island was densely wooded, the foliage being of every conceivable shade of green, variegated in places with blossoms or flowers, in some cases snow-white, in others a delicate pink; here a deep rich golden yellow, there a tender blue, yonder a flaming scarlet, and, perhaps a little further on, a deep glowing crimson or an imperial purple. And even on the larboard hand, where the cliff rose sheer from the water, the rocky face was only bare here and there, the rest of the cliff being thickly clothed with vegetation.

Arrived at the inner extremity of the inlet, the occupants of the gig rounded a rocky point on their starboard hand, and found themselves in a large basin, roughly circular in shape, measuring about two and three quarter miles long, by about two miles wide, and completely sheltered from every wind that could possibly blow, being absolutely landlocked. This basin was formed by a deep indentation in the land on their starboard hand, the shore of which, starting from the rocky point they had just rounded, rapidly rose almost sheer from the water's-edge to about the same height as the precipitous cliff on their left, which it strongly resembled in general configuration, being a steep rocky face densely covered with tropical vegetation, in and out of which, by the way, darted numberless birds of brilliant plumage, whilst monkeys were to be seen here and there gambolling among the branches or staring curiously from some projecting pinnacle of rock at the new arrivals.

This basin, which had a depth of eight fathoms, with a rocky bottom in its centre, terminated, at its inner extremity, in a short passage or channel about half a mile wide between two bold rocky bluffs, beyond which another large sheet of water was to be seen; and toward this the gig was headed, the sounding-line being kept busy during the whole progress. As the gig advanced beyond the centre of the first basin, the water was found to shoal gradually, until exactly midway between the two bluffs, a depth of four and a half fathoms only was given by the sounding-line. The bluffs passed, the explorers found themselves in a second and much larger basin, also roughly circular in shape, like the first, but measuring about three and a half miles long by about three miles wide. This basin also was perfectly landlocked, the water being smooth as a mill-pond, and its surface scarcely ruffled by the faintest zephyr, though it was blowing moderately fresh outside. The shore all round sloped very gently up from the water's-edge, with a gradually increasing steepness, however, further inland, until just before the culminating ridge was reached the inclination appeared to be quite precipitous, giving indeed to the entire basin some similitude to the interior of a gigantic saucer. The slopes here, at least near the water's-edge, were not quite so densely wooded, the aspect of the landscape being exceedingly park-like, the soil being clothed with a velvety green-sward, thickly dotted with clumps of noble trees. A thin fringe of sandy beach ran all round the edge of this inner basin, except at its eastern or farther extremity, where the stretch of sand widened out to about the eighth of a mile for fully a mile in length. The deepest part of this basin was found to be at a point about a mile and a quarter inside the two rocky bluffs, and from thence it shelved up very gradually, the four-fathom line being struck at about a mile from the eastern shore. It was now discovered, however, that what had originally been taken for one island was in reality a group of four, two other channels being noted, one at the north-east, and the other at the south-east extremity of the inner basin. These channels were at once examined by the explorers, with the result that they were found to be impassable, except by boats. Indeed the north-east channel and one arm of the south-east channel—the latter forking into two channels at a mile and a half from its inner extremity—was found to be practically closed, even to boats, by the existence of formidable reefs outside, over which the surf was so heavy that no boat could possibly live in it. There was, moreover, a sandy bar with only one fathom of water on it at the inner extremity of both channels, but that passed, the water deepened again, until in the case of the south arm of the south-east channel, another bar was reached, over which, by watching their opportunity, the explorers succeeded in taking their boat safely, when they once more found themselves in the open sea. This act of crossing the bar they discovered, when it was too late, was rather a bad move on their part, for it placed them some three miles to leeward of the ship, in a fresh breeze and roughish water; but they fortunately had the boat's sails with them, and Ned was rather glad than otherwise of an opportunity to discover what the gig could do under canvas and in such circumstances. The masts were accordingly stepped and the sails hoisted, and in about an hour and a half they once more found themselves alongside of the *Flying Cloud*, those on board her having failed to sight them until they were close at hand, from the fact that the two craft were hidden from each other by a projecting point of land.

It was past two bells in the afternoon watch when the gig rejoined the ship; and Williams was, of course, all anxiety to learn the result of their protracted exploration. There was but one report that could be made— namely, that the place could not be better adapted for their purpose had it been specially constructed for them; and on hearing this, Williams ordered them to at once get their dinners, announcing his intention of taking the ship in forthwith.

Ned was as usual deputed to act as pilot, and accordingly, as soon as he appeared on deck after getting his dinner in the saloon, all hands were called, and sail was made upon the ship. The wind outside was at about west-south-west, which was a fair wind all the way to the spot Ned had fixed upon for an anchorage, except for the passage up the inlet, which trended in a north-westerly direction. This, however, though under ordinary circumstances it would have made the wind rather shy on that course for a square-rigged vessel, gave Ned no concern, as he had observed when passing in with the boat that, owing probably to the height of the cliff on the larboard hand, the wind manifested a tendency to draw up the inlet, and this, when the ship passed in, was found to be sufficiently the case to keep all her canvas full. The passage to the anchorage occupied a considerable time, in consequence of the scantiness of the wind as soon as the ship passed in under the lee of the cliffs, and under other circumstances it might have been tedious; but in the present case it was quite the reverse, the unaccustomed sight of the lofty verdure-clad hills and cliffs, the variegated tints of the foliage, the rainbow hues of the flowers and blossoms, the gaily-painted birds flitting here and there, and the antics of the monkeys fully occupied the attention of all hands, and interested them so completely that the time passed unheeded, and sunset surprised them when still half a mile from their anchorage. Then night fell upon them with the suddenness of the tropics; but the lead was now a faithful guide, and when it announced that the ship had arrived within four and a half fathoms of the bottom the sails were clewed up, the anchor was let go, and the mutineers found themselves at length in a harbour so safe that they might laugh at the winds in their utmost fury.

An anchor watch was kept that night as a precautionary measure, because it was not then known whether the group was inhabited or not; but nothing occurred to alarm the watchers, the only sounds heard being those made by the countless insects on shore or the weird cries uttered by the nocturnal birds. Some of the sounds and cries were certainly uncanny enough to send a creeping thrill through the frame of the listener, but with that exception the night passed peacefully away; and when the hands were turned up next morning to wash decks many was the longing glance which was cast across the water to the bosky glades, which looked so inviting in the bright sunshine.

Williams' alert eye at length took cognisance of these longing glances, and when at length the task of washing down was completed, the buckets and scrubbing-brushes put away, and the running-gear hauled taut and coiled down, he summoned the men into the waist, and informed them that, prior to beginning upon the somewhat lengthy task which he intended to carry through before again leaving the anchorage, he proposed to have the islands thoroughly explored and examined, the exploration to partake somewhat of the nature of a holiday ramble ashore, when each man, properly armed, would be at liberty to go whithersoever he would, and to spend the day pretty much as he pleased, so long as the question of whether the group was inhabited or not was satisfactorily settled. And he further intimated that that same day would be devoted to the examination; an intimation which was received with enthusiastic cheers.

Upon hearing this announcement Ned—who for reasons of his own was most anxious to keep on fairly good terms with all hands, and especially to so shape his conduct as to remove any suspicions against him which might still be lurking in the minds of the mutineers—at once stepped forward and, stating to Williams his desire to take part in the exploration, requisitioned the dinghy for his own and Miss Stanhope's use. His request was favourably received, and acceded to with a promptitude which somewhat surprised him; whereupon he hastened into the saloon, and, encountering the steward, gave orders for the preparation of a substantial luncheon basket, after which he apprised Sibylla of his proposed expedition.

Accordingly, as soon as breakfast was over, the two young people set off in the dinghy, Sibylla being seated in the stern-sheets, with the yoke-lines in her hands and the lunch basket at her feet, whilst Ned faced her, handling the diminutive oars—or "paddles," as the seamen termed them—without an effort. That he had not been unmindful of possible dangers was evidenced by the fact that that he had recommended Sibylla to take with her both her revolvers and a goodly supply of ammunition, whilst, as for himself, he was a perfect walking battery, a pair of revolvers and a small hatchet being stuck into his ammunition belt, whilst a ship's carbine reposed peacefully in the bows on the coiled-up painter of the boat.

Early as Ned and Sibylla were in leaving the ship, the mutineers had got the start of them, and, observing that the rest of the boats were making for the east and south islands, Ned determined to give them a wide berth, and accordingly paddled away for the north island, which was the largest in the group. He headed for a small strip of sandy beach which he had noticed during the examination of the harbour on the previous day, and after a leisurely pull of more than an hour across the placid waters of the basin beached the boat.

Ned was by nature a keenly observant young gentleman, and the first fact which attracted his attention on landing was that the water in the basin was at exactly the same height on the beach as when they had passed it some hours later on the previous day, from which he at once arrived at the conclusion—afterwards proved to be correct—that there was practically no tide in Refuge Harbour, as Williams at once named the place. But to obviate all possibility of the dinghy being swept away he not only dragged her half her length up high and dry upon the beach, but also planted one of the paddles firmly in the sand and then made fast the painter to it. This done, the lunch basket was stowed carefully away in the shade under the stern-sheets, when, loading and shouldering his carbine, Ned strolled along at an easy pace, so that Sibylla could walk beside him without much apprehension, the beach nowhere showing any footprints, as Ned believed it surely would have done had the place been inhabited.

They struck directly inland, and after traversing the narrow bit of sand reached the green-sward, the thick, luxuriant grass on which reached almost up to their waists. The ground here was open, the clumps of trees which they had noticed from the ship—and which now seemed to be as it were the outposts of a dense forest—not approaching in this particular spot nearer than about a quarter of a mile of the water. But even here there was enough and more than enough to occupy their pleased attention for the moment, the long grass being thickly interspersed with flowering plants and shrubs, adorned with blossoms of most exquisite form, hue, and fragrance. Sibylla, woman-like, must needs at once proceed to gather a bouquet for herself, in which pleasing occupation the next half-hour was spent. And here the pair were somewhat startlingly reminded that there is no Eden without its serpent, for as Sibylla stooped over a shrub loaded with magnificent white azalea-like blooms, one or two of which she desired for the completion of her bouquet, a sharp hissing sound was heard, and she started back with a cry, just in time to avoid a vicious stroke from a small heart-shaped head which suddenly upreared itself from among the leaves of the plant. Ned, however, was close beside her, and whipping out his revolver he fired, blowing the head of the snake clean off.

"Did the creature strike you?" demanded Ned anxiously.

"No," answered Sibylla; "I was so startled at its sudden appearance and its malignant aspect that I darted back without giving it time to bite. Do you think the creature was venomous?"

"We will soon see," answered Ned; and searching about in the long grass, which he was careful to divide with the barrel of his carbine, he soon found and held up to his companion's horrified view the severed head.

"Yes," he announced, "the brute was undoubtedly venomous. Note the heart-like shape of the head, the heads of all venomous snakes are shaped more or less like that. And see here," he added, compressing the neck just behind the jaws in such a way as to force the mouth open, "do you observe these two curved needle-like fangs, one on each side of the upper jaw? Those are the poison fangs. And these swellings of the gums at the base of the fangs are the poison bags. They become compressed when the fangs strike into the flesh of a victim, and a drop or two of the venom passes down through the fang, which is hollow, into the wound, and thus the mischief is done. You have had a narrow escape, Miss Stanhope."

After this little adventure the wanderers conducted their perambulations much more circumspectly, and Ned lost no time in providing his companion and himself with a stout pliant switch, which he had heard or read somewhere is a most effective weapon against snakes.

Soon after this they reached the outskirts of the forest, and it was not long before Ned discovered in a little greed patch of sward a small grove of banana trees with huge bunches of fruit, more or less ripe, depending from the crown of immense palmate leaves. He saw that the trees were of two or three different kinds, and, looking more closely, he quickly discovered that of which he was in search. Then, approaching one of the trees, he reached up and dragged the bunch of fruit down toward him, and, detaching several of the bananas, which were small and of a fine yellow colour, he approached Sibylla, saying:

"Now, let me offer you a treat, in the shape of a few 'ladies' fingers;' so called, I believe, because the fruit is so small and delicate. I scarcely think you will have ever tasted this kind of banana before, because I believe it will not bear transportation to England without spoiling."

Sibylla tasted the fruit, which she pronounced delicious, and then they resumed their ramble, enjoying their bananas as they went. A little further on they found some magnificent pine-apples, then some granadillas, and shortly afterwards several other fruits were met with, a few of which Ned was acquainted with, whilst others he had never seen before, and these last they very wisely let alone.

When about half a mile distant from the beach they entered the actual forest. Here the trees grew very closely together, whilst the entire space between their trunks was completely choked with a dense undergrowth of parasitic creepers, the long, thin, pliant tendrils of which stretched from trunk to trunk, or hung in festoons from the lower branches, and were so hopelessly tangled up together that progress was quite impossible, except along and through such openings as were the result of accident. Here the ground was quite bare of grass, a thick carpet of dry twigs and fallen leaves taking its place, and the whole aspect of the wood looked so exceedingly unpromising that Ned proposed turning back. Sibylla, however, was not so easily discouraged; she was very desirous of reaching the ridge or highest part of the island, and was not disposed to retrace her steps without at least making the attempt. They accordingly once more moved forward, Ned leading the way, and directing his steps as best he could with the aid of a small compass which he wore attached as a charm to his watch-guard.

They had advanced but a very few yards into this "bush," as Ned termed it, when they found themselves wandering almost blindly in the midst of a deep, sombre, greenish twilight gloom; the overhead growth being so dense as to almost entirely exclude the daylight, save where, here and there, an accidental break permitted a stray sunbeam to stream down and illumine a space of a few square yards. The effect of these partial illuminations was very beautiful, revealing as they did the long tangled festoons of creepers hanging black and snake-like against the light, and causing the brilliant tints of the variegated foliage and the resplendent hues of the flowers to flash out with dazzling effect against the contrasting shadows. Moreover, these little illuminated patches were alive with huge superbly-coloured butterflies, birds of gaudy plumage, and other winged creatures, whose forms were as novel as the combinations of colours which marked their bodies. They were the scene of a perpetual whirl and flutter of wings, and before they betrayed themselves to the sight their locality could be detected by the sense of hearing from the never-ceasing hum and chirp of the insects and the calls of the birds which frequented them. They were the scenes of an eager, busy, active life; whilst in the twilight depths of the forest everything was deathlike, everything was still—the very air was motionless, not a leaf stirred. The silence was weird, oppressive, and awe-inspiring; and when, at more or less lengthened intervals, a dry twig snapped, a withered leaf crackled, when the soft wafting of the wings of some nocturnal bird was heard among the branches overhead, or the sudden, brief rustling which betrayed the presence of some wild creature smote upon the ear, the effect upon the nerves was startling in the extreme. Through these alternate stretches of gloom and brief illuminated spaces the pair wound their way, Ned leading and clearing the path where necessary with his axe or his stout, serviceable clasp-knife, until eventually, after more than an hour's toil, they emerged upon a bald, ridge-like eminence which, on looking about them, they found was the highest spot in the entire group.

Chapter Eleven
An important discovery

From the point which they had now reached Sibylla and Ned commanded a bird's-eye view of the entire harbour, with South Island—as it soon came to be called—for a background, with the southern horizon showing just clear of its highest portion. Ned was now able to form a very much more correct idea of the entire locality than had before been possible; and as he stood critically examining the two basins, a suggestion as to their possible origin and that of the islands themselves presented itself to his mind. Seen from where he then stood the group bore a very strong resemblance to the crater of a long extinct volcano. To begin with, the ridge-like summits of the islands swept round in a form that was roughly circular, and they would have been continuous but for the breaches or channels which separated the islands from each other. They presented an appearance precisely similar to the rim of a volcanic crater; and the inner and outer slopes of the islands were also strongly suggestive of the inside and outside slopes of a crater. The two basins conveyed the idea of two closely contiguous vents for the subterranean fires, and the channels might very well be breaches in the sides of the crater through which the molten lava had burst its way. And this theory was confirmed by the colour of the water at the seaward extremities of the several channels, which clearly indicated the existence of reefs that might very well have been formed by the outflow. Some of these reefs, it is true, were so deeply submerged that the sea did not break over them at all, at least in fine weather such as then prevailed; this being notably apparent in the case of the channel by which the *Flying Cloud* had entered the harbour. But the mouth of the north-east channel, and that of the north arm of the south-east channel, were so choked with rocks close to the surface that they showed nothing but a wide expanse of white water. In a word, the more Ned thought about it the more convinced he became that he was standing on the summit of a volcanic mountain, the top only of which rose above the surface of the sea. As to the period when the volcano had become extinct, Ned was not scientist enough to form any opinion, but the whole aspect of the place was such as to convince him that it must have been countless ages ago.

Having at length satisfied their eyes with the superb prospect which lay spread out before them and beneath their feet, the happy wanderers—for happy they somehow were, notwithstanding all the unpleasant peculiarities of their position—set out to retrace their steps, reaching their boat about an hour later; when, taking advantage of the shade afforded by a few bushes which grew on the edge of an overhanging bank, they seated themselves on an outcropping rock and did the fullest justice to the luncheon which the friendly steward had put up for them.

It was two o'clock in the afternoon by the time that this meal was disposed of, when Sibylla expressed a desire to have a nearer view of the lofty cliffs bounding the outer basin than she had been able to obtain on the previous day when the ship entered the harbour. The boat was accordingly got afloat and leisurely pulled by Ned close along the northern shore. In due time the dinghy passed between the northern and southern bluffs and entered the outer basin, the water being still smooth enough to allow of her keeping within oar's length of the shore; and now they began to realise the majestic and indeed terrific character of the nearly vertical rocky walls which shot sheer out of the water and towered far away above their heads. The qualifying word "nearly" is used advisedly in speaking of the vertical rise of these cliffs, because, whereas when they were passed in mid-channel they had the appearance of being absolutely perpendicular, it was now seen that they had a slight—a very slight—backward slope.

The faces of these cliffs were, as has before been stated, so densely clothed with vegetation, mostly in the form of thick-growing shrubs—though trees of quite respectable size were by no means wanting—that but little of the actual rock was to be seen; and here and there among these shrubs and trees monkeys could be seen swinging from bough to bough, whilst thousands of birds darted in and out and flitted to and fro among the branches. One of these latter at length so strongly attracted Sibylla's admiring attention that she pointed it out to Ned.

"By George!" the lad exclaimed rapturously, "that is a beauty, and no mistake; I must have him. I have long been intending to make a collection of tropical birds for my father, and I might as well begin now; it seems to me that I shall have an opportunity of making a very respectable collection here whilst the mutineers are busy carrying out their plans at the head of the basin."

"You speak as confidently as though you deemed it an absolute certainty that you will eventually succeed in making your escape from those wretches. Do you still regard the project as a hopeful one?" said Sibylla inquiringly.

"Yes, most certainly," answered Ned, as he carefully withdrew the bullet from his carbine, and substituted for it a charge of small shot. "The fellows are certain to grow careless, sooner or later, and afford us a chance to give them the slip, even if we do not fall in with a man-of-war and get taken. Keep up your spirits, Miss Stanhope; keep up your spirits and your courage, I say, for I am always thinking and planning, and I never mean to rest satisfied until I have taken you out of the hands of those wretches and safe back to England again."

"You are very good to say so, Mr Damerell, nay more than good," answered Sibylla frankly, "and come what may, I shall never, *never* forget your constant watchful care."

"Oh, don't say too much about that," answered Ned cheerfully. "I look upon you almost as a second sister, you know, and I am only doing for you just exactly what I should wish to be done for my sister Eva if she were placed in a similar position to yours. And as long as you are compelled to remain on board the *Cloud*, I hope you will trust me as fully and as implicitly as if I were your brother; it will perhaps make you feel less lonely, you know, if it serves no other good purpose. And now, where is my bird? I am quite ready for him."

The creature was still hopping about among the branches of a tree almost directly overhead, apparently feeding on the fruit or berries which it found there; and taking careful aim, Ned fired. The report of the carbine went echoing back and forth between the cliffs in the most astounding manner, raising a tremendous disturbance, not only by its reverberations along the cliffs on both sides of the basin, but also from the cries of the countless startled birds which suddenly appeared in the air, and the excited chattering of the equally startled monkeys. As the smoke from the piece blew away, Ned saw his quarry tumbling from branch to branch, and bough to bough, until it finally brought up in a small bush which overhung the water some fifty feet above its surface.

"Killed him, by all that's lucky!" exclaimed Ned joyously. "Now, if you do not mind being left in the boat a moment by yourself whilst I slip aloft there—I will make the painter fast to this sapling so that you may not go adrift—I will secure my prize."

"But will it not be dangerous for you to climb up there?" protested Sibylla apprehensively.

"If I find it so I will not persevere in my attempt," answered Ned laughingly, as he grasped a bough and swung himself up on to a projecting ledge of rock.

For a few yards of the ascent Ned's figure was clearly visible; then, as he ascended still higher, Sibylla caught sight of him only at intervals, and soon afterwards he vanished altogether among the greenery, though his upward progress could still be traced here and there by the swaying of the bushes, but at length this also ceased, and then a dreadful silence and feeling of lonesomeness seemed to enwrap the fair girl as in the folds of a sable mantle. Minute followed minute with painful slowness as it seemed to Sibylla, and *every* instant she expected to see Ned's outstretched arm appear from the midst of the shrubs clinging aloft there to grasp the body of the bird. But nothing of the sort occurred, and at length, after a long and tedious period of painful apprehension, she ventured to call his name.

No answer.

Sibylla waited a minute or two, and then called again.

Still no answer.

She now became very seriously alarmed, and, quite losing command of herself, called upon him in piteous accents to answer, or if anything had befallen him to give her some sign of his whereabouts in order that she might be guided to his assistance. Still calling him, she was about to attempt the perilous ascent of the cliff-face in quest of him when she heard him shout, and, looking up, saw him leaning over the edge of a rocky ledge about a hundred feet above her.

"Are you all right, Miss Stanhope?" he shouted. "I thought I heard you call."

"Yes," she replied, steadying her voice as well as she could on the instant. "I am all right, thank you, but I *have* been calling; you were so long away that I began to fear some accident had befallen you."

"No," he answered back, "I am all right, but I have made a most wonderful and interesting discovery that—However, I will come down."

And suiting the action to the word, he at once began to descend the face of the cliff, not vertically, as he had gone up, but in a diagonal direction, and, as Sibylla thought, at break-neck speed. Ned continued his wild career until he reached the water's-edge, at a distance of perhaps two hundred feet to the westward of the boat, when, from what Sibylla could see of his movements, he appeared to break the bough of a bush in such a manner as to leave the branch dangling from the parent shrub, after which he began to make his way along the cliff-face toward the boat.

A few minutes later he reached the dinghy—minus the bird, by the by, which he had set out to secure—and stepping in at once proceeded to cast off the painter. Then, as he stepped aft and tossed the paddles into the rowlocks, he first got a glimpse of Sibylla's still troubled face.

"I beg your pardon, Miss Stanhope," he said. "I am afraid I have frightened you by my long stay aloft there. The fact is I was so interested in my discovery that for the moment I forgot the flight of time.

"I have made a most curious and important discovery, and one that may or may not be of the utmost value to us. When I started aloft to get that bird—by the bye, where is it? Ah! I see it! and I will have it, too, before I go back to the ship; but I will tell you my story first. I had not made my way very far up the cliff when I came to what looked so very much like a flight of roughly hewn steps running up the cliff-face that I determined to follow the indications, and investigate. I did so, and soon came to the conclusion that, though the step-like projections were just as thickly overgrown as the rest of the cliff-face—showing that they had not been used for years, or possibly generations, they had undoubtedly been wrought out by the hand of man. Pushing the shrubs on one side I had no difficulty whatever in making my way upwards, until I at length came out upon a flat platform of rock, in the outer edge of which were two holes or depressions, some twelve feet apart, which I imagined might have been hollowed out to receive the heels of a pair of sheers, an impression which was rendered all the stronger when, on looking more closely, I discovered a groove terminating in a third hole which I immediately guessed must have been formed to receive the heel of the back-leg. All this is, I suppose, Greek to you; but you will perhaps comprehend me when I explain that sheers are used to assist in hoisting heavy articles with. The rocky platform is about fifteen feet square, the cliff-face overhanging it above; and at its back part there is a sort of split in the rock about eight feet wide and nearly the same height. I passed in through this crevice, and at once found myself in a cave perhaps thirty feet wide and about fifty feet deep. And now comes the strangest part of the affair. It is nearly half full of bales and parcels, with several jars, apparently earthenware, their mouths tied over with what looks like a coarse kind of cloth; but everything is so thickly coated with dust and grime that it is quite impossible to guess at the contents of these jars and bales without further investigation. And in one corner there are stacked up a number of weapons—spears and axes—so rusted and decayed that they may have been there for centuries. There are also a number of what I took to be shields by the look of them; but they, like everything else, are so coated with dust that I did not touch them. But I must certainly give the place a thorough overhaul, as it may serve us as a refuge and place of concealment at a pinch. Would you like to go up and have a look at the cave and its contents now?"

"I should like it very much, if you think I could climb the stairs," answered Sibylla.

"Oh, yes," answered Ned, "you can do that easily enough, I should think; and I should like you to make the attempt, if only to find out whether you could accomplish the ascent at some future time, if necessary. I will go before and clear the way for you, using the axe if we meet with any very serious obstacles; but I think you will be able to manage without much difficulty. Ah, here, you see, is the landing at the bottom of the flight"—and Ned indicated to his companion a flat ledge about a yard square, close to the surface of the water.

The dinghy was carefully secured, and then, stepping on to the ledge, Ned assisted his companion ashore.

There could be no doubt as to the fact that from this ledge or landing a flight of step-like projections led diagonally up the face of the cliff; and, thickly overgrown as they were, there could be as little doubt that, if not entirely artificial, nature had been largely assisted by the hand of man in their formation. The flight averaged pretty evenly about a yard in width, each step being about six inches high; so that but for the dense growth of shrubs upon them, the ascent would have been exceedingly easy. Even as things were, Sibylla experienced far less difficulty than she had anticipated; Ned going before and then pressing the shrubs aside to facilitate her passage, using his axe here and there to remove such growth as stood fairly in the middle of the way. Nor was the ascent nearly so dangerous as might have been expected, the dense growth all along the outer edge of the stairway forming a sort of bulwark which rendered a fall almost impossible. So safe, indeed, and comparatively easy was the ascent that it was accomplished in about twenty minutes: when, after pointing out the holes in the upper platform, and fully explaining the structure and uses of the sheers which he believed to have once stood there, Ned led the way into the cave.

For a few minutes after entering everything was so dark compared with the brilliant daylight without that nothing could be seen. At length, however, their eyes became accustomed to the soft twilight gloom of the place, when Ned at once began to direct Sibylla's attention to the various articles that were stored there. The first objects examined were the weapons, all of which were stacked in one corner. The shields—for such they actually proved to be—were circular, about two feet in diameter, and made of a metal which, when cleared of its thick coating of grime and a small portion of its surface scraped with a knife, turned out to be brass. The outer and inner surfaces were both perfectly plain, or, if ornamented at all, the ornamentation could not be discovered without resort to a much more effectual cleaning process than Ned felt disposed to bestow upon them. On the inside two leather straps were rivetted, one for the arm to pass through and the other for the hand to grasp; but so old and decayed were these straps that they crumbled into black dust at a touch. This was also the case with the wooden shafts of the spears, which powdered away like touchwood. And, as for the spear-heads and the blades of the axes, they were so rust-eaten that little more than a rough jagged indication of their original shape remained.

The earthen jars, of which there were twenty-four, next claimed Ned's attention. These vessels stood about two feet high, and were about ten inches diameter, of peculiar though not ungraceful shape, and they were singularly heavy; as Ned discovered when he seized one with the intention of moving it forward into a lighter part of the cave. The mouth was covered with four thicknesses of a kind of wax-cloth, such as Ned had never seen before; the cloth being bound round the neck of the jar with several turns of fine cord, which, like the cloth, seemed to have been treated with a waxy coating, doubtless to assist in its preservation. If such was the purpose of the treatment, it had succeeded fairly well; but the outer or top layer of the cloth covering the mouth of the jar had rotted and split here and there. The second layer, however, was in a very fair state of preservation, and the other two layers were perfect, proving on examination to be a coarse kind of linen which had either been steeped in or painted over with a composition which felt waxy to the touch, and imparted a yellowish tinge to the fabric.

Ned's knife quickly severed the cord, which, however, was so rotten that it came to pieces during the process of unwinding, and he then uncovered the mouth of the jar and peered down into it. The vessel was full of a coarse, dull, yellow glistening sand, a handful of which the young fellow quickly removed and carried out into the daylight. He was back again in a moment, exclaiming to Sibylla in a tone of exultant astonishment:

"It is *gold-dust*, Miss Stanhope! gold-dust, and our fortunes are made!"

"I am very glad indeed to hear it," answered Sibylla. "But are you quite sure you are not mistaken? How do you know it is gold-dust?"

"I know by the look and weight of it," answered Ned. "I have seen too much gold-dust in Australia to be deceived in such a matter. Look at it and feel it for yourself—note the weight of a handful of it, and you will be satisfied that I am right. I expect the contents of all these jars are the same, but I will open one or two more just to satisfy myself."

He did so, and found his conjecture to be correct—the additional three which he opened were all full of gold-dust like the first.

"What shall we tackle next?" asked Ned. "That big bale looks as though it ought to contain something valuable; I think I will pursue my investigations in that direction."

The bale, which had an outer covering of wax-cloth of a much coarser texture than that which closed the mouth of the jars, proved to be too heavy for Ned to move unaided; so his knife was again brought into requisition, and the cloth—which was still tough enough to offer a slight resistance to the blade—was ripped open from end to end of the bale. The orifice thus made disclosed to view a firmly packed mass of several sorts of fabrics, neatly folded, and laid one upon the top of the other. The first three or four layers consisted of fine linen cloth dyed a deep rich purple hue. Then came several pieces of a heavy, rich kind of brocade; then a quantity of thin filmy muslin, fine as if woven of a cobweb, and exquisitely embroidered with a beautiful and intricate design in very fine gold thread. The brocades had been greatly admired by Sibylla, but these embroidered muslins simply threw her into ecstasies.

"Oh!" she exclaimed, clasping her hands in almost childish delight, "they are lovely; never in my life have I ever seen anything half so exquisitely beautiful!"

"Then," said Ned, in the most matter of fact way, "I'll tell you what we will do. The next time we come here we will be provided with the means of carrying off enough of the stuff to make you a dress or two. We cannot do so now, as the men would see it, and questions would be asked; which would never do. But next trip we will contrive to carry away a bolt or two of it."

Sibylla was a true woman; and even in her present predicament her feminine love of things beautiful was strong enough to win from her a ready assent to Ned's proposition. In the meantime the muslins were carefully re-folded—a task of some little difficulty, owing to their filmy texture—and replaced in the bale.

Quite a large pile of small brick-like parcels next came in for a share of Ned's attention. They, like the bales, were enveloped in wax-cloth, and like the jars were singularly heavy. Ned opened one, and on removing the cloth wrapper disclosed to view a block of dull yellow virgin gold. The block was about the same shape as, but a little larger than an ordinary English brick, and stamped or moulded on each side was a sign or symbol of hieroglyphic character.

Ned did not consider it necessary to open any more of the brick-like parcels, as, after his experience with the jars, he felt fairly satisfied that, if opened, each parcel would be found to contain a gold brick similar to the one already disclosed. He was therefore about to suggest a descent to the boat, under the impression that his inspection of the cave and its contents had been completed, when it occurred to him that he might as well strike a match or two and throw a little light into the extreme corner of the cave, in which, now that his eyes were growing somewhat accustomed to the gloom, he fancied he could detect a pile or stack of some kind. He accordingly drew from his pocket a box of matches, and, placing some half a dozen of them together, ignited them. This afforded him light enough to see that there really *was* a stack of long dark curved objects piled in the angle. To get at these it was necessary for him to climb over the heap of gold bricks, which formed a kind of barrier across the corner, and in so doing his eye fell upon one brick quite at the rear of the stack which was very considerably larger than the others.

Reaching the mysterious stack in the corner he selected one of the long curved objects and, brushing the dust from it as well as he could, proceeded to scrape through the remaining coat of dirt with his knife. By this means he soon reached a hard bone-like substance, upon which he presently scraped a white surface, when the expenditure of a few more matches revealed the fact that he had been operating upon an elephant's tusk, of which nearly a hundred he thought must be stacked in that dark corner.

On his return to the lighter part of the cave where he had left Sibylla, his attention was again attracted by the extra large brick-like parcel, which he thought he might as well examine. He accordingly raised it from the floor to carry it further forward into the light, when, though tolerably heavy, the comparative ease with which he lifted it at once assured him that, whatever else it might be, it certainly was not gold.

The grimy cloth wrapping was soon removed, and a casket of discoloured but still recognisable brass of elaborate and curious workmanship was disclosed. The lid was not secured in any way, otherwise than by the hinges; and so perfect had been the protection afforded by the wax-cloth wrapping that these worked without difficulty. The lid was quickly raised, and the casket—which measured about fifteen inches long by nine inches wide, and perhaps ten inches deep—was found to contain a number of neat wax-cloth parcels. The first which came to hand—and which, by the way, was by far the largest one—was at once opened, and there before the eyes of the admiring pair, fresh as if just removed from the shell, lay some two hundred or more magnificent pearls—magnificent not only in respect of their unusual size, but also of their exquisite lustre and perfect globular form. Needless to say that in presence of these superb and incomparable gems Sibylla's admiration of the embroidered muslins dwindled away to insignificance, and her minute examination of the pearls plunged her into a perfect trance of delight. The other parcels were found to contain rubies, sapphires, emeralds, diamonds, and other precious stones, all in their rough state just as they had been unearthed from the mine, but all without exception of extraordinary size. At first the fortunate finders were not greatly impressed at the sight of these stones, for neither of them quite knew what they were—though they judged them to be valuable from the circumstance that they had been deemed worthy of a place in the same receptacle with the pearls—and it was only the gleam of the diamonds which at last awakened in their minds a suspicion that the stones were really precious. When at length, however, this suspicion fairly dawned upon them Ned positively gasped for breath.

"Why," he exclaimed, "we are *rich*! rich beyond the power of computation. There must be at least a hundred magnificent fortunes in this veritable cave of Aladdin; and now all that we have to do is to give those ruffians the slip, when I will find means to return here and recover all this treasure. Now," he went on, "I'll tell you what we will do. We will divide the contents of this box into two about equal portions, one of which we will convey from time to time on board the ship, whilst the other shall remain here; and in this way I think we may make reasonably sure of securing one half of the gems whatever happens. The gold we must leave, I think, as too cumbersome to be dealt with under our present circumstances, but the dresses you certainly *shall* have. Now, slip those pearls into your pocket, and I will take as many of the diamonds and what not as I can stow away, after which I think we had better see about getting back to the ship."

"But," interposed Sibylla, "have we any right to touch these things? Surely they must belong to some one?"

"I have not the slightest idea who was the former rightful owner of all this property," replied Ned, laughing; "but, whoever he was, he has been dust and ashes ages ago, and so too have the rovers who, I expect, brought them to this out-of-the-way place and hid them in this cave. Why, by the look alone of the things, the arms especially, they must have been here at least hundreds of years! There is no doubt a deeply interesting story attaching to this hoard, but what it is we shall probably never know. Of one thing, however, you may rest assured, and that is that we, as the finders, have a better right to everything in this cave than anyone now living."

The reasonableness of this argument satisfied even Sibylla's sensitive conscience, and she made no further demur to Ned's proposed arrangements.

An hour and a half later they reached the ship, just as the sun was setting, and found her still deserted, though the men could be seen mustering on the beaches and preparing to return on board. Advantage was taken of this circumstance by Sibylla to stow away in her own boxes, at Ned's request, all the jewels brought on board, thus leaving that young gentleman free to meet Williams on his return to the ship and to make such a report of his explorations as he might deem fit. Half an hour later all the men had returned on board, and though they were thoroughly fagged out by their unwonted exercise they had evidently enjoyed the day just as much as though they had been so many schoolboys.

On the following morning work was begun in earnest, part of the men being engaged in unbending sails and sending down the upper spars, whilst a contingent under Williams landed and proceeded to cut down trees for the purpose of building stores, a dwelling-house, a kitchen, and so on, on shore. Williams' plans comprised no less than the entire stripping of the ship down to a gantline; the thorough overhauling of her hull, inside and out, including cleaning and scrubbing; and a number of petty alterations in her rigging, which he thought would have the effect of disguising the vessel. And in addition to this he also proposed to construct on shore permanent buildings for the storage of his booty, as well as for the residence of a small contingent of men to guard it. This of course was not only a work of considerable time, but it also involved the complete evacuation of the ship, a circumstance which Ned foresaw would cause very serious inconvenience to Sibylla. This, however, was at length happily surmounted by his obtaining the very reluctant consent of Williams to employ some of the men in the construction of a hut for her sole accommodation, he at the same time locating himself in a small tent, which was pitched close at hand, so that he might always be able to watch over her safety.

Meanwhile the *Southern Cross* duly arrived at Melbourne after an excellent passage; and Captain Spence was intensely gratified when he found that nothing had been heard of the *Flying Cloud*. A week later the *Southern Cross* was lying with an empty hold, waiting for her homeward cargo to come alongside, and still the *Flying Cloud* had not put in an appearance. Knowing what he did of the latter vessel's sailing powers, Captain Spence could only conclude that after the *Flying Cloud* had parted company with him in the Atlantic, she must have met with a streak of foul wind or light airs which his own ship had happily avoided; but when a week later still, the *Flying Cloud* had not arrived, the exultation which the honest skipper had at first experienced was converted into a feeling of incipient anxiety, which increased as time went on without any appearance of his rival. The *Southern Cross's* cargo was slow in coming alongside; but, nevertheless when she was loaded, and her hatches put on, and she finally went to sea on her homeward voyage, the *Flying Cloud* was still numbered among the non-arrivals. And when, after a long passage home, the *Southern Cross* arrived in London, and Captain Spence had time to inquire after his old friend, Blyth, he was not only surprised, but deeply grieved to hear that no intelligence of his arrival in Melbourne had up to that date been received.

But there were others even more interested than Captain Spence in the fate of the *Flying Cloud*, and these were by this time anxiously watching the columns of the "Shipping Gazette" for tidings of the ship. They came at last, in the shape of the following paragraph:—

Missing Vessel

"The following vessel, previously referred to as overdue, was on Wednesday posted at Lloyd's as missing:—

"The ship *Flying Cloud* (Blyth, master), which left London for Melbourne on —, and which afterwards picked up the derelict barque *Umhloti*, of Aberdeen, and sent her into port."

Chapter Twelve
Mr Gaunt goes on an exploring expedition

It is now time to return to the little party of passengers, who, it will be remembered, were left in a situation which was certainly the reverse of pleasant.

Mr Gaunt, whose profession peculiarly adapted him to cope with such difficulties as those which now environed the party, at once naturally took the lead and assumed the direction of affairs—a position which Dr Henderson most willingly accorded him, counting himself indeed fortunate in being thus associated with a man of such infinite resource as the engineer. In their present state, the first thing to be done was to provide a shelter for the helpless women and children of the party; and no sooner was the boat's cargo discharged upon the beach and conveyed in safety above high-water-mark than was this task commenced. A suitable position for the tent, which Gaunt proposed to put up, was soon found among the trees, which grew thickly in clumps on the gentle slopes just beyond the sandy beach. Two cocoanut-trees, growing at a convenient distance apart, were selected as uprights; and a young sapling was then cut down and lashed horizontally from trunk to trunk, at a height of about nine feet from the ground, to serve as a ridge-pole. The sail was next hauled over this sapling and secured to the ground on each side, in such a form as to make an A shaped tent about twelve feet long by eight feet wide, the spare canvas being so split that it fell down at the rear and front end of the tent in such a way as to enable the little shelter to be completely closed when necessary. And, this done, the bedding, as well as such articles as it was important to protect from the weather, were at once placed under shelter, and the interior of the tent made as comfortable as circumstances would permit; thus completing the first portion of their task. The next thing was to construct a shelter for the powder—and in fact their little all, in the shape of worldly possessions, which they thought it undesirable to put into the tent. Two more cocoanut-trees were selected; another stout sapling was cut and secured between them, as in the case of the tent, though not quite so high from the ground, and then a quantity of other and somewhat lighter saplings were procured to form a roof, which by sunset next day they had succeeded in covering with a good serviceable thatch, quite impenetrable to the weather. But before this was accomplished they were unexpectedly reinforced by the sudden appearance of Nicholls, whose presence upon the island up to that moment had been quite unsuspected by them. This individual had been so anxious to avoid all possibility of recapture that he spent the night in the woods, presenting himself to the little party as they sat at breakfast next morning. His sudden appearance created quite a sensation for the moment; but he was almost instantly recognised.

"Why, Nicholls!" exclaimed Gaunt, "what is the meaning of this? What are you doing here? I thought you and the rest of the mutineers were far enough away by this time."

"Well, sir," said Nicholls, twisting his cap nervously in his hands as he spoke, "I hopes the rest of the mutineers are, as you say, far enough away by this time, but I am *here*, and here I intends to remain—with your good leave, sir. The fact is, Mr Gaunt, I've cut and run! That fellow Williams—as, perhaps, you may know, sir—is a rare good 'un to talk, and he managed to talk me, as well as the rest of the hands, quite into the idee that pirating was just the best thing a poor down-trodden seaman could turn his hand to. Lord bless you, Mr Gaunt, if you had heard that man I'm blessed if I don't think he would have persuaded *you* into the same idee! But after I had agreed to jine them I began to think matters over a bit, and the more I thought about it the less I liked it; and at last I made up my mind that I'd slip my moorings aboard the *Cloud* the first chance as ever I got. And when I got to hear that Williams was going to turn you two gentlemen and your respected families ashore here, I says to myself, '*Now's* your time, Tom!' And so I managed to get told off for service in one of the boats, and, watching my chance, I sort of strolled up among the trees and then took to my heels, quite determined not to show up again until the *Cloud's* to'ga'nts'ls had sunk below the horizon. And now, here I am, sir, ready and willing to ship with you. I'm nothing but a poor ignorant man—a blacksmith, rightly, by trade—but mayhap I may be able to make myself useful enough to earn my bread and cheese."

"Well, Nicholls," said Mr Gaunt, "I am heartily glad to see you, my man. And, as to your earning your bread and cheese, a stout, handy fellow like you, and a blacksmith to boot, will be a considerable acquisition to us in our present circumstances. I have no doubt that Williams managed to make his plans very attractive to you poor fellows in the forecastle; but wait and see how they will all end. We know not what is before us. We shall, doubtless, have to endure much hardship and be exposed to countless perils before we once more reach the shores of old England—if ever we are fortunate enough to do so. But, whatever hardship or peril may fall to our lot, I feel confident that in the end you will be better off with us than you would have been with

Williams and his piratical crew. But sit down man; sit down and take some breakfast. You must be nearly famished by this time, if, as I suppose, you have eaten nothing since you left the ship yesterday."

Nicholls, nothing loath, at once seated himself, and was served with breakfast, which he devoured with an eagerness that at least spoke well for the tonic properties of the air he had lately been breathing.

"I should like," said Mr Gaunt, "before we go any further, to say a word or two, whilst we are all present here, upon our future plans. I suppose you have all been thinking more or less upon this subject, and, as for myself, I may safely say that since we landed upon the beach yesterday my thoughts have dwelt upon nothing else. I do not know how it may be with you, Henderson; but, delightful as is the climate of this island, and fertile as its soil appears to be, I have no fancy for adopting it as my permanent home. I am anxious to return to civilisation at as early a date as possible. What are your ideas upon the subject?"

"Precisely similar to your own," answered the doctor. "My tastes and inclinations are, by no means, pastoral; and if they were I do not think I should particularly care about indulging them in this lonesome spot. With all its failings, civilisation has certain advantages which I must say have a peculiar value in my eyes, not the least of which is the ability to live a quiet and peaceable life, free from all possible attacks by savages or the semi-civilised marauders which I have understood infest these Eastern Seas. So, whatever may be your plans for returning to civilisation, you may depend upon me, Gaunt, in aiding you in every way I possibly can."

"Very well," said Gaunt. "Then I will now tell you in as few words as possible what my ideas are upon the subject, and I shall be glad of any suggestions which either of you may afterwards have to offer. When we were in the act of leaving the ship yesterday, that noble fellow Ned slipped into my hand a strip of paper, in which he had noted not only the position of this island but also the important fact that he had detected the presence of what he believed to be a wreck on the reef on the western side of the island. About this wreck I shall have more to say presently. The position of the island, as given by Ned, places us at no very great distance from land; but that land is inhabited by people who would not scruple for an instant to cut our throats if they thought it would suit their purpose to do so; it is useless, therefore, for us to think of making for a nearer port than either Hong-Kong, Singapore, or one of the ports of Western Australia. At first sight it would seem a simple matter enough to build a boat and make our way in her to one or another of the places I have named; for we have wood in abundance here, and apparently of many kinds, and Ned has, I see, provided us with a stock of nails which, carefully used, might suffice us for the purpose. But our island is, unfortunately for us, situated in a sea which is swept at times by the most destructive hurricanes; and it would be madness for us to think of leaving this place in anything but a craft capable of living through the very worst of weather. I have not the slightest doubt of my ability to design such a vessel; but, let her be as small as we dare to make her, her construction will still be a work of exceeding difficulty for our small party, and it will also be a work of time. During that time we must all be housed, and clothed, and fed. And I therefore propose that our first task shall be a thorough examination of the entire island, for the purpose of ascertaining the most suitable spot as a base for our operations; and, that discovered, I think we should next go to work to construct for ourselves such a dwelling as shall bid defiance to an assault by anything but civilised troops; stock it abundantly with provisions, so that, if besieged, we may not have famine to contend with; and, that done, I think we shall then be free to begin our operations upon the boat. With regard to this boat—for, in dimensions, she will not be much more—I think that, in addition to being of a capacity sufficient to conveniently carry us all, she should be fully decked and modelled upon such lines as will not only make her a good sailer, but also a first-rate sea boat."

The doctor in his present situation found himself so utterly strange, that, if left to himself, he would scarcely have known what to set about first, and he was therefore only too glad to find that Gaunt was not only so willing, but also so thoroughly able to grapple with the difficulty. He said as much; and when Nicholls was asked his opinion it turned out that, like a great many more of his class, he was quite unable to advance one, but was perfectly willing to follow the lead of his superiors, let them go where they would.

The next matter for consideration was that of the exploration of the island, which Gaunt proposed to undertake alone. His idea was to advance cautiously inland for a mile or so, and then, if he saw no sign of their territory being inhabited, to make a push for the mountain at about the centre of the island, and from thence onward to its western side. It was, of course, rather hard upon Mrs Gaunt that he should be left, as it were, alone in this way while the disagreeable novelty of her position was still fresh upon her; but there was no help for it, so the brave little woman plucked up her courage, and when her husband was ready to start bade him a cheery farewell.

Gaunt thought it only prudent to start upon this expedition thoroughly well armed, and in addition to his repeating rifle, and the revolvers and hunting-knife which he wore in his belt, he carried an axe, which he thought might be useful in a variety of ways. He hoped to return to camp that evening, but foreseeing that he might meet with delays on the way he cautioned them not to feel in the least anxious on his account should he be absent that night and the whole of the next day.

On taking leave of his companions he at once struck inland towards the mountain, which, looming vast and grey, formed the most prominent object and landmark in the entire island. The ground sloped gently upward, and was thickly covered with long, tangled, and luxuriant grass; and at a short distance from the beach it began to be thickly dotted with clumps of trees, among which the cocoanut, the date-palm, and two or three varieties of the banana were prominent. On reaching the wooded portion of the island, the engineer found, to his great gratification, that although the soil appeared to be most densely overgrown with trees, such was not in reality the case, as the clump-like arrangement which he at first encountered still prevailed, although as he advanced inland the clumps grew much more closely together than they did on the outskirts of the wood. He had very little difficulty in making his way among the boles of the trees, as, contrary to what he had anticipated, there was not much parasitic undergrowth, and where it became inconveniently dense his axe soon enabled him to clear a way for himself.

Advancing steadily and with tolerable rapidity over the gently rising ground, he at length, when not more than about two miles from camp, suddenly found himself upon the verge of a ravine with steeply-sloping sides, through the bottom of which wound what he at first took to be a river, but which, on close examination, he found was really an arm of the sea. Descending the banks of the ravine he followed this stream—which at the point where he encountered it was about a quarter of a mile in width—and after pursuing a somewhat devious route for about another mile and a half, came to a spot where this arm of the sea widened out to a lake-like expanse of water, nearly circular in shape, and rather more than a mile in diameter. Almost in the very centre of this lake stood a small island of about eight or ten acres in extent and thickly wooded, which the engineer at once fixed upon as a most suitable spot on which to establish an encampment. He was very anxious to reach this island and submit it to a closer examination, but he had no means of crossing the intervening water except by swimming, and this, in consequence of the distance to be traversed, would occupy more time than he felt justified just then in devoting to it. But he promised himself that, circumstances permitting, he would do so on his return journey.

So far he had met with no trace or sign of the existence of savages, or indeed of inhabitants of any description, upon his territory; and he therefore relaxed somewhat of the vigilant and anxious demeanour which he had hitherto observed, and pushed forward, with as much rapidity as circumstances would allow, upon his journey. Traversing the borders of the lake, which lay embosomed in the midst of an amphitheatre of steeply-sloping hills, he reached, after a walk of about a mile, a spot where a genuine stream flowed into it. At the point of junction with the lake this stream was about a hundred yards in width, having a current which flowed seaward at the rate of half a knot per hour. Half a mile further on, following the course of the stream, Gaunt found that the channel narrowed very considerably, and, whilst still to all appearance moderately deep, the current became much more rapid. It was at about this spot that he discovered what he thought would serve as a capital site for a mill, if, indeed, the little party should find it in their power to undertake so important a work; and, making a mental note of the locality, he passed on.

He now determined to follow the stream to its source, as his active mind already began to see that it might prove a very useful ally to them in many ways. The ravine-like character of the banks on either side of the stream still prevailed, and this, in conjunction with its winding course, continually opened up such vistas of sylvan beauty, that from time to time the wanderer involuntarily paused in admiration, and once or twice even caught himself asking the question whether, after all, a man might not do worse than spend the remainder of his life in the midst of such grandeur and beauty.

He now frequently encountered streams and brooks of more or less importance flowing down into the main stream on either side of the ravine, but they were scarcely sufficient in volume to account for the large quantity of water which now went dashing and foaming and sparkling over a bed of huge boulders. At length he came to the end of the ravine, and there he beheld a sight which amply rewarded him for all the labour which he had undergone in following the stream. The ravine terminated in a vertical wall of rock fully a thousand feet in height, from an immense fissure in which, near the top, there spouted a column of water which he estimated to be at least twelve feet in diameter. For fully a third of the distance this liquid column poured down unbroken, to be dashed into spray and mist—in which a rainbow softly beamed—upon an immense spike of rock which divided the flow into two nearly equal parts, and formed two superb cascades one on each side of the projecting rock.

At this point it was easy for an active man to cross the stream without wetting his feet, by jumping from boulder to boulder; and this the engineer did, for he saw that in order to reach the mountain he would have to get on the opposite side of the stream and follow its downward course for nearly a mile. When at length he climbed up the steep and lofty side of the ravine and reached its brow, the nearest spur of the mountain was only about a mile and a half distant, and for this he at once made. His route now lay over a flat table-land, out of which the mountain seemed to spring at once, and almost sheer. On reaching the base of the hill, however, its sides proved to be not quite so steep as they had appeared to be, but they were nevertheless steep enough to tax Gaunt's muscles to their utmost extent before he finally reached the bald summit.

He had now spread around and beneath him a prospect of such surpassing beauty as he thought he had never gazed upon before. The sea bounded his horizon on every side, whilst the entire island lay spread out like a map beneath him, with all its bold undulations, its streams, the lake, and the arm of the sea distinctly visible; and with the aid of his telescope he was even able to discern the gleaming white canvas of the tent which marked the position of the little party he had left behind. Nay more, when he had finally adjusted the focus of his telescope, he was even able to detect, upon the white sand of the beach, two tiny moving objects which he knew to be his own boy Percy and little Lucille Henderson. For some time he was unable to withdraw his eyes from those two diminutive objects; but when he did so, and turned his face to the westward, he saw that the remarkable cliff which Ned had noticed as the ship passed the island, and which seemed to divide it into two separate and distinct portions, was distant not more than three-quarters of a mile from the base of the hill on which he stood. The top edge of this cliff bounded his view to the westward so far as the island was concerned; but the bay with its encircling reef was visible, and even with the naked eye he readily detected, on the interior edge of the reef, a small speck-like object which the telescope showed him to be the wreck mentioned by Ned in his note. The day was now wearing on apace, and his long walk had sharpened his appetite; Gaunt therefore thought that he could not do better than sit down where he was and take his luncheon or dinner whilst he noted in fuller detail the topography of the island, of which he there and then made a rough sketch-plan.

His meal over, the solitary explorer descended the mountain and made his way to the edge of the cliff. Arrived there, it soon become apparent that the most difficult portion of his journey still lay before him, for at the point where he then stood, he saw at once that to descend the cliffs face to the slope below would be an impossibility without the aid of ropes or some substitute for them. He turned south and followed the edge of the cliff, hoping to find a spot at which he might descend, but without success, as he at length reached a point where the face of the cliff turned sharply off to the eastward, eventually running into and forming a portion of the cliff proper, which on that side of the island ran sheer down to the water.

Retracing his steps, Gaunt soon found himself back at the spot where he had in the first instance reached the edge of the cliff, and passing on he found, at a distance of about a quarter of a mile beyond, a narrow chasm or gap, which on careful inspection he saw would enable him to descend to the sloping green-sward at the foot of the cliff. Down this gap he cautiously scrambled, narrowly escaping an awkward fall once or twice on his way, and by that means soon reached the foot of the cliff, which appeared to maintain a tolerably uniform height of about three hundred and fifty feet.

From the point where he now stood the ground sloped pretty evenly down to the water, the inclination of the slope being about one foot in every three; and the distance to the water's-edge a mile, as near as might be. The base of this long slope terminated in a narrow strip of sandy beach, which was strewed here and there with timber and what-not from the wreck in the offing. This wreck Mr Gaunt was exceedingly anxious to visit, as he felt it might—and probably would—prove of inestimable value to himself and his companions. She was not more than half a mile distant from the beach, and was lying close to the inside fringe of the white water which broke over the outlying reef. Her bows pointed shoreward, but at an angle which enabled the engineer to catch a glimpse of her entire broadside; and she was lying well over on her side, with her inclined deck towards the island, thus enabling Gaunt to get, with the aid of his telescope, a fairly good view of her, and to form a tolerably accurate estimate of the amount of damage which she had received. She was a large vessel, measuring, as near as he could judge, some sixteen hundred tons, and she appeared to be built of wood. She had been either barque or ship-rigged; but all three of her masts were over the side, and could be seen floating there still attached to the hull by the rigging. Her bulwarks were entirely swept away, as also were her deck-houses—the broken stanchions of which Gaunt thought he could detect still projecting above the surface of the deck. The stem and stern-posts of a couple of boats still dangled from her davits; which seemed to point to the conclusion that when disaster overtook her the crew had been allowed little or no time in which to provide for their safety.

Gaunt was an excellent swimmer, and, having no boat, he thought his quickest mode of reaching the vessel would be by taking to the water. He was on the point of stripping for this purpose when, his eye still fixed upon the ship, he caught a glimpse of two or three small dark objects projecting above the surface of the water and moving slowly about. He had a very shrewd suspicion as to the nature of these objects, and his telescope soon demonstrated to him the fact that he was right in believing them to be the dorsal fins of so many sharks.

He was scarcely prepared for this discovery, as he was under the impression that the bay on the shore of which he stood was completely hemmed in by the reef; and he was fully aware that if such had been the case the smooth water inside would be quite free from sharks, as these pests never voluntarily pass through broken water. Their presence, therefore, pointed to the probability that although he had been unable to detect such a circumstance, there must somewhere be a channel through the reef.

The sight of the sharks effectually put an end to his project of swimming off to the wreck, and he at once began to look about him for the means of forming such a raft as would enable him to make the trip in safety. There was plenty of timber lying strewed about the beach, but he had no nails or tools of any description, except his axe, with which to construct the raft. Under these circumstances the matter required a little thinking out; and whilst deliberating upon his best mode of proceeding, he sauntered along the beach on the look-out for suitable materials. He had been walking slowly along for a distance of about a mile when his quick eye detected certain objects lying on the sand which he instinctively divined to be human corpses, and, making his way to them, he found he was not mistaken. There they lay—seven of them—just as they had been washed ashore, dead, after their last ineffectual struggle with the merciless sea. Three of them were fully clothed; the remaining four were clad only in their shirts, which seemed to indicate that they had leaped from their hammocks, upon some sudden alarm, and rushed upon the deck, to be almost immediately swept overboard. The bodies were in a most revolting condition, from the combined effects of the sun and the attacks of the sea-birds and land-crabs, the latter of which swarmed upon the beach in thousands. It was difficult to judge accurately how long a period had elapsed since death had overtaken these unfortunates; but from their appearance Gaunt believed that it could not have been many weeks. It was a sad sight to look upon, especially for a man in his situation; and he hastened to remove it by roughly sharpening a fragment of plank with his axe and scooping shallow graves in the sand, into which he rolled the bodies and hastily covered them up.

Chapter Thirteen
A visit to the wreck

This shocking discovery diverted his thoughts for a short time from his original project; but, having done all he could for the poor wretches, he was glad to turn anew to the question of the raft. To a man accustomed as he was to the quick devising of expedients it was not difficult to scheme out the plan of such a structure as would serve his purpose. Looking about him and collecting a quantity of such small pieces of wreckage as had nails in them, he formed them into a heap, to which with the aid of some dry grass and withered leaves and a lens from his telescope, he set fire and left it to consume. Then picking out three 6-inch planks of about equal length he sharpened their ends with his axe and laid them on the beach, at a distance of about three feet apart, with their sharpened ends pointing seaward. He next procured three pieces of plank long enough to just cross the first three planks at right angles; and as soon as his bonfire had burned itself out he cleared the nails from among the ashes, and with them fastened his structure together. Two short pieces of plank nailed vertically in midships, with another piece secured on top of that, formed a rough-and-ready seat; and two other pieces secured crosswise on each side to the outer edges of his raft, and at the distance of about a foot abaft the seat, gave him a fairly serviceable substitute for rowlocks. He had already been fortunate enough to find a couple of small oars, and he now thought he might venture to essay a trip to the wreck.

MR. GAUNT BOARDS THE WRECK OF THE "MERMAID"

Small as was his raft, it was still so heavy as to give him some trouble in the launching of it; but he at length got it fairly afloat, and seating himself in the centre, adjusted his oars and began to try its paces. He was greatly surprised to find that he could propel it through the water at a very fair speed, and without much effort; and, this fact ascertained, he at once headed straight for the wreck, which he safely reached in about half an hour.

There were plenty of ropes'-ends dangling from the ship's side, to one of which he made fast his raft, and laying the oars carefully down in such a manner as that they would not be likely to slip overboard, he scrambled on board the wreck and reached the steeply inclined deck.

The wreck appeared to be fully as large as he had supposed; and he was agreeably surprised to find, on investigation, that she had not received nearly so much damage as he had anticipated, indeed her injuries seemed to be confined almost entirely to the loss of her masts, bulwarks, and deck-houses. The cabin had been on deck; but this was swept away. The forecastle, however, was below, and into this he descended. It was arranged in the usual manner on board merchant ships—that is to say, it had standing bunks round each side of it, in which the bedding of the unfortunate seamen still remained, precisely as when the ship struck.

The seamen's chests were also there, showing that they had had no time to make any elaborate preparations for leaving the ship; and the impression produced upon Gaunt's mind by what he saw was, that when the ship struck the watch below must have rushed immediately up on deck, and very soon, if not immediately afterwards, have been swept overboard.

As he was there, not to satisfy his curiosity, but to ascertain of what value the ship might prove to himself and his friends, he did not hesitate to open and examine the chests of the poor fellows; but he found nothing therein except such coarse clothing as is usually worn by merchant seamen, and a few little odds and ends of no particular value, except perhaps a sailor's palm or two, with sail-needles; and in one or two instances a little housewife with sewing needles, thread, etcetera, neatly arranged.

One of the chests, however, proved to be a carpenter's tool-chest; and this, although Gaunt had a small tool-chest of his own among his effects, would be of such priceless value to the little band, that he determined to secure it then and there; and he accordingly dragged it on deck at once, in readiness to transfer to his raft. The floor of the forecastle was quite dry, and this circumstance led Gaunt to hope that the hull had received no damage; but on raising the hatch leading to the fore-peak he saw that the place was nearly full of water. His exploration of the forecastle ended here; and he was about to proceed on deck when he caught sight of a fishing-line suspended on a nail inside one of the bunks. This fishing-line he at once secured and took on deck with him laying it down on top of the carpenter's tool-chest so that it might not be forgotten when he left the wreck.

He now proceeded to the after end of the wreck. Here the cabins had been entirely swept away; and he had no means of ascertaining any particulars as to the ownership of the vessel, the nature of her cargo, or her destination—the ship's papers and the captain's private documents having doubtless gone overboard with the wreck of the cabin. But by looking over the ship's counter he saw that she was named the *Mermaid*, and that she hailed from the port of Bristol.

That portion of the deck which formed the floor of the cabin had been covered with oilcloth; and this oilcloth still remained in place, securely nailed down to the planking. Looking about him Gaunt had no difficulty in discovering the locality of the hatch leading down to the lazarette, which, like the rest of the cabin flooring, was covered with oilcloth, on folding back which he noticed, with satisfaction, that the sea had been prevented from penetrating into the interior. Raising the hatch he descended, and found, as he expected, that the place was well packed with the usual stores supplied to such a ship when bound upon a long voyage. He opened a few of the cases at haphazard and extracted from one a bottle of port wine, and from another a tin of preserved soup; he also found several casks of ship's bread, from one of which he filled his pockets. With this booty he returned to the deck and deposited it on the carpenter's tool-chest. He next turned his attention to the hatches. These were all securely battened down; and he noticed with great satisfaction that the tarpaulins which covered them were quite uninjured, and to all appearance perfectly watertight. He was about to break open the main hatchway, but on further consideration he decided not to do so until he was prepared to hoist out the cargo and transfer it to the shore, as he well knew that when the tarpaulin was removed he would be unable to properly secure it in its place again without assistance.

His preliminary examination of the wreck was now completed, and the position of the sun warned him that it was high time for him to see about returning to the shore. He met with a great deal of trouble in lowering the heavy tool-chest down the ship's side and safely depositing it on his flimsy raft; but so much value did he attach to its possession that he determined not to leave the wreck without it. And he eventually succeeded, though not until the sun was within half an hour of setting. This task successfully accomplished, and the fishing-line, bread, wine, and tin of soup placed in security on the top of the chest, he cast off and cautiously pulled away to the shore, which he safely reached just as the sun's upper rim was disappearing below the horizon.

He was by this time desperately hungry, and the first thing to which he devoted himself was the preparation of supper. His first idea was that he would be obliged to consume the soup cold; but the prospect of such a comfortless meal was so little to his taste that he began to look about for some means of overcoming this disadvantage. What he wanted was a vessel or a receptacle of some description in which he could heat the soup and make it somewhat more palatable; and here he remembered having passed during his morning's ramble on the beach a very large shell of the species *Tridacna gigas*. He bethought himself of its whereabouts whilst busily engaged in moving the tool-chest, etcetera, well up above high-water mark; and having brought the locality to mind he took the tin of soup in his hand and hastened along the beach. The shell was not very far distant, and securing it he dragged it to a convenient position and imbedded it in the soft dry sand, placing the tin of soup in it. He next collected a quantity of dry twigs and brushwood, of which there was no lack beneath the trees at a short distance from the beach. He also collected a quantity of dry leaves, and with these and the brushwood he built the constituents of a fire, which he next lit with the aid of a match, a few of which he had taken the precaution to provide himself with that morning before setting out His next task was to find a few good large pebbles, of which there was a plentiful supply lying about just where the sand and the soil proper met. Selecting about two dozen of the largest he conveyed them to his fire and carefully arranged them in its midst. He then proceeded to fill the shell—which was to serve as his cooking pot—with salt water, no fresh-water being at hand; after which he sat down and waited patiently until the stones which he had laid in the fire should be sufficiently heated for his purpose. About twenty minutes sufficed for this, when the hot stones were dropped one after the other into the shell, by which means the water was very soon brought to boiling point, and maintained at that temperature long enough to thoroughly warm the soup, the tin of which he had, after some difficulty, succeeded in opening with his axe. He then hurried back to where he had left the wine and the bread, both of which he conveyed to his extemporised kitchen, and there, with the aid of a small shell carefully washed, made shift to consume the soup, washing it and the bread down with a moderate draught of wine. This done, he kneeled down on the sand and, commending himself and his dear ones to the care of his Maker, stretched himself out by the side of the fire, and was soon wrapped in a dreamless sleep which lasted until morning.

He was awakened by a sound so homely and familiar to his ears, that when he first started up he almost believed that the experiences of the past few months could have been nothing more than an unusually vivid and circumstantial dream, and that he should find himself a tenant of some pleasant English farm-house. The sound—which was the crowing of a cock—was repeated, and answered from the woods at a distance of perhaps half a mile, and again answered by another shrill crowing nearer at hand, but in a different direction. He was astounded. What could be the meaning of the presence of domestic fowls on this lonely island? He started to his feet and set off, determined to investigate. The crowing was repeated often enough to serve him as an effective guide in his search, and proceeding cautiously he at length found himself quite close to the spot from whence the sounds apparently proceeded. Still advancing cautiously he presently heard not only the crowing of a cock but the loud triumphant clucking with which a hen proclaims to an admiring world the fact that she has laid an egg. A little further away he heard, in addition to these sounds, the softer cluck with which a parent hen calls to her chickens; and presently, peering out from behind the bole of an enormous teak-tree, he saw not only chanticleer but also his harem, consisting of half a dozen hens, two of which had broods of fluffy-looking chickens running at their heels. This was a most delightful surprise to Gaunt; for though the island seemed to promise that he and his party would never be likely to want for the means of sustaining life, here was a supply of food which, carefully looked after, would be the means of affording them many a dainty dish. The fresh morning air had again sharpened the solitary man's appetite, which now admonished him that it was high time to think seriously about breakfast, and the loud continued clucking of the hen which had laid an egg reminded him that fresh eggs were very good for breakfast. His first intention was to confiscate that egg; but a moment's reflection showed him that if left alone it might eventually become a chicken, and thus considerably increase in value. He therefore decided to forego the gratification of fresh eggs for breakfast, and to turn his thoughts in some other direction.

It occurred to him that fresh eggs being, in the existing state of the market, too expensive a luxury for breakfast, fresh fish might serve as a very satisfactory substitute; he therefore made his way to the beach, and taking his fishing-line, launched the raft and went off as far as the inner edge of the reef, wondering meanwhile how the presence of those domestic fowls could be accounted for upon the island. If the *Mermaid* had not obviously been wrecked too recently to admit of the existence of so nourishing a brood, he would have thought that they must have formed part of the live stock of that vessel, and that when she struck and her decks were swept, the coops had been smashed and the fowls had succeeded in effecting their escape to the shore. This, however, was impossible on the face of it, and he knew not how otherwise to account for it, unless they had been landed and left by some passing ship, which seemed even more improbable.

He was not long in reaching the inner edge of the reef, where he laid in his oars, baited his hook with one of a few shell-fish with which he had provided himself for the purpose, and dropped the line into the water, where it had not been above half a minute when he felt a tremendous tug. Pulling up the line quickly, he found that he had captured a magnificent nine-pounder in splendid condition, the fish being very like a salmon in shape, make, and colour, excepting that it had a longer, sharper head, and a finer tail. Securing his prize, he at once put about and made for the shore, as he was anxious to reach the camp on the other side of the island that evening.

Having caught his fish, the next question was how it could be cooked. He had been revolving this matter in his mind on his return journey from the reef, and remembered having somewhere read of a process which he thought would suit his present condition. He remembered having noticed an outcrop of clay not far from where he had camped on the previous evening, and making his way to the spot, he secured a sufficient quantity to serve his purpose. The next thing he required was a quantity of leaves, and he plunged into the woods to search for some which might be suitable. He found plenty, but they were all of a class unknown to him, and as they would come into intimate contact with his food in the process of cooking, he hesitated about making use of them; so pushing on a little further, he was fortunate enough to discover an orange-tree laden with both blossoms and fruit in every stage, from the little hard green ball the size of a marble, up to the perfect fruit just changing from dark olive green to a golden yellow. The leaves of this tree would suit his purpose admirably; so gathering as many as he required, as well as three or four of the finest specimens of the ripened fruit, he returned to the beach. Here he at once proceeded to mould a portion of the clay into a rough semblance of a long narrow dish of dimensions suitable for the reception of the fish. This clay dish he thickly lined with orange leaves, upon which he laid his fish entire as it had come out of the water, covering it with another thick layer of orange leaves, and then with a thick coating of clay, so that the completed structure resembled a roughly moulded clay pie with the fish wrapped in orange leaves in its centre. He now proceeded to light a fire, and when the brushwood of which it was composed had been reduced to a mass of glowing red-hot embers, his clay pie was carefully deposited in the centre; fresh brushwood was heaped thickly on the top, and he then sat down to await results. In about half an hour the clay showed signs of cracking, which told him that his culinary operations were complete; so dragging the mass out from among the embers, he proceeded to carefully break away the top layer of clay, and there lay his fish cooked to perfection, a dish fit for a king. Upon this fish, and a portion of the bread which he had procured from the wreck on the previous evening, he breakfasted royally; washing down the whole with a moderate libation of wine, and topping off with a couple of oranges, after which he was ready to start on his homeward journey. Before going, however, he hauled up his raft as high as he could get it on the beach, placed the two oars in safety beside the carpenter's tool-chest, and roughly thatched over the latter with palm-leaves to protect it from the weather.

The long pull of a mile up the steep slope leading to the base of the cliff tested his unaccustomed energies very severely, and the toilsome scramble up through the precipitous incline of the gap taxed them still more; so that when he at length reached the top of the cliff, he was glad enough to fling himself down in the long grass and allow himself half an hour's rest and the refreshment of a pipe. At the end of that time he once more set forward, shaping his course so as to pass to the southward of the mountain, and from thence down the steep ravine to the edge of the river, the left bank of which he determined on this occasion to follow. As he pursued his journey he could not help being struck, and very agreeably impressed, with the wonderful fertility of the island, and the great variety of its products. The trees were many of them of immense size, and though there were many species, the names and natures of which he knew nothing about, he was able to identify on the upper slopes of the mountain the pine, the fir, and what looked very much like a species of ash; whilst on the table-land and on the slopes of the ravine the teak, mahogany, and jarrah, as well as the cocoanut and two or three other varieties of palm flourished in abundance, to say nothing of the bamboo, several groves of which he passed through during the course of the day. Of fruits also there was a great variety, among others the pine-apple, banana, plantain, pawpaw, granadilla, guava, orange, loquat, durian, and the cocoanut. Several species of cane also flourished luxuriantly, and among them he found what he believed, from its general appearance and its taste, to be a wild sugar-cane. But what perhaps gratified him more than all was to meet here and there with little patches of maize.

Of animal life also there was no lack. Of snakes there were more and in greater variety than he at all cared to see, and in addition to these the forest was alive with monkeys of several varieties, to say nothing of other animals whose quick movements would not permit him to identify them. Insects, as might be expected, swarmed in countless millions, some of them being most grotesque in form and colour. Butterflies of unusual size flitted about from flower to flower, and the upper branches of the trees were fairly alive with birds of the most brilliant plumage, among which he noticed two or three varieties of the parrot tribe, whilst birds of paradise were there in such numbers that he thought he might not inappropriately name his new domain "Paradise Island." Where the ground was sufficiently open to permit of their growth, flowering shrubs and plants with blossoms and blooms of the loveliest colours, and some of them of the most delicate perfumes, abounded; and among the shrubs there were several which he believed to be spice-bearing plants. After a fatiguing but nevertheless very enjoyable tramp, he arrived, at about two o'clock in the afternoon, at the margin of the lake, and at once took measures for swimming across to the islet in its centre. Collecting a large bundle of rushes, he stripped, and placing his clothes and his other belongings upon the flimsy raft thus formed, and stepping into the cool refreshing water, struck quickly out into the centre of the lake, pushing his raft before him.

As he approached the islet he noted with great satisfaction that, so far as he could then see, the place was admirably adapted for the head-quarters of the little party so long as it might be necessary for them to remain in their island prison. There were trees in abundance on the islet, and of many varieties, but they did not grow so thickly together as they did on what we may call the mainland, large spaces of open prairie being discernable here and there, which Gaunt already mentally devoted to the process of cultivation. Swimming quietly he reached the islet with very little fatigue, and, dressing himself, at once set about looking for the wherewithal for a dinner. He had not far to go, for he had scarcely plunged into the first grove of trees when a large bird took wing from among the branches, and, raising his rifle, he succeeded in bringing it to the ground. It proved to be a brush-turkey, which he forthwith proceeded to pluck and prepare for the spit; lighting a fire meanwhile, so that it might burn well up and be in a fit state for cooking when wanted. The turkey was cooked—after a fashion—and if it was not as well done as the engineer could have wished, it was still sufficiently so to satisfy his hunger, after which he set out to explore the islet.

It was of no very great size, being about ten acres in extent, or thereabouts, but its surface was finely broken up into miniature hills and dales in such a way as to not only make the spot appear larger than it really was, but also to present a very pleasing variety of aspect to the eye. He found here a spring of fresh, clear, cool water, which was a source of great satisfaction to him, as the water of the lake, being in direct communication with the sea, was somewhat brackish, too much so at all events to render it a desirable liquid for drinking and culinary purposes; and the presence of this spring would avert all necessity for a search on the mainland and a possible difficulty of securing a sufficient supply without much labour.

Having an eye to the presence of the children upon this islet, Gaunt was peculiarly inquisitive in the matter of reptiles, and it was a great relief to his mind to discover that if any such were on the islet they were so scarce that during his entire search round and through it he did not encounter a single snake. So far as he could see there were no animals to be found upon it, though birds were, of course, in as great variety and numbers as they were on the mainland of the large island.

He was fortunate enough to find, not very far from the spot on which he had landed, a shelving piece of beach running down into deep water, which would serve him admirably as a site on which to build his proposed boat, and near it—distant, in fact, not more than two hundred yards—there was a small grove of palms and other trees which would serve admirably as a shelter from the sun for his proposed house.

His survey of the islet completed, he again entered the water, and, with his raft of rushes ahead of him as before, quietly paddled across to the shore on the right back of the stream, which he now proposed to follow down to its junction with the sea. A walk of about six miles brought him to the mouth of the little estuary, which he found perfectly concealed from the sea, in consequence of the river taking a sudden bend and then doubling again almost upon itself between two low bluffs which rose steeply out of the sea.

At this point there was no beach whatever, the shore being rocky and precipitous; but somewhat further on the slopes of the land became gentle, and a sandy beach was met with which, after a walk of some seven or eight miles, brought him out at the spot on which he had originally been landed from the ship, and within full sight of the encampment where dwelt the rest of the party.

Chapter Fourteen
Gaunt's pontoon raft

His arrival, which took place just as tea was about being served in the camp, was greeted with great rejoicing by all hands, but especially by Mrs Gaunt; who, notwithstanding the assurances of Doctor Henderson, was beginning to feel serious alarm on account of her husband's prolonged absence.

Of course there was much to tell on both sides. The principal item of news from the Doctor was that he and Nicholls had between them contrived, during the two days of Gaunt's absence, to erect a very roomy and by no means uncomfortable shelter for the men of the party; in addition to which the whole of their goods and chattels were now placed in perfect safety so far as the weather was concerned.

No adventures of any description had been met with by any of the party; a circumstance which was no doubt largely due to the especial care which Doctor Henderson had exercised in keeping them all close to the shore, from a suspicion he had entertained that the forest depths might not be altogether safe travelling, at least for women and children.

Gaunt's story of his journey to the wreck, with the vivid description he gave of the fertility and general productiveness of their island-home, greatly raised the spirits of the listeners; and the sanguine way in which he spoke of their ability to build the little vessel which he contemplated, caused them already to feel as if their days on the island were numbered.

The chief point calling for consideration was how they should dispose of themselves in the immediate future. Their position was this: they were then located on the eastern end of the island; the lake and the islet were situated almost in the centre of their domain, or say at a point about six miles distant, as the crow flies, from the point where they then were; whilst the spot where the wreck lay, if measured in the same way, would be about five miles further on.

Gaunt made it so clear to them that the islet was the most fit and proper spot at which to establish their head-quarters that that matter might be considered as already definitely settled. But they would have to draw all, or nearly all, the materials for the proposed craft from the wreck; and that wreck would not only have to be broken up, but the timber, etcetera, would have to be conveyed to the islet before a permanent settlement could be established there. Had the party consisted of men only, there was no doubt their best plan would have been to remove in a body to the western end of the island, and to have established themselves temporarily on or near the beach close to the wreck whilst she was being broken up; but it seemed to be rather a hardship that the women and children should have to be removed there—involving a somewhat lengthy and arduous journey—and to go into temporary quarters only to have to return gain over a great deal of the same ground afterwards, Gaunt's idea was that the ladies and children might be safely placed on the islet, and comfortably housed there in the first place; after which the three men of the party could go over to the wreck and remain there until everything of value were got out of her, he undertaking to visit the islet at least once every day to ascertain that all was going well in that direction. This proposition, however, met with no favour from the parties chiefly interested; and so it was ultimately resolved that, notwithstanding the inconvenience, the entire party should settle down for the time being on the western side of the island.

On the following morning this resolution was put into effect, the little band taking with them nothing but just such arms as were deemed absolutely essential to their safety, and the tinware, knives and forks, and other small table conveniences with which Ned's forethought had supplied them.

On this occasion Gaunt, who of course acted as guide, struck off in a new direction; as, having made a sketch-plan of the island when he was on the summit of the mountain, he believed it possible to reach the wreck by a much shorter route than the one he had followed. Keeping somewhat more to the right, or in a more northerly direction than on the first occasion, he brought his companions out upon the banks of the stream at a distance of about two miles below the lake, where the channel was somewhat wider than in any other portion of its course, and where the current was particularly gentle. Here it became necessary to construct a raft of some description for the transport of the party across the stream; but, as the water was perfectly smooth, anything which would bear their weight and hold together during the passage was considered sufficient, and with the aid of their axes such an affair was knocked together in about three hours. The transit was then safely accomplished; and, climbing the steep slope of the ravine through which the stream flowed, they found upon reaching its summit that they had arrived at a spot overlooking the lake, and from which they were enabled to obtain an excellent view both of it and the islet which occupied its centre. The ladies were especially delighted at the prospect of finding a home in so lovely a spot; whilst Henderson cordially agreed with Gaunt that it would be difficult to find a safer place and one more suitable in every respect for head-quarters.

Pushing on, they arrived about three o'clock in the afternoon at the base of the mountain; and here, in a pretty little meadow which lay between two of its projecting spurs, they determined to encamp for the night, the children, although they had been carried for the greater part of the day, being extremely tired, and the ladies scarcely less so. A little hut of branches and palm-leaves was constructed as a shelter for the weaker members of the party during the night, the men contenting themselves with the soft luxuriant grass for their sleeping place; and, then, whilst Nicholls set to work to build a fire, Gaunt and Henderson went off in different directions to forage for a supper.

The night passed without adventure or alarm of any description, although, as a measure of precaution, the men had deemed it advisable that each should watch for an equal portion of the night; and on the following morning after an early breakfast the march was resumed. The gap in the cliffs was reached about two o'clock that afternoon; and by three the travellers found themselves on the beach at its nearest point to the wreck.

The first matter to be attended to now was the erection of shelters of some description. Henderson undertook to cut down a couple of saplings which Gaunt pointed out as suitable for the purpose; and whilst he was engaged upon this task the engineer, accompanied by Nicholls, went off to the wreck, their object being to procure not only a small quantity of ship's stores, but also one of the sails, which they intended to utilise in the construction of tents. On arriving alongside and making a minute inspection of the wreckage, it was found that the raffle was so complicated that to cut away the sail from its yard as it then lay and to convey it to the shore would be a work of very great difficulty; so, after a short consultation together, Gaunt and Nicholls decided to cut the whole adrift from the wreck and then warp it ashore just as it was. Nicholls accordingly get to work upon this task with his axe; and whilst he was thus engaged Gaunt searched for and found the boatswain's locker, rummaging in which he discovered a small grapnel just suited to his purpose. This he conveyed on deck, and, unreeving as much of the running-gear as he could get at, a good long warp was made by bending the whole together end to end. By the time that his preparations were completed, Nicholls had got the wreckage cut completely adrift from the hull, and the two men now proceeded to carefully coil down upon Gaunt's raft the whole of the warp; the grapnel being bent on to one end, whilst Nicholls, who was going to remain on the wreckage, retained possession of the other. Gaunt then pulled shoreward; and as soon as the full length of the warp was paid out he dropped the grapnel overboard and then made the best of his way back to the wreckage, which Nicholls had already begun to drag shoreward by the warp. The progress of the wreckage shoreward was very slow; but it improved somewhat when Gaunt was able to rejoin his companion. As the warp was hauled in it was carefully coiled down on the wreckage; and when at length the grapnel came to the surface it and the warp were once more promptly transferred to the raft and a fresh cast was made, by which means they managed in about an hour and a half to get the spars with all attached so close to the beach that they grounded. It was now a comparatively easy matter to cut it apart and so obtain the sail, which was the first thing they required. The forecourse was selected, as being of considerable dimensions; and this, when detached from its yard, was dragged up on the beach and spread out to dry. With this sail, and rope procured from among the rigging which had come ashore attached to the spars, they were able to construct two capital tents; and by night-fall the little party found themselves snugly housed.

The two succeeding days were devoted to the construction of a shed of dimensions sufficient to contain all that they thought would be likely to prove valuable to them among the stores and the cargo of the ship. The structure was twenty-four feet long, by eighteen feet wide, and eight feet high to the eaves; and it had a regular pitched roof, with gable-ends, so that when the rainy season came—as come, Gaunt felt certain it would—the wet might be thrown off, leaving the goods beneath its shelter undamaged. It was not a very substantial affair, the four corner-posts being the strongest portion of it, formed as they were by the trunks of four standing cocoanut-trees, the sides and roof being wattled and afterwards thatched with palm-leaves. But the engineer thought it would serve its purpose; and his great object was to get everything he could from the wreck in the shortest possible time, because, lying where she was, she might, and probably would, go to pieces on the occasion of the first heavy gale which might spring up.

The shed completed, their next task was to secure everything which might prove of any possible value to them from the cargo of the wreck. In order to transfer these articles from the hulk to the shore a raft would be necessary; and a raft would also be required to eventually convey those goods round to the islet. The latter transfer would involve the expenditure of an immense amount of labour and time unless the wind or some other motive power could be pressed into their service; and Gaunt had already learned during the course of his professional experience that when any important work had to be performed it was better and more economical in every way to provide efficient "plant" in the first instance. Now the construction of the vessel which he had in contemplation was a simple and easy enough matter to a shipwright with all the usual appliances at his disposal, but was really an important and formidable task to people situated as these were; and, therefore, when talking the matter over together, they had, influenced by Gaunt's arguments, resolved to devote the time and labour required to construct such aids as he seemed to think would be necessary and desirable. To convey from where they then were round to the islet all that they would require for the construction of their vessel would, with an ordinary raft propelled by oars alone, involve a vast amount of labour and time; and it was ultimately decided that it would be more expeditious in the long run if a raft could be constructed of such a character that she could be moved in any required direction by sails.

After a little thinking, Gaunt came to the conclusion that it would be possible to construct such a raft, and he set to work to plan it. The structure, as decided upon by him, consisted of two flat-bottomed straight-sided pontoons, each twenty-four feet long by six feet wide, and six feet deep, their ends being curved up from the bottom until they met the deck in a sharp chisel-like form. These pontoons were built with their fore-and-aft centre lines parallel, and were constructed on separate pairs of ways, the whole of the materials being obtained from the wreckage already strewn along the beach, and such portions of the deck-planking of the wreck as could be removed without exposing the cargo to the risk of damage by sea or rain. The bottom-planking was laid athwartships, and four of the planks at equal distances from each other were carried right through from pontoon to pontoon—the pontoons being built with a space of six feet clear between them—thus securely connecting the two pontoons together. The pontoons were decked all over, the deck-planking for a length of twelve feet in the middle portion being also carried right across from one to the other. The two pontoons were thus securely fastened together above and below, the result being that the entire structure formed a good, substantially-built raft, having in its centre portion a platform or deck measuring twelve feet fore and aft, and eighteen feet athwartships. The craft—if one may dignify the structure with such a name—was rigged with one mast, situated exactly in the centre, and well supported by shrouds on each side, and she was provided with a lateen or three-cornered sail bent to a very long yard composed of a number of bamboos fished together. The yard was hung in its centre, an arrangement by which Gaunt hoped to succeed in making his raft sail with either end foremost with equal facility, his idea being to work the craft precisely upon the same principle as that adopted by the Ladrone Islanders in the working of their flying-proas.

This raft, though of such literal dimensions, was very easy and simple to build, as there was no shaping of timbers and no elaborate workmanship of any kind required, the only matter involving any considerable degree of care being that the two pontoons should be watertight; and this of course was very easily managed. But, simple as the work was, it was fully a month before the raft was ready for service, though when they at length got her afloat and tried her under sail the result was satisfactory, far beyond their most sanguine anticipations.

They were now in a position to attack the wreck in good earnest, which they did by rigging up a pair of sheers on deck and hoisting the cargo from the ship's hold and depositing it directly on the raft alongside. The cargo proved to be, as had been expected, a general cargo—that is to say, it consisted of more or less of almost every conceivable product of a civilised country, from lucifer matches up to railway plant and machinery.

It was a very difficult matter to decide what might, and what might not be of value to the party, and the result was that they eventually determined to land the entire cargo. Of course only a very small portion of it would go into the shed which they had erected; but this was a matter of no very great moment, for a great deal of it was of such a nature that rain would not very materially injure it. It took them another month to empty the wreck, and then they set about the task of breaking her up.

To break up a ship is, under ordinary circumstances, no very difficult matter, but as they expected that they would be dependent almost entirely upon the wreck for the timber necessary to the construction of their little ship, they had to go carefully to work; and as it was all manual labour, and they were very weak-handed, they found the task one of no ordinary difficulty. At length, however, after nearly another month's arduous toil, they had cut her down to the water's-edge, and there they were obliged to leave her.

Hitherto they had not allowed themselves time to very closely investigate the nature of the cargo which they had so laboriously conveyed to the shore, their chief anxiety being to secure from the wreck every scrap likely to be of the slightest use to them, before the change of, the season and the break-up of the weather should render this impossible. Now, however, they had leisure to give their booty a thorough overhaul; and this was the next task to which they devoted themselves. As, however, they were now no longer pressed for time, and one man could easily do most of what was required to be done in that way, it was arranged that Doctor Henderson should examine the cargo as far as he could, and prepare a detailed list of the various goods and articles of which it was composed; whilst Gaunt and Nicholls should proceed in the raft on a trip of exploration round the bay, for the purpose of discovering an outlet in the reef which the former believed to exist, and, if such an outlet could be found, to proceed through it and make a short trial trip to sea for the purpose of testing the sailing qualities of the raft.

On the morning following the completion of their work of dismemberment, therefore, these two tasks were taken in hand. Such cases and packages as it was thought the doctor would have a difficulty in breaking open unaided were attacked by the three men, and their contents laid bare; and then Gaunt and Nicholls got on board the raft—which was berthed at a short distance from the beach and made thoroughly secure by being moored with the ship's smallest kedge—and, hoisting her huge lateen sail, cast off from the mooring-buoy, and proceeded to execute a few trial evolutions preparatory to the exploration of the reef. The mode of working the raft under sail was, as has already been intimated, the same in principle with that in vogue among the Ladrone Islanders; that is to say, the vessel was sailed indifferently, with either end foremost, the sail being always kept on the same side of the mast. In order to accomplish this two broad-bladed steering-oars were necessary—one for each end of the craft—and a long tripping-line, with its ends bent on to either end of the yard, hanging down in a bight on deck, so that by its means the end of the yard which was to form the tack might be hauled down on deck. It will be understood that when plying to windward a craft so rigged is never thrown in stays, but when it is necessary to go on the opposite tack her stern is thrown up to windward by means of the steering-oar, which is then laid in; the end of the yard which is down on deck and made fast is released, and the opposite end of the yard is hauled down and secured; the sheet is transferred from one end of the vessel to the other; the steering-oar at that end is laid out; and the vessel, gathering way, moves off in the required direction. It is probably the most simple mode of working a craft known to navigating mankind, and it obviates all possibility of missing stays; a difficulty which mainly induced Gaunt to adopt it on board his raft. This was the first occasion upon which it had had a fair trial, and it was found to answer admirably; the raft proving to be not only so stiff as to be absolutely uncapsizable, but also remarkably fast considering her shape, a speed of six knots being got out of her unloaded and with a good fresh breeze blowing.

As soon as the somewhat novel mode of working her had been satisfactorily tested, the exploration of the reef was begun in earnest. They cruised along its inner edge to the southward in the first instance, and discovered several places where it would probably have been possible for them to pass out to sea; but in every case the channels, if indeed they were worthy of the name, were so narrow and tortuous that Gaunt had no fancy for attempting them unless as a last resource. They next tried the northern side of the bay; and here they were more successful, for just where the reef seemed to join the land there was a channel of about one hundred feet in width, nearly straight, and trending in a north-westerly direction, with so much water in it that the sea only broke in one or two places throughout its entire length. This channel was all that they could desire; for as the prevailing wind seemed to be about south-west, they were enabled to pass in and out of the bay with the sheet slightly eased off.

Standing through this channel, which was only about a quarter of a mile long, they soon found themselves in the open sea, with a considerable amount of swell, over which the raft rode with a buoyancy which was most satisfactory to her designer. If Gaunt had any doubt whatever about the strength of any portion of his novel construction it was in the transverse bracing which connected the bottoms of his two pontoons, and he was therefore rather anxious for the first ten minutes or quarter of an hour after he found himself fairly in the open sea. But the bracing was found amply sufficient to give the required rigidity, and this fact once demonstrated he kept away before the wind, and coasted along the northern shore of his island, keeping at a sufficient distance from the tremendously lofty cliffs to prevent his being becalmed. With the wind over her quarter the raft travelled remarkably fast, and within an hour of the time when she passed out through the channel she was abreast of the entrance to the river—which, by the way, was so effectually masked that Gaunt actually ran past it, and arrived off a point which they had seen from their original landing-place before he became aware of the fact. Retracing his way, the engineer, after a careful search, found the opening and passed into the river. Their course for the first two miles was dead to windward; but the raft sailed remarkably near the wind, and held her own even better than her designer had believed to be possible—the long, flat sides of the two pontoons seeming to act the parts of leeboards, and so preventing her from making any perceptible leeway. They reached the lake, sailed round the islet, landed there, and procured a liberal supply of fruits of various descriptions, which seemed to grow more luxuriantly and of a finer flavour there than on the mainland, and then embarking once more made the best of their way back to the bay, where they anchored the raft and proceeded on shore in a small boat, which had been built as a sort of tender to the larger craft.

They found Henderson still busy with his examination of the cargo, and Gaunt in particular was highly delighted with its multifarious character. There were many articles which he foresaw would be of the utmost use to them in the construction of their little ship, but perhaps the find which delighted him most was a large circular saw. When his eye fell upon this his vivid imagination at once pictured it as in operation in a mill erected upon a spot which he had already recognised as most suitable for the purpose; and he saw, too, that now they need no longer be dependent upon the old ship-timber, full of bolt and trenail holes, for the timber and planking of their craft, as they would be enabled with the assistance of the saw to provide themselves with all the planking, and, indeed, timber of every description which would be necessary in their work, from the magnificent teak and other trees which grew in such abundance on the island.

Chapter Fifteen
Captain Blyth and young Manners reappear

Having now secured from the wreck every scrap which it was possible to obtain, the little party had more leisure than they had had since the moment of their landing; for there was now no longer any fear that if a gale sprang up they would sustain any material loss. True, the greatest part of their work still remained to be done; but there was no longer the same necessity for hurry that there had been whilst any portion of the cargo remained at the mercy of wind and wave, and they therefore resolved that in future they would take matters a little more easily. The next portion of their task consisted in the conveyance of everything landed from the wreck round to the islet; which the ladies had suggested should be called "Fay Island," its exquisite and fairy-like beauty seeming to them to render such a name appropriate. The men of the party were by this time beginning to feel that of late they had somewhat overworked themselves; they needed rest, and they determined to indulge in a couple of days' holiday before engaging in the task of transhipment. Up to this time the ladies had found themselves unable to render any very material assistance; yet they had not been altogether idle, for under Doctor Henderson's directions, and with his assistance, they had succeeded in luring into large wicker-work baskets, which the doctor had very ingeniously framed, the whole of the fowls; the capture consisting of three cocks, fourteen or fifteen hens, and a couple of broods of chickens. So that, with a little careful management they now believed they need never be at a loss for eggs, or even an occasional dinner of roast fowl.

During the two days of holiday which the men permitted themselves Henderson employed himself in wandering about the island, gun in hand, in search of botanical and natural history specimens; and he not only secured several rare birds, the skins of which he managed to cure, but also some very valuable medicinal plants. Gaunt and Nicholls, on the other hand, chose to devote their time to a further and more complete examination of the island, the result being that they discovered a very much more suitable site for the shipbuilding-yard than the one already fixed upon; a site which, though somewhat further away from the spot where they had intended to build their house, was much more secure and less liable to discovery by an enemy, should such unhappily make his appearance.

Nothing worthy of mention occurred during these two days, and on the morning of the third work was once more resumed with a will. The task of reloading the raft proved, as had been anticipated, a somewhat laborious one, and, indeed, their first idea had been that instead of discharging on the beach it would be better to convey the goods direct from the wreck round to the islet; but the loss of time which this would involve seemed to them so serious that, rather than incur it and the loss which might possibly result therefrom, they had decided to put up with the inconvenience and the extra labour of an additional handling of all their goods. The real value of the raft and the wisdom which had suggested her construction now became fully apparent, for she made two and sometimes three trips a day between the west bay and Fay Island with loads averaging about ten tons on each trip.

The day at length arrived when this part of their task drew so near its completion that they expected to finish the transfer before evening; and on this particular day they experienced a most agreeable surprise. For, as the raft, with Gaunt and Nicholls on board, was running down with its last load, Nicholls caught sight of what he took to be a tiny sail in the offing to the northward, to which he drew Gaunt's attention. The latter, who usually carried his telescope with him, at once brought the instrument to bear upon the object, and found that Nicholls was right; it was indeed a sail. The craft, a very small one, was some four miles to leeward when first descried, and notwithstanding the loss of time which such a step would involve the engineer promptly bore up to examine it. As the two craft closed with each other it was seen that the small sail was heading in for the island, and a few minutes later she was made out to be an out-rigger canoe with two persons on board. Her construction was of so primitive a character that Gaunt naturally expected to find that the persons on board her were natives who had possibly been blown off the land, and, failing to make their own island again, had perhaps been wandering aimlessly about the ocean for many days. What was his surprise, then, when he observed one of the individuals rise in the canoe and lift something to his shoulder, the movement being followed by a flash, a little puff of smoke, and the faint report of a gun. Keeping his glass fixed upon the canoe, Gaunt next observed that the individual who had fired the gun was gesticulating violently, the gesticulations being such as to convey the idea of rejoicing rather than an effort to attract attention. A few minutes later the raft was so close to the canoe that the engineer, almost doubting the evidence of his senses, was able to identify the two persons in the canoe as none other than Captain Blyth and young Manners. At the proper moment the raft was rounded-to, the canoe shot alongside, and Captain Blyth, closely followed by young Manners with the canoe's painter in his hand, sprang upon the deck of the raft and gave Gaunt a hearty hand-grasp.

AN UNEXPECTED AND HAPPY REUNION

"My *dear* fellow!" he exclaimed, "how *are* you? And you, too, Nicholls, my lad—I did not expect to see *you* here! How are you, my good fellow? Well, Mr Gaunt," he continued, "this is the happiest day I have known since the mutiny. I am heartily glad to meet you once more, sir, and to see you looking so well. And how"—with a slight shade of hesitation—"how are the rest of your party?"

"All perfectly well, thank you; and as happy as can reasonably be expected under the circumstances," answered Gaunt. "But where on earth have you come from?" he continued; "and how did you manage to effect your escape from the *Flying Cloud*?"

"We have come from a bit of an island away yonder, one hundred miles or so to the eastward of the spot where we *now* are. And we did not *escape* from the *Flying Cloud* at all, sir—John Blyth is not the sort of man to voluntarily desert his ship as long as she will hang together or float with him—no; we were simply shoved ashore by those scoundrels of mutineers, and left to shift for ourselves as best we might. And a precious poor shift it would have been, I can tell you, but for Ned, who—fine fellow that he is—managed somehow to scrape together for us not only a fair supply of food, but also arms, a few tools, and nails enough to knock that bit of a canoe together. He gave us the exact position of your island, and told us that *we* might possibly get a sight of the top of yonder mountain on a clear day—which, as a matter of fact we did, once or twice—so that I knew exactly how to steer in order to make a good land-fall. And so you are all in good health, eh? Well, I am delighted to hear that. And where are the rest of your party? It will be a pleasant sight for my old eyes when they rest upon the ladies and those dear children once more—bless their sweet innocent little hearts!"

"You shall see them in good time—in the course of two or three hours—as soon as we have landed our cargo and can work back to the western end of the island, where our camp is at present located," answered Gaunt, with a smile. "But, tell me," he continued, "before our conversation drifts away from the subject, where and how is Miss Stanhope?"

"She is—or was, when I saw her last—on board the *Flying Cloud*," answered the skipper. "You must understand that I was landed from the ship on the day following that on which they put you ashore here; so I know nothing whatever about what may have happened to her since then. But they let me wish her good-bye before I was landed, and I had a few minutes' conversation with her; and, from what passed then and in a chat I previously had with Ned, I am in hope that she is as safe as a girl can be in the hands of such a set of ruffians. It seems that they are keeping Ned to navigate the ship for them; and they are keeping Miss Stanhope as a hostage for his good faith, and to insure his dealing honestly with them. And from what I know of Williams I am not altogether without hopes that so long as Ned faithfully obeys their orders the young lady will be perfectly safe. But, at best, her situation is a very terrible one, and I would give my right hand this moment to see her safe once more among us. And now, tell me, what have you been doing all the time, and what is the meaning of this raft and her cargo?"

Gaunt, in reply, gave a pretty fully detailed account of all that they had done, and of their future plans; winding up by expressing the exceeding satisfaction he felt that the little party would now be benefited by the aid and advice of two such valuable auxiliaries as the skipper and young Manners.

Captain Blyth listened most attentively to everything the engineer told him—the raft meanwhile being worked to windward toward the harbour's mouth—and when he had heard everything he remarked:

"Well, so far you have done admirably; I do not believe matters could have been managed better had I been here myself. And as to this raft of yours—if raft you call her—she is simply a wonder; why she turns to windward like a racing cutter. I am sure *I* should never have dreamed of scheming out anything half so handy. You engineers are very clever people, there is no denying that, and can even give an old salt like myself a wrinkle now and then, as I have learned before to-day. But now, to say a word or two about the future. You tell me that this is your last cargo; and that on your next trip you propose to transfer all hands to this bit of an islet that lies away inland there somewhere. Now, let me ask you, have you had any craft of any description prowling about in the neighbourhood lately?"

"We have not sighted a sail of any description since we saw the *Flying Cloud's* canvas sink below yonder horizon," answered Gaunt, pointing to the eastward.

"So much the better," said the skipper; "and I am right glad to hear it. These waters, as you may perhaps know, are not often traversed by the craft of civilised nations; indeed, so far as I can make out, we are quite out of all the regular ship-tracks. But Manners and I have been alarmed on two or three occasions on our own island yonder by the appearance of proas—a class of craft which, I may tell you, are usually manned by Malays, or semi-savages of a somewhat similar race and character; and if any such should come prying about here they will certainly beat up our quarters and give us no end of trouble. Indeed, to speak the whole truth, my dear fellow, I would as soon be in the hands of a crew of mutineers as in theirs. So, if you will listen to my advice, our first job should be the building of a house large enough to accommodate all hands; and, if possible, it should be so fortified as to enable us to hold out with some chance of success against such an attack as those fellows would be likely to make in the event of their looking in here."

This was news indeed, the gravity and importance of which is would be difficult to over-estimate. Gaunt already knew something of the Malays by reputation; and he was aware that Captain Blyth was speaking no more than the truth when he asserted that the party would be certainly no worse off in the hands of the mutineers than they would be in those of a horde of Malay pirates, whose calling only fosters their natural propensity for rapine and bloodshed. He had heard one or two perfectly hideous stories of atrocities committed by those wretches when unfortunate ships' crews had fallen into their hands. And he shuddered, and his blood ran cold as his vivid imagination pictured the women and children of the party in the hands and at the mercy of such a band. In this, as in every other case of difficulty or danger, the safety and welfare of the women and children would naturally be the first consideration; and Gaunt's first mental question was how would they be affected by these tidings. It was true, he reflected, that the proas might *not* visit the island; but, as it was evident that they were cruising in the neighbourhood, it would be the height of folly to rely only upon chance in such a matter. And he forthwith began to turn over in his mind what would be the best steps to take in the emergency. It would be possible for the weaker members of the party to find concealment somewhere among the spurs of the mountain; but any such arrangement as this, whilst highly inconvenient, would be open to many other disadvantages. And he could not help thinking of what their fate would be, supposing that whilst lying thus concealed the men of the party should be attacked and made captive or slain. Were such a catastrophe as this to befall them, the fate of those poor women and children would be little better than a living death; left as they would be to shift for themselves unaided, unprotected, and their hearts wrung with anguish for the loss of those to whom they were naturally in the habit of looking for help and protection, and with little or no chance of ultimate escape from their island prison. And, to add to the difficulties of the situation, the little party were so weak-handed that to construct such a fortified habitation as Blyth had suggested would be, if not an absolute impossibility, a work of such time and labour that for all practical purposes it might as well be unattempted. This was no case of ordinary difficulty; it was not a difficulty which could be overcome by the skilful and judicious application of a practically unlimited supply of manual labour. And almost for the first time in his life the engineer found himself confronted with a question which he was unable to satisfactorily answer.

Whilst Gaunt was still revolving this difficult matter in his mind the raft arrived at her usual berth at Fay Island, and her cargo was as rapidly as possible discharged; after which she sailed at once for the western settlement. Here the unexpected appearance of Captain Blyth and Bob Manners was greeted with every manifestation of surprise and delight; and the former had, as a matter of course, to recount to his interested friends the whole story of his sojourn upon, and escape from the island upon which the pair had been landed. The ladies were naturally most anxious to learn the latest news concerning Miss Stanhope; and the wary skipper, whilst telling them what little he knew about her, did his best to allay their fears with regard to that young lady, carefully concealing his own somewhat gloomy anticipations as to her future. And so successfully did he manage this business that Mrs Henderson's heart was considerably lightened of the load which had for so long a time been secretly pressing upon it.

As soon as it could be done without exciting suspicion in the minds of the ladies, Gaunt contrived upon one pretext or another to draw away all the male members of the party, to whom forthwith he disclosed the alarming intelligence which Captain Blyth had brought to the island with him; pointing out to them the new danger which thus threatened the very existence of them all, and earnestly begging them to give the matter their most serious consideration. Suggestions were, of course, at once offered in plenty, but they all possessed one very serious drawback; they lacked practicability. The least unpromising of them all was that of Captain Blyth, who boldly advocated the abandonment of the scheme for building a vessel; and proposed that, instead of incurring the delay and risk involved in the carrying out of such a plan, the raft should first be strengthened as much as possible, and that he, Manners, and Nicholls should then sail in her to Singapore, from whence it would be easy to dispatch a rescue vessel to the island to take off the rest of the party.

But when this proposal came to be canvassed more in detail, it was found that there were several very grave objections to it, the most grave of them all lying in the fact that, according to their calculations, the stormy season must now be close at hand; and, strengthen the raft as much as they would, or could, Gaunt believed that if she happened to be caught in a hurricane, nothing could prevent her going to pieces. Moreover, Singapore was well to windward of the island they were then upon, and, though the raft did very fairly upon a taut bowline in fine weather and in a moderate sea-way, Gaunt expressed very grave doubts as to how she would behave in a strong breeze and a heavy sea. Then, again, the absence of the skipper, Manners, and Nicholls would reduce the defensive strength of those left behind to two men only, and that, too, without any artificial protection, save such as their united strength might enable them to throw up. On the whole, after canvassing the question thoroughly, it was decided that the skipper's plan was very much too risky for adoption under the then existing circumstances of the party, and they eventually came to the conclusion that no better course seemed open to them than to carry out Gaunt's original plan—namely, the construction of a house which should be strong enough to serve also as a fort in case of need.

The next point to be decided was, of what material should the house be constructed? Of timber of a suitable character there was a superabundance upon the island; nay, even on the islet itself there was more than sufficient for their purpose. But it would have to be cut, sawn to the required dimensions, and hauled to the site of the building before it could be made use of; and all this involved a very great deal of labour, to say nothing of the fact that, when finished, the structure could easily be destroyed by fire. Gaunt was strongly of opinion that stone was the most suitable material for the purpose; but, unfortunately, he was by no means certain that a quarry could be found in a convenient position, and at a convenient distance for transportation. If it could, he believed that shells in sufficient quantities for the manufacture of lime could easily be collected on the beach; and he had no doubt as to his ability to construct a kiln in which to burn them. As the engineer warmed with his subject he made the superiority of stone over wood so evident that it was finally decided he and Henderson should devote the next day to a search for a suitable quarry; whilst the skipper, with Manners and Nicholls for his assistants, was to essay the task of knocking up a temporary but somewhat more efficient shelter for the party than the tents would afford, pending the completion of the house or "fort," as they seemed inclined to style the proposed structure.

In accordance with this arrangement, immediately after breakfast next morning the tents were struck and placed on board the raft, and the ladies and children also embarked in her to proceed round to Fay Island in charge of Captain Blyth and his two assistants; whilst Gaunt and Henderson, armed with their repeating rifles and an axe each in their belts, set out in company for the gap in the cliffs, their intention being to proceed overland, and to separate at the head of the river, each taking one of its banks with the object of ascertaining whether any suitable quarry-site could be found in a situation convenient for the shipment of stone on board the raft.

The quest occupied the two friends for the greater part of the day, they arriving abreast the islet within half an hour of each other, and reaching its friendly shores just in time to assist the working party there in putting the finishing touches to quite a respectable structure—half tent, half bower—for which the skipper had acted the part of architect-in-chief. This structure had cost Captain Blyth a vast amount of almost painful cogitation, and was the result of a little fit of excusable, and perhaps natural pique, which had come over him on finding how exceedingly well the two landsmen had managed without him. From the moment of their being thrust out of the ship to that other moment when he had rejoined them, they had scarcely been out of his thoughts for an hour, and his commiseration for them—abandoned, helpless, and deprived of the priceless advantage of his counsel and experience—was dinned into the ears of young Manners to such a wearisome extent that that officer, dutiful as he was, sometimes felt inclined to wish he had been carried away like Ned by the mutineers, instead of being accorded the privilege of the skipper's society. And now, behold! all the anxiety and commiseration which had been felt for them turned out to have been wasted, thrown away. The two quiet undemonstrative men, whom the honest skipper, when ruefully meditating upon their forlorn condition, had often likened to babes in arms, had proved themselves to be fully equal to the situation in which they had so unexpectedly found themselves, and had indeed managed so exceedingly well that Captain Blyth found himself at a discount; and, whilst heartily welcomed by them, was fully conscious that, save in the matter of purely physical help and companionship, his presence was in no wise an acquisition to them. Hence the little fit of pique, the outcome of which had been a resolve to show these two resourceful men that he, plain, unpretending seamen though he was, knew a thing or two besides how to handle or navigate a ship, and that, even when it came to such a matter as the knocking up of an impromptu house, he was not disposed to give way to anybody. The house, or shelter rather, for it was too rough-and-ready an affair to be worthy of the former appellation, was really a very creditable production—roomy and weather-tight, though it was doubtful whether it would prove capable of withstanding the buffeting of a hurricane—and Captain Blyth was very justly proud of it; and when Gaunt and Henderson (both of whom read the worthy man like a book in large print) seemed to vie with each other as to who should speak of it in the most complimentary and appreciative terms, the fit of pique vanished like snow beneath a summer sun. The wound to the skipper's *amour propre* was completely healed, and he was once more happy.

On comparing notes it was found that both the explorers had been successful in their search, both had found stone of a more or less suitable quality, some of it, indeed, being excellent; but the honours of the day fell to the doctor's lot, he having discovered not only a quarry-site in a most convenient situation, with stone of a quality far superior to anything that Gaunt had met with, but also an outcrop of coal! This discovery was of infinitely greater value to the party, situated as they then were, than would have been the finding of a gold mine, and Gaunt in particular—who perhaps realised more fully than any of the others the exceeding importance of the discovery—was greatly elated thereat.

Fully alive to the importance of developing these new resources without delay, the five men started in the raft at daybreak next morning, well provided with picks, shovels, crowbars, sledges, and such other implements as it was thought might be useful, together with a keg of powder from the magazine of the *Mermaid*, and made their way up stream, Henderson acting as pilot. The quarry was first reached, being situated only about half a mile above Fay Island, and a single glance sufficed to satisfy Gaunt that here was stone not only of splendid quality, but amply sufficient in quantity for every possible want of the party. The quarry-face consisted of an almost perpendicular cliff of grey limestone springing out of the soil at a distance of only some fifty feet from the margin of the stream; it was about thirty-five feet in height, and fully one hundred and fifty feet long, and of course of unknown depth, though a very hasty examination of the top showed that it extended fully fifty feet back from the face. Captain Blyth and Nicholls landed here, provided with the powder and such tools as they needed, and instructed by the engineer—who promised to rejoin them, as soon as he had inspected the coal outcrop—began at once to lay bare the stone at the top of the cliff. The rest of the party then proceeded in the raft to the "mine," as they already began to term it, which they found about a quarter of a mile further on. The outcrop proved, as Henderson had asserted, to be a genuine coal, and of very fair quality, too, with a prospect of its improving as it was worked down into; and, most important and fortunate for the discoverers, it, like the stone, was situate close to the river bank, near enough in fact to permit of its being loaded direct on the deck of the raft by means of a long wooden shoot. The doctor and young Manners willingly undertook to "get" such coal as might be required—not a very large quantity in all probability—and, stripping to the waist, at once set to work, whilst Gaunt, who by this time had learned to manage the raft single-handed, made his way back in that singular-looking craft to the quarry.

On rejoining the skipper and Nicholls, the engineer found that the two men had worked to such excellent purpose that they had already laid bare an area of some forty feet of stone, and disclosed a small fissure which Gaunt thought would serve admirably to receive a blasting charge, which he at once proceeded to prepare. This operation was soon accomplished, the fuse—a chemical preparation "made up" by Henderson the night before—was lighted, and the trio hastily retreated to a place of safety. A minute later a faint *boom* was heard, followed by a tremendous crash and the rattle of falling fragments; and, hurrying back to the spot, the workers found that, by a lucky accident, the charge had been so placed as to dislodge and hurl down on to the bank beneath upwards of twenty tons of stone. After this there was no further difficulty, for the layers happened to so run that a very little labour with the bars sufficed to send the stone down on to the bank ready for loading; and when any especial difficulty was experienced, a small quantity of powder always proved sufficient to overcome it. Such capital progress, indeed, did they make, that in less than a month they had not only quarried, but had actually transferred to the islet as much stone as it was thought they would require. By that time a very fair quantity of coal was also ready for removal; and when this important task was accomplished, a kiln was built, and Gaunt himself undertook the manufacture of lime, whilst Henderson and the skipper proceeded to erect a shed for the storage of the same, Nicholls meanwhile essaying the task of putting up a smithy on the site of the future ship-yard, whilst Manners busied himself in getting out the ground for the foundations of the fort.

But before they were ready to begin their building operations in earnest, the long-expected change of weather—or rather the change of the seasons—had come upon them, and their work was somewhat retarded by the setting in of heavy rains, accompanied by terrific thunderstorms and occasional heavy gales of wind. The course of the wind, too, had changed; for whereas its prevalent direction hitherto, ever since their landing upon the island, had been south-west, it now blew almost unintermittently from the north-east.

Chapter Sixteen
The skipper goes in chase of a strange sail

The violent atmospheric disturbances which accompanied the change of the seasons lasted about a month, after which the weather became tolerably settled once more, though rain now fell, more or less heavily, every day. To work out of doors in the midst of pelting rain was by no means pleasant, although there was no perceptible variation in the usual temperature of the climate. Still there existed in the breasts of all so strong a feeling of insecurity so long as the "fort" remained unbuilt, that they determined rather to suffer the unpleasantness of being daily drenched to the skin than to protract the uneasy feeling of defencelessness which haunted them.

The building, then, was pushed forward with all possible expedition, and, thanks to the indefatigable energy with which they laboured, was so far finished as to be habitable within a couple of months of its commencement, though of course a great deal still remained to be done before it could be regarded as absolutely secure.

The site for this house or fort—for when finished it really was strong enough to merit the latter appellation—was finally fixed so as to include within its limits a spring of pure fresh-water—an adjunct of the utmost importance if it should ever fall to the lot of the occupants to be placed in a state of siege, and it possessed the further advantage of completely commanding both the land and water approaches to the proposed shipyard. It was built in the form of a hollow square, enclosing a small courtyard (which the ladies determined to convert into a garden at the earliest opportunity) with the spring in its centre. One side of the house was set apart for the purpose of a general living-room; the two contiguous sides were divided unequally—the larger divisions forming respectively the doctor's and the engineer's sleeping-rooms, whilst the smaller divisions served as kitchen and larder; and the fourth side afforded ample sleeping accommodation for the remainder of the party, with a store-room in one angle of the building, and the magazine and armoury in the other. The windows all looked outward, but were small, and strongly defended with stout iron bars built into the masonry, and with massive wood shutters inside, loop-holed for rifle firing. The doors giving access to the rooms all opened upon the court-yard, and were as high and wide as they could be made, so as to let in plenty of light and air. For still further security there was no doorway whatever in the exterior face of the building, egress and ingress being possible only by means of a staircase in the court-yard leading up on to the flat roof, and thence down on the outside by means of a light bamboo ladder which could be hauled up on the roof in case of need. The roof, or roofs rather, had only a very gentle slope or fall inward, just sufficient to allow of the rain flowing off, and afforded a fighting platform at a height of about fourteen feet from the ground, the defenders being sheltered by the exterior walls, which were carried up some five feet higher and were also loop-holed. It seemed at first sight a great waste of labour to build so strong a place as this for what they hoped would be a comparatively brief sojourn; but, as Gaunt pointed out to them, there was no knowing precisely how long their stay on the island might be protracted, and if they were going to construct a defence at all, it was as well, whilst they were about it, to construct something which should effectually serve its purpose. And after all, when the work came to be undertaken, it was found that it took but little if any longer time than would have been required to put up a wood house, and to surround it with an effective palisade.

Another month saw the fort so far completed that Gaunt thought he might now safely take in hand the saw-mill upon which he had set his mind; and he and the skipper accordingly devoted themselves henceforward to that undertaking, finishing it within a few days of the date when Henderson reported that all was done at the fort which at that time was deemed necessary. The doctor and his party now took to the woods armed with their axes, and began the important task of selecting and felling the timber for the proposed boat, the design for which Gaunt had been diligently working upon whenever he could find a spare hour or two to devote to the purpose. As ultimately worked out this design was for a cutter, to be of twelve feet beam, forty feet long on the load-water line, and of such a depth as would not only afford comfortable head-room in the cabins, but also give the craft a good hold of the water and make her very weatherly. These dimensions, it was considered, were sufficient for perfect sea-worthiness, whilst the various timbers would be of a scantling light enough to permit of their being handled and placed in position with comparative ease with the limited power at their command. The greatest care was exercised in the selection of the timber, it being necessary to choose not only that which was thoroughly sound, but also such as could without very much labour be conveyed to the saw-mill. This latter necessity, or rather the actual labour of conveying the timber to the mill, caused their progress to be somewhat less rapid than they had anticipated, especially as Nicholls was now busily engaged at the smithy preparing the bolts, fastenings, and other iron work for the little craft; but, notwithstanding all, the work advanced with fairly satisfactory rapidity. It had been decided that the whole of the timber should be cut, sawn, and stacked in the ship-yard before even the keel-blocks were laid down, so that it might become at least partially seasoned before being worked into the hull, and this was accomplished in rather less than a couple of months.

At length the day arrived when, everything being ready, the keel of the vessel was to be laid down—a task which, the keel-piece being cut out of one log, it took the little band an entire day to accomplish satisfactorily. And it was on the evening of this particular day, or rather during the ensuing night, that the little colony sustained a loss which plunged its members into grief so deep that its shadow never entirely left them until long after the termination of their sojourn upon the island.

It happened thus. During the numerous passages of the raft to and fro between the west bay and Fay Island a small reef had been discovered some six miles north of the island, upon which reef, it had been further discovered, a certain fish of peculiarly delicate and agreeable flavour was to be caught between the hours of sunset and sunrise. So very delicious had this particular species of fish been found, that it had become quite a custom for one or more of the men to take the raft after the day's work was over and go off to the reef for an hour or two's fishing, thus combining business and pleasure in a most agreeable manner. Captain Blyth especially always partook of the fish with quite exceptional relish; and, it happening at this time that all hands had been too busily occupied for any of them to go out for several days past, the skipper thought he would celebrate so momentous an occasion as the laying of the keel by a few hours' fishing upon the reef. Accordingly, as the evening meal was approaching completion, he announced his intention, at the same time inquiring if any of the others felt disposed to join him. All, however, confessed themselves to be too tired to find pleasure in anything short of a good night's rest; and the skipper therefore departed alone, Henderson calling out after him as he went:

"Don't go to sleep and fall overboard, captain; and keep a sharp eye upon the weather. To my mind the wind seems inclined to drop, and if it does it will probably shift. And I suppose you have noticed that heavy cloud-bank working up there to the westward?"

"Ay, ay, I've noticed it," answered the skipper good-humouredly, but slightly derisive at what he considered the presumption of a landsman in thinking it necessary to caution *him* about the weather. "Another thunderstorm, I take it—they always work up against the wind; but I shall be back again and safe in my bunk before it breaks. Good-night!"

So saying, Blyth, pipe in mouth, strolled down to the tiny cove in which the punt was moored, cast off the painter, and paddled out to the raft, which rode to a buoy anchored about fifty yards distant from the beach. Arrived alongside the raft he made fast the punt's painter to the buoy, loosed the raft's huge triangular sail, mast-headed the yard by means of a small winch which Nicholls had fitted for the purpose, cast off his moorings, and began to work down the stream seaward, the wind being against him. He was not long in reaching the open water, and as he shot out between the two headlands which guarded the mouth of the harbour he noticed with satisfaction that the cloud-bank to which Henderson had warningly directed his attention had already completely risen above the horizon, and was slowly melting away under the moon's influence. True, the atmosphere was somewhat hazy, and the breeze was less steady than usual; but the general aspect of the sky was promising enough, and if a change of weather was impending it would not, the skipper told himself, occur for several hours yet, or without giving him a sufficient warning to enable him to regain the island in good time.

Arrived on the reef—over which, by the way, there was plenty of water, four fathoms being the least the party had ever found upon it—the expectant sportsman dropped his grapnel, lowered the sail, and threw his lines overboard. The sport, however, was not by any means good that night, for it was fully half an hour before he got a bite; and the interval which followed his first capture was so long that the skipper's interest waned and his thoughts wandered off—as indeed they very often did—to his ship; and he fell to wondering what had become of her, whether the mutineers had actually gone the extreme length of carrying into effect their piratical plans, whether Sibylla and Ned were still on board, and, if so, how matters fared with them. He was full of commiseration for the two young people, both having taken a strong hold upon his warm and kindly heart, and he scarcely knew which to pity most—whether Sibylla, cruelly and perhaps permanently cut off from all intercourse with her own sex and constantly in association with a band of lawless men; or Ned, likewise a prisoner, with all his life's prospects blighted, and in addition to this the never-ceasing care, anxiety, and watchfulness which he must endure on Sibylla's account. Most people would have been disposed to say at once and unhesitatingly that the girl's lot was infinitely the worse of the two. But the skipper did not; he understood pretty well, or thought he did, the position of affairs on board the *Flying Cloud*; and he knew to an absolute certainty that so long as Ned had life and strength to protect her Sibylla was reasonably secure. But Ned, he repeated to himself, would always have her safety and well-being upon his mind in addition to his other cares and anxieties. It was a miserable plight for both of them, he mused, and he didn't see how they were to get out of it—unless, indeed, they could manage to steal away in a boat and give the ship the slip some fine dark night. And what would become of them then? he asked himself. What chance of ultimate escape would they have? He knew Ned well enough to feel assured he would never attempt so extreme a step without first making the fullest possible provision for the safety of his companion and himself; but when all was done, what prospect would they have of being picked up in those lonely seas? He pictured them to himself drifting helplessly hither and thither, exposed to the scorching rays of the sun all day and the pelting rain at night; their provisions consumed, their water-breaker empty, and hope slowly giving way to despair as day and night succeeded each other, with no friendly sail to cheer their failing sight and drive away the horrible visions which haunt those who are perishing of hunger and thirst. He saw Ned's stalwart form grow gaunt and lean, and Sibylla's rounded outlines sharpen and waste away under the fierce fires of hunger; and his soul sickened within him as their moans of anguish smote upon his ear. And at last he heard Sibylla, in her agony and despair, entreat Ned to take away the life which had become a burden to her. And he saw and heard too how Ned, his speech thick and inarticulate with torturing thirst, first tried unavailingly to soothe and comfort and encourage the suffering girl; and how at last, in sheer pity for her and mad desperation at their helpless state, the lad drew forth his knife and stealthily tested the keenness of its edge and point. And as he watched, with feverish interest yet unspeakable anxiety and horror, he saw that the long-protracted suffering of himself and his companion had at last proved too much for the poor lad and that his brain was giving way; for look! the baleful light of madness gleams in his bloodshot eyes! Madness gives new strength to his nerveless limbs as he rises and bends over his companion. As he slowly uplifts his arm its shrunken muscles swell beneath the skin as though they would burst it, his talon-like fingers close with a grip of steel round the haft of the upraised knife, Sibylla closes her eyes in patient expectancy of the stroke, the blade quivers and flashes in the sunlight, and Captain Blyth, with a cry of horror, starts forward—to awake at the sound of his own voice and to find himself at the edge of the raft, in the very act of leaping into the jaws of a shark which is eyeing him hungrily from the water alongside! He luckily checks his spring in time. To seize the boat-hook and strike savagely at the waiting shark with its point follows as a matter of course; and then the skipper piously returns thanks to God not only for his escape, but also that the events he has just been witnessing are nothing more substantial than an ugly dream.

Blyth's next act is to haul in the lines which have dropped from his nerveless hands during sleep, and which would unquestionably have been lost had he not taken the precaution to make them fast; and he finds to his chagrin that not only the bait but also the hooks have been carried off. He therefore neatly coils up his fishing-tackle preparatory to shaping a course for home; for the moon is on the very verge of the western horizon, and he knows therefore that it is past midnight. Moreover, though the breeze is rather fresher than it was and the horizon is clear, there is a murkiness in the atmosphere overhead which portends a change of weather; and as he looks knowingly about him he gives audible expression to his opinion that there will be but little work done in the ship-yard on the morrow.

The grapnel is lifted, and the skipper, attaching the handle to the winch, begins to mast-head the yard of the solitary sail which propels the raft. As he does so his eyes are directed towards the moon, now slowly sinking beneath the horizon. Ha! what is that? The labour at the winch is suspended, a hasty turn is taken with the halliard, and Captain Blyth strains forward, his eyes shaded by both hands the better to observe that black spot which is slowly gliding athwart the moon's pale face. Little need is there, though, for him to look so intently to ascertain what that black spot really is; it is more for the purpose of assuring himself that his eyes are not playing him false, or that he is not once more the victim of a dream. No; this is not a dream. He is wide awake enough now, and his mind is busy with a thousand tumultuous thoughts, for, as he watches, clear and unmistakable glide the upper sails of a large ship across the face of the sinking planet. She is steering south, but whether easterly or westerly it is impossible to say as she stands out black and silhouette-like against her golden background; but one thing is plain—she is moving very slowly. The skipper darts to the compass—one of a pair saved from the wreck of the *Mermaid*—and striking a match, which he carefully shelters from the wind in the crown of his cap, he manages to take her bearing before she vanishes from his sight. He next completes the setting of his sail, hauls aft the sheet, and, jamming the raft close upon a wind, asks himself what is the best thing to do.

To return to the island will consume an hour of most precious time; and when there what could he do to attract the stranger's attention? Nothing more than light a huge bonfire; and the only spot suitable for this is the western side of the mountain, to reach which will consume at least another hour. Then there would be wood to collect, occupying say another half-hour, making a total of at least two hours and a half before such a signal could be rendered visible. And perhaps, after all, those on board the ship might not see it, or, seeing it, might not understand its meaning—might suppose it to be nothing more than a fire built by the natives, and so pass on their way. No; that would not do—the risk of failure would be too great. What then? There remained nothing, in Captain Blyth's opinion, but to pursue the stranger. She could not, he thought, be going more than five knots, judging by the strength of the breeze and the momentary glimpse he had obtained of her; whilst the raft, light as she was and with the wind well over her quarter, would go nearly or quite seven. The strange sail was about twelve miles off; therefore, if he could overhaul her at the rate of about two knots per hour, he ought to be near enough to attract her attention by sunrise. But he must bear up in chase at once, there was no time to waste in running ashore to make known his intentions; and as for help, he wanted none, he was quite capable of managing the raft single-handed. Moreover, he began to suspect that Henderson would prove to be right in that suggestion of his respecting a change of weather, which made it all the more important that the strange sail should be overhauled before the change should occur.

These reflections passed through the skipper's brain in a single moment—not perhaps quite so definitely as here set forth, but to the same purpose—and in the next he jammed his helm hard up, eased off the sheet, and bore away upon a course which he conjectured would enable him to intercept the stranger.

For a few minutes after the disappearance of the moon Blyth was able, or fancied he was able, still to distinguish the canvas of the chase looming up vaguely like a dark shapeless shadow upon the horizon; but either the sky grew darker in that quarter or the weather thickened, for he was soon obliged to admit that he could see it no longer. But that circumstance gave him not the least concern; he had set his course by a star, and he knew that so long as he continued to steer for it, so long would the course of the raft converge toward that of the stranger. He *was* concerned, however, to notice later on that not only was the weather thickening overhead, necessitating a frequent changing of the star by which he was following his course, but also that the wind was becoming unsteady; sometimes falling away to such an extent as to cause the raft's sail to flap heavily as she rolled over the ridges of the swell, and anon breezing up quite fresh again, but with a change of perhaps a couple of points in its direction, the change generally being of such a character as to bring the wind forward more on his starboard beam. Gradually the haze so thickened overhead that such stars as were not already obscured grew dim and soon disappeared altogether, leaving the solitary man dependent only upon the somewhat fickle wind for a guide by which to steer his course; for though he had a compass on board the raft, he had no binnacle, and no lamps by which to illuminate the compass card. It is true the island was still in sight, some four miles astern, but the night had grown so dark and the atmosphere so thick that the land merely loomed like a vast undefined blot of darkness against the black horizon, being so indistinct indeed that only the practised eye of a seamen could have detected its presence at all; it was therefore useless as an object to steer by, even to so keen-eyed an old sea-dog as Captain Blyth.

It had by this time began to dawn upon the skipper that his adventure was likely to prove of a far more serious character than he had at all contemplated; and he was earnestly debating within himself the question whether his wisest course would not, after all, be to abandon the chase and make the best of his way back to the island, when the breeze once more freshened up so strongly, and that too dead aft, that it made everything on board the raft surge again as she gathered way and skimmed off before it. And Blyth, calculating that even if the chase were sailing away from instead of toward him it would shorten his distance from her at least a couple of miles before she caught it, grimly held on his course, determined to risk everything rather than lose so good a chance; his chief fear now being that the sheet would part under the tremendous strain brought to bear upon it by the immense sail. The raft, as has been elsewhere stated, was of very peculiar construction, her shape and build being such as to peculiarly favour speed, especially when running dead before the wind; and, light as she now was, she skimmed away before the fierce squall at a rate which made Blyth's heart bound with exultation as he looked first to one side and then the other and noted the furious speed with which the phosphorescent foam from under her bows was left behind. There was now no longer any thought of turning back, for, be it said, Captain Blyth—good honest soul—was a devout believer in Providence; and he had by this time arrived at a firm conviction, first, that it was by the special intervention of Providence that he had been led to undertake his fishing excursion that night, and next, that the freshening up of a dead fair wind just when it did was a second special intervention of Providence to prevent his giving up the chase. And so he held on everything, and the raft rushed away dead before the wind through the pitchy darkness, the mast creaking ominously in its step every now and then, and the tautly-strained gear aloft surging from time to time in an equally ominous manner; whilst the sea rose rapidly—showing that the solitary voyager was fast drawing out from under the sheltering lee of the island astern—and the foaming wavecrests, vividly phosphorescent, momentarily towered higher and more threateningly, and hissed louder and more angrily in the luminous wake of the flying craft.

The squall lasted a full hour, when the wind died away even more suddenly than it had arisen, and the raft was left tumbling about with little more than steerage-way upon her. The skipper had no means of ascertaining the time, it being too intensely dark to permit of his reading the face of his watch even when it was held close to his eyes, though he made two or three unsuccessful attempts to do so; but, anxious and impatient as he was for the dawn, he knew that it must be at least another hour, perhaps nearer two, before he could reasonably expect its appearance. Two hours more of sickening suspense! One hundred and twenty minutes! With the weather in such a threatening state what might not happen in the interval! If he could only have obtained an occasional glimpse of the compass, or if the night had been less opaquely dark he would not have cared so much. For in the one case he would have been enabled not only to keep a mental reckoning of his own course, but also that of the chase as well, and to follow her attentively no matter how capricious the breeze; whilst in the other case he might have stood some chance of catching a momentary glimpse of her. As his reflections took this turn he stooped and looked ahead under the foot of the sail; looked more intently; rubbed his eyes, and looked again. What was it he saw? A light—lights? Yes, surely; it must be so, or were those faint luminous specks merely illusory and a result of the over-straining of his visual organs due to the intensity of his gaze into the gloom? No; those feebly glimmering points of light were stationary; they maintained the same fixed distance from each other, and he could count them—one, two, three—half a dozen of them at least, if not more, he could not be certain, for they were so very faint. What could it mean? Was there a whole fleet of ships down there to leeward? That there was *something* was an absolute certainty; and as it seemed an impossibility that it could be anything else it was only reasonable to conclude that it must be a ship or ships. At all events there could be no question as to the course he ought to follow; it would be worse than folly to continue in pursuit of an invisible ship with those lights in comparatively plain view only a couple of points on his lee-bow. So the skipper bore away until the faint luminous spots opened out just clear of the heel of the long yard—which, it will be remembered, was bowsed down close to the deck—and there he resolutely kept them, the wind having by this time fallen so light that it was necessary for him to make frequent sweeps with the steering-oar in order to keep the raft's head pointed in the required direction.

Suddenly, a greenish spectral radiance beamed down upon him from above; and, quickly casting a startled glance aloft, Blyth shudderingly beheld a ball of lambent greenish light quivering upon the upper extremity of the long tapering yard and swaying to and fro with the roll of the raft, much as the flame of a candle would have done under similar circumstances. Clinging lightly to the end of the yard, it alternately elongated and flattened as the spar swayed to and fro, now and then rolling a few inches down the yard as though about to travel down to the deck, but as often returning to the extremity of the yard again. Presently another and similar luminous ball gleamed into shape at the mast-head, swaying and wavering about the end of the spar like its companion. They were *corposants*, and whilst they conveyed to the skipper the only additional warning needed of the impending elemental strife, they also at once explained the mystery of the lights to leeward for which he was steering. They also were undoubtedly corposants glimmering from the spars of the strange sail of which he was in pursuit, and which, from her present proximity, must have been steering to the eastward, and consequently toward him, instead of to the westward and away from him, as he had feared.

Blyth believed she certainly could not be more than a mile distant, his conviction being that the feeble, sickly lights of the ghostly corposants could not penetrate further than that distance in so thick an atmosphere, and it now became of the utmost importance—nay, it might even be a matter of life or death for him—to reach the stranger before the hurricane should burst upon them. He looked over the side to ascertain the speed of the raft through the water, and his heart quailed as he observed that, save for an occasional tiny phosphorescent spark on the surface or a faintly luminous halo lower down in the black depths slowly drifting by, there was nothing to indicate that she had any motion whatever. Her speed was not more than half a knot per hour; and the stranger was probably a mile distant—two hours away at the raft's then rate of progress! Something must be done, and quickly, too; for out of the darkness round about him there now floated weird, whispering sighs, faint, dismal moanings, and now and then a sudden momentary rush as of invisible wings, telling that the storm-fiend was marshalling his forces and about to make his swoop. What was to be done? There were only two oars on board the raft—the steering-oars—and they were so firmly secured that it would be next to impossible to cast them adrift and use them as means of propulsion, even if one man's strength were sufficient to handle them both simultaneously. Moreover, if a little puff of wind should come, as is sometimes the case, before the great burst of the hurricane, they would, one or both, be wanted where they were. Perhaps hailing might be of use. At all events, he would try. And, placing his hollowed hands on each side of his mouth to form a speaking trumpet the skipper drew a deep inspiration or two, hailed with the utmost strength of his lungs; "Ship ahoy–oy!"

And then listened.

No response. Nothing save the faint murmurings and railings of the gathering gale.

"*Ship ahoy–oy!*"

Hark! what was that? Did he, indeed, hear a faint answering halloo from away yonder in the direction of those weird lights, or was it merely that the wish was father to the thought?

"Sh–i–ip A—hoy–oy–oy!"

"*Halloo!*"

Quite unmistakable this time; and the skipper, in a perfect frenzy of excitement, repeats his hail time after time, waiting only long enough to receive the answer before hailing again. Presently a bright star suddenly appears under the faintly gleaming corposants. It is a ship's lantern held up over the rail. A minute later a tiny spark appears close to the lantern, immediately bursting into a keen bluish glare from which a cloud of white smoke arises and flakes of blue-white flame drop now and then as a portfire is burnt. By its brilliant though ghostly radiance the skipper can see, less than half a mile distant, a brig under nothing but close-reefed main-topsail and fore-topmast staysail—evidently fully prepared for the worst that can come to her in the shape of weather—with a little group of figures gathered about the port-fire, and a smaller group, consisting of two men only, abaft the main-rigging, all peering eagerly in his direction.

He sees one of the figures raise his arms; and presently there comes floating across the inky water:

"Halloo, there! Who hails?"

The skipper again raises his hands to his mouth, draws a mighty inspiration, and replies, as the readiest means of bringing succour to him:

"Shipwrecked m–a–an. Broad—on—your—port—b–ea–eam!"

The figure who had hailed waves his hand to show that he has heard; and just at that moment the port-fire burns out. Another is quickly ignited, however; and as the blue-white glare once more illumines the brig Blyth sees that there is but one man now on the forecastle—the man who holds aloft the port-fire—and that the rest are gathered aft, busy about the davit-tackles by which a boat is suspended on the larboard quarter.

At this moment the whole firmament from zenith to horizon is rent asunder, and for a single instant the entire universe seems to have been set on fire by the fierce blaze of the lightning which flashes from the rent, whilst the accompanying thunder crash is so deafening that even the skipper, seasoned as he is, quails beneath the shock of it. For a single instant the sea and everything upon it, from horizon to horizon, is illumined by a light brighter than that of day; and in that single instant Blyth sees not only the brig, enveloped in a perfect network of fire, but also the huge piles of cloud overhead, twisted and distorted into a hundred fantastic shapes by the forces at work within them, and the black glistening water, carved into countless hollows and ridges by the agitation of its surface; the whole apparently motionless as if modelled in metal. Then comes the blackness of darkness, so thick and impenetrable that the half-stunned skipper, scarcely conscious of where he is, dares not move by so much as a single footstep lest he should step overboard. The next moment down comes the rain, not in drops, not even in sheets of water, but in a perfectly overwhelming deluge of such density and volume that Blyth, bowing to his knees beneath it, gasps and chokes like a drowning man.

But he speedily recovers his senses—he had need to, for he will soon want them all—and, staggering to his feet, makes toward the mast, which with the yard and dripping sail is now distinctly outlined against the milky background of sea, milky by reason of the phosphorescence of its surface being lashed into luminosity by the pouring rain. He grasps the halliard of the sail, and with feverish haste proceeds to cast it adrift from its belaying-pin, murmuring the while:

"Now God be merciful to me, a sinner: for I am too late. The time for rescue is past!"

With utmost haste, yet with all the coolness and skill of a finished seaman, he lowers the sail on deck and proceeds to secure it as well as he can, for he knows only too well what the next act in the drama will be; he knows, too, that those on board the brig—invisible now—are as well versed as himself, and are at this moment far too busily engaged in preparing for the stroke of the hurricane to have a thought to spare for him.

Now the rain stops as suddenly as it began, and an awful silence ensues, scarcely broken even by the lap of the water alongside, for the terrific downpour has completely beaten down the swell, and, save for an occasional gentle heave, the raft lies motionless.

Now stand by! Summon all your nerve and all your courage to your aid, skipper, for you never stood half so sorely in need of them as you do now. And, above all, lift up your heart to God in fervent prayer, be it ever so brief. Call upon Him whilst you have time; for time, so far as you are concerned, may soon be merged in eternity!

Listen! What is that low murmur in the air which so rapidly increases in volume until it becomes a deep, hoarse, bellowing roar? The sound is broad on your starboard beam, skipper! Aft to your steering-oar for your life, man; sweep her head round quick, in readiness to run before it! That is well; round with her; again; another stroke. *Now* stand by! here it comes! Seize that rope's-end and hold on for your life!

A long line of milk-white foam appears upon the horizon, spreading and advancing with awful rapidity; the roar swells in volume until it becomes absolutely deafening; the air grows thick with vapour; a sudden whirl of wind rushes past lashing the skipper's face with rain-drops as it goes—rain-drops? no; they are salt, salt as the brine alongside—and then, with a wild burst and babel of hideous sound and a shock as though the raft had collided with something solid, the hurricane strikes her. The white water surges up over her stern, and the skipper is hurled forward, face downward and half-stunned, upon her already submerged deck.

Chapter Seventeen
The Malays!

The occupants of the fort retired to rest that night, as usual, at the early hour of ten o'clock; and, thoroughly fagged out with the day's labour, soon sank to sleep. Nobody felt in the least degree anxious about the skipper, because, when Gaunt and Henderson took a last look at the weather before turning in, there was nothing particularly alarming in its aspect; they agreed that there was going to be a change, and that it would probably occur before morning; but Blyth, they considered, was not the man to be caught napping; moreover, he had already been absent long enough to make his return possible at any moment; so, with this opinion expressed and understood, all hands sought their bunks with perfectly easy minds.

Manners and Nicholls were the first to awake, which they did simultaneously when the hurricane burst over the island, their sleeping-room happening to be on the weather side of the fort, or that upon which the gale beat with the greatest fury, and they were therefore naturally the first to be disturbed by the uproar of the storm.

"Whew!" whistled Manners, as he settled himself more comfortably in his cosy bunk; "it's blowing heavily! I'm glad I have no watch to keep to-night. Listen to that!" as the wind went howling and careering past the house, causing it to tremble to its foundations; "if it's like that down here in this sheltered valley what must it be outside in the open sea?"

"Bad enough, Mr Manners, you may depend on't," answered Nicholls, who, occupying the adjoining bunk, had overheard this muttered soliloquy, "bad enough! This is the worst bout we've had since we've been on the island. Why—listen to that, now!—and did ye feel the house shake, sir? Why, it must be blowing a regular tornado—or typhoon, as they calls 'em in these latitudes. The skipper sleeps pretty sound through it, don't he, sir?"

"He does, indeed," replied Manners; and then, a sudden recollection of the fishing expedition coming upon him, he added, "I suppose he *is* asleep—I suppose he is in his berth. Did you hear him come in?"

"Not I, sir," was the answer. "I dozed off to sleep almost before I had time to make myself comfortable, and I never woke again until a minute or two since when the roar of the gale disturbed me."

"Are you awake, Captain Blyth?" demanded Manners sharply.

No answer, and both men listen as well as they can through the awful roar and shriek of the gale, hoping to hear the measured breathing of the sleeper. But no such sound is heard; and after listening breathlessly for a few seconds Manners bounds out of his berth, and fumbling about for the matches, finds them at last and strikes a light. The skipper's berth is empty and undisturbed; it has evidently not been slept in that night.

Manners and Nicholls—the latter having also turned out—look blankly at the bunk and then at each other, the same dreadful suspicion dawning upon them both at the same instant.

"Good heavens!" gasped Manners. "It cannot be that - and yet it looks like it—is it possible, Tom, that the skipper has not returned—that he is at sea on the raft in this awful gale?"

"I'm blest if it don't look uncommon like it, sir," is Nicholls' reply, uttered in a tone of desperate conviction. "Tell ye what 'tis, sir," he continued, as he hastily proceeds to don a garment or two, slipping his bare feet into his shoes as he does so, "I'm off down to the creek to see if the punt is there. If she ain't, you may depend on't she's ridin' at the raft's moorin's—if she ain't swamped—and that the raft's at sea, with the poor skipper aboard of her. The Lord have mercy on him if it is so, that's all I says."

"Stop a moment; I will go with you," says Manners, also hastily dressing; "but before we go we had perhaps better inquire of Mr Gaunt or the doctor whether they know anything about him; they are certain to be awake."

A minute later the two men are groping their way along the wall of the court-yard toward the door of Gaunt's room, in which they can perceive a light. Manners knocks, and instantly receives the response:

"Yes. Who is there?"

"Manners and Nicholls, sir. Do you know anything about the captain, Mr Gaunt? He is not with us, and his bunk has not been slept in to-night."

"Stay where you are, I will be out in a moment," is the reply. And almost in the short space of time named Gaunt emerges.

"Now, then," he demands, somewhat sternly, "what is it you say about the captain? Surely I cannot have heard you aright?"

"Indeed I am afraid, sir, you did," answers Manners, by this time in a state of deep distress as the conviction forces itself upon him that the skipper really is missing.

"I said, sir, that the captain is not with us, and that his bunk has not been slept in to-night."

"Then God help him, for I fear he is beyond all human aid!" ejaculates the engineer hoarsely. "Have you been down to the creek yet?" he continues.

"No, sir," says Manners; "we were about to go down there, but I thought it best to speak to you first."

"Quite right," assents Gaunt; "I will go with you."

The engineer re-enters his room, hastily explains the situation to Mrs Gaunt, and then, returning, leads the way up the staircase to the roof; that, it will be remembered, being the only mode of exit from the building.

It is not until the trio reach this comparatively exposed situation that they at all realise the strength of the gale; but, once there, though the building is surrounded on all sides by the high ground of the ravine through which the river flows, the tempest seizes upon them and beats and buffets them and dashes them hither and thither with such irresistible power and fury that they are in absolute peril of their lives whilst they remain there, and to avoid being actually hurled off into space they are constrained to go down upon their hands and knees. To add to their difficulties the darkness is so intense that they can see absolutely nothing; they have to grope their way like blind men, relying solely upon their remembrance of localities for guidance. And, search as they will, they cannot find the exterior ladder by which to descend to the ground outside. It has doubtless been blown away. This misfortune, however, is soon remedied by the substitution of a rope from the store-room for the missing ladder, and with its assistance the three men quickly reach the ground.

Arrived there, they find that their difficulties have only just begun, for they are no sooner clear of the house than, what with the profound darkness and the awful buffeting of the wind, they soon get confused and lose their way. At length, however, after more than an hour's aimless wandering, they find themselves at the ship-yard, which is in quite another direction, and once there, they are enabled, by keeping close along the water's-edge, to reach the creek.

As each had by this time expected, the punt is not there; and now any lingering hopes as to the skipper's safety which either of them may have cherished disappears, and in his own mind each mutely gives the poor fellow up as lost. The punt being missing, there is no means of crossing to the main, for the stream, swollen by the recent rain, is rushing past at a speed swift enough to sweep away the strongest swimmer that ever breasted wave, to say nothing of the fact that the gale—which is opposed to the current—has churned and lashed the waters into a sheet of blinding foam. They can do nothing, therefore, except make an ineffectual attempt to light a fire, in the hope that its blaze, reflected in the sky, may serve as a beacon to their unfortunate friend in the improbable event of his still being alive and within sight of the island; but this attempt also is frustrated by the wind, which not only renders it impossible for them to kindle a flame but also sweeps away all their materials as fast as they are gathered. There is nothing left for them, then, but to wend their way back homewards as best they can and await the dawn of day.

The dawn that morning was long in coming, and when at length the grey murky light slowly forced its way through the overhanging canopy of rent and tattered cloud which obscured the heavens, wreck and destruction everywhere became visible. Fay Island, it is true, had escaped almost unscathed, doubtless owing to its sheltered situation; but on the main—as the party had got into the way of designating the larger island—thousands of trees were lying prostrate, many of them uprooted, and the rest snapped off close to the ground.

As soon as it was light enough to see anything, Gaunt, with Henderson this time for a companion, once more made his way down to the creek, but there was nothing to be seen from there. Even the buoy attached to the raft's moorings was invisible; but just where it ought to be there was a strong ripple on the roughened surface of the water which seemed to suggest that the buoy, and possibly the swamped punt as well, was still there, but dragged under water by the strength of the current.

It continued to blow very heavily—though not with the same awfully destructive violence which marked the first burst of the hurricane—all that day and part of the ensuing night, when the gale broke, and by sunrise the wind had dropped to a strong breeze. Then once more did the four men set out from the fort in the, by that time, almost hopeless effort to obtain some clue to the fate of poor Captain Blyth.

Descending the outer ladder—which had been discovered on the previous day at some distance from the fort—the search party first made for the creek, from the shore of which—the stream having by this time subsided and its current sunk to its normal speed—they descried not only the buoy marking the moorings of the raft, but also, as they had quite expected, the swamped punt hanging to it. The latter was promptly secured; Manners swimming out to it with the end of a line from the shore, by means of which the craft was drawn in and grounded upon the beach and baled out. The oars having been washed out of her and swept away, the next thing to be done was to work up a new pair; a task which was soon accomplished, since they now had an abundant store of suitable material close at hand in the ship-yard. This done, the searchers made their way down stream and crossed to the main, there separating into two parties, one of which was to skirt the shore to the northward and westward, whilst the other was to proceed in the opposite direction until the two parties reunited; their object being not so much to look out seaward—for they knew that if the raft had missed the island it would by that time be far enough away—but rather to examine the shore for any sign of wreckage or—the poor skipper's dead body. Henderson and Nicholls constituted one party, whilst Gaunt and Manners formed the other. They had not only a long, but also a most difficult journey before them, the difficulty arising chiefly from the nature of the ground they had to traverse; and it occupied them until well on in the afternoon of the following day, both parties camping in the woods for one night—and finding it anything but a pleasant experience; but neither party found anything to throw the least light upon the fate either of the raft or of the unfortunate man who had gone to sea in her; and when at length they met they had at least the negative satisfaction of being able to say that, after a thorough search of the entire seaboard of the island, they had discovered no actual *proof* that the captain had lost his life.

Very fortunately for them no damage had been done either to the mill or in the ship-yard; there was therefore no time lost in making good deficiencies of that kind, and they were consequently enabled to resume and carry on their shipwrights' work forthwith. But not until a full fortnight after the gale did they finally give up the skipper as lost, young Manners being despatched every morning to the top of the mountain with instructions to remain there all day and maintain a constant look-out, the party still hoping, against their better reason, that after all the raft *might* have held together, and that Blyth *might*, in such a case, strive to regain the island. But at the expiration of that time they felt that it was useless to hope further, and the watching was discontinued.

Doctor Henderson was the hero of the next adventure which befell the party; and a pretty state of consternation he managed to throw everybody into for the time being, his poor wife and little Lucille especially.

It happened thus. It had been the custom of the party ever since their landing upon the island to observe Sunday as a day of rest, the prayers of the Episcopal Church being read, with their proper lessons, both morning and evening; whilst the rest of the day was devoted to such much-needed recreation as they thought in their consciences might legitimately be indulged in. Manners and Nicholls, after the manner of seamen, usually devoted a great deal of time on this particular day to the requirements of the toilette and the patching up of their clothes; whilst the two married men devoted themselves entirely to their families, taking their wives and the youngsters for tolerably long walks when the weather permitted. Sometimes the two families took these excursions in company, sometimes separately, according to their inclinations at the moment; and, whether separately or together, Gaunt usually carried his sketch-block and colours, whilst Henderson always took his specimen box; the one being as enthusiastic an amateur artist as the other was a botanist and chemist. When the weather was unfavourable for these walks Gaunt was in the habit of routing out some interesting book from his large stock and reading from it aloud; whilst Henderson, in the privacy of a little laboratory he had managed to fit up, prosecuted his researches into the nature of the various plants and herbs he had collected in former rambles.

They were all thus engaged on the afternoon of an atrociously wet Sunday, about a month after the mysterious disappearance of poor Captain Blyth, when the rest of the party were suddenly startled by a loud cry for help from Henderson, the call being instantly repeated twice or thrice in a much weaker tone of voice.

Tossing aside his book and springing to his feet Gaunt at once rushed off to the laboratory, with all the others close at his heels, and there they discovered the unfortunate doctor in a most extraordinary state of mind and body, and at the same time became conscious of a faint fragrant odour pervading the atmosphere of the room. Pale as death, with all his limbs hanging limp as if paralysed, the poor fellow was huddled up in a chair upon which he had evidently hung himself when the seizure—or whatever it was—first came upon him. His eyes were rolling wildly, his teeth chattered as though he were suffering from an ague fit, and his moustache and beard *were* flecked with foam. But it was evident that he still retained his reason, for the moment that he saw the little crowd pouring into the room he cried out in a weak but piercing voice:

"Fly! fly for your lives, every one of you but Gaunt! *Fly!* I say; stay not a moment. My dear fellow," turning to Gaunt, "*drive* them out; *throw* them out if they will not go otherwise! And throw open that window at once; this atmosphere is *deadly*, I tell you."

This statement had the desired effect; the room was cleared promptly, everybody beating a somewhat precipitate retreat but the engineer and Mrs Henderson, the latter quietly but firmly refusing to be removed, upon the double plea that it was no more dangerous for her than for Gaunt, and that, whether or no, her proper place was beside her husband. As for Gaunt, he acted with his usual decision, first dashing the window wide-open, and next stooping to raise his friend and convey him into a presumably more healthy atmosphere; and if any additional motive beyond solicitude for the sufferer were needed to impel him to this step he had it, first in the awful pallor which suddenly overspread Mrs Henderson's features, and secondly in a curious sickly feeling of lassitude and languor which he felt stealing over himself. But, to his unspeakable surprise, no sooner did he approach Henderson than the latter shrank away from him with a cry of fear, beseeching him in a weak voice not to come near him. Gaunt, however, by no means saw matters in this light; if the atmosphere were deadly, or even deleterious, as his own increasingly unpleasant sensations made him perfectly ready to believe, then the sooner they three were out of it the better. So, disregarding the unfortunate doctor's protestations and entreaties, he raised him in his arms and, notwithstanding the increasing sensation of feebleness and numbness which oppressed him, staggered with his burden into the outer air of the court-yard, closely followed of course by Mrs Henderson. But it was a most trying business altogether, for no sooner did Gaunt lay hands upon the sufferer, though he did it ever so gently, than the poor fellow rent the air with his screams, crying out between whiles that Gaunt was crushing him to death and that he was stripping the flesh off his bones. It was a most extraordinary affair altogether, for they could get no intelligible explanation from the patient even after they had with infinite trouble and care—seemingly at the cost of the acutest agony to Henderson—conveyed him to his own room and laid him on his bed. He could do nothing but shiver and moan and cower down among the coverings, and entreat that nobody—not even his wife or child—would go near him, or, least of all, touch him. The little party were almost beside themselves with anxiety and terror, which feelings were increased when poor Mrs Henderson exhibited symptoms of a similar character. As for Gaunt, he was thoroughly alarmed; for not only did the feeling of feebleness increase, but he also found himself gradually becoming the victim of a blind unreasoning terror for which the term "abject cowardice" afforded but a very inadequate description. And to this very unpleasant sensation was added that of a morbid sense of touch, so acute that even the very pressure of his clothes became almost unendurable. Fully alive, however, to the possibly critical state of affairs, he battled desperately against the influences at work upon him, and, with infinite patience, at length succeeded in extorting from Henderson a few suggestions toward the adoption of remedial measures, which he put in force first for the benefit of the doctor, next for Mrs Henderson—who had also succumbed to a similar though much milder attack—and lastly for himself. Nothing that was done, however, appeared to be of the slightest service, the symptoms continuing with unmitigated severity for fully eight hours, after which they gradually subsided. Gaunt was quite himself again by noon next day; Mrs Henderson recovered about eighteen hours later; but as for the doctor, it was fully a week before he entirely shook off the effects of the attack. But in less than twenty-four hours from his first seizure he had sufficiently recovered to give an explanation of the singular affair to the following effect. He had, it would seem, been investigating the nature of a hitherto unknown plant growing in considerable abundance upon the island, and had found it to possess several very remarkable qualities, some at least of which he believed might be rendered of the utmost value in medical practice. Anxious to make his researches thoroughly exhaustive he had, upon the day of the catastrophe, been distilling the essence of the plant; and, his task completed, he was in the act of bottling the extract for future examination when its peculiarly pleasing fragrance caused him to take several deep inhalations from the bottle. He had hardly done so when he felt his strength rapidly leaving him, and he had only time to deposit the phial, open, upon his table and stagger to a chair when something very like a fit of paralysis seized him. He at once cried out for help; but by the time that his cries had evoked a response his nerves had begun to give way, and in a very few minutes he was enduring such an agony of fear of everybody and everything as words utterly failed him to describe. And with this terrible fear came the equally terrible morbid sensitiveness of touch, which he found himself equally unable to describe. So excruciating was it, he said, that even the sound of an approaching footstep caused him more suffering than he had ever before experienced; and as to the moving of him from the laboratory and again into his own room—his silence and the convulsive shudder which shook him from head to foot were far more expressive than words. His first act when he was sufficiently recovered to move about once more was to secure the phial containing the liquid which had done all the mischief, and—with Nicholls to manage the punt—go right out to sea, where, hastily uncorking the bottle, he flung it as far from him to leeward as possible, at the same moment ordering his companion to give way for home again with all speed. This was done whilst the terror of his attack was still upon him; but it was not in the nature of a man of Henderson's training to give way for long to so irrational a fear as that which prompted this action, and in less than a month afterwards he had, with the adoption of all proper precautions, secured another and far more liberal supply of the singular essence, with a view to future experiments and analysis.

Meanwhile, the work at the ship-yard was pushed forward with all possible energy, and to such good purpose that in an incredibly short time, all things considered, the timbers for the new boat were raised into position and secured, the planking carried up to the gunwale, the deck laid and caulked, the joiners' work advanced, and the spars put in hand. Everybody was in the highest possible spirits, for they saw the end of their labours rapidly approaching; they were, moreover, not only pleased but absolutely proud of their work, for, though of course only amateurs, they had wrought so carefully and conscientiously that everything was finished off not only as strongly but also as neatly as if they had every one served an apprenticeship to the handicraft. Then the little vessel herself was a perfect beauty; graceful in shape, notwithstanding her extreme breadth of beam; powerful, yet buoyant; and with lines so cunningly moulded that, whilst it would doubtless require a good strong breeze to show her off to the utmost advantage, Nicholls and Manners—who might both be expected to know a good hull when they saw it—confidently predicted that she would prove very nimble even in light airs. And so confident were they of her sea-going powers that they averred, again and again, they would not be afraid to face in her even such a hurricane as that which had robbed them of poor Captain Blyth; indeed, they even went the length of volunteering to take her home to England after she should have accomplished the primary mission of her existence in conveying the party to a civilised port. Matters were in this satisfactory state, the work having reached such a stage of advancement that the rigging of the *Petrel*—as they had decided to name the little cutter—had already been begun, and some talk was being indulged in of hopes that the launch might be accomplished within the following week, when, on a bright Sunday afternoon, Gaunt left Fay Island for the main, taking the two children with him, the object of the little party being to gather a few of the strangely-shaped and exceedingly beautiful shells to be found on the sea-beach, as mementoes of their long sojourn on the island. The ladies preferred to remain at home, deciding that the day was far too hot for walking exercise; and the doctor remained with them for company. It was getting on toward sunset—indeed, the sun had already disappeared behind the high ground to the westward of the fort—and the doctor with his two fair companions had ascended to the flat, rampart-like roof of the building to enjoy the cool, refreshing breeze and watch for the return of the shell-gatherers, when the sound of a musket-shot, quickly followed by some five or six others, broke upon the air with startling effect, and immediately afterwards the head of a lofty triangular sail glided into view from behind some tall bushes which had hitherto concealed its approach. That a strange craft of some sort was in the river was the first idea which presented itself to Henderson's mind; that Gaunt—who was unarmed—and the children were but too probably at that moment crossing from the main, and consequently in full view from the deck of the strange craft, was the next; and that the firing must necessarily have proceeded from the unlooked-for visitor and be an indication of hostility, possibly directed against Gaunt and the youngsters, was the third—the three ideas following each other with the rapidity of a lightning flash. To these succeeded a fourth—the Malays! So long a time had elapsed since poor Blyth had arrived with his alarming intelligence respecting the propinquity of these rascals and his disquieting suggestions as to a possible visit from them, that, though an anxious watch had been for some time maintained, the uninterrupted absence of any alarming indications had at length resulted in so complete a relaxation of vigilance that even the very existence of these pests of the Eastern seas had been forgotten. What if the wretches were upon them now? It seemed only too probable. As these thoughts darted through Henderson's brain, and with them the frightful suggestion that those three—the unarmed man and the two helpless children, one of them *his*—might at that moment be beset by a cruel and bloodthirsty foe, a cold shudder went through his frame, and, hurriedly speaking to his companions a few words which he intended should be reassuring, but which his manner rendered quite the reverse, he dashed down the inner stairway to the court-yard, and seizing Gaunt's repeating rifle, which he knew to be loaded, and directing Manners and Nicholls—who had rushed out of their room at the sound of the firing—to arm themselves and follow him, he rushed up to the roof again, and descending to the ground by the outer ladder, hurried away off in the direction of the creek. He had not advanced in this direction much beyond a hundred yards, along the pathway through the bush, when a child's screams—little Lucille's—smote upon his distracted ear, and, darting forward in a very frenzy of apprehension, as he sprang round a bend in the path the poor child, her head uncovered and her long fair hair streaming behind her, her sweet eyes wild with terror, and her little hands outstretched, rushed up to him and with an inarticulate cry of joy sank exhausted and almost lifeless at his feet. Behind her, not a dozen yards distant, followed a fierce-looking Malay, his parted lips revealing the white teeth clenched in the eagerness of pursuit, his cruel black eyes gleaming with the ferocious joy of anticipated success, and with a murderous-looking creese with a long wavy blade uplifted in readiness to strike the moment he should have brought the poor innocent little victim within reach of his lean muscular arm.

To spring over the prostrate form of his darling child, thus placing himself between her and her pursuer, whilst he raised his rifle to his shoulder, was an act of such lightning-like rapidity with Henderson that he and his foe were almost within striking distance before either could check his career. The next instant the crack of his rifle rang out sharp and clear, and the Malay, with a convulsive bound, crashed face downward at his feet dead, with the bullet through his brain.

Breathless with excitement and the exertion of his short run, his teeth clenched, and the fierce eagerness for battle suddenly awakened to full activity within him, the doctor stood waiting impatiently for the next foe to present himself. But none came; only Manners and Nicholls now appeared upon the scene with their rifles in their hands, and eager questions in their eyes and on their lips for an explanation of the sudden and tragic turn of affairs. To them in a few terse words Henderson stated what had already taken place, adding an expression of his apprehension that Gaunt and little Percy had fallen into the hands of the enemy, and finally directing the two men to advance with caution as far as possible with the view of ascertaining the whereabouts of the missing ones, and of affording them help if help were indeed still possible, and, when they had done all that they could, to the best of their judgment, to return to the fort with intelligence. Having thus dismissed his companions, the doctor tenderly raised the now insensible Lucille in his arms, and, pressing her to his breast with a sob of inarticulate gratitude to God for her preservation, he wended his way back to the fort with a heavy, grief-stricken heart, wondering meanwhile how he could best meet the anxious inquiries which he knew would be made by poor Mrs Gaunt.

Chapter Eighteen
An anxious night at the fort

As Henderson approached the fort he saw the two ladies watching for him; and anxious not to unduly alarm them, he cried out—referring to Lucille—as soon as he had approached within shouting distance:

"It is all right; she is not hurt, only frightened a little. Get her bed ready."

Upon hearing this, Mrs Gaunt, taking the notion into her head that her husband and Percy were following at their leisure, hurried away to prepare Lucille's bed for her, leaving Mrs Henderson to receive her child. This afforded the doctor an opportunity which, to speak the truth, was most welcome to him. He knew from experience the consummate tact which women are wont to exercise in the breaking of bad news, and he resolved forthwith to delegate to his wife the task to which he had been looking forward with so much mental perturbation. So, as soon as he reached his wife's side, he said hastily:

"Look here, Rose dear, you need not be alarmed. With the exception of being frightened very nearly out of her wits, poor child, there is nothing wrong with Lucille; she has swooned with terror, but I can soon put her all right again. The Malays, however, have landed on the island; and I am dreadfully afraid they have got Gaunt and poor little Percy, but we can know nothing for certain until the return of Manners and Nicholls, who have gone forward to reconnoitre. There is no time now to enter into particulars—they can be told by and by; but poor Mrs Gaunt is certain to inquire presently for her husband and child, so I want you to go to her *now*—leave Lucille to me; take her to her own room, and break to her as gently as possible what I have just told you, laying stress at the same time upon the fact that we *know* nothing certainly as yet, and that matters may turn out much better than we apprehend. Look! there she is. Now go to her and be as gentle with her as you can."

Full of sympathy, Mrs Henderson at this hurried away upon her painful errand; whilst her husband, as soon as the coast was clear, made his way down to his own room with the unconscious Lucille.

Arrived there, he laid the child upon her bed, and then opened the compact medicine chest which, on leaving England, he had happily taken the precaution of adding to his personal outfit, and this done he forthwith set about the task of restoration.

The task proved more difficult and of longer duration than he had anticipated; and before success rewarded his efforts his wife rejoined him, in tears.

"Well," he said nervously, and without desisting a moment from his occupation, "how have you managed?"

"Oh, Duncan!" sobbed Mrs Henderson, "it was dreadful! Poor dear Ida is quite prostrated with grief and terror, though she did, and is still doing, her best to bear up under the awful agony of suspense. Fancy, dearest, both husband and child—oh, it is horrible! Can *nothing* be done to save them?"

"Nothing, just now, I fear," was the gloomy response. "You see there are but three fighting men of us now, and we do not know how many of the enemy there are. It is quite useless to attempt the devising of plans until the other two return with intelligence; *then*, indeed, we will see what can be done. And it shall go hard but we will rescue them somehow. Where did you leave Mrs Gaunt?"

"In her own room on her knees, praying for her lost ones; it is all she can do, poor soul. Ah! the dear child is reviving at last, is she not, dear?"

"Yes, yes," answered Henderson hurriedly. "Now reach me that glass of medicine from the table. Thanks. Here, Lucille, my dear, drink this, little one, it will do you good."

A faint tinge of returning colour had at length appeared in the child's pale cheeks and lips. This had been succeeded by a-fluttering sigh or two, and then her eyes had opened suddenly with a look of terror, which had given place to one of joy and relief as she recognised her father and mother bending over her. Upon which Henderson had gently raised her and promptly administered the draught which he had prepared.

Presently the little creature spoke. "Oh, mamma," she exclaimed, looking somewhat wildly about her, "is it morning; is it time to get up? I have had such a dreadful dream—"

"There; never mind your dream, dear; forget all about it, and try to go to sleep again," said Mrs Henderson soothingly; "it is not quite time to get up yet."

"Yes; go to sleep again like a good girl," agreed Henderson; "but you can tell us your dream first, dear, if you very much wish to do so. You forget," he added in an undertone to his wife; "she may be able to throw a great deal of light upon the state of affairs, and afford us information of the last importance. What was your dream, darling?"

"Oh," began the child, "I dreamt that we—Mr Gaunt and Percy and I, you know—had been to the beach gathering shells; and as we were coming back in the boat a great ship suddenly came round the corner, full of ugly, wicked men; and they fired guns at us, and one of them hit Mr Gaunt, for I saw the blood running down his face. And then they came after us in a boat, and were quite near us when we reached the creek; and then Mr Gaunt told Percy and me to run home as fast as ever we could; and he took one of the boat's oars and got out and stood on the beach, and looked as if he was going to fight the men. So Percy took my hand, and we ran—oh, ever so fast; and I looked round and saw Mr Gaunt fighting all the men with the oar; and then we turned a corner, and I felt tired and wanted to stop; but Percy wouldn't let me, and we kept on running, and I began to cry. And just as I wanted to stop again we heard somebody running after us, and I thought it was Mr Gaunt, but it wasn't; it was one of the ugly men out of the ship; and he had a long knife in his hand. So we ran faster, and then dear Percy fell down; but I ran on, and the ugly man caught Percy, and—oh, mamma!" Here the poor little creature's eyes filled with tears, and the frightened look returned to them. "*Was* it a dream, or did it really happen?"

"It really happened, dear," answered Henderson, who made a point of never deceiving his child about anything; "it really happened; but never mind; you are with us now, you know, and *quite* safe, so lie down and try to go to sleep. And do not trouble about dear Percy; we will have him and his papa both safe back with us by to-morrow morning, please God. What a horrible experience for the poor child—and what dreadful news about those two!" he murmured to his wife as Lucille sank back and closed her eyes again under the influence of the soothing draught he had administered. "Fancy that poor little fellow Percy in the hands of those fiends. Hark! is not that Manners' voice hailing outside? Stay here with Lucille and hold her hand, it will soothe her, and I will go and lower the ladder."

With that Henderson hurried away, leaving his wife to watch by the bedside of their child, with a heart brimful of pity and sympathy for her bereaved friend, and of unspeakable gratitude to God for the safety of her own loved ones.

Arrived at the head of the staircase, Henderson approached the parapet, and, leaning over, peered down into the gathering darkness.

"Is that you, Manners?" he asked, seeing a couple of figures standing close underneath him.

"Ay, ay, sir; here we are," answered Manners for himself and his companion. "Will you kindly lower the ladder, please, doctor?"

The ladder was lowered, and in another moment Nicholls made his appearance above the parapet, closely followed by Manners, who immediately hauled up the ladder after him.

"Well," questioned Henderson impatiently, seeing that neither of the men evinced a disposition to speak; "well, what is the news?"

"The worst, sir; the very worst," answered Manners with unusual emotion. "They've got both Mr Gaunt and little Percy; and, would you believe it, sir? the devils have actually been ill-treating the poor little fellow, just for the sake, seemingly, of tormenting his father."

Henderson groaned aloud in sheer bitterness of spirit at hearing this.

"It's awful, isn't it, sir?" continued Manners, grinding his teeth with rage. "Nicholls here wanted to open fire upon them, there and then, and board in the smoke—dash in among them in the midst of the confusion, you know, sir, and see if we couldn't cut the two of them adrift and bring them off with us. There's nothing would have suited me better, for it made me fairly mad to see the brutes striking that poor little innocent child, and he and his father lashed to the trunks of a couple of trees; but it wouldn't do; it *wouldn't* do, sir; there were too many of them for us. I counted twenty-seven of them, all told, after the second party had come ashore from the proa; we couldn't have done any good. And, besides, there was you and the ladies to be thought of. So, after we had watched them for some time, I thought our best plan would be to come back here and consult with you, especially as they seemed to be getting ready to beat up our quarters. But we're determined, Nicholls and I, to have a slap at them some time to-night in some shape or form; and the only question is, how it is best to be done?"

Henderson stretched out a hand to each of them, which was cordially grasped, as he said, huskily:

"Thank you; thank you, my staunch and trusty friends, both; we *will* have a slap at them, as you say. But we must do nothing hastily or without careful consideration; the issues involved are too many, the stake too great for us to risk anything by over-rashness. Let us each think the matter over carefully. And, meanwhile, as we shall need all our strength, you, Nicholls, go down and bring us up here something to eat and drink, as this may be our only chance to snatch a morsel of refreshment. And whilst he is doing that, perhaps you, Manners, will kindly go down and bring up all the arms and ammunition you can find, so that if the Malays come this way we may be prepared to give them a warm reception. I will keep watch here for the present."

In another minute Henderson was alone upon the parapet, with the deep violet star-studded sky above him, and on every hand the black outline of the high land and the dense growth of trees and bush which hemmed in the fort. Not a sound met his ear save the continuous *chirr* of the myriads of insects with which the island abounded, the distant wash and gurgle of the river, and the mournful sighing of the night breeze through the foliage; but the whereabouts of the Malay camp was faintly indicated by an occasional gleam of ruddy light flashing upon the branches and leaves of a lofty tree in the direction of the creek; and, most gratifying sight of all, away to the eastward the sky was brightening into silvery radiance, showing that the full moon would shortly shed her friendly light upon the scene.

The two men soon returned from below in the performance of their several tasks, Manners having had the forethought to load the firearms by the light of a lantern whilst still in the armoury.

A few minutes later the moon rolled slowly into view from above the low-lying land beyond the Malay encampment, flooding the whole scene with her soft subdued light; and Manners then cautiously went from loophole to loophole looking for signs of the enemy, but without detecting any indication of their presence. Though neither of them had the slightest appetite for food, the three men now proceeded to force a little refreshment down their throats, knowing full well that ere long they would have need of all their strength; and, whilst they ate, the conversation naturally turned upon the two hapless prisoners, and the best means for effecting their rescue. Henderson, indeed, had been able to think of little, else since the moment when his child had recovered sufficiently to relate her terrible experience; and whilst turning the matter over in his mind a hopeful thought had suggested itself. What, he asked himself, could have been the motive of the Malays in making prisoners of those two? Was it not likely that their object was plunder, and the extortion of a ransom? And, if so, he was resolved that *anything* in reason which might be demanded—anything, in short, which should leave the party with the means of defending themselves and providing for their ultimate safety—should be granted. Let the wretches but be persuaded to give up their prisoners unharmed, and to leave the island, and he would not haggle about the price to be paid.

The trio were anxiously discussing together this hopeful view of the matter when the watchful Manners, who had stationed himself at a loophole for the purpose of maintaining a ceaseless look-out, suddenly raised his hand warningly, and then pointed in the direction of the pathway to the creek. Springing to their feet, his companions at once stationed themselves in positions which gave them a view of the spot indicated; and, looking intently, they presently detected in the deepest shadow of the bush two or three other shadows, which they speedily identified as human figures, the more readily from the fact that a stray moonbeam occasionally fell upon and glinted from their naked weapons. The two or three were quickly joined by others, who emerged silently from the pathway through the bush until the watchers were able to count a dozen in all.

"Now, sir, what do you say? Shall we open fire upon them, you and I, with Mr Gaunt's repeaters, and Nicholls with his rifle? We could bowl over at least half of them before they could get away," eagerly whispered Manners in Henderson's ear.

"No, no; not for the world," was the answer. "Let us watch them and see if we can get an inkling of what their intentions may be. They at least cannot get at *us* here; and any precipitate action on our part may only make matters worse for poor Gaunt. Our policy is to keep them in the dark as long as possible as to the number of their opponents."

The Malays having gained—unperceived, they doubtless hoped—the cover afforded by the deep shadow of a dense clump of bush, some two hundred yards distant from the fort, were now clustered closely together therein, apparently engaged upon a careful inspection of the curious building before them, and probably comparing notes thereon. They evidently seemed quite unable to arrive at any satisfactory conclusion with respect to it; and the fact that everything was perfectly dark, silent, and motionless about the fort—all the shutters in the exterior walls having been carefully closed—seemed to excite misgiving rather than confidence in their breasts, for a figure would now and then detach itself from the rest and, on hands and knees, advance cautiously a little way through the long grass into the open, as though to gain a nearer view of the building, and then somewhat precipitately retire again, as though the courage of the adventurer were not equal to the task which he had undertaken. At length these tactics ceased, and the party, seeming to have finally made up their minds to be at least doing something, began, still clinging tenaciously to the deepest shadow, to move quietly along in a direction which would eventually lead to their discovery of the ship-yard.

"That will not do," whispered Henderson to his companions as soon as he observed this. "They must not be allowed to reach the ship-yard, or they will doubtless set fire to the cutter and everything else there. I was in hopes they would make up their minds to attack the building, when the advantage would be all on our side, enabling us to greatly reduce their numbers without risk of loss to ourselves; but apparently they do not like the look of the place. Now, you see that broad strip of moonlit sward over there which they are approaching. The first man who attempts to cross I will fire at; you, Manners, taking the second, I the third, and so on, you and I firing alternately so that we may take the better aim, and Nicholls reserving his fire in case of a rush. Should such take place, we must all fire as rapidly as possible with the object of checking it. But remember this, both of you, we must each make absolutely certain of his man before pulling trigger. Not a single bullet must be wasted, because in this case it will give us an immense advantage if we can impress the enemy with a conviction of the deadly character of our fire. Now, make ready, and recollect I fire first."

As the doctor spoke he carefully levelled his repeating rifle through a loophole and brought the sights in line with the trunk of a young sapling which stood full in the moonlight, and in front of which the stealthily advancing figures would have to pass. His heart throbbed so loudly that he could count its pulsations—one, two, three, four. The first figure is on the verge of the moonlight; he pauses a moment, looks anxiously at the fort, and then starts at a run to cross to the next patch of friendly shadow. Poor wretch! he little knows how true an eye is watching behind the sights of a rifle, waiting for him to come in line with that sapling. Another stride will bring him in line with it—*crack*! a flash of fire, a little puff of white smoke, and he flings up his arms as he falls heavily forward into the grass. A second figure has already emerged into the bright moonlight, following the first; it pauses at the flash and the report, as if about to turn back. Too late! A second flash, a second report, and he, too, falls forward on his face. A third now springs out of the shadow and stoops forward as if to drag the fallen man back into shelter; but before he can reach him he, too, falls before Henderson's deadly rifle. That stops the advance most effectually, the remaining figures huddling close together where they stand. A most fatal mode of grouping themselves this, for the doctor, whose blood is now fully up, gives the word to fire into them as they stand; and instantly out flashes the fire of three rifles from as many loopholes, followed by such a commotion over there among the shadows as seems to indicate that the fire has not been in vain. Two more shots, one each from Henderson and Manners, complete the enemy's discomfiture, and a hasty retreat is commenced.

"Follow them up, now; fire away!" exclaims Henderson eagerly; "but take careful aim. Now is our opportunity to teach them a wholesome lesson!"

And follow them up they did, with such deadly persistency that four only out of the twelve succeeded in making good their retreat and regaining the path leading to the cove.

"Splendid! admirable!" exclaimed the doctor with exultation, as he hastened with a parting shot the disappearance of the last figure. "We shall neither see nor hear anything more of those fellows to-night. And now, let us once more see if we cannot hit upon some scheme for the deliverance of those two, our valued friend Gaunt and his little son."

He was mistaken, however, in supposing that he had seen the last of the Malays for that night; for about two hours later, whilst they were still anxiously discussing the one question which, above all others, absorbed their thoughts, and were seemingly just as far as ever from any practicable solution of it, a gleam of ruddy light suddenly appeared in the pathway leading from the creek, and a minute later two Malays stepped boldly into the open, one of them holding aloft a lighted torch in one hand and a palm branch in the other, whilst the second man displayed what looked like a sheet of paper.

"A flag of truce craving a parley!" exclaimed Henderson, as he critically examined the two men through a loophole. "Let them approach; we will hear what they have to say — that is, if they can make themselves intelligible."

The Malays advanced boldly enough across the open toward the fort, evidently quite satisfied that the palm branch afforded them full and absolute protection, and at length came to a halt beneath the walls.

"Well, what do you want?" demanded the doctor of them in English, as he leaned over the parapet.

The one who bore the paper seemed quite to comprehend the purport of the question, for he said something unintelligible in reply, made a motion of writing upon the paper, and then held it aloft toward Henderson.

"Um! a letter," muttered the doctor; "possibly from Gaunt. Have you any string, either of you?" turning to his companions.

Nicholls happened to have a small ball of spun-yarn in his pocket, and this being produced, was unwound and the end lowered down to the letter-bearer, who gravely attached the letter, or whatever it was, to it, made an oriental obeisance, and promptly retired, followed by his companion.

"Now, Nicholls," said Henderson, as he hauled up and secured the document, "you mount guard here, keep a sharp look-out, and give the alarm the moment you note anything suspicious. Mr Manners and I are going below to see what news this letter contains."

That the letter was not from Gaunt was evident the moment it was opened, for it consisted of nothing more than a series of roughly but vigorously executed drawings.

The first sketch, or that which occupied the top of the sheet, consisted of a straight horizontal stroke with markings underneath it, which were evidently intended to represent waves; and on the centre of the horizontal line stood a semicircle with straight lines radiating from it, with a bold single upright stroke to the left of it. Though roughly executed, there was no doubt this was intended to represent either the rising or the setting sun, probably the former, the upright stroke being perhaps intended to indicate the first sunrise, or that of the next morning; at all events, so Henderson interpreted it.

The second sketch rudely but unmistakably represented the fort, with the exception that, in order to make his meaning perfectly clear, the artist had been obliged to add a door. Out of this door several white men were walking, with guns in their hands, which the leading figures were either delivering up, or had already delivered up, to a body of Malays. A second group of whites and Malays were shown to the right of the sketch, the Malays being represented as handing over to the unarmed whites two prisoners with ropes round their necks and their hands tied behind them. One of the prisoners was an adult, whilst the other was much smaller; and there could be no doubt whatever that they were intended to indicate Gaunt and Percy.

The, third and last sketch was also a representation of the fort, but in this case it was drawn without a door. Looking over the parapet were a number of white men with guns in their hands, which they were pointing at a party of Malays on the ground below, who in turn were pointing guns at the whites; whilst to the right of this picture was drawn another group, a most sinister one, for it represented Gaunt and Percy bound to two trees and surrounded by a pile of—presumably—branches, to which other Malays were in the act of applying *a blazing torch*!

Henderson and Manners studied this document most attentively for some time, and they at length agreed that only one meaning could possibly be intended to be conveyed by it—namely, that if the fort and all it contained, including weapons, were surrendered by sunrise, or sunset—but most probably the former—next day, Gaunt and Percy should be delivered up by their captors; but if not, then the fort would be attacked, and the two captives *burnt alive*!

"Why, this is horrible!" exclaimed Henderson, as he finally folded up the document and carefully placed it in his pocket. "We cannot possibly make the unconditional surrender which they demand, it would simply be placing the entire party, Gaunt and his child included, at the mercy of a pack of treacherous, bloodthirsty scoundrels, who would probably slaughter us all in cold blood as soon as we had delivered up our weapons. On the other hand, it is equally out of the question that we should abandon those two poor souls to the frightful fate with which they are threatened. What is to be done, Manners?"

"Let us go up on the parapet and talk the matter over with Nicholls, sir," was the reply. "He is a quiet, inoffensive fellow, but thoroughly to be depended upon in a fight, and he is pretty long-headed too, perhaps he may be able to help us out with a suggestion. At all events, sir, you may depend upon it neither Mr Gaunt nor little Percy—poor little chap!—shall be burnt, alive or dead, whilst I can strike a blow to prevent it."

"Come, then," said Henderson, "let us go and hear what Nicholls has to say upon the matter." And he led the way up to the parapet once more.

But Nicholls, honest man that he was, seemed completely to lose in horror the long-headedness with which Manners had credited him, as soon as he was made acquainted with the terms of the singular document handed in by the Malays, and beyond the utterance of several very hearty maledictions upon the heads of those scoundrels, and the reiterated declaration that they should kill him before they harmed a hair of the heads of either of the prisoners, he had nothing to say.

Henderson was reduced to a condition of absolute despair, for neither of the trio could think of any plan of rescue promising even the remotest prospect of success.

"Leave me, both of you," he at length exclaimed in desperation—"leave me to watch and to think out this matter alone; lie down and rest if you can for an hour or two, husband your strength as much as possible, for we shall have need of it all before sunrise"—he shuddered involuntarily as he uttered the last word—"and fear not, I will call you in good time."

The two men turned, and without a word retired below to their room, leaving the doctor to wrestle alone with the difficult question of what was his actual duty in this terrible strait.

Reader, do not mistake this man's character. No braver or more gallant Englishman—no nobler or stauncher friend—ever lived than he. Had he been an unmarried man, or had those two women and that helpless child, his daughter, been in a place of safety, he would have unhesitatingly accepted the hints which Manners and Nicholls had so repeatedly thrown out, and placing himself at their head, would have marched with a light heart against the Malays, and either have rescued the captives or have perished with them. But the odds against him and his companions were so great—a little over seven to one even now, after the losses already sustained by the enemy—that he felt he *dared* not indulge in any hope of success, especially as those odds would be so greatly increased by even *one* casualty on his side; and if failure ensued, what would be the result to them all, including the women and the child still safe in the shelter of the fort? It would not bear thinking about.

"God help me!" he cried in his despair. *"What* shall I do?"

"Ay, and why should not God help him?" was the thought which followed close upon the heels of his exclamation. And feeling that he had already too long neglected to seek the only counsel upon which he could safely rely, this simple-hearted, noble-minded gentleman went down upon his knees there and then, and laying the whole case before his Creator, humbly, yet fervently, sought for guidance and aid, for Christ's sake.

When he rose from his knees it was with a feeling of almost ecstatic relief, for—be it said with all reverence—he had cast his burden upon the Lord. He had sought for guidance and help; the one had been given him— for he had formed his resolution what to do; and the other he doubted not would be accorded to him in his time of need; there remained therefore nothing for him to do but to make his arrangements and then to carry them out.

He looked at his watch. Two o'clock, just four hours to sunrise; he had not much time to spare, for when the sun next rose. Gaunt and his child must be once more safe within the walls of the fort, or—well, that must not be thought of.

So taking one more keen glance around, to make quite sure that all was safe, Henderson went softly down the staircase leading to the courtyard, and quietly directed Manners and Nicholls to rejoin him at once upon the parapet. This done, he entered his own room. A lamp, turned low, was burning upon the table, and by its light he was just able to see that his little Lucille was sleeping calmly where he had laid her; but his wife was absent, he needed not to be told where she was. He stood for a moment looking with unspeakable fondness upon the sleeping child, and then bending softly over her, he pressed one long lingering kiss upon her forehead. As he did so she smiled in her sleep, her rosebud lips quivered a moment, and then he heard her whisper, "Dear Percy!" It was enough; had he felt the least lingering hesitation about the carrying out of his plan, that unconscious appeal made by his sleeping child would have effectually banished it, and dashing away the tears that rose to his eyes, the doctor quietly withdrew. There was a light burning in Mrs Gaunt's room; and as he passed the door on tiptoe and stealthily, as though he had been engaged upon some unlawful errand, he caught the low murmur of his wife's voice, and a stifled sob. That was another appeal not to be resisted; and without venturing to disturb the two mourning watchers—though he never before yearned so hungrily for a parting word with his wife, or a sight of her sweet face—he passed noiselessly on, and so regained the parapet, where Manners and Nicholls already awaited him. To them he fully unfolded his plan, minutely explaining not only his own but also their part in it; after which he gave them his final instructions, and then taking *both* of Gaunt's magazine rifles in his hand, and thrusting a brace of revolvers into his belt—having previously loaded each weapon most carefully with his own hands—he quietly lowered the outer ladder, cautioning his companions to draw it up again after him, and stepped briskly but noiselessly out through the long dew-laden grass in the direction of the ship-yard.

Chapter Nineteen
Doomed to die

The story told by little Lucille relative to the first appearance of the Malays was so graphic and accurate up to the point of Gaunt's capture, that little or no addition is needed to complete it. The shell-gatherers had been most successful in their quest, and returning to Fay Island laden with their delicate and beautiful spoils, were about half-way across the stream—which, it will be remembered, was of considerable width at the point where they would have to cross—when the proa suddenly hove in sight round a bend of the channel. There was only one possible explanation of the reason why Gaunt had not seen her in ample time to avoid capture, and that was that whilst he had been busy with the children on the eastern beach, the proa must have been approaching from the westward, which would cause her to be hidden from view by the intervening high land. By what means, however, her crew had discovered the entrance to the harbour must remain a mystery; probably it was the result of pure accident, for—as has already been mentioned—it was so artfully concealed that even Gaunt himself, when voyaging to and fro in the raft during the earlier period of his sojourn upon the island, had upon more than one occasion been puzzled to find it.

Be this as it may, the moment of the proa's arrival in the river was a most unfortunate one for the occupants of the punt, who were seen and chased by the Malays the moment that their vessel rounded the point. Gaunt at once saw that escape for himself as well as for the children was impossible; he was as near Fay Island as he was to the main, and in whichever direction he headed he must inevitably be overtaken before he could make good his retreat, and with his usual promptitude he at once decided to continue his course for the islet, hoping to be able to make a sufficiently long stand against the enemy to permit of the children gaining the safe refuge of the fort. He was hailed as soon as seen; but, of course, the only notice he took of this was to urge the clumsy, heavy punt with redoubled speed through the water. Finding him so contumacious, the Malays then fired upon him several times, and succeeded in slightly wounding him in the head. As the proa advanced further up the stream, and drew closer and closer still in under the lee of the high land, the wind grew light and shy with her, and then, perhaps fearing that after all their prey might escape them, the crew hastily launched a boat and gave chase in her. But for that unlucky wound in the head it is possible that Gaunt might have succeeded in his plucky effort; but though the bullet inflicted but little actual damage the blow stunned and dazed him, so that for a minute or two he scarcely knew where he was or what he was doing. Trifling as was the amount of time thus lost it was sufficient to ruin what little chance he originally had; for when the punt at length grounded with a shock on the sandy beach of the creek the Malays were scarcely a dozen yards astern of her, and Gaunt had only just time to lift the youngsters out on the sand, to give the hasty injunction, "Run away home, children, as fast as ever you can," and to seize an oar in self-defence, when the enemy—nine of them—were upon him. Of course, armed as he was with no better weapon than a clumsy oar, he had no chance whatever against such overwhelming odds, and though he managed to fell three of his antagonists the fight had not lasted two minutes before his arms were pinioned from behind, his feet tripped from under him, and himself made a prisoner. He was quickly rolled over on his face and his arms securely lashed behind him, when, this being satisfactorily accomplished, his captors raised him to his feet, and, conducting him to a tree, firmly bound him to its trunk. The idea then seemed to occur to the Malays that possibly the children might not yet be beyond the reach of capture, for two of them set off at a run in pursuit along the path leading to the fort. Gaunt guessed only too surely at the object of this sudden and hurried departure, and his heart sank with dismal apprehension as he thought of the distance those little feet would have to traverse ere the refuge of the fort could be won, of their liability to become fagged and to lag upon the way, and of the fleetness of foot displayed by their cruel pursuers when starting upon their relentless errand. And when, from the prolonged absence of the pursuers, apprehension was beginning to yield to a hope that the children were safe, he was plunged into the bitterest distress by the reappearance of one of the miscreants, roughly and cruelly dragging along by the arm his darling and only son, Percy; the poor child crying bitterly with terror and the ruffianly usage to which he was being subjected. Upon seeing his father the little fellow managed, by a sudden and unexpected effort, to break away from his captor, and, running up to Gaunt, embraced him, crying:

"Oh, father, make that cruel man leave me alone; he has been whipping me and twisting my arm and hurting it so much that I can scarcely use it. Oh, don't let him touch me again, father," as he saw the Malay approaching him with a scowl of hideous malignity upon his already sufficiently ugly features.

"My darling boy, I cannot help you," groaned Gaunt. "Would to God that I could! but you see they have bound me to this tree so that I cannot move. Listen, Percy dear; we can do nothing at present but submit to these men, who have us in their power, so you must just let them do what they will with you, my precious one; go with the man very quietly, and then perhaps he will not ill-treat you any more."

"*Must* I, father?" asked the little fellow tearfully, and looking at his father in vague surprise at so seemingly heartless a command.

"Yes, dear boy; yes. It is for your own good that I tell you to do this," answered Gaunt brokenly, for he keenly felt the unspoken reproach which he saw in the child's eyes as the little fellow forlornly turned away and with a piteous sob quietly surrendered himself to the brute, who now again with ruffianly violence seized upon his helpless victim.

"Oh, don't! you hurt me so," the poor little fellow suddenly screamed out; and the father's heart swelled almost to bursting with impotent fury as he saw the cruel clutch with which the wretch was digging his long thin sinewy fingers into the tender flesh of the boy's shoulder as he forced him toward an adjoining tree, to which he forthwith proceeded to lash him, drawing the cord so tightly round the slender wrists that the little fellow fairly screamed and writhed with the intolerable pain.

"Curse you!" yelled Gaunt, now fairly stung to madness and foaming at the mouth with fury; "curse you, fiend that you are!" And as he hurled forth words of rage and defiance he tugged and strained with such superhuman strength upon his bonds that the stout rope fairly cracked whilst it cut into the flesh of his wrists down to the bone. But the lashing was too strong to yield to even his frenzied efforts, apart from the fact that, with his arms lashed behind him, he had no opportunity to exert his strength effectively, and at length, completely exhausted, he was fain to desist, to the undisguised delight of a little knot of the Malays who had gathered round and were keenly enjoying the scene. So much pleasure, indeed, did they derive from it that they said something to little Percy's tormentor which was evidently an incitement of him to continue his ill-treatment of the child, for the fellow, with an acquiescent grin, had no sooner finished his task of lashing the little fellow to the tree—a task which he performed with the utmost deliberation and gusto—than he retired a pace or two, contemplating the helplessness of his little victim with malignant satisfaction, and then, with a glance toward Gaunt and a few laughing words to his companions, he stepped forward and dealt the poor child a savage blow upon the mouth with his clenched fist—so cruel a blow that it extorted another piercing scream of pain and terror from the sufferer and caused his quivering lips to stream with blood.

Gaunt said nothing this time, nor did he renew his worse than useless efforts to burst his bonds, but he directed toward the fellow a look of such deadly ferocity that the wretch actually quailed under it, and seemed glad enough to slink away into the background under cover of an order which another Malay, apparently one of the officers of the proa, now stepped forward and gave him. Possibly the order given may have been to desist from further ill-treatment of the child, for the new-comer next said something to the group of onlookers which caused them also to retire, with many a backward glance of animosity at Gaunt—which he returned with interest; and, these dismissed, the officer, if such he was, looked at the sobbing child's bonds and, with a muttered word or two, proceeded to loosen them sufficiently to relieve the little fellow from the cruel suffering they had caused him—a proceeding which won for him a look of unspeakable gratitude from Gaunt which seemed to be not wholly unappreciated.

The loosening of his bonds afforded the poor child so much relief that he now felt almost comfortable, comparatively speaking; and, exhausted with the pain and terror he had already endured, he soon sank into a kind of stupor, which, if it did not amount to actual insensibility, approached it so nearly as to afford the poor little fellow at least a temporary forgetfulness of his situation and surroundings. Gaunt, speaking quietly once or twice to him without obtaining a reply, at once saw with intense satisfaction the state his child had fallen into; and to such a state of despair had he now been brought that he would have been positively happy could he have been assured that his darling boy was dead and beyond the reach of further suffering. For as he now had leisure to reflect, the future, so far as they two were concerned, was without a single ray of hope to brighten it. He knew, of course, that those staunch comrades of his at the fort would not abandon him and his child to the mercy of the Malays without making some attempt at a rescue; but there were only three of them, and what could three men, however brave, do against such overwhelming odds unless acting upon the defensive and behind stone walls? *There*, indeed, but not in the open field, he had some hopes for them, and there he fully expected they would all very shortly have their hands full, for he momentarily expected to see the whole body of the Malays—except, of course, a man or two to guard himself and his boy—move off to the attack of the fort. And if the attack failed, as he hoped and believed it would, the Malay loss would doubtless be very heavy; and he had heard quite enough of their vindictive nature to feel assured they would take their revenge upon him and Percy. Yes, the more he thought about it the more convinced did he become that it was their doom to die. "Well," he murmured, "God's will be done!" It was best, perhaps, that his child should die now, young and innocent as he was; and as for himself, if he could but be satisfied that the little fellow's death was quick and easy, he cared not how soon he followed him.

But if this was to be the end of the matter so far as they two were concerned, there was a task before him to which he must at once give his best attention—the task of preparing his little son for the awful ordeal before him. To paint Death in colours so attractive as that they should rob the grim king of his terrors and make him welcome, was, he felt, a task of no ordinary difficulty; and coupled with this was the fact that the poor child had been dreadfully terrified already. How was this task to be accomplished—how even begun?

As he cogitated painfully over this problem he saw a party of twelve Malays detach themselves from the rest and move off in the direction of the fort. Then after a considerable interval came the sounds of firing, followed some twenty minutes later by the return of four only out of the twelve. A sickening fear came over him at first that those in the fort had succumbed to the attack, and that the eight absentees were remaining behind in charge of the prisoners. But a little reflection led him to believe that, had such been the case, the prisoners would have been brought in triumph to the Malay camp. Could it be possible, then, he asked himself, that the missing eight had fallen in the attack? It might be so. The bearing of the four who had returned was anything but triumphant; and then there was a great deal of excited talk and gesticulation on their part, seemingly in the nature of an explanation, and more excited talk among the others, followed, after a long and stormy debate, by the preparation and despatch of the letter, the delivery of which we witnessed in the preceding chapter. This last act of the Malays completely reassured Gaunt as to the safety of the fort and its inmates, but it also confirmed him in his belief that his own fate and that of his child was sealed.

The messenger soon returned, a few questions were put to them and answered; a couple of sentries were posted with loaded muskets at the entrance to the bush-path leading to the fort; a man was detailed to keep watch upon the two prisoners; the watch-fire was bountifully replenished with brushwood; and then the camp sank gradually into a state of repose.

Then again the question arose in Gaunt's mind. In what manner could he best set about the task of preparing his child to meet death unflinchingly? Whilst he was painfully grappling with the problem Percy himself afforded his father an opening of which the latter at once gladly availed himself. Stirring uneasily, and with a sobbing sigh seeming to recover his recollection of where he was and what had happened to him, the little fellow looked up and asked shudderingly:

"What will the Malays do to us, father?—will they kill us?"

"That is as God wills, dear boy," answered Gaunt with an affected cheerfulness which he was very far from feeling.

"They may or they may not, I cannot tell. But if they do you will not be sorry to die with father, will you?"

"I—I—don't know," answered the little fellow, looking terrified. "Will it hurt us?"

"Oh, no," answered Gaunt, "not at all—nothing, that is, worth thinking or troubling about. It will *very* soon be over; and then—*then*, dear boy, when we come to ourselves again, we shall find that, hand in hand, you know, we are going up, and up, and up, higher and higher, toward heaven. And very soon we shall see the glorious light shining upon the jewelled walls of the heavenly city, the New Jerusalem. And as we draw near we shall see the pearly gates unfold to admit us, and God's holy angels coming to meet us, clad in their white robes. And we shall hear the first sweet sounds of the celestial music. And as we enter in at the gates we shall meet all those dear ones who have gone before us. Dear grandpa, whom you never saw, my precious one, but about whom, you know, I have told you so many pretty stories—he will be there to welcome us; and—"

"Oh, that *will* be nice!" exclaimed the child with kindling eyes. He meditated for a moment, and then, looking up, he asked eagerly: "When are we going, father?"

"Oh, very soon now, dear," answered Gaunt, "*very* soon—perhaps in two or three hours' time. We can wait patiently until then, can we not?"

"Yes," answered Percy in a perfectly contented tone of voice. And the father was inwardly congratulating himself upon the ease with which his difficult task had been accomplished—though he of course felt that it would be absolutely necessary to keep the child in that frame of mind by constant conversation until the arrival of the supreme moment—when the little fellow looked up and with sudden anxiety asked:

"And will mother be there too?"

How little the poor child knew what poignant anguish he inflicted upon his father by asking this innocent and perfectly natural question! Gaunt would have given worlds, had he possessed them, for the priceless privilege of saying farewell to his idolised wife; but he knew it could not be—it was impossible. And the child had still to be thought of, still to be cheered and encouraged and strengthened to meet death with a smiling face—*nothing* must be allowed to interfere with that; so, choking back his anguish as best he could, the father answered:

"Well—no, dear boy; I scarcely think she will be there quite so early as ourselves. But she will not be long in following us. When she finds that we are gone she will be anxious to come, too; and she will not delay for one unnecessary moment, you may depend upon it."

"Oh, father!" exclaimed the poor little fellow in sudden distress, "let us not go without mother; it will be so lonely for her to be down here all by herself. Let us wait for her and all go together; it will be ever so much nicer. I don't want to go without her, father. I would rather not go without mother, if you please." And the poor little fellow began to cry piteously.

Here was a catastrophe! The fabric of joyous anticipation which the father had been painfully building up within his child's breast had collapsed completely, and in a moment, when he found that they were "going without mother!" Gaunt argued and reasoned with the little fellow for a full half-hour, taxing his ingenuity to its utmost extent to recover the advantage he had lost, but it was all unavailing; to this poor child it seemed that heaven itself could not be heaven "without mother." His father was fast giving way to despair when a brilliant idea shot through the childish brain.

"Father," he exclaimed suddenly, looking up with renewed hope, "cannot God make the Malays not kill us?"

"Certainly He can, if He chooses," was the ready answer.

"Then let us ask Him," was the triumphant rejoinder. "I am quite sure He will let us wait and go all together if we tell Him we would rather."

What could the father do but acquiesce in a request founded upon such perfect trust in the love and mercy of the Almighty? Indeed, it was no sooner made than he wondered how it was that he had been so utterly faithless as never to have thought of it himself. So he forthwith offered up, audibly, just such a petition as the child had suggested, taking care to clothe it in language which the little fellow could fully comprehend; and, though it must be admitted that the prayer was begun more to satisfy the child than from any feeling or belief that it would be answered, yet, as Gaunt proceeded, with all the earnestness of which he was capable, hope revived in his heart, and his conscience began to rebuke him for his practical infidelity.

The prayer concluded, Percy expressed himself as perfectly happy and satisfied; but it distressed his father not a little to find that the child's thoughts now persistently turned in a direction precisely opposite to that in which he wished them to incline; over and over and over again did Gaunt strive to rekindle the little fellow's enthusiasm about heaven, but it would not do; life, not death, was what the child was now looking forward to; and all his father's most earnest exhortations failed to elicit from him anything beyond the question:

"When do you think they will come and set us free, father?"

"I do not know that they *will* set us free, dear boy; it may not be God's will," was the substance of Gaunt's reply to this oft-repeated question; at which the little fellow would look at his father in surprise and retort:

"But, father, you used to tell me that God is *always* pleased to hear and answer the prayers of little children!"

In short, the child at length got the better of the man in this curious theological discussion, and Gaunt was finally obliged to give in.

"He is right," the father at length admitted to himself, "and I am wrong. After striving with all my might during the whole of his brief little life to inculcate in him an absolute belief in the unalterable truth of God's promises, why should I now allow the weakness of my own faith to undermine his? My child is in the hands of a merciful God; there will I leave him."

And so, when, from time to time, after that, the little fellow repeated his question of "When do you think they will come and set us free, father?" Gaunt would reply hopefully:

"Oh, very soon now, I should think, dear boy; very soon."

The long, weary, trying night was wearing to its close. The moon hung low in the western sky; the horizon to the eastward was paling from violet-black to pearly-grey; and the stars in that quarter were beginning to lose their lustre. The air, which during the earlier hours of the night had been oppressively sultry, now came cool and refreshing to the fevered brows of the anxious watchers; the insects had subdued their irritating din, as is their wont toward the dawn; the watch-fire had smouldered down to a heap of grey, feathery, faintly-glowing ashes; the two sentinels at the entrance of the bush-path had ceased their alert pacing to and fro, and, having grounded their muskets, were now drooping wearily upon them with their hands crossed over the top of the barrels; whilst the Malay who had been detailed to watch the prisoners, having some half a dozen times during the earlier hours of the night tested their bonds and satisfied himself of their perfect security, was now seated on the ground before his charges, with his ringers interlocked across his knees and his head bowed forward, manifestly napping. The weariness of the long night had told upon both the prisoners; their conversation had first languished and then ceased altogether; but now the cool, fresh, sweet-smelling breeze had aroused them both, Gaunt first, and the poor, tired-out, suffering child soon afterwards; and whilst the first was looking abroad over the tree-tops at the brightening sky to the eastward and thinking that *now*, surely, their fate must be drawing very nigh, the little fellow by his side stirred uneasily, roused himself, and once more put the stereotyped question:

"*Now*, father, when do you think they will come and set us free?"

Gaunt, with their probable fate now apparently so near at hand, was debating within himself what answer to return, when his attention was arrested by a curious vibrating movement of his bonds, as though they were being tampered with from behind the tree to which he was bound; and ere he could collect his faculties sufficiently to even ask himself what it meant, a low whisper from behind him caught his ear:

"Hush! it is I—Henderson!"

And at the same instant the ropes which bound him suddenly slackened about his limbs and disappeared behind him. Then an arm appeared round the bole of the tree, and Gaunt felt the cold barrel of a rifle being thrust into his hand, whilst the voice again whispered:

"Your own repeater fully loaded. Now to loose poor little Percy."

Then Gaunt turned to his child—how white and haggard the dear little fellow looked in the pallid light of the dawn—and, with a heart brimful of gratitude to God for His priceless gift of restored freedom, said, in reply to his question:

"*Very* soon, now, my precious darling—now, *at once*, in fact. But Percy, dear boy, take care that you do not move or cry out when you feel the rope loosening; stand perfectly still and quiet, my son, until I tell you what to do."

The little fellow looked eagerly up into his father's face, and whispered, "Yes, father." And then Gaunt saw his look of surprise as he felt Henderson's hand releasing him. The bonds fell away; the child was free; and presently Gaunt saw a shadowy figure bend forward and whisper in the little fellow's ear. There was a start, a faint cry of rapture, the little arms were flung lovingly round the neck of the bending figure, and Gaunt caught the murmured words:

"Thank you, dear doctor, oh, *thank you*!" followed by the soft sound of a kiss.

But that childish involuntary cry of delight, faint as it was, had caught the quick ear of the dozing guard; the fellow raised his head, and, seeing that something was wrong—though he was still too drowsy to distinguish what it was—scrambled to his feet and advanced toward Gaunt. Up to that moment the engineer had not moved; he was waiting for the blood to circulate once more in his cramped limbs, and also for Henderson to give him the cue for their next movement. He remained perfectly still until the Malay had approached within arm's-length of him, and then, with a single lightning-like blow of his fist fair between the eyes, he dropped the fellow senseless upon the grass at his feet.

Then, swift as light, he glided behind the tree, where Henderson stood with Percy in his arms, and, convulsively gripping the other's outstretched hand, he murmured:

"A thousand thanks, old fellow! Now, which way are we to go?"

"I arranged for Manners and Nicholls to join us in the bush-path yonder; never dreaming that those two men would be posted there," whispered Henderson in return.

"Well, come along, then," cheerily observed Gaunt. "Never trouble about the Malays; it is their misfortune that they happen to be in our way. We must shoot them down if they offer to oppose our passage—ha! we shall be *compelled* to fight whether we will or not; that fellow whom I knocked down is reviving, and he will raise the alarm before we have gone a dozen feet. Give me the child, my arms are still benumbed and scarcely fit to hold a rifle, but I can carry him. So, that is it"—as Henderson handed over little Percy—"now let us make a run for it."

Therewith the two friends started at top speed for the entrance of the bush-path, running straight toward the two Malay sentinels. No sooner, however, did they appear in the open than a cry was raised, and in an instant the whole camp was on the alert, some of the Malays running to intercept the fugitives whilst others hurriedly sprang for their muskets and opened a wild fusillade upon them. The two sentinels faced about, and seeing the white men running at once raised their weapons to their shoulders.

"Halt!" cried Gaunt, setting Percy down on the ground and facing about toward their pursuers. "Drop those two sentries, Henderson, for Heaven's sake! I will deal with the others!"

No sooner said than done. Henderson pulled up at once and, coolly receiving the fire of the two Malays—which, however, owing to their being hurried, proved harmless—deliberately covered and dropped them, one after the other.

"Are they down?" demanded Gaunt, as he also knocked over the leader of the pursuing party.

"Yes, both down!" was the response.

"Then, on again!" exclaimed the engineer, snatching up his frightened child and regaining Henderson's side. As they ran, Henderson placed a whistle between his lips and blew a single short piercing call upon it. "That will soon bring the other two to our help," he gasped.

They were by this time within a hundred feet of the bush-path; but the light-heeled Malays were close behind them. The time for decisive action had arrived. Seeing this, Gaunt once more placed his child on the ground and said:

"Now run home as fast as you can, dear boy, and tell mother that the doctor and I hope to be with her in a quarter of an hour."

Then, as the little fellow made off at top speed, the father added: "Thank God, *his* retreat is secured if we can hold out for ten minutes. Now, Henderson, true and trusty comrade, let us make a stand here and, shoulder to shoulder, show these rascals how Englishmen can fight."

So, without another word, the two friends turned and stood at bay, finding time to bring down two more of their foes by a couple of lucky snap-shots before they were closed with.

And then began a battle, fierce and grim—sixteen Malays to two Englishmen! Luckily for the smaller party the Malays had, at the outset of the disturbance, emptied their pieces ineffectually, and had found no time to reload them, whilst Henderson had provided himself, in addition to the two repeating rifles, with a brace of loaded six-chambered revolvers, one of which he now handed to Gaunt. With these and their clubbed rifles the two men fought so desperately, that not only were the Malays effectually checked in their attempt at an outflanking movement, but actually foiled in their intention to bear down the two men by sheer force of numbers and brute strength. Swinging their rifles club-wise with one hand and firing their revolvers with the other whenever they saw a chance of making a shot tell, the Englishmen wrought such terrible execution that at length the Malays drew back confounded. At this moment a cheer was heard close at hand, and in another instant up dashed Manners and Nicholls, breathless with hard running, and placed themselves one on each side of their two countrymen.

"*Now* let us give them a volley!" cried Gaunt—who, his blood fairly boiling at the recollection of the past night, had been fighting like a demon—and, at the word, up went the four rifles to the "present."

"Choose each his man!" ordered the inexorable engineer: and then out rang the four pieces, leaving three foes the less to deal with. Hark! what was that? Not an echo of the rifle-shots, surely; no, it was the *boom* of a distant gun, unless the ears of all strangely deceived them. Whatever it was, the Malays also heard the sound, and, looking for an instant in consternation at each other, wavered, turned, and fled.

"Hurrah!" cried Gaunt exultantly, "rescue is at hand. After the rascals, and give them a lesson they will never forget!"

It was, perhaps, an imprudent thing to do, but away after the flying foe went the four men, popping away with their revolvers, and so severely galling the Malays that *sauve qui peut* quickly became the word with the latter, who now evidently thought of nothing but how to reach their boats alive. One in his frantic haste stumbled and fell, revealing his features to Gaunt as he did so. It was the wretch who had so cruelly ill-treated little Percy on the night before. With a couple of bounds the engineer was upon him. Wresting the creese from the fellow's hand, Gaunt seized him by the collar and dragged him along the ground, writhing, to a clump of canes growing close at hand. With his foot on the man's neck to keep him down, the engineer then cut with the creese a stout, pliant cane, lifted the wretch to his feet by main strength, and, dropping his weapons to the ground and still retaining his grip upon the fellow's collar, deliberately thrashed him until the cane was split to ribbons and the clothes literally cut from his back, finally dismissing him with a kick which—apart from the thrashing—it is safe to say, that Malay will never forget so long as his life shall last. The unfortunate wretch hobbled off with quite remarkable celerity—considering that every bone in his body must have been aching—eager to overtake his comrades, whose "way" had been very materially "freshened" not only by the heat with which they were pursued but also by the booming of the guns in the offing. But he was too late. When he reached the beach the boats had shoved off; so, rather than remain where he was, the fellow unhesitatingly plunged into the stream and swam off to the proa, reaching her just in time to be hauled up over the side as, with slipped cable and hastily-hoisted sail, the craft paid off and gathered way on her road out to sea.

Gaunt followed more leisurely, for, in common with his three friends, he had suffered somewhat in the *mêlée*—though, fortunately, none of them were seriously hurt—and he reached the cove just in time to witness the hasty departure of the proa. He seized this, the first opportunity which had presented itself, to heartily thank his companions for their gallant rescue of himself and his child, inquired anxiously after the safety and welfare of the little Lucille, and then said:

"I have been wondering what can be the meaning of that firing in the offing. I cannot help thinking it is intended as a signal of some kind to *us*, and, assuming that to be the case, I can only account for it upon the pleasant supposition that Captain Blyth, instead of perishing in the hurricane as we feared, must have in some miraculous manner escaped; and that it is he who is now outside, on board a rescue ship, come to take us all off the island. I think it would be well if you, Manners, were to take the punt, and, with Nicholls, go out as far as the harbour's mouth to reconnoitre, taking care not to show yourselves until you are quite certain that the craft is a friendly one."

The two men named eagerly adopted the suggestion, and a minute later were afloat and pulling rapidly down stream. As soon as they were fairly off Gaunt turned to Henderson and said:

"And now, my dear fellow, I think I will walk as far as the fort to exchange a word or two with Ida, and assure them all of our safety; and then I will rejoin you here to await the tidings from outside."

Meanwhile Manners and Nicholls, pushing off into the strength of the current, sped rapidly toward the two headlands which guarded the harbour's mouth; arriving at which they landed, hauled the punt up on the beach, and made their way through the bushes to a point from which, themselves unseen, they could get a clear view of the open sea outside.

And then what an exhilarating sight met their delighted eyes. A large full-rigged ship lay in the offing, about a mile distant, hove-to under her three topsails, spanker, and jib. At first they took her for a corvette, her gear being all fitted in regular man-o'-war fashion; but this mistake was instantly corrected upon their noticing that she flew the *red* ensign from her gaff, in addition to which she showed a burgee with a long name on it at her main-royal mast-head, and the *pilot-jack* at the fore. By the greatest good luck Manners happened to have in his pocket a small telescope which he had a trick of always carrying about with him, and this he quickly brought to bear upon the stranger. Watching him eagerly, Nicholls observed him change colour; a perplexed expression passed over his face, his hand trembled. For two long minutes he remained steadfastly peering through the telescope; then he suddenly closed it with a snap, and exclaimed excitedly:

"Away to the punt and pull out to sea for your life, Nicholls. It is the dear old *Cloud*, as I am a living sinner! and Miss Stanhope is on the poop watching the island through the ship's glass. There goes another gun!"

Chapter Twenty
A daring plan successfully executed

In accordance with Williams' plans the *Flying Cloud's* cargo was in due time discharged and warehoused on shore in the newly-built stores; the ship herself stripped, hove down, scrubbed, and re-painted from her keel up; her interior re-arranged—particularly the forecastle, which was extended sufficiently to accommodate a hundred men; the upper spars replaced by new ones, somewhat higher in the hoist, cut on the island; her canvas altered to fit the new spars, skysails being abolished as causing more trouble than they were worth; the running-gear re-arranged; the deck-houses, with the exception of the poop, swept away; the bulwarks strengthened and pierced; the breech-loading guns, twelve in number, mounted on carriages and placed in position; and, generally, the ship made to look as much like a man-of-war as possible, though she as much resembled the old-fashioned sailing sloop which then still performed duty on our more distant stations as a swan does a goose, her sailing powers far exceeding those of the fastest of them, whilst Williams' metamorphosis of her only had the effect of imparting to her an extremely rakish and wicked appearance.

In due time—and not a very long time either, taking into consideration the amount of work done—the ship was once more ready for sea; and ballasted carefully down to her very best sailing trim, she left Refuge Harbour for an extended piratical cruise. It is not necessary to describe in detail where she went, or the various adventures met with by her crew; suffice it to say that the cruise proved wonderfully successful, several very valuable prizes being taken—no less than three being vessels with large amounts of specie on board. When Williams first mooted to the crew his proposal to seize the ship and convert her into a pirate, he met the strongest objection raised by the more scrupulous of the men by asserting that he had a plan whereby all bloodshed could be avoided; this plan being no less than to practically enslave such portions of the crews of the prospective prizes as refused to become pirates, and to confine them at Refuge Harbour, there to perform the large amount of work necessary to the complete furtherance of Williams' ambitious schemes. But, as may be supposed, this plan, when put to a practical test, failed. Capture was not in all cases tamely submitted to—resistance was offered, blood was shed in the conflict. And when this had once happened all scruples vanished, and the further step of murdering such prisoners as proved contumacious or were inconvenient to keep was an easy one; the worst passions of the men asserted themselves, and breaking loose from all restraint speedily converted their possessors into very demons.

Miss Stanhope was daily and hourly in peril during the latter part of that dreadful cruise. Still, thanks to the compact with Ned and the hold which he still had upon the crew, the unhappy girl had so far escaped direct threats and open insult. But toward the end of the cruise matters had reached such a stage that she foresaw the absolute necessity for effecting her escape immediately upon the arrival of the ship again at Refuge Harbour. The state of horror and terror into which she was continually thrown was such that death itself seemed preferable to a further continuance of such a life as she was then living.

At length the ship once more glided into the secure haven of Refuge Harbour, and about five o'clock in the evening let go her anchor. The sails were furled anyhow—discipline having by this time grown very lax on board the *Flying Cloud* notwithstanding all Williams' efforts to maintain it—and then the men, without going through the formality of asking leave, lowered the boats and went ashore in a body; Sibylla, Ned, and Williams being left to follow, if they chose, in the dinghy, which they did, the steward being ordered to remain on board for the night as anchor watch.

When the dinghy reached the shore its occupants discovered that the ship's crew—among whom were several new hands who had joined from the prizes—had already seized a cask of spirits, and were evidently bent upon a carouse in celebration of the successful completion of their first cruise. They were then only rough and noisy, the liquor not having had time to operate; but an hour later the entire band, with a very few exceptions, had become converted into a howling mob of drunken desperadoes, ripe and eager for any species of ruffianism which might suggest itself. Sibylla was at this time busy putting matters to rights in the hut which Ned had caused to be erected on their previous visit to the island, and Ned was busy in the same way in his tent when Williams, happening to pass by, looked in at the latter.

"Hark ye, youngster," he gruffly remarked, "you and the young woman had better keep well out of sight to-night, for if either of you are seen, mischief may come of it; and whilst those beasts up there are in their present condition neither I nor anybody else could help you. The rascals are mad drunk, and hungry for mischief. They positively *laughed* at me just now when I tried to bring them to something like order! But if I don't make them smart for it to-morrow when we start to overhaul the rigging, call me a Dutchman."

Coupled with what he had already seen and heard, this warning of Williams' so seriously impressed Ned that he went to Sibylla's door and called to her to put on her hat and join him outside. As soon as she appeared Ned said:

"Look here, Miss Stanhope, Williams has just been here to tell me that the men up there are mad with drink and—as he phrased it—*hungry* for mischief. Judging from the frightful noise and commotion among them I should say he is right, and I have called you out to tell you that I think it will be best for you and me to return on board the ship; the steward is there, you know, and he and I can keep the anchor watch between us, whilst you take your rest as usual in your own cabin."

Sibylla had long ago come to the conclusion that she could do no better than follow poor Captain Blyth's advice and unreservedly follow Ned's instructions, so she at once announced her readiness to do whatever he thought best. Upon this Ned, believing that no time was to be lost, at once extinguished the lights and, locking the door, placed the key in his pocket; after which, taking a somewhat circuitous route in order to avoid attracting attention, he and Miss Stanhope made their way down to the spot where they had left the dinghy.

The boat was still there, with her oars and rowlocks in her just as she had been left, so handing his companion in and instructing her to sit steady, Ned placed his shoulder against the stem of the boat, and with a powerful shove sent her stern-foremost off the beach, springing in over the bows as he did so. There was a bright moon, nearly full, riding high in the sky, and Ned was rather apprehensive that his movements might attract attention and provoke pursuit. But the men had, for some reason or other, kindled a large fire, round which they were holding their carouse, and Damerell could only hope that the brilliant blaze would dazzle their eyes, and blind them to everything beyond the circle of its influence. Perhaps it did so, for when they reached the ship there was no sign of pursuit.

Ned had never allowed the idea of escape to be absent from his thoughts for a single day since the memorable one upon which the ship had first been seized; but, fertile as he usually was in resource, he had never been able to think of anything practicable except that of seeking a refuge in the treasure-cave; and this scheme was open to so many serious objections that he and Sibylla had agreed together that it must not be adopted except as a very last resource. Now, however, as the dinghy approached the ship and Ned gazed admiringly aloft at the tall graceful spars and complicated network of rigging, and reflected that at that moment the beautiful fabric was in charge of only one man—and that man friendly to him, as he had long ago ascertained—a daring idea suddenly took possession of him; and, without giving himself time to reflect, he there and then resolved upon its execution.

The wind was blowing moderately fresh from the north-west; but so secure was the anchorage and so good the holding-ground that, on arriving on board, Ned was not at all surprised to find that the steward, instead of keeping watch, had gone below and turned in, trusting to luck that, once on shore, nobody would dream of going off again to the ship that night. This arrangement, however, though it might be perfectly satisfactory to the steward, by no means suited Ned, who at once went below and unceremoniously routed the poor man out of his berth.

"Price," said he, "I have something of the utmost importance to say to you. I have noticed that in the course of conversation, when nobody else has been present, you have frequently gone out of your way to remind me that I am an unwilling member of the piratical crew in the midst of which we find ourselves, and you have also dropped sundry hints that if ever I happen to hit upon a way of escape you will be more than pleased to accompany me. Now, I want to know exactly what you have meant by this."

"Just exactly what I have said, Mr Damerell—or rather what *you* have just said," answered Price. "I joined the party because I had no fancy for being left to die on a desert island, like those unfortunate passengers or the poor skipper and Mr Manners; but I didn't then know what was before me, sir. I am a peaceable man, I am, and though I've had no hand in any of the bloodshed that has occurred since we sailed from here, I know that murder has been committed, and I want to separate myself from the murderers. If I could I would have prevented the mutiny in the first place; but I never knew that anything serious was intended—"

"Well, never mind about that just now," interrupted Ned; "the present question is this. If I happened to have formed a plan of escape—a plan, we will say, involving a considerable amount of risk and a great deal of hard work, would you be willing to join me in it?"

"Would I? Only try me, Mr Damerell—try me, sir! Why, there is *no* risk, *no* labour I would not willingly face for a good chance to escape from that pack of yelling savages over yonder. Why, what are they doing now, sir? Blest if it doesn't look as though they had been and set fire to the hut, sir!"

Ned ran into the saloon and brought the glass on deck.

"*They have!*" he exclaimed, looking through the instrument at a bright blaze which was leaping up among the trees on shore. "Well, never mind," he continued; "it does not matter, for I intend attempting an escape from them to-night—now, at once—and glad enough shall I be to have your assistance. I intend nothing less than to run off with the ship; so—"

"To run off with the ship?" echoed Price. "Oh, Mr Damerell, we can never do that, sir—"

"I shall *try*, at all events," interrupted Ned. "So whilst I slip out and cast loose the jib, do you go below to the boatswain's locker and bring me from thence a cold chisel and a good heavy hammer."

Without further parley, Price did as he was bidden, and very soon he and Ned were busy knocking out the pin from the shackle in the cable which happened to be nearest the hawse-pipe. The job occupied them fully a quarter of an hour, for the pin was rusted-in; but at length out it came, and in another minute away went the end of the cable out through the hawse-pipe and into the water with a loud rattle and a splash.

"So far, so good," said Ned. "Now, Price, I want you to take the glass and keep a sharp watch upon the shore. The ship is now adrift, and driving slowly stern-foremost toward the outer basin. So long as we see no sign of alarm from the people on shore I shall let her drive; that will increase our chances of a good start. But the moment you see any indication of an attempt to launch a boat give me the word; and we must then get the jib on the ship and put her head round. There is a fine breeze blowing, and if we can only get outside the heads without being overtaken, I have no fears whatever."

So saying, Ned ran aft and placed himself at the wheel, which he manipulated in such a way as to keep the ship head to wind with her bows pointing toward the shore, thus keeping up the appearance that she was still riding to her anchor. Price meanwhile posted himself on the forecastle, and kept the telescope levelled at the shore.

For some time all went well. The ship, under the influence of the fresh breeze, which effected her with increasing power as she lengthened her distance from the land, drove steadily astern; and still no warning word came from Price. At length, however, when she had drifted about a mile, and had arrived within about a mile and three-quarters of the contracted channel between the north and south bluffs which divided the inner from the outer basin, the steward cried out:

"They are after us, Mr Damerell; I can see the flash of oars in the moonlight!"

"All right!" answered Ned, sending the wheel hard over with a spin, and leaving it to rush forward. "Now, Price, aft with the starboard jib-sheets, and belay them—not too flat, man; let them flow a bit—so, that's well! Now tail on here to the halliards with me and let us set the sail. Up with it! that's your sort! Now take it under the belaying-pin and let me browse it up. Yo-ho; ho-hip; ho-ho! Belay that! Now, the main-topmast staysail. Let go the down-haul; that is it, that rope you have your hand on—cast it off! That's right. Here are the sheets; hook the clips into that ring-bolt there close to the second gun. That is all right. Now take a turn with the running part round that cleat! Capital! Now wait a moment."

The ship was by this time broadside-on to the wind and gathering headway under the powerful influence of the jib, necessitating a hand at the wheel. Ned therefore ran aft, and, summoning the astonished Sibylla from her cabin, where she was making her preparations for passing another night on board, he sent her to the wheel, with instructions how to act, but concealing from her for the present the fact that they were pursued. Most fortunately for the runaways, the young lady was by this time quite a practised helmsman—or *helmswoman* rather. She could not only steer straight, but she also knew the difference between port and starboard, and understood in which direction to turn the wheel upon receiving either of those mystic words of command. She consequently now proved a most useful auxiliary, and left Ned at full liberty to devote himself to the toilsome task of getting canvas upon the ship.

With the aid of the winch the two men succeeded in getting the main-topmast staysail set, after which they hauled out the spanker. They were now running for the passage between the two bluffs, with the wind over their starboard quarter, the ship in her best possible sailing trim going through the water at a speed of nearly three knots. This, however, was not fast enough to suit Ned, for though they had secured a capital start, and he conjectured that the pursuers were too thoroughly intoxicated to be capable of pulling a boat at any very great speed, he knew that at the south-western extremity of the outer basin they would reach the most difficult part of their navigation. This consisted of a channel only half a mile in width by about a mile and a quarter in length, bending to the south-east, where the ship would be almost completely becalmed under the high land. And it was here, if anywhere, that he expected to be overtaken. So, without wasting time to ascertain the whereabouts of the pursuing boat, he hurried aloft and cast off the lashing from the main-topgallant-staysail, and, sending the sheets down on deck, descended and helped Price to set the sail. He now had as much canvas upon the ship as he believed he and the steward could conveniently manage for the present. He was, therefore, compelled to content himself with making a tour of the decks and so trimming the sheets as that the different sails set should draw to the utmost advantage. Then, and not until then, did he allow himself leisure to take a peep through the glass at what was going on astern. The sight which met his eyes was by no means reassuring, for he now saw that there were no less than *three* boats in pursuit, the foremost of which—one of the gigs—was distinctly gaining upon him.

"If they have no firearms with them," said Ned to Price, "I think we may perhaps be able to keep them from boarding, even in the event of their overtaking us; and, in any case, I think it will be advisable to have up on deck and load a few of those rifles from the arm-chest, for having gone so far it will never do now for us to allow ourselves to be taken. Get the keys of the arm-chest and magazine, Joe, and bring up a couple of dozen rifles and a few packets of cartridges."

The rifles were brought on deck and loaded carefully, half of them being stacked in the waist of the ship, whilst the other half, with a liberal supply of ammunition, were taken up on the poop.

By the time that this was done the ship had reached the passage between the bluffs, and as soon as she was fairly through Ned kept away dead before the wind for the mouth of the "Narrows," as the contracted entrance channel was called. The ship being under fore-and-aft canvas only, this alteration in her course was a disadvantage rather than otherwise, the staysails refusing to stand properly; moreover the high land was now once more close aboard of them on both quarters, rendering the wind light and shifty, in consequence of which the ship lost way perceptibly. Ned became increasingly anxious; so much so, indeed, that he resolved to get more canvas upon the ship, and running out to the flying-jib-boom he loosed the flying-jib, set it with Price's assistance, and then went aft and set the mizen-topmast staysail—a very large sail, reaching from the mizen-topmast head down to within twelve feet of the main deck. This addition to the amount of canvas spread had an immediately perceptible effect; and going aft to the taffrail, and from thence watching the approach of the boats, Ned believed he should be fairly in the Narrows before the gig reached him.

The ship was fully half-way across the outer basin when the gig—the leading boat—opened fire upon her. The weapon employed was evidently a rifle, for though the boat was half a mile astern Ned distinctly heard the whistle of the bullet overhead, showing not only that they were well within the range of the piece, but also that it had been skilfully and steadily aimed, a circumstance which led him to conjecture that Williams, probably the only perfectly sober man in the entire crew, must be in charge of the boat. The ship being thus proved to be within range, Ned now took the wheel himself, sending Sibylla below to the saloon, with instructions not to venture from thence out on deck until he should intimate to her that she could do so with safety. The firing, however, was not maintained, and a quarter of an hour later Ned had the satisfaction of putting his helm down and rounding East Point at the inner extremity of the Narrows. The sheets now had to be trimmed over, but the ship being found to steer herself, this was not a matter of any very great difficulty, Ned leaving the helm to itself for the short time necessary to enable him and Price to perform the operation; but when he returned to his post he was greatly concerned to discover that the gig was less than a quarter of a mile astern, and coming up rapidly, though, from the unsteady way in which the oars were being handled, it was evident that the crew were pretty nearly exhausted with their long pull.

The fugitives were now fairly within the Narrows, and in their narrowest part, moreover; the shore being within a quarter of a mile of them on either hand. This of itself would have been a matter of no consequence, however, had the configuration of the land been different; but, unfortunately, the cliffs towered high above the mast-heads on both sides of the ship, and as the wind happened to be blowing athwart the channel the canvas was almost becalmed; indeed, had it not been for a little draught of air which now and then came down the channel astern of her, the *Flying Cloud* would have lost headway altogether. As it was she still moved through the water, though at a speed barely sufficient to give her steerage-way; and the crew of the gig, seeing her almost helpless condition, raised a loud confused shout, which they doubtless meant for a cheer, and redoubled their efforts at the oars.

Ned lashed the wheel and took up one of the rifles, Price taking another.

"Now," said Ned, "I have no wish to shed blood if I can help it, so we will not fire until the very last moment; but if the gig approaches near enough to enable us to distinguish Williams' eyes—there he sits in the stern-sheets with the yoke-lines in his hands—we *must* fire in self-defence. And mind, Joe, it is the oarsmen we must fire at; we must disable *them*, and so prevent the nearer approach of the boat, for if she once gets alongside and they succeed in boarding us, our throats will be cut within five minutes afterwards. Look out! Williams is going to fire again!"

THE ESCAPE OF THE "FLYING CLOUD"

They saw the pirate raise his rifle and take a long steady aim; then came the flash. The bullet struck the taffrail just at their feet. Williams dashed the piece down, savagely disappointed at his ill-success; and Ned stepped to the wheel and gave it a slight adjusting touch. When he turned again Williams was standing up in the boat, with his hands to his mouth, and next moment came the hail:

"*Cloud* ahoy! If you will heave-to at once I solemnly swear that no harm will come to either of you. I will pass over and forgive your mad attempt to run away with the ship; but if you compel us to pull alongside and recapture her, look out! Your punishment shall be such that I will make you positively *pray* to be put out of your misery. Do you hear me, there?"

"I can see his eyes now," said Ned. "I will fire first; and directly the smoke clears away you must follow suit, taking care to fire into the thick of the crew so as to do all the mischief possible. Now!"

As Ned spoke he levelled his piece, and aiming carefully, pulled the trigger. Simultaneously with the report came a sharp yell of agony and a groan, and as the smoke drifted away two oars were seen to drop overboard and two forms to sink down into the bottom of the boat. Then Price's piece spoke out, and Williams himself sprang convulsively from his seat and fell forward. This caused a great deal of confusion and a temporary suspension of the pursuit, during which Ned again went to the helm. By this time the ship, having drifted past the highest point of land to windward, once more began to feel the breeze; and when the gig—having lost a good hundred yards' distance—again resumed the chase the ship was creeping ahead at a speed of fully three knots, with the wind coming truer and fresher at every fathom of progress. The men in the gig now pulled most furiously, and actually crept up to within about twenty feet of the ship's quarter, but—she increasing her speed every moment—they could get no nearer, try as they would. At length one of them bethought himself of the rifle, which he picked up and with some difficulty loaded; then, standing up unsteadily in the stern-sheets, he pointed and fired the piece, harmlessly so far as the fugitives were concerned, but not so for himself, for the recoil and his intoxicated condition together combined to upset his equilibrium so completely that as the piece exploded he staggered backwards and, amid the jeers and loud laughter of his comrades, disappeared with a splash over the stern of the boat. The pause made to pick him up terminated the pursuit, which had now become hopeless, and ten minutes later the *Flying Cloud* glided past West Point and was rising and falling on the swell of the open ocean.

Chapter Twenty One
The arrival home of the "Flying Cloud"

As soon as the ship was fairly clear of the harbour Ned kept her away on a south-west by west course for the island on which the skipper and Manners had been landed; and then, resolved to make the most of the fair wind and the fine weather, he ran aloft and loosed the three topsails, which, with a considerable amount of labour, and with the aid of the winch and a snatch-block, he and Price actually succeeded in getting sheeted home and mast-headed. The yards being laid square, the adventurers had now nothing to do but to steer the ship, Sibylla spending the greater part of the day at the wheel—thus affording her companions an opportunity to snatch a little rest—whilst Ned and Price alternately steered and kept the look-out through the night; and such excellent progress did they make that at noon on the day but one following that of their escape from Refuge Harbour, they had the satisfaction of heaving-to the ship off the skipper's island. Here the colours were hoisted and a gun was fired at frequent intervals, a keen scrutiny of the island being maintained meanwhile with the aid of the telescope, so that if the captain and Manners were still there they might have an opportunity afforded them to paddle off to the ship, or at least to signal their presence. Hour after hour passed away, however, without any sign being discoverable of the existence of living beings upon the island; and at length, just as the sun was setting, Ned once more filled upon the ship and headed for Gaunt's island, shrewdly surmising—what he afterwards found to be the truth—that the skipper and Manners had found means to rejoin the passengers.

The mountain on Gaunt's island was made about three o'clock next morning, from the deck of the *Flying Cloud*, the atmosphere being somewhat hazy at the time; and daybreak found the ship off the north-eastern extremity of the island, some two miles distant, when the colours were again hoisted and guns fired as before, the reports serving, as has already been seen, to greatly disconcert the Malays and expedite their departure.

The first thing seen by the anxious watchers on the ship's deck was the proa crowding sail out of the harbour, a sight which filled them with the keenest anxiety; and Ned, thinking it possible that his friends might at that moment be prisoners on board the vessel, was busying himself in making preparations to open fire upon her, with the hope that he might be able to dismast her and so frustrate her attempt to escape, when his mind was set at rest by the sight of the punt pulling off to him with Manners and Nicholls in her. Filling upon the ship and running down toward the tiny craft, Ned and his companions soon had the satisfaction of shaking hands with their two former shipmates, after which came mutual hurried inquiries and explanations, in which, on the part of the islanders, the adventures of the past night naturally occupied an important place. To hear that the entire party were safe, with the exception of a few comparatively trifling scratches, was a great relief to the minds of the new arrivals, as also was the statement that a capital harbour existed, into which the ship could be taken and moored with perfect safety. For the mouth of the harbour the *Flying Cloud* was now headed, under Manners' pilotage, and half an hour later she rounded-to and let go her anchor in mid-stream exactly opposite the creek, to the unbounded astonishment and delight of Henderson and Gaunt, the latter having rejoined the doctor just in time to witness the arrival.

The halliards were let go and the sails rolled up as smartly as possible by the four men on board; and then, the side-ladder being rigged for Sibylla's accommodation, all hands descended to the punt, the paddles were tossed out and the boat was headed for the beach.

The unbounded delight and exultation on all hands when at length a general meeting took place at the fort must be left to the lively imagination of the reader; an entire chapter would be needed for its adequate portrayal, and time presses. Suffice it to say that there was only one bitter drop in the cup of happiness quaffed by the party that morning, and that was the sad loss of poor Captain Blyth, which Ned felt with exceptional keenness, not only because it was wholly unexpected by him, but also because he had, ever since making good his escape, been looking forward with pleasurable anticipation to the moment when he should be able to hand over the ship to her rightful commander.

The whole of that day was spent by the party in the interchange of a full and detailed recital of the various events which had transpired since the moment of their separation; and when it came to Ned's turn he was, as may be supposed, especially eloquent upon the subject of the treasure which he had discovered. His description of the contents of the cave, together with the exhibition of the pearls and precious stones already secured, made a profound impression upon his hearers, who fully agreed with him that such vast possibilities of wealth were not to be lightly abandoned. How to secure it was, however, the question—a question which Ned solved the moment he set eyes upon the *Petrel*. He proposed that she should at once be completed and launched, and that, whilst the rest of the party should effect a leisurely removal of themselves and whatever they wished to take with them on board the *Flying Cloud*, he, with Manners, should proceed in the cutter to Refuge Harbour, and, watching their opportunity, run in during the night, secure the treasure, and leave again next morning—as they could easily manage to do—before the pirates could gain an idea of their being at hand. It was a risky thing to attempt, certainly, though not nearly so risky as it at first sight appears; and after a full and exhaustive discussion of the chances for and against success the bold scheme was agreed to.

Accordingly, on the following morning all hands went to work with a will; and they laboured to such good purpose that the last finishing touches were put to the little craft on the Friday following, leaving nothing to be done on the Saturday but the actual launching, and such trimming of the ballast as might be found necessary when she was afloat. The launch was effected successfully, the ceremony of christening being performed by little Lucille; and, it being found when the craft was afloat that only a very trifling alteration was necessary in the distribution of the ballast, the alteration was at once made, after which all hands repaired on board, sail was made, and they went outside to try the cutter's paces. The result was more than satisfactory—it was a delightful surprise; for not only in her sea-going powers but also in the qualities of speed and weatherliness did the *Petrel* far exceed the most sanguine anticipations of everybody, including her designer. They worked to windward for about three hours and then returned to the harbour, where the remainder of the day was spent in getting on board the provisions, water, and other necessaries for the projected trip.

On the following Monday the *Petrel* sailed for Refuge Harbour, with Ned as skipper and Manners as mate, cook, steward, and crew, all rolled into one—the adventurers receiving all sorts of cautions and good wishes as they said good-bye at the cove. The course to be steered was east-north-east, or nearly dead to windward as the wind stood at that season, and the distance was about three hundred miles; so it was calculated that the trip there and back would occupy about a week. But no sooner were they fairly outside the harbour's mouth than Ned and Manners exchanged the opinion that a smart little weatherly fore-and-aft rigged craft like the *Petrel* ought to do the distance in considerably less than the time specified; and they forthwith took measures to practically demonstrate the soundness of that opinion, "carrying-on" sail to such a daring extent that even poor Captain Blyth would have remonstrated had he been with them. The craft, however, was staunch, the spars and rigging sound, the canvas new; and the youthful mariners, though daring, were by no means reckless. The weather also was settled and the wind steady, if somewhat fresh. All, therefore, went well with them, and so thoroughly did the cutter answer the expectations of her crew that at dawn on the Wednesday morning—the second day out—the high land of Refuge Harbour was distinctly visible from the deck, showing just above the horizon like a sharply-defined purplish-grey blot upon the primrose-tinted sky to windward. At the same time the adventurers also made out something else, to wit, a fleet of five sail of small craft dead to windward—in fact, immediately between the cutter and the island. At first they were considerably puzzled to determine the character of these small craft, which were steering due west; but at length, as they closed and became more distinctly visible, Ned was enabled to solve the riddle. The fleet was none other than *the boats belonging to the Flying Cloud*! And Ned conjectured that the hasty abandonment of Refuge Harbour, indicated by the appearance of the boats at sea, arose either from a fear that Ned might give such information of the existence of the place as would lead to the speedy capture of its occupants, or a determination on the part of the discomfited pirates to seek at sea a substitute for the noble ship of which they had been so cleverly deprived. Whichever—if either—of these surmises might have been the correct one, a very lively interest in the movements of the *Petrel* was speedily manifested by the occupants of the boats, makeshift signals of distress being promptly displayed on board each craft. Ned paid attention to these to the extent of closing with the fleet sufficiently to enable him to establish their identity beyond all question, after which he calmly made arrangements to avoid them. When this was seen the boats hauled up in pursuit, but they might as well have attempted to pursue the sea-birds which hovered in their wake. Ned so manoeuvred as to pass the nearest boat well out of rifle-shot, at the same time steering such a course as would be unlikely to excite any suspicion that he was bound to Refuge Harbour; and though the pursuit was maintained for nearly an hour, its hopelessness had by that time become so apparent that the boats again bore up and were soon afterwards lost to view in the western board.

For the information of those interested in the ultimate fate of the pirates it may be as well to mention here that they were from that time never more seen or heard of.

It was just noon that day when the *Petrel* entered the narrows; and, all fear of discovery by the pirates being now at an end, Ned took her directly alongside the cliff immediately underneath the entrance to the treasure-cave and began the shipment of the treasure. This was an easy and expeditious task, the jars of gold-dust and the gold bricks being simply slung at the end of a line and lowered down the cliff-face to Manners, who received them below. The casket with the remainder of the gems was not forgotten; and one particular bale of embroidered stuffs which Sibylla had declared to be of priceless value was also taken; as were such of the shields and weapons as would bear handling—Gaunt and Henderson having expressed a very particular wish to possess some of these, as quite unique curiosities. But the ivory and the other bulky articles were left for the benefit of whosoever might choose to go after them. The shipment was completed in about three hours, after which Ned entered the inner basin and worked up as far as the anchorage, which spot was indicated by the buoy still watching over the slipped anchor. But though nobody was to be seen, and the storehouses had all the appearance of being completely abandoned, the voyagers were far too prudent to land—for which, indeed, there was no inducement—and, having satisfied their curiosity, they wore round and proceeded at once to sea, passing out through the Narrows again just as the sun was setting. Thirty-six hours later, or about six o'clock on the following Friday morning, they once more entered Gaunt's harbour and let go their anchor, to the accompaniment of a surprised and delighted shout of welcome from Nicholls, who—the entire party having removed on board the *Flying Cloud*—happened to be keeping the anchor watch at the time.

But little more remains to be told. Being so shorthanded, the party found it impossible to take the *Petrel* away from the island with them; she was therefore moved to a snug berth well up the river—her cargo, of course, being first transferred to the *Flying Cloud*—and there well thatched over with palm-leaves to protect her from the weather, in the hope that if ever any unfortunates should be cast away upon the island she might prove of service in enabling them to effect their escape; and there she may possibly be at the present moment.

This done, the party made sail in the *Flying Cloud* for Batavia, the nearest port, which, the weather still favouring them, was reached after a short but toilsome passage. Here they were fortunate enough to pick up a shipwrecked crew of Englishmen who were only too glad to ship for the passage home, especially as Ned felt justified in offering them the top scale of wages; and the owners of the *Cloud* having been telegraphed to and letters written by all hands, advising their friends of their safety, sail was once more made, this time for Old England direct. On the voyage home the *Flying Cloud* fully justified the name which had been bestowed upon her; for, carrying on night and day, Ned succeeded in making the fastest passage on record from Anjer to the Lizard. The latter, or rather the light, was sighted one fine April night in the first watch, nearly two years after the ship had last passed it; and on the following day she hauled in round Portland, stood across into Weymouth Bay to show her number, and then bore away up channel again, a fine westerly breeze prevailing at the time, which Ned was anxious to make the most of. At daylight next morning a tug came alongside in the Downs, and after the usual amount of chaffering, the tow-rope was passed on board her and she went ahead, the ship's crew at the same time going aloft to stow the canvas under the watchful eye of Manners, who was acting chief-mate, and who was particularly earnest in his exhortations to them to "be careful that you make a *harbour* furl of it, lads!"

Gaily the good ship stemmed the tide as she ploughed her stately way up the river in the wake of the grimy little tug; and a right noble and beautiful sight did she present, in all the glory of fresh paint and newly-blacked rigging—laid on during a spell of fine weather experienced just before entering the channel—with her white canvas snugly stowed, yards laid accurately square, running-rigging hauled taut and neatly coiled down, with the house-flag floating at the main-royal-mast-head, the burgee at the mizen, and the red ensign at the gaff-end. Many were the admiring glances bestowed upon her from the craft which were passed either going up or down the river—for, being only in deep ballast trim, she towed light, and passed ahead of nearly all the inward-bound craft—and at length a great bluff-bowed, deeply-laden barque was overtaken, the quarter-deck occupants of which appeared to manifest not only admiration but quite a surprising amount of curiosity as the two vessels closed. For a little group of men and women had gathered aft on board this barque for the evidently express purpose of getting the longest and best possible view of the *Flying Cloud*, many of them being provided with opera-glasses, which seemed glued to their eyes, albeit it was evident from their occasional gestures that they were listening intently to the eager and excited utterances of one of their number, a shortish, thick-set, grey-haired man clad in blue serge garnished with gilt buttons, whom our friends naturally supposed to be the skipper of the craft. At length, as the *Flying Cloud* ranged up on the larboard quarter of the barque, the excited blue-clad figure appeared to suddenly go demented altogether, for, rushing to the barque's gangway, he threw himself over rather than descended the vessel's side into a boat which was towing alongside, and with imperious gestures seemed to command the boatmen to convey him to the approaching ship. They obeyed, and the distance of the two vessels being but short, in less than a minute a voice—well known, notwithstanding its excited, exultant ring—hailed:

"*Flying Cloud* ahoy! heave us a rope's-end, will ye, and let your captain come on aboard!"

With a delighted shout the *old* hands rushed to the gang way, Ned foremost; the rope's-end was thrown, the boat sheered alongside, and in another moment Captain Blyth, alive, well, and as hearty as ever, stood once more on his own quarter-deck, shaking hands convulsively with everybody who came near him, with the unheeded tears chasing each other down his cheeks as he huskily replied to the enthusiastic greetings of those who had long ago given him up for lost.

His story was a long one, but it may be condensed into a few words. The raft, contrary to all expectation, had held together and lived through the terrific hurricane, before which it was driven furiously to the southward, to be wrecked eventually upon a small islet, whence, after many months of hardship and privation, the skipper had been rescued by a sandal-wood trader and conveyed to Singapore. He there joined the barque, homeward bound, the hospitable skipper gladly offering him a passage home, and, by a singular coincidence, had arrived in the river only an hour or two ahead of his own ship. He was full of pride and delight at the way in which Ned had outwitted the pirates at last and run away with the ship; and could find no words in which to express his admiration of Sibylla's courage under her long-protracted and trying ordeal, and his gratitude at her escape; and when at length the stories of the various actors in this little drama had been fully told, and he had congratulated them upon their marvellous deliverance, he wound up all by saying:

"Well, I took the ship out, it is true, and I lost her; but, thanks be to God, I can now face my owners with the words, 'There is your ship, in as good order and condition as when you placed her in my charge; and if I didn't get her back from the pirates for you, I at least had the training of the man who did, which is almost as good, I take it.'"

The arrival home of the vessel, so long overdue, and the publication of the adventures of those who went out and came home again in her, created a profound sensation almost throughout the length and breadth of England, and proved quite a god-send to the daily papers for a few days; but it was soon obliterated by the occurrence of events of greater importance to the community at large, and the chief personages of the story were allowed to sink back into a welcome obscurity, although the public interest in the subject was fitfully revived from time to time by accounts of proceedings in connection with the restoration, as far as possible, to its rightful owners of the booty brought home in the *Flying Cloud's* hold; but even this complicated matter was settled after a time, and now the good ship's name never appears in the public prints except in the advertising columns as being "for Melbourne direct," or among the shipping news as "spoken" or "arrived."

Like most seamen, Ned was generosity itself, and had he been allowed to have his way, the treasure found at Refuge Harbour would have been equally divided among all those who had participated with him in that adventurous voyage; but to such a proposal, of course, not one of the interested parties would listen. Nicholls and Price, however, eventually consented to accept a moderate pension, and the doctor and the engineer point proudly to their trophies of ancient arms as they tell the story connected with them to their friends. Captain Blyth still commands the *Flying Cloud*, ship and captain alike being the most popular in the trade; and Bob Manners was, at latest accounts, superintending, on full pay, the building and equipment of a magnificent yacht, in which Mrs Damerell, *née* Stanhope, hopes to accompany her husband on a luxurious trip round the world.